WORKING
CLASS

For more information or to leave a comment about this book,
please visit us on the web at:
www.nathanlowell.com

Publishers Note:

Science Fiction

The Golden Age of the Solar Clipper

Traders Tales

Quarter Share
Half Share
Full Share
Double Share
Captains Share
Owners Share

Seekers Tales

In Ashes Born
To Fire Called
By Darkness Forged

SC Marva Collins

School Days
Working Class*
Hard Knocks*

Smugglers Tales

Milk Run
Suicide Run
Home Run

Shaman's Tales

South Coast
Cape Grace
Finwell Bay

Dark Knight Station: Origins

Fantasy

Tanyth Fairport Adventures

Ravenwood
Zypherias Call
The Hermit Of Lammas Wood

The Wizard's Butler

The Wizard's Butler
The Wizard's Cat*

* Forthcoming

WORKING CLASS

NATHAN LOWELL

Durandus

To Blue Wave Ogee
"Say more."

Not her real name, just the name we all loved her by.
A teacher who had a such lasting effect on me
that ten years later I still think of her almost every day.

Yet I never had a chance to meet her in person.

RIP

CHAPTER ONE
NEWMAR ORBITAL: MAY 28, 2379

Zoya, Natalya, and Pip had already settled with their breakfasts by the time I hit the hotel dining room.

Pip gave me a smirk. "Nice of you to join us, Captain. Caught in traffic?"

I laughed and slid into my chair to wait for the server to notice me. "Figured I better clear out the room. I won't get a chance later, will I?"

Zoya shook her head. "Not likely."

The server sailed up to the table and swapped out the old carafe for a new one. "Having the usual this morning?" he asked.

"Buffet."

He nodded. "The egg bake is really good today."

"Thanks."

He wandered off as Pip checked the time. "Get some food. I've got to catch the shuttle shortly."

A couple of ticks later I settled again with a full plate. As much as I enjoyed a good breakfast buffet, after almost a month of this one I wouldn't be sorry to see the end of it.

The server hadn't steered me wrong on the egg bake. I savored it for a moment before looking to Zoya. "Where are we?"

"Looks like the ship is ready for habitation," she said. "Chief Bashar's got the galley functioning, planning on a limited lunch mess for the transplants from the Chernyakova. Franklin has moved over to help in the galley already. The rest will be coming over around 0800. Department head meeting at 0900. First shuttle load from the Academy at 1030, then every half stan until they're all up. Fire watch changeover with station services at 1800."

Pip took a sip of his coffee. "How many did we end up with?"

"Ten for the Chernyakova, sixteen for the Marva." She helped herself to the coffee from the carafe.

Pip nodded. "You have rosters for who's coming when?"

"We do," Zoya said. "We'll tap a few of our people to act as traffic controllers. I can meet the shuttles and get them pointed in the right direction. We'll need somebody watching the docks to catch the strays who miss the exit to long-term parking."

"What about the ones that can't find the docks?" Pip asked.

Natalya laughed. "I'm pretty sure they can find the docks. If they can't, it'll be a learning experience for them."

"Station security," Zoya said. "I've alerted them to watch for strays carrying duffle bags."

"They've got shipsuits?" I asked.

Pip nodded. "I arranged for them to be outfitted at the Academy before graduation. Basic setup. Just needed to tell their chandlery what colors for the Chernyakova. We're adopting the Academy standard for ours. They all got quarter share stripes. The halfs can upgrade when they get here."

"So when they get here, they only need to check in and head for the berthing areas," Zoya said. "Fire watch has the rosters and knows how to check in new crew for mass allotments."

"What are we missing?" I asked.

"If we knew that, we'd have planned for it," Zoya said, finishing off her breakfast and sitting back in her chair.

I lifted my coffee cup in a toast. Natalya chuckled.

"So the plan is get them in, assign them to watch sections, establish a portside rotation, and take over from the fire watch at 1800?" I asked.

Natalya and Zoya both nodded.

"How long do you want to stay before we undock?" Pip asked, looking at each of us in turn.

Zoya chewed through a mouthful of pancake, frowning and staring into the distance.

"Two days?" Natalya asked, looking at Zoya.

"Three?" Zoya asked, looking back. "We've got the basics for deck division covered. We could get underway in one, but you've got fewer seasoned hands and will need to get more people up to speed."

They shrugged, almost in unison, and looked at me.

"Let's do this," I said. "Get them aboard today. Give everybody a day to settle. Move the ship to a regular dock the day after."

"Seems slow," Pip said.

"Can you fill the cans by then?" I asked.

He nodded, but it didn't look like his heart was in it.

"Really?" I asked.

"Not good quality, but I could fill them this afternoon."

"You're getting cargo cadets," Natalya said. "What can you teach them about picking cargo?"

"And how long would you need?" I asked. "No sense in rushing things. Cargo and steward are the two divisions that have the most to do in port."

"Abe already has a can for Dark Knight."

"Yes, but you picked that can last week, didn't you?" Natalya asked, casting him an amused side-eye.

"No," Pip said, looking down at this empty plate. "I might have pointed him to it, but he did the actual picking."

"How do you know?" Zoya asked. She cradled her mug in both hands in front of her face. "In the Toe-Holds it's easy. How do you find them up here?"

"Secret cargo-master knowledge," he said, a teasing gleam in his eye.

She pursed her lips and raised an eyebrow.

"There's a clearing house for Toe-Hold cargo requests, if you know where to look. It's not exactly hidden, but CPJCT doesn't put it front and center."

"You get it from the back doors," Natalya said.

He nodded. "Same places we land the cans from the Toe-Holds. They keep a record of cargoes that 'might, theoretically' be bound for one. And which one needs which can." He shrugged. "It's cross-referenced by CPJCT sources when it's available."

"That's where you'll get the cargoes for us?" Zoya asked.

He nodded. "We've got a lot more to do because we've got a lot more than one can, but it also gives us a lot of flexibility. Cargo brokers have goods that need selling. We can buy those here to sell in the Toe-Holds."

"Have you ever done that before?" she asked, her eyes narrowing. "Seems like kind of a risk."

"It is," he said. "I've taken Barbell cans on spec before. It was common when I ran the Prodigal Son, but the scale was really small. This is my first real chance to play with more than one can."

"When did you take a can on spec?" I asked.

"About half the time we left The Ranch." He shrugged. "Everybody needs food."

Zoya looked over at me. "You didn't know?"

I shook my head. "Never asked. Not my problem. I'm—"

"Just the bus driver," she said, interrupting me. "We know."

I looked around. "So, crew up today. Shake them down tomorrow. Move to a regular dock the day after. How long before we get underway for real?"

"You wanna give us a target?" Zoya asked.

I shook my head. "Too many variables and it really doesn't matter if it takes a day or a week. I'd much rather find problems here at the dock than halfway to the Burleson limit."

"If we do four days in the trade docks, that's our normal rotation," Zoya said. "Gives everybody a chance to find their way around. Even the people coming over from the Chernyakova aren't going to know their way around here."

Natalya nodded. "I like this plan."

I looked at Pip. "CEO?"

He nodded. "Yeah. Good."

"We aren't going to have a problem, I don't think." Zoya glanced at me. "Chernyakova?"

"Is Skaggs still a problem?" Pip asked.

"I talked with Beth yesterday. She's senior to me and has a lot more experience. She wasn't happy with him, but it's not my place to butt in." I looked around the table. Natalya looked satisfied with the answer. Pip looked like he had something he wanted to say but kept his lips pressed together. Zoya saw me looking at her and gave me a nod, along with a small smile.

I didn't think I needed her approval but it felt good to know I had it.

Before I had a chance to think about that in any detail, Pip said, "I also talked to her. She's promoted all the people who earned it and moved them into their posts. She's swapped the sections around so that the people who are coming over here will be free to move." He looked at Zoya and Natalya. "You're both happy?"

"With the people coming over?" Zoya asked. "I am."

Natalya nodded. "I worked with Reynolds in sorting out engineering staffing. He's got some solid people to help with the influx of quarter shares."

"That'll help," I said. "Getting even a few of them up from wiper to engineman would help, too."

Natalya shrugged. "Engineering watch is mostly about knowing when to call for help."

"How do you feel about taking a watch section?" Pip asked, looking across the table at me.

"I'm fine with it." I frowned, wondering what he meant by the question.

"You know the people in your section are gonna take heat from the rest," he said.

"What kind of heat?" Natalya asked.

"For having access to the captain that they don't," Zoya said.

I sat back in my chair. "Is that a good thing or a bad thing?"

Zoya shrugged.

Natalya looked at Pip. "You have a solution, or are you just stirring the pot?"

"Just something I thought we should consider."

"There isn't another officer who can take the watches," I said. "If we have four deck watches, we'll need four deck officers."

"We could rotate them through," Zoya said, glancing at me. "You cover the eight to noon watch. Whatever section gets the morning watch gets you instead of their usual officer."

"Is that how you set it up?" I asked.

Zoya nodded, glancing at Natalya. "It's not cast in stone yet."

"So we're running four on and eight off?" Pip asked. "Get them used to watchstanding on shorter, faster cycles?"

"Quarter share is a quarter share," Zoya said. "We'll have a lot of completely green crew, so breaking them in easier might make sense."

"Is it better for the crew in general?" he asked. "Running fours and eights?"

"Research isn't conclusive," Natalya said. "Nothing I've found has been really significant except in some particularly high-stress environments."

Pip's head turned and he frowned. "You just happen to know that?"

Zoya hid a smile behind her coffee cup.

Natalya sat up straight in her chair and scowled at Pip. "Does that surprise you? I've got the most people in any division on the ship. You think I don't keep up with the field?"

He held up both hands palm out. "No, not at all. I thought you'd be reading, you know, more technical stuff."

Her normally sunny disposition clouded over. "What? Like Grease Monkey Quarterly? Journal of Wrench Wrangling Science instead of Command Staff Research Monthly? I can't do both?"

"Of course, you can." Pip shook his head. "I didn't mean to imply—"

"Put the shovel down, Pip," I said.

He looked at me from behind his upraised hands. "Shovel?"

"When you discover you're digging yourself into a hole, the wise choice is to put the shovel down," Zoya said, a wry grin lifting one corner of her lips.

Pip lowered his hands and gave Natalya a sheepish grin. "Sorry. That was dumb. I am honestly impressed you know that. I didn't mean it as a criticism."

She gave him a scowl and picked up her coffee cup. I caught the wink she gave Zoya when her face turned away from Pip.

"That was mean," I said, tilting my head toward Natalya and lowering my voice.

Zoya nodded. "Probably."

Pip frowned across the table at us.

I shook my head at him.

"So, fours and eights," I said, looking between Natalya and Zoya. "I take the eight to noon watch and we rotate the sections through?"

"Probably a good choice," Zoya said. "Gives all the mates a dedicated free slot every day."

I considered that for a moment. "You think MacBradaigh can use that?"

"I don't know." She shrugged a shoulder. "It had crossed my mind. He mentioned something about doing some work with cognitive apprenticeships, but hypotheticals don't work as well as authentic work situations. Usually that means having an expert explain their thinking while they're actually doing it."

Pip stared at Zoya, but, wisely, kept his mouth shut.

"You don't think he's going to try to do this on the bridge, do you?" I asked.

She gave me a "how would I know" shrug, but the look in her eyes said "of course."

I blew out a breath. "We'll have to see how that goes, I guess."

Pip's eyes twinkled. "Worried about having somebody second-guess you?"

I laughed. "Maybe revealing how little I think about what's happening on the bridge at any given moment."

He laughed. Natalya shook her head, grinning.

Zoya looked at me with a small frown but didn't say anything. It made me wonder what she was thinking at that given moment.

"We'll make that jump later," Pip said. "It's coming up on 0700. Is everybody out of the hotel?"

"It's just us four, isn't it?" I asked. "Cartwright moved aboard yesterday."

Pip nodded. "I still have my trunk here, but that's a small matter of grabbing it before I close the tab for the rest of us." Pip gave me a grin. "Are you going to move into the cabin this time?"

"This time?" I asked.

"You only camped out in the Chernyakova."

I snorted. "We'll see. Right now, we're on a one-stanyer contract. I may just live out of my grav trunk for a while to see if I like it."

Pip grimaced, and Natalya laughed at his consternation.

"You're going to set a terrible example for the cadets," he said.

"Quarter shares," I said. "Not cadets. Stop thinking about our crew as students and start thinking about them as crew."

Pip frowned. "Really? You're going to pretend they're not all going back to their classrooms and marching drills?"

I nodded. "I am, yes. They might not."

"Alys would love that," he said. "Take them on a cruise and she loses paying students when they don't come back?"

"You say that like it's a bad thing," Zoya said, leveling a stare at him.

"What?"

"What if this is part of her plan? They've been in the program long enough now to begin understanding what tiger they're riding. How many of them are only holding on because they either don't know what to do or are trusting they can get off later?"

"You think she's using it to screen out people?" Natalya asked.

Zoya shrugged. "I'm saying the cadets we're turning into crew are the people most likely to flounder in the last half of the program. We should be able to help those who want to continue. We're also going to be showing them that being in officer country isn't the only way to ship out."

"I'm still back on why they'd want to leave," Pip said.

"That's because it's all you ever wanted," I said. "Regardless of how hard you fought it. You'd have wound up there sooner or later. You only fought it because you thought your father made you do it."

Pip clamped his mouth shut and sat back in his chair. He glanced at Natalya, then Zoya. "Maybe."

"Some of the cadets I interviewed seemed almost ambivalent about continuing," Zoya said. "I wouldn't say they weren't motivated. You have to be, just to make it to the second year, but a lot of them mentioned things like 'my parents' or 'don't want to disappoint my family.'"

Natalya nodded. "I had some of that. Also had the 'when am I going to get my hands dirty' people. They might be happier as ratings instead of officers."

"Oh, and you get your hands dirty so often," Pip said with a smirk.

She scowled at him. "I have to do a lot of walking around and pointing. I don't get to do a lot of doing any more."

"You miss it?" he asked.

She shrugged.

My tablet bipped, interrupting whatever Natalya might have been going to say. I read the message. "Orbital security. We have cadets on the dock asking for the Marva Collins."

"They're early," Zoya said, frowning and pulling her own tablet out.

Pip stood and waved us off. "Go. I'll deal with the hotel here before I have to go play ringmaster for the symposium."

The three of us headed for the lobby. It took only a moment to reach the lift and Zoya pressed the call button. The doors opened almost immediately to an empty car, and we trooped in.

"If you want to hit the shuttle docks, I'll grab the people at security," I said, looking at Zoya.

She nodded. "Aye, Cap. I'll buzz the Chernyakova and let them know. See if we can find a couple of people to help herd."

"What do you want me to do?" Natalya asked.

"Check the docks," I said. "Look for lost sheep dragging duffle bags around. They should be easy to spot. They'll be wearing their shipsuits and have funny haircuts."

Natalya laughed and glanced up at my head.

I knew what she meant. One of the benefits of growing older was that I didn't need to cut much off the top when I got a trim. I thought I should get a discount, but the barber didn't agree.

The doors opened on the main deck with a ding.

"Git," I said, with a grin.

"Gitting, aye, Skipper," Natalya said with a jaunty two-fingered salute. She took off down the docks.

"No plan survives first contact, eh?" I said.

Zoya looked up from her tablet. "Ever true. Seems some eager beavers left the dorms early this morning without actually checking out at the Academy. No morning muster because they're between sessions."

"Not like they're excited or anything, huh?" I asked.

She smiled. "Wouldn't you have been?"

"You wouldn't have taken me. I already had full share ratings when I went."

"Probably so." She nodded and holstered her tablet. "I better get to the shuttle docks and see if anybody's waiting."

She strode off in the opposite direction from Natalya while I checked the message headers to figure out which security station held our new crew.

It felt like it was going to be a long day, but I was surprised to find I was looking forward to it.

CHAPTER TWO
NEWMAR ORBITAL: MAY 28, 2379

I got down to the security checkpoint on the oh-two deck and found four young people in Academy colors. They stood propped against the bulkhead except for one enterprising individual who'd turned his duffle into an impromptu seat. They all looked up when I entered, each one straightening into something approximating attention. One of the two women looked nervous; the other squinted her eyes like maybe she couldn't see that well. The fellow standing against the bulkhead gave me rather a surly sneer that had no place on a cadet's face, but the one on the floor just glanced up at me before coming to his feet and shaking out the bag before bracing.

The duty officer nodded to me. "These belong to you, Skipper?"

"Possible," I said. "I'm expecting some new crew."

"We got the memo. The teams are keeping an eye open for strays."

"Thanks. They're early. We've got crew heading for the shuttle docks now to help direct traffic."

"Appreciated, Captain."

"They being charged with anything? Loitering? Littering? Spitting on the decks?" I asked, giving them a side-eyed glance.

The officer laughed. "No. Just lost. You can take them."

I nodded my thanks and turned to them. "You're all for the Marva Collins?"

They all nodded. One of the women said, "Sar, yes, sar."

"All right. Follow me."

They gathered their bags and followed me in a line like ducklings. They weren't exactly marching, but I could hear them walking in step even over the noise on the promenade. I led them to the lift and pushed the call button. "Whose idea was it to come up early?"

"Sar, early, sar?" the surly one asked.

I read his name off the tape on his chest. "Early, as in why didn't you wait until the Academy shuttles started ferrying you up, Mr. Jacobs?"

He shrugged. "Sar, didn't know it was important, sar. They published the list but I wasn't scheduled until midafternoon. I caught one of the training flights this morning, sar."

I looked around. "The rest of you?"

The other guy—Smelser, according to his tape—said, "Sar, I came with her, sar. She seemed to know what she was doing, sar." He nodded at the woman who had looked nervous at the security station.

"Ms. Vincent?"

"Sar, I'm sorry, sar. I didn't realize it was going to be so difficult to find the ship, sar." She looked around. "Sar, Laura and I thought it would be good to beat the rush and get settled in, sar."

I looked at the other woman. "Ms. Huber?"

"Sar, yes, sar. What she said, sar."

"Well, you're cadets, all right." The lift doors opened with a double ding, and a small herd of spacers tramped out and headed down the promenade, half going one way, the other in the opposite direction.

I led my people into the lift and pressed the button for the main deck.

They lined up as if on parade, Smelser at attention and the two women at something approaching parade rest. Nobody said anything as we rode up the two decks but I could see Jacobs glance at me periodically in the reflection of the doors. When we hit the docks, the doors opened and I led them out. Again they followed in single file.

It amused me a little bit but it also troubled me. I hadn't factored in their Academy indoctrination as something that would need addressing.

Mr. Bentley stood at the entrance to the maintenance dock wearing his new Academy-dressed shipsuit with spec/3 helm insignia. "Morning, Skipper."

"Good morning, Mr. Bentley. Congrats on the promotion."

"Thanks, Captain."

"You're on traffic duty, I take it?"

"Yes, sar. Ms. Usoko is at the shuttle docks now and sending them on to me. Are these our new crew?" He smiled at them.

"Some of them. Early birds."

"Welcome," he said, nodding.

Smelser nodded back. "Sar, thank you, sar."

Mr. Bentley bit his lips and glanced at me. "Is this going to be a thing, Skipper?"

"For a few days, probably."

Jacobs stepped up. "Sar, is there a problem, sar?"

I turned to look at the group, noting the stripes and various insignia on their shipsuits. "Before we go any further, we need to get clear on something. From this point forward and until we release you back the Academy's tender mercies, you are no longer cadets. Cadet rules don't apply. You don't need to start and end every utterance with 'sar.' You are expected to treat officers with the appropriate respect. I'm the captain. You're the crew. Mr. Bentley here is spec/3 helm and has sailed with me for the last three stanyers."

"Four, Captain. Since Breakall."

"Has it been that long?"

He nodded.

"At any rate, one day you will likely be officers and you can have crew address you as 'sar.' You should address the officers on the Marva Collins as 'sar.' Or by their rank. You're second years, you should have sorted rank insignia out by now." I fingered the tabs on my collar. "Collar tabs are a giveaway, if you haven't memorized them yet.

"The good news is that there are many fewer officers that you need to worry about. We usually wear these brown uniforms most of the time. Crew wears shipsuits like yours. You don't need to use 'sar' when addressing fellow shipmates."

"There's not that many of them," Mr. Bentley said. "You'll get used to it."

I gave him a look. "Are you through, Mr. Bentley?"

He nodded, and grinned. "Yes, Captain."

"Thank you, Mr. Bentley."

"My pleasure, sar."

I held back the chuckle and looked to the new crew. "Any questions about any of this?"

Ms. Huber half raised a hand, and I nodded to her. "Sar, what do you mean we're not cadets, sar?"

"For the next stanyer, you're crew. Not cadets. Academy rules don't apply. You will go back to being cadets when we're done. In the meantime, you'll all be treated as if we hired you off the dock."

Mr. Jacobs raised a hand and waited for me to nod. "Sa— I mean, Captain, is that why we're all quarter shares?"

"It is. You'll each be given a rating assignment based on your underlying area of study. You're in engineering, Mr. Jacobs?"

"Sar, yes, sar." He bit his lips. "S-sorry, Captain."

"It's a hard habit to break, and you're going to have to relearn it when you go back." I shrugged. "So you're a quarter share wiper. Ms. Huber, steward?"

She nodded. "Yes, sar."

"So, mess deck attendant. Mr. Smelser, Ms. Vincent. You're both deck so you're spacer apprentices."

"We're the lowest ranks on the ship, sar?" Ms. Vincent asked.

"For the moment, yes. Over the next stanyer you can work your way up the ladder just like any of the other crew. For example, Mr. Bentley here had some experience as a deck hand, so he started as an ordinary smartass and look at him today."

"Took me almost a stanyer to make able smartass, Skipper." He never cracked a smile.

14

"Thank you, Mr. Bentley."

"My pleasure, sar."

I gave them a minute to see if anybody would break but nobody dared say anything. I held back the sigh. "With that out of the way, any other questions?"

They looked around at each other. Smelser glanced at me and then Bentley a couple of times. Eventually they shook their heads.

"Anybody want to back out and go back to the Academy?"

Mr. Jacobs looked like he might be weighing the idea but eventually joined in with the collective head shaking.

"All right, then. Let's go get you signed in." I led them through the airtight hatch that separated the maintenance docks from the main.

When we got to the ship, the fire watch checked them in. Ms. Heath stood ready beside the console.

"Welcome to the Marva Collins," I said. "Your home for the next stanyer. We'll have a formal welcome and instruction session later this evening when the rest of the crew gets up from below. In the meantime, Ms. Heath has volunteered to show you to the berthing areas and help you get set up. You're first, so you get to pick your bunks."

Ms. Heath nodded to them. "Come on. I'll give you a quick tour on the way."

"One question, Captain?"

"Yes, Mr. Jacobs?"

"Sar, liberty, sa—ah—liberty?"

"What about it?"

"Sar, are we free to leave the ship and visit the orbital?"

He made me grin. "You're not even settled on the ship and you already want off, Mr. Jacobs?"

He shrugged. "Sar, I thought since we're early, we might take advantage of the opportunity to learn more about the station."

"Nice try, Mr. Jacobs. Liberty has not been granted, but you have earned some extra time to learn about the ship and your new duties. The section heads will run some instructional sessions tomorrow. The day after that we're getting underway, so learn all you can now."

He looked like he might be ready to object but wisely refrained. "Sar, thank you, Captain."

I nodded to Ms. Heath who waved them on before heading into the ship.

"He's going to be a handful," the fire watch crewman said, grinning.

"Eh, he's no worse than others I've known. I bet they jumped the gun because they thought they could get some extra time to play on the orbital." I shrugged. "I don't blame them, but I'm also not going to deal with a bunch of quarter shares who're half in the bag before we get them settled."

"That's a lot of green quarter shares, isn't it, Skipper?"

"It is, but the department leads are all solid. The ship is new to all of us. It's going to take us all a bit to learn our way around, but most of us know what needs to happen once we get there."

"Aye, Cap. That doesn't change much." He was an older man with a nice smile and the look of somebody who knew his way around the docks.

I nodded to him. "Sounds like the voice of experience."

"Twenty stanyers, off and on, Cap. Spec/1 ship handler when I left."

"Retired?"

He shrugged. "Beached. Banged around until I got this job. Found somebody who could put up with me and settled down."

"You ever miss it?" I asked, curiosity boiling the question out of me before I could think better of it.

"What? The Deep Dark? No." He shook his head and drew the word out. "Missed the credits at first. Won't lie. I made do. This is easy duty and steady. We get a lot of long-term parking jobs here between regular maintenance and the Academy effect. It's not as steady as someplace with a full production yard, but it's steady enough. At the end of my shift I get to go home and cuddle my husband and kids."

I stuck out my hand. "Ishmael Wang."

He shook my hand with a firm grip and a short nod. "Christopher Powell."

"Pleased to meet you, Mr. Powell." I nodded at the passageway into the ship. "Duty calls."

"Good luck with it, Skipper."

I smiled. "I knew the job was dangerous when I took it. It'll be fine."

I heard him chuckling as I made my way into the ship.

Eventually we got our new crew corralled, settled into berthing areas, and gathered on the mess deck a few ticks before 1800. I heard them chattering away among themselves as I came down the ladder from officer country. The ship's layout owed a lot to the Barbell, or vice versa. It wasn't quite the same as I remembered it from the Lois, but it had been a long time since I'd been on a mixed-freight hauler. It was close enough that I kept having flashes of my own early days trying to be a spacer. It was a bit disconcerting.

I stepped onto the mess deck and one of the new ratings barked. "Captain on deck."

"As you were," I said.

The quick jolt made everybody start and then resettle as their necks craned around and eyes focused on me. The only sounds came from the galley, Mr. Bashar's deep voice against the clatter of cutlery and pans. By the time I got to the center of the mess deck, the galley door had opened and the new galley crew had lined up against the bulkhead. Mr. Bashar propped himself in the doorway and gave me a nod.

I gave them all a moment as I scanned the faces—some new, some familiar. "Normally, I don't make speeches, but since this isn't exactly a normal situation, I'm going to. We've got a lot of work to do over the next stanyer, so making sure we're all on the same course from the start seems worth the effort."

Except for Pip, the rest of the officers filtered into the back of the mess deck, including Mr. MacBradaigh wearing a shipsuit without insignia. They took up station against the bulkhead nearest the entry.

"As soon as you signed on as crew of the Marva Collins today, you became quarter share crew. Some of you have the experience necessary to step up to half share, but you need to take and pass the appropriate exam to make that happen. You'll get a chance to do that before we leave Newmar.

"Your lives as cadets are on pause. Your mission here is to learn what it's like being crew on a commercial vessel. The expectation is that you'll apply what you learn here to your own careers, assuming you eventually graduate from the Academy and take up the mantle." I made a point to smile and got a few chuckles in response.

"Along the way, we expect you to be crew. Not act like crew. Not pretend to be crew. You are the crew. You'll be required to stand watches, do the work necessary to keep the ship flying, safe, and profitable, and improve your skills." I let that sink in a moment, turning to look more directly at those who sat behind me. "In return, you'll have all the rights and privileges accorded to your rank. That includes a paycheck and a share of the profits." I gave them another few heartbeats.

"All of you should have met your section heads by now, so let me introduce the officers you'll be working with." I ran through them starting with Zoya and ending with Chief Bashar. Each nodded in acknowledgment. "Our cargo master, Phillip Carstairs, is busy running the data symposium on campus but he'll be joining us when that's over. Any questions?"

Virgil Bentley raised his hand. I shouldn't have been as surprised as I was.

I chuckled a little. "Yes, Mr. Bentley?"

He nodded at Mr. MacBradaigh. "What about him?"

"This is Caoimhin MacBradaigh. He's here to observe. As we go along, there might be some instructional activities and the whole crew is encouraged to participate. Even you, Mr. Bentley."

Mr. MacBradaigh frowned and started to speak, but Zoya nudged him with an elbow, giving him a small shake of her head.

One of the new people, a wiper according to the insignia on her sleeve, raised a hand.

"Yes? I'm sorry, I can't read your name from here."

"Sar, what kind of instructional activity, sar?" she asked.

I held my palm up facing her. "One moment." I looked around at the room. "This is going to be hard to deal with, but you're crew. You're not cadets. The first and last word does not need to be 'sar,' although by now I know it's second nature to you and you don't even think about it. There's no penalty for doing it, but it's not necessary here. Clear?"

A couple of the new people chanted, "Sar, yes, sar," before looking sheepish and ducking their heads to a round of gentle laughter.

I turned back to the questioner. "Your name?"

"Sar, Nunnelee, Jennifer, s—Captain."

"Thank you, Ms. Nunnelee. I'm not exactly certain. That will be up to Mr. MacBradaigh. Mr. MacBradaigh is an instructional designer, here to observe this first trial of the Marva Collins and possibly design new curricula for the Academy based on what he learns over the next stanyer."

Mr. MacBradaigh shot me a dark look, no doubt planning to object.

I gave him a smile back. "I'm looking forward to seeing what he learns from the experience."

One of the new mess deck attendants raised his hand.

He stood close enough that I could make out his name. "Mr. Armengol, is it?"

"Yes, sar."

"Your question, Mr. Armengol?"

"First trial, Captain?"

"One of Mr. MacBradaigh's jobs will be figuring out how to use the Collins most effectively as a training vessel. We're all his lab rats, I'm afraid. Even me." I smiled at him.

Another unfamiliar person raised a hand near the bulkhead across the from me.

"Yes? Your name?"

"Sar, Dayton Healey." He bit his name off and managed to not say sar.

"Your question, Mr. Healey?"

"What about the other ship, the Chernyakova, sar?"

"What about it, Mr. Healey?"

"Some of our classmates went there instead of here. Do they have their own instructional designer, sar?"

"Do they have to attend classes, too, you mean?" I asked, grinning at him.

He blinked. "Well, no. Yes. Sort of. Sar."

"No. They don't have an instructional designer. Not at the moment. But you're not required to attend classes here, either, even though Mr. MacBradaigh may offer them." I saw Mr. MacBradaigh stiffen against the bulkhead and his eyebrows met over his nose. Zoya turned her head and stared at him. He clearly noticed the look and kept his mouth shut, but he didn't look happy about it.

"Then why offer them, Captain?" Mr. Healey asked.

I gave him my full attention. "For starters, learning more is the best way to get ahead. Your copy of the Spacer's Handbook has everything you need to improve your skills and rank. We'll have at least four opportunities over the next stanyer for you to gain another stripe or two. Even earn a specialization, if you can push yourself that far. Group educational activities help that by giving everybody in the group the benefit of everyone else's questions and answers."

"But why, Captain?" Mr. Healey's frown fell just short of a scowl. "If we're just going to quit and go back to the Academy again. What does it matter?"

"Maybe it doesn't, Mr. Healey." I shrugged. "You've got a year to learn the nuts and bolts of your division from the deck up. You're engineering?" I asked, tilting my head to see his sleeve.

He turned to display it. "Yes, sar. Wiper, sar."

"Well you're going to be working for one of the best engineers in the Western Annex. You've got the opportunity to observe how a professional chief engineer keeps the ship sailing. Do you think she doesn't know how to change a water filter? Or how to diagnose a scrubber problem?"

Mr. Healey swallowed and glanced to where Natalya grinned at him.

"No, sar."

"Do you know how to do that now, Mr. Healey?" I asked.

He shook his head. "No, sar."

"By this time next week you will," I said. "Or next month. Depends. Certainly by the time you put your cadet uniform back on. Do you think that knowledge will be wasted when you earn your engineering third license?"

His frown relaxed a bit and he gave Natalya a more thoughtful look. "No, sar. I don't."

"Me, either, Mr. Headley." I looked around the room. "Any other questions?"

A lot of heads shook and no hands went up. "If nobody has questions for me, I have one for Chief Bashar."

He grinned at me. "Yes, Captain?"

"Is dinner ready, Chief?"

Everybody laughed and he nodded. "It is, indeed, Skipper. Line 'em up."

"Thank you for your attention, everyone. Settle in tonight. Your department and division heads will meet with you tomorrow. We're getting underway the day after, so pay attention. It's cold and dark out there. You don't want to have to walk home."

I left the mess deck to the rattle of the serving line shutters opening and a rising tide of conversation. I knew we had enough of the right ratings aboard to get things going. Having everybody locked in the ship overnight would give them something in common to complain about.

Zoya and the rest of the officers followed me out, around the corner, and into the wardroom.

Mr. Franklin met us in the pantry door, wearing his new steward uniform of black slacks and white jacket. "Good evening, sars."

"You're looking dapper, Mr. Franklin," Zoya said.

"Thank you, sar. It's going to take some getting used to."

"I need to check on the brow watch," Ms. Fortuner said. "We're letting the fire watch company go. Don't hold dinner on my account."

I nodded. "Thank you, Ms. Fortuner."

Mr. MacBradaigh pushed his way past Zoya to get in my face, a dark scowl pulling his hairline toward his eyebrows. "What was that?" He practically spat the words at me.

"What was what, Mr. MacBradaigh?" I turned to the sideboard, grabbed a plate from the rack, and began working down the buffet. It smelled wonderful and looked very good in the shiny new fixtures.

"I'm not here to train the crew. I'm here to observe and train cadets."

I paused, contemplating the steamed vegetable medley. "There are no cadets aboard, Mr. MacBradaigh. I thought I made that clear." I took a helping of the vegetables and moved down the line. "My understanding is that you're here to observe, to learn all you can about the Toe-Holds, and to start working up the curriculum design to replace the Academy's current courses." I plucked a dinner roll from the basket with the tongs. "Did I miss something?"

His chest puffed up as he took in a deep breath. "Those people are cadets. This charade doesn't change their status."

I nodded to Mr. Franklin. "Thank you, Mr. Franklin. Everything looks great."

"The carafes are full. I'll leave you to your dinner, sar." He gave a little bow, stepping back into the pantry and closing the door.

I looked at Mr. MacBradaigh. "You might want to grab a plate and get some dinner, Mr. MacBradaigh. Or at least get out of the way so others can." I cast a pointed look to the people lined up behind him.

"It's customary to go in rank order, top to bottom," Zoya said, nodding to Mr. Cartwright at the end of the line.

I crossed to the head of the table and placed my dinner down before taking a seat. "I don't stand much on ceremony. Some rituals get established early and they're hard to break."

Zoya picked up a plate and stared at Mr. MacBradaigh until he stepped out of the way. "Thank you," she said.

He looked at me and at the lineup for dinner. "This is madness."

"This is the wardroom," Natalya said, grabbing a plate and following on Zoya's heels. "Madness is down the passageway and to the left."

Mr. MacBradaigh fumed, his face getting redder. He looked as though steam might come from his ears from the built-up pressure. "You are not taking this seriously." He bit off each word as if each word were a sentence of its own.

"It's meal time. I assure you, we take it very seriously." I gave him a raised eyebrow as I poured some coffee into my cup. "Plate, Mr. MacBradaigh. Food. Seat."

He turned to take his place behind Mr. Cartwright, continuing to cast dark looks in my direction as the rest of the officers took their seats.

Kim entered and hustled to the serving line. "Fire watch has been dismissed. Third section has the watch, Skipper." She paused to look at MacBradaigh, then at Natalya and Zoya, and finally Mr. Cartwright, who'd taken a seat near the foot of the table. "What'd I miss?"

"Mr. MacBradaigh thinks there are cadets aboard," Natalya said. "He's taking some umbrage over the captain's cavalier treatment."

She worked down the line, elbowing MacBradaigh out of the way at the end to finish and take her seat. She glanced at MacBradaigh. "You can sit, you know." She nodded at the empty chairs across the table.

MacBradaigh walked all the way back down the length of the wardroom, around the foot of the table, and took a seat across from Mr. Cartwright. His lips pressed together in a tight line. "I don't appreciate this."

"Mr. MacBradaigh," I said, waiting for him to look up. "I apologize for making light of a serious situation. I don't apologize for standing up for my crew."

He took a deep breath and blew it out his nostrils before responding. "You're undermining my position, Captain."

"In what way, Mr. MacBradaigh?"

"There most certainly are cadets on this vessel. Opening up the instructional sessions to the whole crew? What am I supposed to teach them?"

I put my coffee cup down in its saucer, wondering how to make it plain. "Mr. MacBradaigh, were you paying attention at the session on the mess deck?"

"Of course, I was. Why do you think I'm upset?" He didn't shout, exactly, but his agitation spewed forth with his words clearly enough.

"I think you're upset because your understanding of the matter varies from mine to a significant degree, Mr. MacBradaigh."

He blinked. "Are you ignoring the reality of this? How can you say that?"

"No," I said, purposefully trying to pull back, to remember that he worked for the Academy but had no idea about how ships actually ran. I took a deep breath and started again. "The people we employ are not cadets. They are quarter share crew. You see them as cadets because you're ignoring the context. As soon as they came to work for us, they were no longer Academy students. When they return, they will no longer be employed by us and will return to being cadets."

He frowned. "You can't just wave your hand and make that happen. Alys Giggone doesn't see it that way."

"Are you sure?" I asked. "Nobody else around this table thinks they're cadets. They're not being graded on their assignments. They're not being hazed by upper classmen. They're not marching between duty stations. They're not attending physical training under arms. They won't get gigged or accrue demerits. The only activities aboard that correspond to the Academy are daily musters and watchstanding. In what manner are they cadets?"

"They're enrolled at the Academy. What more do you need?"

I looked at Zoya. "Are they?"

She shrugged. "They're on the rolls, yes, but their status is 'sabbatical,' I think. The other choices weren't applicable for getting them the time away without also jeopardizing their student status."

Mr. MacBradaigh stared at her. "Sabbatical only applies to faculty."

"Sabbatical only means a break to pursue interests outside of regular duties. According to the Student Handbook at least."

"That's not right," Mr. MacBradaigh said. "It can't be right."

Zoya shrugged. "You have a copy of the Student Handbook? Look under 'authorized interruptions of studies' in the appendix."

"It's so cadets could take extended leave for exceptional opportunities in the field," Natalya said. "Some of the engineering cadets earn internships with various companies around the Annex. It's a trade-off in terms of graduation dates, but it opens doors for them after graduation." She looked over at me. "We could have done this on the Chernyakova from the beginning. It never occurred to me."

"Onesy-twosy," Zoya said. "We've got a large percentage of the crew as green quarter shares. That's very different from one or two new people on the rosters."

She nodded. "Think it will make a great deal of difference?"

Zoya shrugged. "I'd like to think not, but department heads can only do so much. We won't have much trouble in deck, but engineering?"

"We'll be all right, I think. We've got some solid people and at least three of the wipers can be enginemen before we leave here."

MacBradaigh looked up from his tablet, shaking his head. "This doesn't say anything about them not being cadets."

"You're hung up on semantics," I said. "What makes them cadets? Beyond their Academy IDs?"

He settled back in his chair a bit. "They're getting academic credit for this work."

"Really?" I looked over at Zoya.

"They are, but it's half a credit a month for pursuing work in a related field."

MacBradaigh frowned at his tablet again, flipping screens with his finger.

"If we go back to the cadet question, Mr. MacBradaigh?" Zoya got his attention and he looked up. "What were you planning on teaching in these instructional sessions?"

Color rose up the back of his neck and he cleared his throat. "I thought a series of lessons based on a cognitive apprenticeship model. I want to highlight how experts approach a problem, the things they think about as they're going about their work."

"Experts, meaning us?" she asked, waving her hand to encompass all of us at the table.

"Exactly. Knowing how officers like yourselves approach the problems of command and control should give them insights that will help them create their own internal processes." He warmed to his subject, seeming to forget his objections.

"You haven't actually started the development of those lessons yet, have you?"

"No, Ms. Regyri. I've just come aboard."

"So, the reality is that you don't have any lessons at the moment. You could change that focus, couldn't you?"

His frown came back. "I could, but why would I? That's what cadets need to know."

"Setting aside that assumption, Mr. MacBradaigh, in the absence of actual materials, materials that, presumably, you need each of us to help you with, what prevents you from using existing materials and your expertise in education to teach all the crew how to do their jobs? We encourage all the crew to improve their skills and knowledge by working up the rank ladder. Having an expert teacher guide them can only help. Not just the lowest tier, but all of them." She picked up her fork again and began eating, letting Mr. MacBradaigh chew on her words.

He gaped at her for several long moments while the rest of us ate. "Assumption?"

Zoya looked up from her plate and swallowed. "That it's what cadets need to know? Isn't that what you said?"

"Of course. It's the whole point of the Academy. To train the next generation of officers."

"Yes, but is it what these people need to know right now?"

"What are you getting at?"

"That your idea of a cognitive apprenticeship is a good one, but it's going to take a lot more than just us. How Captain Wang solves problems will be different from the way Captain Case does. Every officer solves problems differently. Same with mates. Same with engineering officers and stewards. Collecting those might be a good idea, but you're going to need more officers to do that.

"These people are coming from the end of second year and will be going back to begin their third. They're here to learn what it's like to be crew on a commercial vessel, not how officers solve problems. It's to give promising students the background some of their peers already have." She paused to sip her coffee. "It seems to me, that you'd want to teach the lessons they need now even as you plan for the lessons you might teach back on the ground later."

I kept my head down and focused on my meal to hide my smile. He had no chance against her logic. I wondered if he'd see it.

MacBradaigh stared at her for several long moments, his meal apparently forgotten as the rest of us ate. "What do they need to know?" The question ground out of him as if pulled by a chain. It wasn't the dismissive sound I expected, but rather a statement of pure inquiry, put into the atmosphere almost to himself as his gaze lost focus.

"She's right, you know," Kim said around a mouthful of chicken. "She makes a habit of it."

MacBradaigh blinked at her, coming to his senses. "A habit of being right?"

Kim nodded and toasted Zoya with her water glass.

Zoya laughed and addressed her dinner again.

Natalya caught my eye and nodded to where Mr. Cartwright sat on the far side of Ms. Fortuner, looking a bit off his stride.

"Mr. Cartwright," I said. "As this is your first formal meal with us in the wardroom, welcome." I raised my cup in his direction.

"Thank you, Captain." He looked around and nodded at each of us in turn.

"It's not usually this animated," I said.

Kim leaned over to him. "Mostly, we're just here for the food. The floor show is just icing on the cake."

He looked back at her, but she'd already turned back to her dinner.

"Do you have any observations after a few days on board, Richard?" Natalya asked. "Is it Richard? Rich? Rick? Dick?"

"Richard is fine. Rich works. I answer to most everything but I try not to be a Dick."

The words floated across the table in a bubble of silence. He sat there for a couple of heartbeats and I saw the uneasy look in his eyes for just a moment before Natalya burst into laughter and everybody but MacBradaigh joined in.

Kim leaned over to him. "You're gonna get along just fine here, Rich."

He smiled and tried to hide his embarrassment by looking at his mostly empty plate.

Mr. MacBradaigh seemed more puzzled than amused but he made no comment. He looked down as if suddenly noticing his rapidly cooling dinner and proceeded to make up for lost time.

I turned to Natalya. "You find any problems in the engine room?"

"Nothing yet." She finished with her plate and took up her coffee mug, taking a sip. "The first cut at a spares order should be delivered the day after tomorrow at the regular docks. It's massive. It may take them a couple of days to get it all delivered."

"What about the potable water? I noticed it doesn't taste as bad."

"Flushed the tank. Drained the lines. Changed the filters. It should get better as we go."

"You notice anything about the ship itself?" I asked, looking at Zoya.

"Nothing odd, Captain, but the consoles?" She raised an eyebrow.

"Yeah. I noticed that, too."

"What about them?" Kim asked.

"They're in the fancy housing, but they're not the latest release," Zoya said. "They look good, but they're nothing special."

Kim's eyebrows rose a fraction. "All I noticed was that they're newer than the Chernyakova's. Didn't realize there was one newer?"

"Two, actually," Natalya said. "From what I hear, the latest one isn't really all that much better, so it's no great loss. They just moved components around on the boards and made the displays a centimeter bigger."

"Interesting." I looked at Natalya. "Should we be looking into upgrading the Chernyakova so it's the same level as here?"

Natalya shrugged. "Chief Stevens picked those consoles, didn't she?"

"Yeah."

She shook her head. "I didn't see anything wrong with them. They're solid gear. Do the job well. Is there a reason to upgrade? Beyond for the upgrade's sake?"

"No. Not from my perspective. Is there any technical reason why we should?"

She shook her head again and finished off her meal. "I wouldn't if she were mine."

Zoya nodded. "We upgraded the Madoka to that model when they came out, didn't we?"

"We gave it a stanyer to see how they performed, but yes."

"Any obstacles to moving the ship to the main docks?" I asked, looking around the table.

"We should be fine," Zoya said with a nod to Natalya.

"It's no big strain on the plant. We'll be under tow, so basically getting them to pull us out and push us in again."

"That's what I thought. Thank you."

Mr. MacBradaigh looked up the table at me. "You do this every time?"

"Do what, Mr. MacBradaigh?"

"Consult your senior officers about routine actions?"

His question puzzled me. "Why wouldn't I?"

"You're the captain."

The way he said it made me chuckle. "Yes. I've noticed that."

"Shouldn't you be telling them?" His brow carried just the tiniest wrinkle, like he didn't understand.

"Telling them what? That the divisions they're in charge of are ready for a ship movement? How would I know that if I don't ask?"

Mr. MacBradaigh settled back in his chair, perhaps suddenly aware of all the eyes pointed in his direction.

Natalya leaned a little sideways toward Mr. MacBradaigh. "Not going exactly the way you thought it would?"

Mr. MacBradaigh shook his head as he looked around the table, taking a moment to look at each of us. "No, Ms. Regyri. No, it's not. It seems I've a lot to learn before I can begin to teach anything here."

She grinned and nodded. "Welcome aboard, Mr. MacBradaigh. Glad you could join us."

———————————

The next day, section heads worked with the crew, getting them up to a base level of 'finding the head.' It worked out well enough. Junior hands shadowed their senior counterparts through portside watch procedures and then demonstrated them to show what they'd learned. We only logged the actual watch reports, but everybody went through the motions. They'd have more time once we got across to the main docks. I also planned to grant liberty there, at least on a limited basis. I wanted our four-day stay to be as close as possible to what passed for normal, while still getting the quarter shares up to speed enough to be able to work while underway.

In the afternoon, we ran a whole series of emergency practice drills. Everybody learned where the suit lockers were and how to put their suits on. We went through fire drills and lined up for the lifeboats.

The Collins had two pods of life boats, a small one aft in engineering and a bigger one in the forward nacelle with the gym. A narrow running track ran over the top of the boat bays there, with gym equipment taking up much of the center deck space. As the largest open volume in the ship, it felt cavernous after my stanyers of working on Barbells.

Zoya caught me inspecting the boat deck after a successful drill. The last of the crew had headed back to the mess deck for a fire safety lecture. "Don't get used to it, Skipper. We won't be on this ship that long."

"What makes you say that?"

She shrugged. "We're here for a stanyer. You thinking beyond that yet?"

"I don't think I've even got that far yet."

"Any ideas about what will happen when we bring back silk and spices from the Orient?" she asked.

I looked at her, drawn by the half smile on her lips and the question in her eyes. "Serious amounts of commercial disruption, I should think."

"I think it'll be more like all-hands damage control. The trustees are going to want to shut this down as soon as they can." One eyebrow rose in challenge.

"Too risky?"

She shook her head. "Doesn't align with doctrine. We're getting away with it now because they don't know, but they're going to lock down the docking clamps when we get back."

I nodded. "Good point. I wonder if Alys knows that."

Zoya grinned at me. "I'd bet you credits to crullers she's planning on it."

"No bet." I shook my head and looked around the boat bay. "They won't be able to keep this ship docked forever."

"Probably not," she said. "But long enough that we're going to need to do something else for a while."

I glanced at her. "You're probably right."

"I could be wrong, too," she said, folding her arms and looking away. "Be a shame, though."

"No argument from me." I looked over to see her giving me a long look. "What?"

She shook her head and dropped her arms. "Just thinking we're two of a kind."

I raised an eyebrow at that, wondering how I could even compete with someone with her background and advantages. "How do you figure?"

"I didn't know about the Toe-Holds until Nats dragged me out. For you? Pip. We both found something good out there and we're having to figure out how to deal with the universe that is rather different from the one we thought we knew."

I watched her lips moving, heard the words as if from an oracle. When they stopped moving, I almost had to force myself to look up to her eyes. "True."

Her head tilted to one side, just a fraction off vertical, as she looked back at me.

"All I ever wanted was to have a place I couldn't be evicted from," I said. "You always had a star to guide you."

Her eyebrows did a little dance and her lips curled. "Yet we're both here."

"You should have time in grade by the time we get back."

She nodded and looked away for a moment before looking back. "I know you can't control whether the board convenes, or when."

"They'll convene."

"You sound pretty sure."

"I am." I grinned, offering her own words back to her. "I could be wrong, too."

She laughed. The sound echoed around the boat deck and took root in me.

I turned away and headed for the ladder. "I'm heading aft to see how it's going."

"Good idea, but Nats has them eating out of her hand by now."

She made me laugh and look back at her. "Probably. Nothing like ridiculous levels of competence to garner support."

"She's got that," Zoya said with a grin. "If I'm ever stranded on a desert island, I hope it's with her. Within two days she'll have hot and cold running water, a fish farm, and a three-bedroom house—all made out of sand and coconut husks."

The image made me laugh again, but Natalya wasn't the only one who had the new crew in the palm of her hand. I headed for the spine trying not to think about who I might like to be stranded with. I'd been down that road once already.

It hadn't ended well.

CHAPTER FOUR
NEWMAR ORBITAL: MAY 30, 2379

I had Zoya call the ship to navigation stations at 0900. We'd run through the drill with the whole crew a couple of times. I had faith that the department heads would deal with the inevitable few who had missed the memos. We had time. The ship only carried enough power to keep the environmental systems alive and the lights on. I waited until the bridge crew had taken their posts before leaving the cabin and climbing the ladder. Familiar faces smiled at me as I took my seat on the bridge and clipped my belt into place.

"Status, Ms. Usoko?"

"Engineering reports shore ties are disconnected and secured. Fusactors are supplying all necessary power. All external field generators are locked and safed. We have departure clearance from orbital local for transition to main dock. The tug is standing by. Ship is green for departure."

"Well, let's move then. Let the tug know we're ready to move, Mr. Cartwright."

"Calling the tug, aye, Captain."

I watched over Cartwright's shoulder and saw the ship's schematic on his screen. I almost forgot that I had screens of my own, but I really didn't need them and left them stowed.

"Tug is on approach, Captain. Contact in five." He paused.

I looked over my shoulder at the stern and saw the familiar yellow and black shape of the tug easing up to our stern plates. They mated with us, giving us only the slightest of bumps. If I hadn't been looking, I probably wouldn't have noticed.

"Tug has locked, Captain."

"Thank you, Mr. Cartwright. Release the docking clamps, Ms. Usoko."

"Docking clamps, aye, Captain." She keyed a command into her console and I felt the docking clamps release with a thunk that carried through the ship's frame. "Brow reports docking clamps released, Captain."

"Signal the tug for pullback, Mr. Cartwright."

"Signal for pullback, aye, Captain."

The pullback started so smoothly, the station seemed to be moving away from us rather than the other way around.

"Log it, Ms. Usoko."

"Logged, Captain. Helm, status?"

"Helm zeroed. Tug has the ship, sar," Mr. Bentley said. "Ten meters per second."

"Thank you, helm," Zoya said.

The tug slid us out of the maintenance dock without a hitch. We all sat on the bridge and watched it happening around us until we cleared the station.

"Tug reports traffic hold for ten minutes, Captain. Incoming vessel."

"Thank you, Mr. Cartwright. Signal the tug that we acknowledge the hold."

"Acknowledge hold, aye, Captain." He tapped a few keys. "Hold acknowledged, sar."

"Thank you, Mr. Cartwright." Most of us looked around at the sight. Ships moving silently, sliding around with tugs. Fast packets easing into dock with small flashes of maneuvering rockets. I watched a shuttle drop away from the station and begin the long curving course back to the surface. I glanced over to see Mr. Cartwright staring fixedly at his console screen. "Mr. Cartwright?"

He looked back at me. "Yes, Captain?"

"What do you think?" I waved a hand around, indicating all the activity outside. "Pretty spectacular, isn't it?"

He sat up at his console and took a cursory glance around. "Yes, sar." He went back to his console.

Zoya gave me a quizzical look and nodded at Cartwright.

I shrugged. His jacket didn't indicate he had a lot of experience on the bridge, having just graduated, but I knew only too well how little the jackets actually said.

"Tug reports the hold has cleared, Captain. We're cleared to move."

"Thank you, Mr. Cartwright."

The orbital seemed to rotate around as the tug yawed us to the new heading. The tug's crew used a delicate touch on us, for which I felt grateful. It wouldn't take much to get a ship our size into trouble this close to other ships and the orbital itself. I admired their skill even as my belly flipped anytime it looked like a cargo hauler veered into our path or another ship crossed our bow. Eventually we made it around the far side of the orbital and the tug eased us into the dock not far from where the Chernyakova rested. The last few meters felt very long but soon enough the docking clamps triggered with a thump and a shudder.

"We are docked, Captain. Clamps have us solid green."

"Thank you, Ms. Usoko. Mr. Cartwright, notify the tug. Thank them for their gentle touch."

"Notify tug, aye, Captain."

"Mr. Cartwright, notify me when the tug has released."

"Notify on release, aye, Captain."

It took only a moment. "Tug has released, Captain."

"Thank you, Mr. Cartwright. Set shore ties and fittings, Ms. Usoko."

"Shore ties and fittings, aye, Captain." She tapped a few keys. "Chief Regyri reports we are now on shore power, Captain. Fittings for fuel, water, and gases are connected."

"Thank you. Log us in, Ms. Usoko."

She tapped her screen. "Logged, Captain."

I took a moment and looked around the bridge. "Well, not a long trip, but a necessary one."

Zoya grinned at me, lights from the orbital casting sharp shadows in the bridge.

"Secure from navigation stations. Set portside watch throughout the ship, Ms. Usoko."

"Aye, Captain." She picked up the mic and made the announcements while I unbuckled my belt and stood up from the chair.

Call me crazy, but it felt good to be moving again, even if we only moved from one side of the orbital to the other. I ducked down the ladder and into the cabin. I'd grant liberty later, but they didn't need to know that.

I finished my dessert, a delightful vanilla pudding, and sat back in my chair. "Where are we on getting cargo, Pip?"

He picked up his coffee mug and waggled his head from side to side. "You still shooting for Saturday?"

"Unless you've got a reason to stay another night."

"We'll have most of the cans full by then. I'm working on a couple of deals that might give us a few more, but we're not going out full unless we stay another couple of days."

"Worth staying?"

Pip shrugged. "Not for cargo, but if we need another day or so to get the hands up to speed?"

"Zoya?" I asked.

"Deck is about where I expected. Martinez got her half share rating this morning and has some aptitude for helm so we have enough for bridge watches with Jenson, Bentley, and Heath. Chief Bashar finished loading stores this afternoon. He said he's missing a few odds and ends but expects them tomorrow before lunch."

"Natalya?" I asked.

Natalya sighed. "Most of them have slotted in well. Jacobs hasn't made the adjustment yet. I've put him with Bell and Harris in power for the time being. I thought Nunnelee would move up to engineman but she failed the exam. She's in environmental with Penna."

"What's Mr. Jacobs's problem?" I asked.

"Attitude, what else?" She shook her head. "Hasn't quite figured out that his place in the pecking order shifted."

"Will another day in port help?"

"I don't think so, Skipper. Maybe getting underway will help settle him down."

"Any word from our counterparts on the Chernyakova, Pip?"

"I talked to Captain Case this afternoon. Her new people have settled. The existing crew is feeling a bit restive."

"Any back channel you want to share?" I asked.

He shook his head. "Didn't hear anything worth repeating."

"Can they be ready to go by then?"

"Should be," he said. "She says so. Everything I've heard and seen makes me believe her."

"Kim? Astrogation?"

"All the charts are up to date, Skipper. At least until we get out to Dark Knight and I can get the refresh there."

"Systems, Rich? I realize there's not much there by way of backup yet, but can you get an offsite set by tomorrow?"

"Yes, Captain. Kim's clued me in on how that works. I'll spin out a full set Saturday morning and get them stored with the Chernyakova's here on the orbital."

"Mr. MacBradaigh? How are you settling in?"

He stiffened when I called his name, and took a moment to brush his lips with his napkin before looking over at me. "I have no idea." He said it without any heat, just a bemused smile. "All I've done for the last few days is watch you people run drills, quiz the cad—" He cut himself off with a little shake of his head. "Quiz the new people. There's nothing for me to teach here."

"What have you learned?" I asked.

He chuckled, almost bitterly. "I've learned that nothing I thought about this job is right."

"You say that like it's a bad thing," Zoya said.

He frowned at her. "It's disconcerting, Ms. Usoko. When I take an assignment, I usually get a brief of some kind. Right now the only guidance I have is to learn all I can about the Toe-Holds so I can redesign the curriculum."

"We're not in the Toe-Holds yet," she said. "What did you expect?"

He looked around at us, taking a moment to collect himself. "I thought I'd be working with the cadets—" He winced. "Sorry, the new crew members to help them understand more about what goes into running a ship. Observing their progress." He shook his head. "Now? I don't know what I'm supposed to be doing."

Zoya shrugged. "Who told you to do that?"

"The commandant, when she asked me to take the assignment."

"You just said the only brief you got involves the Toe-Holds." She picked up her coffee cup and took a sip. "Maybe you should check with her before we get underway."

"I threw a wrench into your preconceived notions, didn't I, Mr. MacBradaigh," I said.

"Yes, Captain. I know a lot about what the new people will be going back to. I can help prepare them for that while we're out here so they hit the ground running. The rest of the crew? Honestly, what can I teach them?"

I shrugged. "What's your normal process for creating instruction?"

"It usually starts with a need. Some knowledge domain. You seem to have that covered. Every time I turn around, I see somebody studying something on their tablet. I have no idea what the need might be."

"There's a need," I said. "Every person on this crew wants to advance. The Spacer's Handbook is a do-it-yourself manual for ratings."

"I've looked it over, Captain. It's self-directed, self-guided for the most part. It appears comprehensive in the extreme."

I nodded. "Each step gets more and more difficult. The practice makes way for theory. It's quite good up to a point, but I think you put your finger on the problem."

His eyebrows shot up. "I don't even see a problem. How could I have identified it?"

"It's self-directed. Every crew has a few people who never advance," I said.

Zoya chimed in. "Some advance a step or two, then quit."

Natalya leaned forward to talk around Pip. "Same in engineering. I think we all have the same problem with people getting past full share and then not making the step into one of the specializations."

"It's not universal," I said. "A few take to it like they were born to it. Too many of them stall out even before making the step to full share in their divisions."

"What are you suggesting?" he asked.

"Self-directed, self-guided," I said. "The most success I ever had with a crew was when we ran study sessions on the mess deck."

"Many hands make lighter work," Ms. Fortuner said.

"But everybody is studying something different. How can you teach a lesson like that?" Mr. Mac-Bradaigh asked.

"You know the hammer-nail metaphor?" Pip asked.

Mr. MacBradaigh shrugged and frowned at him. "Of course."

"Put down your hammer."

Mr. MacBradaigh blinked a couple of times, his frown deepening.

"Learning happens all the time," Zoya said. "It doesn't depend on a lesson. How could you facilitate learning without standing up and delivering a lesson?"

He stared at his empty plate and reached for his fork, fiddling with it without actually picking it up. "They're not all studying something different, are they?"

"The early levels? It's only a question of degree, of depth. The basics of shipboard life within a specific context. Everybody studies the same drills, the same routines. Shipboard life with watchstanding and day workers. Basic ranks and requirements," Zoya said. "Most of them have the basic rank and insignias down. They know the fundamentals of watchstanding, I should think."

"They get more specialized around the full share level," Natalya said. "The specializations are where the skill trees branch and the instruction becomes more directly applicable to a specific job."

"But only a fraction of spacers even get to spec/3," Pip said. "We push it in our crews. Incentivize it by paying them for the rank even if they don't have the job."

Mr. MacBradaigh shook his head and looked at Pip. "Why would you do that? Pay them for the higher paying job?"

"To keep them," Pip said. "Otherwise they can get a job somewhere else for that pay and we'd lose them."

"It's not as good as you think," Kim said. "The shares glue our crew together. They've earned multiples of their base pay here instead of the fractional amounts that are more common across the fleet. The small amounts they get in their pay packets represent goodwill more than any real leverage for their loyalty."

Mr. MacBradaigh's head tilted all the way over to the left as he peered across the table at her. "Multiples?"

"Anything from three to six times base pay, depending on the cargo."

He looked at me. "That can't be right."

"I'm sitting right here, Mr. MacBradaigh," Kim said, tapping the side of her plate with her fork.

"I'm sorry, Ms. Fortuner." He offered her a sheepish half smile. "I'm just shocked."

"It's true," she said.

"It's true," Zoya said.

"I believe you," he said. "It's just one more thing I can't reconcile with what I know. Or thought I knew."

Pip chuckled and leaned over to him with a grin. "You'll get used to it."

I noticed Mr. Cartwright giving everybody at the table a wide-eyed stare. "Not exactly what you were expecting, Rich?"

He started and leaned forward, looking up the table at me. "Not at all, Skipper."

"Well, as third mate, you're also training officer." I nodded at Mr. MacBradaigh. "You've got an instructional designer here to help you."

"Training officer?" Mr. Cartwright asked.

"And morale," Ms. Fortuner said, giving him an evil grin. "That usually falls to the junior officer, which isn't me anymore." She let him panic for a few heartbeats before relenting and laughing. "I'll help with morale. It's not that bad."

"Training officer?"

"You keep track of the testing schedule, and administer the rating tests when we're underway," Ms. Fortuner said.

"Ideally we have everybody on the ship taking a test during each cycle," I said. "In practice, that's not always possible."

"Why not?" he asked.

Mr. MacBradaigh leaned in for that one, too.

"The higher you go, the more complicated it gets," I said. "Spec/3 to spec/2 is a lot harder than full share to spec/3."

"Spec/1 is a bugger," Ms. Fortuner said. "We have testing days once a quarter, but it can take a stanyer or more to get those higher ratings down."

Mr. MacBradaigh sat back, his gaze focused somewhere over Kim's head.

Zoya nudged my arm and jerked her chin toward our education specialist.

I gave her a wink and nodded.

"So," I said, reclaiming the conversational baton. "Saturday afternoon. 1500?"

"Good by me, Captain," Natalya said.

"I'll check with Chief Bashar. Make sure he's got what he needs for boxed dinners," Zoya said.

Pip nodded. "I'll have what we can get by then."

"Good by me," Ms. Fortuner said.

I looked at Mr. Cartwright.

He swallowed. "Can I say no?"

"Yes." I nodded. "I'd rather you tell me now than Saturday when we have a tug tied on. Or halfway to the Burleson limit. Is there a problem?"

He shook his head. "No, Captain. I just wondered if it had to be unanimous."

"I like unanimous. But, if there's a problem, I'd want to know about it so I can address it before it gets worse."

He nodded, not like he agreed with me but more like he'd reached a decision about something. He glanced at Ms. Fortuner before answering. "Good by me, Captain."

"Thank you, Mr. Cartwright. Mr. MacBradaigh?"

"Do I get a vote?" he asked, surprise written on his face with raised eyebrows.

"It's not really a vote, Mr. MacBradaigh. I'm asking you if there's any reason you need the ship to stay docked longer." I paused to let that sink in. "Is there?"

"No, Captain. No reason to stay."

"Thank you, Mr. MacBradaigh." I looked around. "With that settled, let's plan on going to navigation stations around 1430 with pull back at 1500."

Everybody nodded, but Mr. MacBradaigh looked at me like he didn't actually see me, a kind of half focus that shared its center with something over my left shoulder.

I stood. "Thanks, everyone. We've got a few stans for the last-minute things." I started for the door.

"Liberty tonight, Skipper?" Zoya asked.

I stopped halfway out the wardroom door and glanced at the chrono on the bulkhead. "Let's let them off 2000 to 0800 until we get underway," I said. "I want them all aboard during the day. We can run normal liberty once we hit the Toe-Holds. Will that do it?"

"Very nicely, Captain. Thank you."

"Keep me honest, Ms. Usoko."

She winked at me before I got out the door and I chuckled as I climbed the ladder to officer country.

"Captain?"

I stopped at the top of the ladder and waited. "How can I help you, Mr. MacBradaigh?"

He caught up with me and nodded at the cabin door. "If you have the time, I'd like to ask how to keep from tripping on myself any more than I have to."

I laughed and led him into the cabin. "Come in. Have a seat. I can't promise the answers you need, but I'll give you the ones that I have." I settled behind the console and waited for him to make up his mind whether or not to close the door.

"Can I close this?" He had one hand on the knob.

"You can," I said. "I usually leave it open, but it's good for it to be closed every so often."

He closed it, pushing on it until it latched, before taking a seat across from me. "I'm lost. I'm not good at improvisation. Never have been. I had this image of officers that seems completely at odds with everything I've seen you and your crew do for the last few days, culminating in this evening's festivities."

I shrugged. "Not every ship runs this way. It's just the way that works for me."

"It seems to work for your officers, too," he said. "I seriously underestimated Ms. Usoko and Ms. Regyri."

"Yes. You did." I shrugged. "What have you learned, Mr. MacBradaigh?"

"Every book on command I've read, every lesson, they're all based on a solid, even rigid, chain of command."

"You think our chain of command isn't solid?"

He sat back and frowned. "I think I need to re-evaluate what that means."

"What has you so puzzled?"

"That exchange with Cartwright, for one. You expected him to say no?"

I shook my head. "I expected him to say yes, but the point I hope I made with him is that it's his job to say no if there's a reason."

"That makes sense, of course." Mr. MacBradaigh shook his head. "It's fighting with my image of the captain in command of the ship, passing orders down through the officers to the crew."

"What makes you think that's not happening? Just because I ask those same officers for the input I need to make the decisions?"

He licked his lips and frowned down at where his hands wrestled with each other in his lap. "I think that's it." He paused. "The model in my head is one-way. Top down. Captain is the boss."

"And here we have my boss sitting at the wardroom table. He won't argue when it comes to decisions about the ship. I don't fight him when it comes to running the company."

"Can you explain what happened in there?" he asked.

"I surveyed my officers on their readiness to get underway. I usually do it closer to pull back, but we usually only have a few days in port to get things ready to go again."

"I guess that's the thing that puzzles me. Why didn't you just tell them?"

The question caught me sideways, but I realized where his thinking had taken him. "They know what it takes to run the ship. What it takes to keep the crew happy. I asked them because I needed to know if there were reasons we shouldn't follow the course I had in mind."

"None of them objected," he said. "Would they have? Could they have?"

He surprised a short laugh out of me. "Of course. Just like Mr. Cartwright, I'd have expected them to."

"But doesn't that weaken your position at the head of the chain of command?"

"Why? Because I demonstrate good leadership? That I get their buy-in on actions I intend to take before I commit to taking them?" I shook my head. "How can I expect them to take orders like that?"

"Because that's your job." He frowned.

"That's where we're coming at this from different directions, Mr. MacBradaigh."

He blinked a couple of times in confusion. "It's not your job?"

"There's an old, old saying. Never give an order you know won't be, or can't be, obeyed."

"I've heard it. It always struck me as odd. Why wouldn't it be obeyed?"

"In our situation, the most obvious answer might be that obeying the order could blow up the ship."

"That's absurd."

"No. I assure you it's not. The key element is trust. I have to trust my officers, my whole crew, to tell me if something is wrong. They have to trust me not to blame them for factors beyond their control. We go through this exercise every time we get underway. They all expect it, except for Mr. Cartwright, and will make sure I know that the ship is ready. If it's not? If there's an issue? They all know they can pull the plug and we'll stop the process until the ship is ready."

He pursed his lips and frowned.

"You ever tried to push a chain, Mr. MacBradaigh?"

"Excuse me?"

"The chain works both ways, Mr. MacBradaigh. It pulls up. It pulls down. It can't be pushed. A captain who doesn't trust and respect his crew is a captain who probably lacks the trust and respect of his crew."

"But how do you maintain discipline?"

"I'm not sure I understand the question."

"How do you get people to do what you say?" He shook his head. "I don't understand."

"First thing, the Academy is not a good example of shipboard management. It exists to scrape all the edges off. To put the cadets in the right frame of mind for making command decisions. It's terrible at helping them understand what a command decision is or how one comes about."

Mr. MacBradaigh frowned as if I might be speaking a foreign language, one he didn't speak.

"I've been through the program. I'm speaking from direct experience."

"But in an emergency, somebody has to take charge," he said. "That's you."

I tried to think of a way to make him understand. "No." I floated the word across my console in his direction. "Well, yes. In an emergency somebody needs to take charge. You are correct that in some emergencies that person is me. If the emergency is in the engine room? That person is whoever discovers the emergency. It's not me. It may not even be Ms. Regyri. It's going to be the person who sees it first. It's imperative that they act to mitigate the emergency as quickly as possible. They have to take charge. They have to take the correct action." He started to speak but I held up a hand. "Most of the time the correct action is telling somebody higher up the chain of command, but sometimes it's pulling the breaker on the sail generators. Every single person on this ship, including you, needs to know they have some responsibility for keeping us all alive. It's not just me. The only time it comes to me is if everybody else in the chain has failed or the situation requires a decision that nobody else can make. Then it's mine. Until that happens, the decision rests on the person who sees the problem. They either fix it or report it. Usually both."

"How can a ship operate like that?"

"How can it not? I'm only one person. I can't make every decision. That's why I have officers. That's why they have department heads. That's why we maintain watches. The first commandment for a quarter share crew is 'tell somebody.' It's what we've drilled into them for the last few days. We don't expect them to know everything. To be quite honest, we don't expect them to know anything more than who they're supposed to call. We expect them to know what's normal because it's what they've been looking at all week. When it's not normal, tell somebody. They have to take charge, take responsibility for addressing the issue."

"There must be lots of situations where that doesn't work," he said. "A lot of normal things happen irregularly, don't they?"

I nodded. "They do, yes. Department heads are going to get consulted on a lot of those over the next few weeks, especially once we get underway."

"You're going to let cadets just wake people up for no reason?"

I sighed. "They're not cadets." I stared at him until he nodded.

"All right, quarter share crew."

"It's not for no reason. It's because something doesn't look right. A few people will have trouble discerning what looks right and what doesn't. Especially at first. Which would you prefer, Mr. MacBradaigh? Being woken up for something that isn't a problem, or not woken up for something that is?"

His jaw worked as his forehead crinkled, but eventually he nodded. "I can see the logic."

"So, back to your first question about who makes the decisions. Everybody. All the time. My job is to make sure they have what they need to make the right decisions, to the extent that I can and they can. Mostly that hinges on education and experience, but the core that drives it all is trust and respect. I can respect somebody who errs on the side of caution. I can trust them because caution is what keeps us alive a billion kilometers away from home. Somebody who's afraid to wake their supervisor or notify the bridge? I can't trust that person to do what needs to be done. It's my job to make certain that everybody from me all the way down to the lowest wiper knows that our survival depends on trust and respect, wherever you fall on the chain of command."

"I've never heard it put that way before, Captain."

"I've had a lot of time to think about it. I started as a quarter share. It wasn't the first lesson I learned, but it was one of the early ones. It's stood me in good stead ever since."

"But it's not taught at the Academy," he said.

"It's not. At least it wasn't when I went. Even though many of my instructors were officers or former officers themselves, that basic core belief was nowhere in the curriculum. Chain of command. Respect the chain of command. Don't jump the chain of command. That was the common thread." I shrugged. "Nowhere did anybody mention the reality that the chain goes both ways and that respect and trust can't be created by fiat. It has to be earned, and it has to be earned both ways."

He sat there for several long moments. He looked in my direction but his focus wasn't on me. "That seems like a good lesson, but the best lesson is grounded in the work."

"It is." I nodded. "Which is why helping them move up in their rating is the right way to approach it."

He squinted a little. "I get why knowing how to do the jobs they'll be supervising is good. How does that address the core values?"

"By underscoring the purpose of that training isn't only for advancement. Not simply so they earn more credits."

"Isn't that the main motivation?"

"For some. Probably many, which is why having a trainer-led session helps. It's not just for the accountability factor helping to keep them on task. The idea of jobs shared are jobs made lighter. Those are good reasons, but it's so the trainer can point out that everyone who knows more makes the ship safer for all of us. They're more likely to recognize a problem. More likely to have a better response. More likely to keep all of us safe."

Mr. MacBradaigh took a deep breath and blew it out. "You've given me a lot to think about, Captain."

On a hunch, I asked, "Do you get to do much classroom teaching, Mr. MacBradaigh?"

He shook his head. "I design the curriculum. Deal with assessments. Update content sometimes, but that usually falls to the specialists. Teaching effectively requires more than subject matter knowledge. That's important, but understanding how people learn, what motivates them to learn. That's at least equally important. Good classes aren't an accident."

"That's where you're the expert," I said. "The Spacer's Handbook works for self-motivated, self-guided learning. The content is solid and gets updated regularly. I don't know how good the methods are or whether there might be better ones. Most of the ratings learn from a combination of lessons, experience, and on the job training. Too many don't go past the rudimentary knowledge needed to get a full share. If you can come up with ways for officers to more effectively motivate and encourage the crew, that would be a significant undertaking. Something you can look into while we're hauling ourselves out of the gravity well here."

"Who does that training? You said you did it on previous ships."

"I've done it, yes. As far as I know it's not common. I did my own studying and worked up from a quarter share to a full share before I left for the Academy."

He smiled. "Deck division, I suspect."

"All four," I said. I nodded at the master's license above my console. "That supersedes those ratings, but I earned them."

He chuckled. "Overachiever?"

"Insecure." I shrugged. "I was almost deported from a company planet when my mother died, and I never wanted to feel that helpless again. I reasoned that I'd improve my prospects by increasing the number of jobs I was qualified for."

"Good logic," he said.

"But flawed." I grinned at him. "I never got the chance to follow through on it because I went to the Academy."

"I'm guessing that background helped, though, didn't it? Cadets with that level of self-discipline are going to do better."

"It didn't hurt." I grinned at him.

"So you think I could make a difference with these—" He cut himself off for a moment, with obvious effort. "—these quarter shares by helping them understand this idea of a two-way chain of command?"

"I think the real lesson is getting them used to the idea that the more they know individually, the safer we all are collectively." I shrugged. "The chain of command won't change but their understanding of it will, if they remember that even a quarter share can save the ship if they know what they're doing."

"And the corollary?" he asked.

"Even a captain can destroy it if they don't," I said. "Perhaps leave that nugget of truth for them to consider on their own."

He chuckled a little and nodded a couple of times before getting to his feet. "Thank you, Captain. You've given me a lot to think about."

I stood and offered him my hand. "Welcome aboard, Mr. MacBradaigh. I'm looking forward to what you're able to learn about training on the ship."

He shook my hand. "Thank you, Captain. I don't know that I'll discover anything you haven't thought of yet."

"Don't sell yourself short. Alys believes in you. I believe in Alys. She always has her own agenda but it frequently aligns with mine, so it works out."

He laughed at that. "You've known her longer than I have, but even I've learned that much. You think she'd tell me her real agenda if I asked?"

I shrugged. "She might. You've got time to go down and ask her."

He shook his head. "She's here on the orbital. I'd bet on it."

"Because of her husband?" I asked.

"Because she won't let the Marva Collins or the Chernyakova get underway without giving the quarter shares a sendoff."

I laughed. "Yeah. That's Alys."

He grinned and headed for the door. He stopped with his hand on the knob and looked back. "This isn't what I expected."

I laughed. "Yeah. I have a feeling you and I will share that sentiment before we're done. Just not about the same things."

He laughed and nodded. "Thank you, again, Captain. Good night." He left the door open and disappeared down the passageway toward his stateroom.

"At least I hope it's not about the same things," I said, and went back to trying to figure out where to hang Al's painting of the Chernyakova. It seemed almost out of place in the main cabin, but perhaps in the sleeping quarters.

CHAPTER FIVE
JUNE 2, 2379: NEWMAR ORBITAL

Saturday morning, I woke up to a breakfast invitation from Captain Case at Eggs-Zackly, the current breakfast eatery on the oh-two deck. Seemed like every time I came back to Port Newmar it had changed hands. I had plenty of time. The crew would still be on liberty for a couple of stans. I couldn't help worrying that she'd run into a problem as I ran through my morning routine and put on undress khakis. On my way off the ship, I stuck my head into the wardroom. Ms. Fortuner sat in her seat, reading something on her tablet and sipping coffee.

"I'll be skipping breakfast, Kim."

She looked up. "Problem, Skipper?"

"Meeting Captain Case. I should be back by 0800."

She nodded. "Understood. Have fun." She grinned and turned back to her tablet.

It only took a tick to get off the ship and walk to the lift, getting myself there just as Captain Case pressed the call button. She looked over at me when I stepped up beside her. "Oh, good. Thanks for coming, Captain."

"Breakfast is my favorite meal of the day. How could I refuse?"

She laughed through a yawn. "Sorry. I haven't had enough coffee this morning."

"You're ahead of me. I haven't had any yet."

She laughed again. The lift doors opened to an empty car and she led me in, pressing the oh-two button on the way.

"Problem?" I asked.

"No. It's going remarkably well." She glanced at me. "Thanks for Reed. He's a blessing."

"He is that. I think he knows more about how the Western Annex works than almost anybody I've ever met." I didn't believe he knew more than Maggie Stevens, but that wasn't an opinion I wanted to share with Beth Case yet.

The doors opened and she led the way across the promenade to the restaurant. The Eggs-Zackly sign over the door featured a comically exaggerated rendition of "Zack" with a spatula in one hand and a plate of eggs in the other. The place was busy but not packed, which surprised me given the hour.

"Booth or counter?" she asked, eyeing the dining room.

"How much business you want to talk?"

"Booth might be better," she said.

I nodded at one tucked in the corner nearest the door. One of the staffers was just laying out fresh cutlery.

She nodded and we slid in opposite each other as soon as the staffer cleared away.

A waiter came up before we could do more than sit. She brandished a carafe in one hand and a pair of mugs in the other. "G'morning. I'm Pauli. Coffee?"

Captain Case nodded with enthusiasm. "Please."

"Yes," I said.

She filled the mugs before putting them on the table. "Know what you want?"

I nodded to Captain Case.

She looked up at the waiter. "Two scrambled, potatoes, hash?"

"Toast?"

"Hold the toast."

The waiter nodded and looked at me.

"Two over easy, potatoes, bacon, wheat toast."

She nodded again. "Be right back."

Beth took a moment to sip her coffee. "Thanks for joining me, Captain."

"We might want to make this a tradition," I said. "Make sure we're still on the same chart before getting underway."

"Since we're going the same way at the same time," she said with a nod. "What time you pulling out?"

"Navigation stations at 1430. Tug at 1500. You?"

"Right after lunch mess."

"Mr. Skaggs have any problems with the course?"

She took another sip of coffee. "Not that I'm aware of. He and Mr. Reed spent some time on the bridge yesterday."

The waiter brought our breakfasts and laid them out in front of us. "Anything else?"

I checked out my plate and shook my head. "I'm good."

Beth nodded. "Same here. Thank you."

"Has he settled down any?" I asked.

"Mr. Reed has helped. Julie seems to make him nervous for some reason."

"Past experience?"

She shrugged. "Their jackets don't show them being in the same sector at any point in time."

We paid attention to our food for a few moments.

"Did you ask Alys?"

She nodded and finished chewing before answering. "I did. She wasn't terribly forthcoming about it. She made some vague comments about differences of opinion between him and his skipper."

"You have any problems with his work?"

"No. None." She sipped her coffee, shaking her head. "Of course, I haven't seen much yet. Portside duty is pretty much the same for everybody. I haven't heard anything from his watch section."

"Who's with him?"

"Torkelson and one of the new quarter shares."

"She'll tell you if there's a problem. How are the new people?"

"Quarter shares. They've all got good attitudes and understand the basic job." She toasted me with her cup. "Yours?"

"They seem willing enough."

"And MacBradaigh?" Her wry grin showed around the edges of her coffee mug.

"I'd really like to ask Alys about him."

Beth chuckled and looked up as somebody stopped by our table.

"Ask me what about whom?"

"Good morning, Commandant." Beth slid over on her bench. "Have a seat."

Alys took the offered slot and I waved at Pauli who nodded and came right over.

"G'morning. Know what you want?"

Alys looked up. "Just coffee, thanks."

Pauli took a survey of the table and nodded. "Be right back."

"Ask me what?"

"MacBradaigh," I said. "What's the real story there?"

Alys gave me a wide-eyed, innocent look. "Story? You think there's a story?"

Pauli came back with a mug and carafe, filling all the cups before drifting along to the next table.

"What'd he do?" she asked after taking a sip. "Besides flail like a drowning man?"

The deadpan question made me laugh and made Beth look at us both like we'd gone crazy.

"Why'd I tap him for this?" she asked.

I nodded.

"He's the best instructional designer we have. Credentials up one side and down the other. Highly recommended." She shot a small grin at Beth before lifting her cup again. "Why do you ask?"

"What does he know about shipboard life?" I asked.

She laughed. "I suspect you already know that answer."

Beth finished her breakfast and placed the utensils on the plate before turning a little sideways in her seat. "Nothing?"

I shrugged. "I wouldn't say nothing. Exactly." I took a sip and glanced at Alys. "What he knows is largely wrong." I winced a little at my own words. "Not wrong. Just not quite there."

"Wrong is the right word," Alys said. "I didn't warn you because I wanted you to make up your own mind. What happened?"

"We had a few words in the beginning about the new crew no longer being cadets and that he had to stop calling them that. He had to start treating them like crew."

"Plugging that many green hands into a roster is a heavy lift," Beth said. "It's hard not to think of them collectively as 'the cadets.'"

"Yeah. I know. I have to catch myself. He had plans to teach classes while underway."

Alys frowned. "What kind of classes?"

"He didn't seem too sure. He talked about taking videos and creating a course around cognitive apprenticeships to teach the cadets how experienced officers approach problems."

"Videos of you?" Alys asked.

"I suspect he planned to work right through the roster."

Alys's gaze went to the bulkhead over my left shoulder. "That might be worth doing. I could see that being useful." Her focus came back to me. "That's not a bad idea. What's the punchline in this shaggy dog story?"

"I opened up his instructional sessions to the whole crew. He took some amount of umbrage with that."

"Not wanting to teach ratings about command decisions or some such crap?" she asked.

"I'm not sure. His basic argument was that the rest of the crew weren't cadets and he rejected the notion that none of the crew were cadets."

"I sort of see his point," Beth said.

"Yeah. I do, too, but my objection to it is that it's counterproductive to the actual reason those cadets became crew to begin with."

Alys tried to hide a smile behind her coffee cup.

"To learn to be crew, isn't it?" Beth asked.

"Exactly. What does crew do? Besides their jobs?"

She frowned for a moment. "Learn the next job?"

"Yeah. That. One of the new quarters had some thoughts about 'why bother' early on until I pointed out that the knowledge wouldn't expire when they returned to the Academy."

"What did Caoimhin have to say about that?" Alys asked.

"I think he got that point, but he focused on opening up his training to the whole crew, and what he'd planned to teach wouldn't work."

"Had he already started recording you?" Alys asked.

"No. Still hasn't. I think he planned to develop the courses on this first leg and start teaching in the next."

She nodded. "That would fit with what I know about him." She sipped her coffee and gave me a long look. "That's not the whole story, though, is it?"

"No. We had an early pre-departure dinner the other night in the wardroom. He seemed confused that I wasn't telling people what to do."

Alys bit her lips together. It looked like she was smothering a laugh. She took a sip. "How'd that go?"

"We had a talk about decision-making and who has to step up in an emergency. We also had a discussion about how to get quarter shares moving up the ladder and why it was important. I suggested that if he really wanted to help the crew, he should focus on how to facilitate that."

"I'd love to hear how to do that," Beth said. "It's endemic."

"Your ratings will show you the way," I said. "Once we clear the safety limit and get watches set, they'll start organizing study parties on the mess deck."

"Study parties?"

"Particularly when it gets closer to the testing period, but there's a push on to get everybody as high up the ladder as they can get. Phoenix pays them at their rating level, not their job. That's why we had so many full shares waiting to move up the ladder and could fill in the departments with experienced crew on the Collins. Not all of them have much seat time in those slots, but all of them were understudies to the people who had them."

"Go back to study parties," Alys said. "I haven't heard that part."

"Sure you have. We used to do it on the Lois," I said. "Bunch of crew gets together on the mess deck and studies? Fulls help halfs. Halfs help quarters. Everybody learns."

She nodded. "I remember that. I didn't realize it was so organized."

"Organized might be an overstatement. Cookie always put out a tray of fresh cookies in the afternoon for them. We did the same thing on the Tinker while I was there. I asked Ms. Sharps to do it on the Chernyakova and Al prodded a few people to step up in leadership positions before she left." I nodded at Beth. "Give them a day or two underway and you'll be able to find anybody not sleeping or on duty on the mess deck with their Spacers Handbook."

"That's kinda brilliant," she said. "How do you keep from going broke?"

"Earn more revenue," I said with a grin.

"Having a smarter crew doesn't help that, does it?" she asked.

"Doesn't hurt, and we have very little turnover."

Alys snorted. "You have zero turnover, and your payroll is a monster compared to any other Barbell in the fleet."

"It's the shares that keep them," I said. "The payroll is just our way of saying thank you."

"I'm not complaining. Just pointing out the facts."

"Back to my question. What's the real reason you picked Mr. MacBradaigh for this?" I asked.

"He's the best we have. Great ideas. Brilliant instructional designer."

"He's got tunnel vision," I said.

"That's why I picked him. He needs to get out of his tunnel. I figured you could help him with that."

"And he's got the credentials to stand up to the backlash when this new curriculum hits the fan?" I asked.

She gave me a wry grin. "That, too." She turned to Beth. "How's Mr. Skaggs?"

"Better. He's not scowling as much but he still avoids any contact with anybody but Tom Reed."

"Even his watch section?"

"He's aloof with them but can't very well leave the compartment when they enter."

Alys nodded and took a sip, glancing at me. "He had a rough time. A long run of bad luck with skippers and first mates. You can probably relate, Ishmael."

"You're thinking Rossett and Burnside?"

"Yes." She bit down on anything else she might have said before looking back at Beth. "He's a good officer, or was once. Got held down as third and beaten down as second. He's damaged and gun-shy. Risk averse. I think you're the right person to bring him back. He'll make somebody a damn fine first mate eventually."

"You couldn't have told me this before?"

Alys shrugged. "I wanted to give you more time to work with him. You're pushing all his buttons with women in the number one and two slots in his chain. You're going into the Toe-Holds, which he has zero understanding of. He's going to be under a lot more stress than your typical second mate."

"Why me?" She jerked her head in my direction. "He's the skipper with Toe-Hold experience. Wouldn't he be a better choice for rehab?" She gave me a short shrug. "Sorry. I'm not advocating for making your life more difficult."

"Keep going," I said. "I don't agree with you but I'd like to know, too."

Alys gave me a squinty-eyed look. "What are you thinking?"

"I'm thinking you're setting up everybody on the Chernyakova." I took a sip of coffee and watched Beth's brow crinkle slowly into a frown. "Maybe not Tom Reed. He's more the linchpin that binds the old crew with the new."

"Keep going," Alys said, echoing my words back at me.

"Mr. Skaggs needs to rebuild his trust in having women above him in the chain of command. He needs building up in general. The kind of work that needs something extra. The Toe-Holds are perfect. Terra incognita. He's not exactly blazing new trails but discovering a whole new section of the universe that's existed right under his nose. He's joining an in-group that a lot of people don't even know exists. That will help him a lot by giving him something that's his, more or less.

"I don't know what Ms. Southern's deal is, but I'm guessing it has something to do with the way she was treated by a past crew." I looked at Beth. "You were thinking of hanging it up, weren't you?"

She took a sip of coffee before nodding. "The thought had crossed my mind."

"I suspect you got shafted by a lot of people, but you're a good captain. I think you'll do great and that success will either remind you why you became a captain, or convince you that it's time to do something else. The Toe-Holds represent that same kind of new beginning for you that it does for Mr. Skaggs." I paused and tilted my head to the side. "I'm not trying to psychoanalyze you."

"You're doing a bang-up job of it," she said, her lips turned down.

"Sorry," I said. "I know about wanting to hang it up."

"You should," Alys said. "It wasn't that long ago you were in the same boat."

I toasted her with my coffee cup. "And you engineered getting Pip to shanghai me into taking the Chernyakova."

She laughed at that. "No. That was you two idiots' doing all on your own. I admit I was happy to take advantage of it." She looked back and forth between Beth and me. "It worked out for you."

I nodded. "It did."

"You manipulated us," Beth said, frowning at Alys.

Alys sighed and hunched over the coffee cup in front of her. "Reynolds needed a place after spending too long with Federated. Abe Kotawalla just needed a slot he could move into." She glanced at Beth. "You needed a solid company and a good crew. Julie Southern needs a good role model after too many assholes with stars on their collars. Skaggs, you know."

"Cartwright?" I asked.

She chuckled. "Cartwright reminds me so much of you. He just needed a leg up. One of you was going to need a third mate." She took a sip of coffee and looked at Beth. "I offered you a job. Well, more precisely Phoenix Freight offered you a job. All I did was introduce you. You were already here. I brought the rest in on the Academy's dime, true. Well, except for Bashar."

"Yeah, what's with him?" Beth asked.

"He wants to join the faculty." Alys shrugged. "He can't get past the faculty review board. This gets him closer to what he's always wanted to do."

Beth's frown didn't relax any with all the revelations.

Alys glanced at her. "So, you can call it manipulation, I suppose. I brought you all together. That's true. I have my own reasons for wanting to see everybody succeed and my own methods for trying to help people." She waited a beat. "You want out? We can make that happen."

"It's rather late in the game for that, isn't it?"

Alys shook her head. "You're still docked. I'm still the chair of Phoenix's board, and Pip won't make you sail if you've changed your mind."

"You'd just find another captain?"

"It would take a bit, but yes." She shrugged. "It would delay things, but you're not locked on this course."

"You're pretty free with assuming you know what I need."

"She's always been that way," I said. "You know how she got me to the Academy."

"Was I wrong?" Alys asked, grinning into her mug and taking a sip.

"I don't know. What would you have done if I hadn't agreed?"

"If I remember correctly, I would have had to beach you because of Federated Freight's rules."

I nodded. "I remember."

"You'd have landed on your feet. You could have had your pick of full share berths out of Dunsany." She shrugged. "You weren't going to turn it down, though."

"Clearly I didn't."

"You regret it?" she asked.

I shook my head. "It wasn't a path I would have picked for myself, but that's probably because it's not a path I could imagine myself having the opportunity to follow." I looked at Beth. "It's what she does."

Nathan Lowell

Alys sighed and turned halfway toward Beth. "Before I took this job, I used to identify those people I thought needed to be officers. I wrote recommendations for over a hundred people before I took over from my father here."

"Did he ever turn them down?" I asked.

Alys grinned and shook her head. "Never. Once I got here, I started getting recommendations from the people I'd helped up the ladder." She gave me a mock glare. "Except you. Get on that, will you?"

"Al already gave me that speech," I said. "I'll work on it."

She looked back at Beth. "My point being that now my flock is the fleet. It's huge and growing, but I keep my ears open. Once in a while I can help people like you and Julie and Patrick. I can't make your decisions for you, but I can put opportunities in front of you that you might not otherwise consider. Same as I used to do with potential cadets. I still hear of too many people taking the long walk out an airlock. Of people hanging up their licenses too soon." She sighed and looked at me. "I was never able to help Al. I tried often enough."

"She retired before I could put her up again," I said.

"She'd been at it a long time, Ishmael. I don't blame her for stepping back and focusing on her art. A loss for the fleet, but a win for her, I think."

"I can't say I don't miss her," I said. "Although Zoya's one hell of a replacement."

Alys gave me a rather enigmatic grin and looked back and forth between Beth and me. "You two set? Anything you need from me?"

Beth put her cup back on the table. "I suppose I need to get back to the ship. Rumor is we're getting underway today."

Alys took the hint and scooted out of the way. "Hang here a moment, Ishmael?"

I nodded and she walked Beth out into the passageway.

Pauli swung by and started picking up the empties. "Can I get you anything else, Captain?"

I pushed my cup forward. "I'd take a refill. I think she will, too." I nodded to the empty sitting by itself.

She finished grabbing all the dirty dishes and nodded. "I'll be right back."

Alys returned before Pauli but only by a few steps. Coffee refills done, Pauli left us.

"So that was quite a performance," Alys said.

"I call it like I see it." I picked up my mug and blew across the surface before taking a small sip. "Was I wrong about any of it?"

"No." She took a sip from her cup, then shook her head. "No, you weren't wrong."

"You having second thoughts?" I asked.

She raised her eyebrow. "Are you?"

"I'm quite looking forward to it. Any idea what you'll do when we come back?"

She narrowed her eyes and took another sip. "Why?"

"You've sent us out to pick up a bomb. Figuratively speaking. You think they're going to let us continue when we bring it back and it goes off?"

"They who?"

"Trustees? CPJCT? Whoever?"

She hunched over her mug, cupping it between her palms and staring at the table for a few moments. "I don't know." She glanced up at me. "You're planning on staying out for the whole stanyer?"

"That's the plan."

"Might make more sense to make port in a few other places before you get back here. Dunsany Roads, Diurnia."

"Show them how it's done?" I asked.

"Show the flag. As the Academy training vessel, you're going to get a lot of local attention from the newsies."

"Is that a good thing?"

She shrugged. "Maybe. Harder to pull the plug on a program that's become known as helping to train the next generation of officers."

"Zoya seems to think they'll lock the docking clamps on us as soon as we come back."

She shrugged again. "I wouldn't be surprised if they tried."

"You don't think they'll succeed?"

"The trustees can shut down any Academy offering. They'll have a harder time shutting down the holding company without making a nasty scene. Restricting trade on one hand while promoting it on the other wouldn't be a good look."

"Can they bring pressure though the CPJCT?"

"Possible. I don't know how likely."

"You're preparing for it, I take it?"

"I'm hoping that you'll be in and gone again before they know it the first time," she said, looking over at me from under her brows. "If we can get through two cycles without getting shut down, I think they'll have a harder time finding the political clout to do much, especially since I think most, if not all, of them know the truth about the Toe-Holds."

"They're playing a defensive game against it, though. Won't they fight harder with their backs to the wall?"

Alys sighed and picked up her mug. "Speculation all around. Next stanyer? Who knows which way the wind will blow. There's already a pretty strong breeze away from the High Line right now."

I shrugged. "I'm out of that loop. I'll trust your word on it. Is that what you wanted to talk about?"

"No. Mostly I wanted to make sure you understand explicitly why Caoimhin MacBradaigh is with you."

"I thought I had that dialed in, already."

"You're partway there." She held up a hand, one finger extended. "He's very good at creating courses that teach the cadets what the instructors want taught." She held up a second finger. "He's very bad at pushing into the content. He relies on subject matter experts too much."

"You can't expect him to question them, can you?"

"I can and do," she said. "The problem with subject matter experts is that they're experts and they generally stink when it comes to making things understandable to people who aren't. I'm impressed that he's questioned you already."

"Thanks, I think. What's third?"

She put her hand down and picked up her coffee. "He's going to take over the curriculum design department. He doesn't know it yet, and I need somebody in that post that understands what we're doing. He's not going to learn that by talking to the academics."

"Don't most of them have experience?" I asked.

She frowned at me. "Seriously? You went through the program. How many of the math and science people had actual shipboard expertise?" She gave me a wry grin. "We're an engineering and science school first, after all."

I nodded. She had a point. "What're you thinking?"

"We're using a centuries-old model. The officer training is a tacked-on military model. It has its place, but it's also only part of the equation. The problem is that it works."

"Why is that a problem?"

"Because it stops us from considering what might be better." She gave me a hard look. "You and Pip are doing things that are anathema to CPJCT fleet doctrine."

"Toe-Holds? I thought it was common knowledge."

"It's known, but not common. I'm talking about how you treat the crew."

I frowned. "I learned from you. How is it different?"

She shook her head. "Paying them their rank and not their post? You didn't learn that from me. I had to follow the Federated Freight rules. Getting the credits from trading your galley turnover stock? That's not pure Pip, but he's taken it from hobby to art form." She paused. "That 'chain of command goes both ways' thing? I'm stealing that. Do you know just how many captains sit in the cabin and pass down orders, expecting the crews will make it happen even when it's not feasible?"

I laughed. "Honestly? No. I've only served under two. Well, three, counting Rossett."

She shook her head and took a slug from her coffee. "Leon Rossett was a disgrace to his stars. Maloney should have cashiered his abusive butt instead of promoting him from the tractor."

"You knew about him?"

"My father was commandant." She shrugged as if it that explained it. Perhaps it did.

"What are you aiming for?" I asked. "With the Academy?"

"We put too many martinets into service. The military discipline is well and good here, but the ship is a business unit, too. Too many rigid skippers pushing too many new officers into rigid patterns of thinking at a time when rigid thinking is going to swamp the Western Annex."

"And you think Caoimhin MacBradaigh is going to help that?"

She sighed and looked away from me, scanning the nearest diners. "By himself? No. He's only part of it. Another part of it is having a cadre of cadets who know that the curriculum around the Toe-Holds lacks credibility. There's a small population of them who come from the Toe-Holds already, but they keep their heads down and their mouths shut."

"Like Pip and Natalya," I said.

"Yes. Growing that small population makes it more likely that the Toe-Holds will become common knowledge." She grinned at me. "You and your team are the final leg of my triangle. You're going to show them how an effective crew gets managed firsthand. Some of your new quarter shares come from family and co-op ships that are barely squeaking by. They're the third child or the cousin. The only model they know is the one they've seen. Most of them aren't set in the mold yet. They're still reeling from the first two years, and now you and your crew are going to blow their minds by running a ship in ways they haven't ever seen and can't imagine based on the bootcamp rigor they're currently steeped in."

"Are we really that unusual?"

She laughed. "Zoya may be one of the single richest individuals in the Annex at this point. She's almost certainly the most well-off officer in the fleet. Natalya owns and runs a shipping company from your engine room instead of a board room. Pip? His structural equation modeling is taking off. He's been pretty dug in with Phoenix, so I'm not sure he's aware of his effect in the wider fleet, but everybody from Federated and Consolidated to Allied and Saltzman have built up their own routes and cargo based on his work."

"Too bad he's not earning a credit from it."

"Oh, he is. He gets a piece of the conference pie every stanyer, and that pie keeps growing. He's also the CEO of two shipping companies now in addition to running your cargo operation."

I laughed. "I hadn't thought of it that way."

She leveled a stare at me. "I haven't forgotten about you. You are the reason this team runs. Pip thinks he's the mastermind, but you're the hand on the helm. Don't keep selling yourself short, mister. Don't underestimate what a good role model can do for a fledgling officer."

I chuckled and raised my mug in toast. "Back at you, Commandant."

CHAPTER SIX
NEWMAR SYSTEM: JUNE 2, 2379

Pull out went without a hitch. The tug eventually tossed us in the direction of Lesiter in New Caledonia by way of Dark Knight Station. We set normal watch as soon as we cleared the safety limit and I settled into the cabin to continue my review of the quarter share jackets. I'd put most of it off while getting the ship ready for departure, knowing I'd have fewer distractions and more time as we climbed out of the Newmar gravity well.

I hadn't gotten very far before Mr. MacBradaigh knocked on the open door jamb. I waved him to a chair. "Come in, Mr. MacBradaigh. How can I help you?"

"I've been looking over the lessons in the Spacer's Handbook, Captain." He settled into the seat. "They're very good."

"Tried and true," I said. "Motivation is the problem. Once you've done a few, they're cookie cutters. You can pick out the keywords that will be important later even before taking the quiz at the end."

"Does anybody take the quiz first?"

I nodded. "The first couple of lessons are really the quarter share indoctrination. You can take the quiz first and skip the lesson if you pass. You could skip it altogether, if you're so inclined. Half share is mostly more of the same. The Handbook lets you skip ahead to whatever level you want. The practice tests provide a reasonable approximation of the actual exam."

"That's what I wanted to talk about. The practice tests. I presume the questions are drawn from a pool?"

"That's my assumption. The Handbook itself is less a book and more an application. You can look up facts, but I suspect most of it consists of repackaging those facts into lessons, quizzes, and practices."

He pursed his lips and nodded. "How good are the practice tests?"

"Good?"

"What score on the practice test is good enough? I noticed they only give a numeric."

"Unless it's changed since I took it, at least 90 percent. Ninety-five is better. We recommend ratings keep trying until they can hit ninety-five at least three times in a row. Five times is better."

"That's another thing." He shifted in the chair and pulled out a tablet. "I didn't realize everybody in the fleet takes the tests over the same few days."

"I have no idea why, if that's your question."

He shrugged. "It was one of them, but what effect will that have, if we're in the Toe-Holds?"

"None. As far as CPJCT is concerned, we're just between ports somewhere in the Deep Dark. We run the same testing schedule, and file the appropriate updates as soon as we're in range of a communications buoy."

"So the Toe-Holds are on the same network?"

"More accurate to say that CPJCT is on the same network. The Toe-Holds were here first after all."

He frowned and rested his tablet on his lap. "You mentioned that before. You're suggesting that the Toe-Holds created the network and CPJCT simply extended it?"

"No, I'm not suggesting it. I'm saying it flat out." I smiled. "It was hard for me to grasp at first, too. We each see history through our own lens. If something happened before I was born, it's history. If I remember when it started, it's not. The Confederated Planets has always existed for me, even though I know perfectly well it didn't spring fully formed with the universe."

"I'm familiar with the idea, Captain, and a little embarrassed that I'm caught up in that perspective myself."

"CPJCT does that. It's part of the propaganda we're steeped in. It's a lot easier to see through once you've been out there and seen it firsthand."

"So, our Mr. Cartwright will oversee the testing? Did I gather that correctly from our dinner?"

"Ms. Fortuner will help him for the first one, but yes. The testing packets will come to us, usually a month ahead and sealed. The seal breaks for the test period and the crew who want to test will get the opportunity to take it. Mr. Cartwright will safeguard the tests, certify the results, and update their jackets. The jackets get updated when we pass a comms buoy."

He glanced down at the tablet in his hand. "I've been living in the academic world for so long, I have no frame of reference for this."

"No reason you should have. Officers have to take their license exams in CPJCT orbitals. It's the only place they exist. Crew can take ratings exams there at any time as well."

"Which helps reinforce the notion that CPJCT is the authority," he said.

"To be fair, it's the only place that the licenses matter."

He frowned at me. "What?"

I shrugged. "You don't need a license where there is no enforcement. There's no enforcement in the Toe-Holds. CPJCT has the Trade Investigation Committee, but there is no unified enforcement branch in the Toe-Holds. Everybody looks out for themselves."

"What? Different rules for different orbitals?"

"Stations. Orbitals are CPJCT. In the Toe-Holds they're always stations."

"The question stands," he said.

"Yes, Mr. MacBradaigh. Different stations have different rules. Some are quite harsh. Most are pretty lenient and involve station security more than personal morality."

He frowned. "What does that mean for us? In practical terms?"

"Are any of us likely to be arrested? Is that what you're asking?"

He shrugged. "In essence."

"No. It's unlikely unless you do something particularly stupid or dangerous."

"Who defines those terms?" he asked.

"I'd like to say 'common sense,' but that's probably less reliable than admitting that station management defines them. The station regulations for Dark Knight, Mel's, and The Ranch are all on the shipnet already. You can look at them."

He nodded, opening his tablet and making a note.

"They all basically follow the same template. Don't screw with the machinery. Don't poke holes in the walls. Don't screw with people. Pay your bills before you leave."

He looked over at me. "That's it?"

I shrugged. "What else is there? The station is a fragile island in an unforgiving sea. It keeps its inhabitants alive, so messing with the equipment, especially if you don't know what you're doing, can be deadly for everybody. The inhabitants have to put up with visiting spacers all the time. Spacers bring needed cargoes and credits but also can become disruptive guests. It behooves us all to pay attention to that disruptive tendency. Stations don't expect perfection. They're more than happy to deal with the disruptive elements and see that they get safely reunited with their ships. Sometimes that involves a fine. Mostly it's a warning for the first offense. Anybody who repeats learns that stations have very long memories. The situations that need extreme measures are few."

"But they exist," MacBradaigh said.

I nodded. "They do, but there's a saying for that."

He raised his eyebrows in question.

"Not on my watch," I said.

He uttered a short bark of a laugh. "Fair enough."

"What about credits?" he asked. "I don't see anything about currency exchange in the Handbook. Does each station have its own scrip?"

"It's all the same bank. There's only one source. No exchange needed."

"You said something about that before. You're serious."

"Toe-Holds were here first."

"That's what makes them Toe-Holds, yes. I remember." He frowned at his tablet. "Clearly I'm having trouble dealing with that concept on an intellectual basis."

"Now you know why Commandant Giggone wants you to build the new curriculum. Contrary to a lot of very closely held beliefs, the Toe-Holds aren't just part of the history of the Western Annex. They are very much its present. Communications, banking, trade. The Toe-Holds made it possible for the CPJCT to create the High Line, and they're what's keeping the High Line going. Without the High Tortuga Holding Company and its subsidiaries, the CPJCT would have to create their own networks and bear the cost of them alone."

He frowned, looking over at me. "And you believe that all the growth in the Annex happens in the Toe-Holds."

"At the moment, yes. I haven't seen the data but I believe that to be the case. The High Line is stagnant. In the decades I've been sailing, I have not seen a single new orbital established."

"That doesn't mean they haven't been," he said.

"A good point." I frowned. "I should ask Pip about that. He'll have the dates or know where to find them."

"Have you seen new stations get established?"

"I haven't seen them forming, no, but Zoya and Natalya established a new station while I was still a first mate. It's flourishing now. You could ask either of them about it. They've been operating in the Toe-Holds since they graduated from the Academy."

His eyes widened. "Fresh third officers?"

I laughed. "Yeah. It's a long story, but a good one. Buy them a coffee sometime and ask about it."

"That's this Vesta Moya they mentioned?"

"Zvezda Moya. And yes."

"Back to licenses. You don't need a license to operate a vessel in the Toe-Holds?"

"Yes. That's true. If you can convince somebody to trust you with a multi-billion credit ship, you can be captain. That's another interesting aspect. Ask Zoya about being a first mate while holding a third mate's ticket. Natalya skippered her own ship for a few stanyers before they got back on the CPJCT path."

He frowned. "How did that work?"

I shook my head. "You need to ask them. They're not my stories to tell."

He sighed but nodded. "Fair enough, but how can they operate safely without license standards to certify the skills?"

"Reputation matters more than credentials." I grinned at him. "Makes sense when you think about it."

"How?" he asked. "That seems like a recipe for disaster."

"It's no different than the High Line," I said.

"You're going to have to spell that out for me, Captain. You need a license to operate in CPJCT space. You have to prove that you know what you're doing."

"You're right. You need to prove you know what you're doing. The license is only documentation that you satisfied somebody else that you know what you're doing. When everybody is required to have one, they don't matter anymore."

"That's nonsense."

"Not at all. Think about it. You're an owner and need to hire a first mate. Four people show up for the job. Which one do you pick?"

"The most qualified, of course," he said, his head tilting to the right about five degrees.

"How do you know who's the most qualified?"

He sighed. "Well, probably by looking at their experience, checking references. An interview." He raised his eyebrows. "You do interviews, right?"

I chuckled. "We do, yes." I paused a moment. "So you look into their experience. You talk to people who worked with them in the past. You talk to them. Where does the license come into play here?"

"Well, they have to have it before we'll even talk to them."

"I get that, but it's not enough to make a decision, right? Why is that?"

He settled back in his seat and pulled at his lower lip with thumb and forefinger, seeming to weigh me with his gaze.

After a few moments he said, "It demonstrates a base level of competence. Everything else stacks on top of it."

"Agreed, but when everybody has the credential, you're left evaluating the candidates based on demonstrated work, prior relationships, and personal presentation. Right?"

"Granted." The word almost a grunt.

"The Toe-Holds cut out the middle man. If everybody has a certificate, they don't matter anymore."

"But that's the base level of skill."

"No," I said. "It's not. No certificate, no diploma, no license demonstrates the underlying skill or knowledge. It's only documentation that you convinced somebody that you have that skill or knowledge."

He scowled at me. "You're splitting hairs."

"Am I? The Academy grants engineering and management degrees. At any point in time do the students actually do any work that we'd recognize as engineering or management?"

"They study the knowledge. They have to show that they've learned it."

"Really? I remember taking those tests, even now. I have no idea what we were tested on. At least half my coursework went poof at the semester change. Some as soon as I passed the test."

He chuckled. "Well, it's been that way as long as there have been students and tests, I think."

"So I didn't learn it," I said. "I just convinced the teacher that I learned enough to pass the test."

A shadow crossed his face for a moment. "Yes. All right. There are limitations on assessment. What happens inside your mind doesn't show up on a brain scan."

"That's my point. You don't know. You make a good faith effort to pass on the knowledge. You train rudimentary skills. You can test to see if the student can recite the knowledge or apply it to a problem. You can see if the student can execute the skill on demand. You can't actually determine whether the student learned it. That's a test that comes long after the class is over. It's a test no teacher will grade."

"You're painting with a pretty broad brush there, Captain." He paused for a breath. "Are you saying your Academy degree is useless?"

"Not exactly, no." I shrugged. "I learned a lot about navigating bureaucracy. Time management. Balancing priorities. I picked up a broader grounding in management. A better understanding of the business of hauling freight."

"But your contention is that none of that matters in the grand scheme?"

He made me think about it for a few heartbeats. "It made things a bit easier. I'll grant you that. I also picked up a fair amount of propaganda. Your understanding of the Toe-Holds is a prime example." I shook my head. "That's only the beginning. I did not learn anything that the Confederated Planets Joint Committee on Trade didn't approve of."

"Like what?" he asked.

"We learned that TIC maintains the peace in the Western Annex. That's a lesson I remember well from our courses on provenance and compliance."

"What's wrong with that?"

"You mean, other than it's not true?" I asked.

"Of course it's true."

"I'd be willing to entertain the idea that it might be true in the High Line, but TIC has no enforcement authority in the Toe-Holds."

He squinted a little. "You're getting a bit circular in your argument, Captain."

I shook my head. "No. Even if there weren't more Toe-Hold stations than orbitals, even if many of their stations weren't larger than orbitals, even if they didn't have the larger population, they're still part of the Western Annex. Asserting that CPJCT-controlled space is synonymous with the Western Annex constitutes propaganda. Even the characterization of Toe-Hold space as largely deserted and lawless puts the lie to the argument that TIC keeps the peace, because the Academy teaches that TIC has no authority there."

"Well, CPJCT space is the only space that matters," he said.

"And I'm the captain of the Western Annex? Because this ship is the only one that matters?"

"Now you're being ridiculous." He put no heat behind the words.

"Yes. That's exactly the word. Ridiculous. I can no more argue that none of the other ships in the Annex matter than CPJCT can argue that none of the Toe-Holds matter."

He opened his mouth as if to speak but closed it without carrying through. After a moment he asked, "If credentials don't matter, why are you insisting that the ratings earn them?"

"I didn't say they don't matter. The rating steps, in particular, help the crew learn more about what they're already doing. They're grounded in their daily duties and activities. For the most part they can close the Handbook and practice what they just studied. They're immersed in it every day. The practice tests are only a gauge for them to measure against the official one. The real tests happen as soon as they attend their duties."

"Authentic assessment," he said, almost to himself.

"They matter in this context because the High Line puts a premium on those skills, tying pay to position in the skill tree."

He blinked, focusing on me again. "You mean tying pay to performance, don't you?"

"No. You don't get extra pay for performing at higher skill levels. That would be performance. You get paid based on how far up the ladder you climb. In most cases, that only means how far up the ladder your company will pay you. If the job is rated for a half share, that's what they pay. Even Phoenix doesn't pay for extra ratings outside of your core duties. If you're a full share rating, we pay you as a full share, even if you hold a half share rated job. The only incentive for branching out is that it opens more opportunities for future employment."

He stared at me for a few heartbeats. "You have some strange opinions, Captain."

He surprised a laugh out of me. "I get that a lot. I think it comes from being a land rat."

"You're not a spacer, then?"

I looked around the cabin. "Well, maybe now. I didn't start out that way. Alys Giggone plucked me off Neris and kicked me to the Academy. I've always been an outsider."

"You're about as far inside as you can get now, aren't you?"

"Maybe. But I'm not a native. That's both good and bad."

He nodded and stood. "Thank you, Captain. It's been illuminating."

"Alys seemed to think your idea of the video lessons might be worth pursuing," I said.

"You spoke with her about it?"

"Yeah. It could be a bigger project than you think, though."

He laughed and headed for the door. "With Commandant Giggone, it always is."

"I can't argue with that. See you at dinner, Mr. MacBradaigh."

He nodded and disappeared down the passageway, leaving me to return to reviewing the records for the new crew.

I relieved Ms. Fortuner at 0745 and took my first bridge watch in what felt like a very long time. She didn't go easy on me.

"You sure you remember how to do this, Skipper?

"It's like riding a bicycle," I said.

"I've heard that saying. Can you ride a bicycle?" she asked.

"Never tried, but I've held a lot of bridge watches." I grinned at her.

She laughed and logged the changeover. "Good luck, Skipper."

"Thank you, Ms. Fortuner."

Dale Jenson relieved Virgil Bentley and settled into the helm while I ran through the log from the previous watch. I didn't see anything worthy of note. We hadn't come that far from the orbital overnight and the ship still had that "getting underway" feeling.

"How are the new shipmates coming, Mr. Jenson?"

He glanced over from the helm. "Green as grass, Skipper, but most of them are taking it pretty well."

"Anybody I should look out for?"

He shrugged and turned to his helm. "Nobody has risen to the top or sunk to the bottom yet, sar. There are a few early contenders but no clear leader yet."

I chuckled. "Fair enough."

We settled into the routine while I finished scanning through the quarter shares' records. I secured their files and checked course. Without any pressing emergency or shipboard activity, I had very little to do.

I stood up from the console and stood at the aft armorglass, considering the orbital receding from view. Before long it would all but disappear, overwhelmed by the planet's orb until that too reduced to a pin prick in the dark sky. I turned and looked toward the port bow. The Chernyakova sailed somewhere out there, too far away to see. They had a couple of stans on us at pull out, and nobody sailed that close together.

At 1000 Ms. Vincent brought up a tray of coffee and a couple of cookies. "Compliments of Chief Bashar, Captain."

I took a cup but left the cookies for Mr. Jenson. "Thank you, Ms. Vincent. How are you settling in?"

She offered the tray to Mr. Jenson, who took his coffee and a cookie. "It's not exactly what I expected."

"What did you expect?" I took a sip and remembered how much I liked Chief Bashar.

"The Academy makes it sound like life and death all the time, sar." She shrugged. "It's been intimidating, to be honest."

"And you came back for your second year anyway?"

She gave a little laugh and nodded. "Sucker for punishment, I suppose, sar."

"Since she's here already, head call, Skipper?" Mr. Jenson asked.

"Granted. Ms. Vincent? You're about to take Mr. Jenson's place at the helm. You ready?"

"What? No." She took a step back. For a moment I thought she might fall backwards down the ladder.

Mr. Jenson waved her over. "Might as well get used to it. It's easy."

She looked at me before crossing to the helm. I held out my hand for her tray since she seemed to be having trouble figuring out what to do with it. "Is this really part of my duty, Captain?"

"It is. Messenger of the watch. Sometimes you'll get paged to the bridge so you can relieve the helm for a bio break. The watches are only four stans long, but that's a long time to hold it." I grinned.

Jenson made the notation on his log, unfastened his seat belt, then stood. "Here. Sit. Buckle in. The log notation is your initials and the letters T-R. The system will take care of it. I'll be right back."

He grinned at me as he ducked down the ladder.

She jumped into the chair and scrambled to fasten the belt. "What do I do, Captain?"

I crossed to stand behind her. "Type your initials. Figure out what initials you want and always use them. Some people use two, others three. A few people actually have more than that but we have the watch rotation and the logs so we know who K-V is. The T-R is Temporary Relief."

She reached up and typed on the keyboard. The system filled in date and time followed by a current course and speed notation.

I leaned around her and pointed to the tattletale on the front of the console. "Our course is here. That dot needs to stay inside the inner circle unless we're maneuvering." I pointed to the joy stick mounted beside her screen. "That's how you steer the ship, but it's currently on autopilot. You can tell because this little light is green." I pointed to it.

"So what do I have to do, sar?"

"For the moment, just sit there and enjoy the view." I straightened up and looked around. "Mr. Jenson can fill you in more on what a helmsman does, but your Spacers' Handbook lessons on Deck Division Half Share should fill you in on the basics."

"They mentioned the Handbook. Should I be studying it already, sar?"

"Sooner the better, Ms. Vincent. If you make half share and move up to ordinary spacer, we can pay you the higher rate, double your share payout, and you'll get a few more kilograms of mass for souvenirs." I grinned at her. "Or start at the full share section. You don't need to do them in order."

She glanced up at me. "Really, sar?"

"Really, Ms. Vincent. Don't get used to that. Most ships in the fleet only pay you for the job you're doing, not the one you're rated for."

She nodded and went back to staring at the tattletale. After a few moments of sitting there, some of the tension left her shoulders.

I went to my station and settled at the console, bringing up the navigation plot on my screen, just in case. Mr. Jenson returned shortly and I cleared my console as he topped the ladder. It took only a tick for them to swap back and for Ms. Vincent to escape the bridge with her tray.

"How'd she do, Skipper?"

"Very well, although about the only thing she needed to do was sit there and not touch anything."

He chuckled. "Better than I did, then. First time I relieved a watch like that, I grabbed the stick and held on for dear life. I was sure that if I didn't stay on the bubble the ship would crash."

"How'd that go, Mr. Jenson?"

"We didn't crash, sar." He glanced over at me. "I didn't discover the autopilot locked out the stick until much later. I provided a great deal of amusement to the bridge crews."

"And yet you pursued ship handling."

He nodded. "Not much to it on a ship this size. Unless we get caught out in a storm."

"We've been pretty lucky," I said, hoping that wouldn't jinx us. "They're worse in the High Line because we have to get so deep in the well."

He grinned over at me. "Another reason to work the Toe-Holds."

I saluted him with my coffee mug and settled back in the chair. "Let's hope our luck stays."

"Amen to that, Skipper."

Zoya and Ms. Heath relieved us at 1145.

"Nothing to report, Ms. Usoko."

"Thank you, Captain. You stand relieved."

She settled in to make the notations in the log while I dropped down the ladder and slid into the cabin to do the needful. It was going to be a long trip out of Newmar, and Mr. Jenson's comments about the Toe-Holds kept running through my brain. He was right about having to get so deep into the gravity wells to get to the liquid water zone. The probability of running into eddies in the solar wind became larger the longer we stayed and the closer we got to the system primary. As far as I knew, only Margary lacked the planetary anchor for their orbital. I pondered that anomaly as I headed for the wardroom and lunch mess. Why had Usoko joined the Confederated Planets? Simple geography?

I shrugged it off as irrelevant. Still, it made me wonder how the early Board of Exploration and CPJCT classified commercially viable systems and whether other systems like Margary existed within the imaginary boundaries of the High Line. Systems that weren't deemed viable because they lacked rocky planets.

I shook my head to dismiss the wool gathering and pushed into the wardroom. "I'm ready for lunch," I said, smiling at the gathering. "Anybody else?"

CHAPTER SEVEN
NEWMAR SYSTEM: JUNE 8, 2379

The first few mornings covering the eight to noon watch dragged on. Within a week, the routine report handling gave me something to do during the long, uneventful mornings. The watches also gave me a window into the crew as they rotated through. I got to sit with all the deck ratings at least once during any given week. I'd asked "How's it going below decks?" so often that the helms started offering their answers before I asked.

We got halfway to the Burleson limit before Mr. MacBradaigh convened his first study party on the mess deck, disrupting the effort already in progress. In hindsight, I should have anticipated the problem. I learned of it indirectly from Virgil Bentley on the morning watch.

"With all due respect, Skipper, Mr. MacBradaigh needs to mind his own business."

I leaned back from my console to get a better look at Mr. Bentley. "I take it there's an issue?"

Bentley shrugged. "He's taken over the mess deck. We can't study there anymore, sar."

"What's he doing?"

"He's driven us out. We have to study in the berthing areas now."

His words made little sense. "What do you mean, driven you out? He's supposed to be leading the sessions."

He sighed. "He's trying to teach us, sar." While it didn't manifest physically, Mr. Bentley's eye-roll came through loud and clear.

"Teach you? What is he trying to teach?"

"You know how the half shares have a lot of the same stuff across divisions?"

I nodded. "Go on."

"He's gone through the Handbook and pulled all those together. All the quarter shares have to follow along while he lectures. He's just read it himself and mashed it up."

"Why is that a problem?"

"For one, after the first few days, most of the quarter shares stopped coming. For another, those of us trying to work keep getting interrupted by his yammering. When we do start to work together, he interrupts us, telling us to be quiet because we're disrupting his class."

I suppressed the sigh I felt building in my chest. "So, is he still doing this?"

"Morning and afternoon, sar. At least I presume so. A few of the new people seem to think they have to attend or they'll be marked down when they return to the Academy."

"Thank you for bringing this to my attention, Mr. Bentley. What's the ideal outcome in your mind?"

He sighed but kept his own counsel for a few heartbeats before answering. "He's supposed to be some brilliant teacher or something from the Academy?"

"Instructional designer, yes."

He glanced over at me. "Maybe he needs to revisit his design."

"You think he has value?"

"Honestly, Skipper. I'm not sure. What he's doing now is obstructing. It's certainly not helping, and I don't think he realizes it."

"Good insight, Mr. Bentley."

Bentley shrugged. "Not sure how good. I'm not the only one, but we may be in the minority."

"I appreciate the feedback in any case. Other than that, how are the new crew doing?"

"A couple of them are still wearing their riding pants. Most of them seem to have settled in and relaxed into the flow."

"Riding pants?"

"Riding the 'I'm better than you because I'm going back to the Academy' horse." He shot me a grin over his shoulder. "They've got more of that in engineering than deck. We started out with a couple who didn't quite know to behave, but they've settled down."

"How do they feel about going into the Toe-Holds?"

"At least half of them think we're hazing them, sar."

"Hazing them?"

He nodded. "Yeah. Like it's some kind of prank. Whenever it comes up they just look at each other and laugh."

"What of the other half?"

"They just keep their heads down and don't say anything."

Mr. Hoag interrupted our conversation as he climbed onto the bridge. "Morning, Captain. Virgil. Got your coffee."

I took the offered cup but kept my hands away from the sweets. While the chief made a darn fine cookie, it was too easy for me to eat them so I tried to avoid them between meals.

"Tom, tell the skipper about the study sessions," Mr. Bentley said.

Mr. Hoag froze at the top of the ladder and looked at me, eyes wide. "What about them, sar?"

I held up a hand, palm out. "Don't say anything you're not comfortable sharing. Mr. Bentley says the study sessions on the mess deck have been disrupted. What's your opinion, Mr. Hoag?"

He glanced at Mr. Bentley. "Disrupted, Captain?"

"Mr. MacBradaigh?" I prompted.

"Yes, sar. He's there, sar."

"Are you attending, Mr. Hoag?"

"Not always, Captain. No."

"Why is that?"

"He's not particularly helpful, sar. I can read the material on my own much quicker than he can. Sar."

"Are you concerned that your lack of attendance will reflect badly on you when you return to the Academy?"

"I was at first, Captain, but it makes very little sense."

"Why is that, Mr. Hoag?"

"He's not keeping records. Not grading. He's not even taking attendance, sar." He paused. "Will it, sar?"

I shook my head. "No, Mr. Hoag. Other than adding another stanyer to your program, there are very few downsides to this effort."

"Are there downsides, sar?" he asked.

"Well, no more than you might expect from random chance in a year away from the hallowed grounds." I grinned at him. "There's always the chance you could fall down a ladder and break your neck."

"That's true at the Academy, too, Captain."

"Exactly my point."

"Is there anything else, Captain?"

"What would you like to see happen with the study groups, Mr. Hoag?"

"I've been in study groups before, Captain. They've been very helpful to me at the Academy. Having the senior ratings like Mr. Bentley help us when we get stuck? Very valuable, sar."

"So you feel comfortable asking for help?"

"Yes, sar. The senior ratings have all been very generous."

"How would you organize the study groups, if you were in charge?"

He frowned. "We're all at different places." His words leaked out of him, drips from a tap but gathering speed as he went. "That's good and bad. The people who are ahead help those coming up behind. Mostly."

"Would it help if you were all at the same place in your studies?" I asked.

"No, sar. That's the Academy. Everybody at the same place at the same time. It makes sense there and, well, sar, even there the people who have a good handle on a subject help the rest of us get a grip, if you know what I mean, sar."

"I do, Mr. Hoag. Keep going."

"Mr. MacBradaigh isn't helping because he's last in line, sar. He takes everybody back to the beginning without consideration of where we might be. I'm halfway through the fourth unit. Kathleen, Ms. Vincent, is almost done with the fifth while Mr. Schneider hasn't even started yet." He shook his head. "I don't even know where the engineering people are. There are a lot more of them than deck, sar."

"We're just the bus drivers, Mr. Hoag. They keep the bus running."

He laughed. "I can see how that plays out, Captain."

"Tell me about the Toe-Holds, Mr. Hoag."

His eyebrows lifted at that. "Sar?"

"In a few weeks, we'll be at the Burleson limit, Mr. Hoag. We're jumping into the Deep Dark on an alleged route to somewhere in New Caledonia."

"Yes, sar. I'm aware, sar."

"Are you also aware that we're not going to New Caledonia?"

He swallowed and looked at Mr. Bentley.

Mr. Bentley, for his part, seemed intently focused on the tattletale on his console and didn't look up.

"I've heard something to that effect, Captain, yes."

"What have you heard, Mr. Hoag?"

"That we're going to spend the next stanyer visiting Toe-Hold stations, sar. That we're not going back to an orbital any time soon."

"That was my original plan, yes, Mr. Hoag. I think it'll be sooner than I originally intended. Commandant Giggone seems to think we should show the flag around the Western Annex a bit."

He swallowed.

"Our next port will be Dark Knight Station. Have you heard of it, Mr. Hoag?" I asked.

"No, sar."

Mr. Bentley cleared his throat and glanced at Mr. Hoag.

"Well, yes, sar. I've heard of it from the senior ratings, sar."

"But you think they're hazing you," I said.

"Yes, sar. I'm not alone in that."

"Why, Mr. Hoag?"

"Why what, sar?"

"Why do you think they're hazing you?"

"Well, it's impossible, isn't it, sar?" He shook his head. "There's nothing out there. Just a long series of hops from here to New Caledonia."

"Why do you think that?"

"I've seen the charts, sar. There's nothing on them. It's empty space, sar. I mean there's a lot of rocks and stars and gas and the like, but the senior ratings keep talking about these fantastical cities in space. What are we supposed to think, sar?"

"Mr. Bentley, what's your favorite watering hole on Dark Knight?"

"Toss up, Skipper. Molly Malone's is handy. Good beer. Decent food. Not too rowdy. Knight's End is a little better for blowing off steam."

"You think Mr. Bentley is lying to me?" I asked, raising an eyebrow at Mr. Hoag.

"I—I don't know, sar."

"You think I'd be in on the plot to haze the entire quarter share contingent?"

Mr. Hoag stiffened a bit, his lips pressing together. "It's not beyond the realm of belief, sar."

"Good answer, Mr. Hoag."

"I am lying," Mr. Bentley said, looking over at Mr. Hoag. "I hate Molly Malone's. Their beer is only average, and they're too close to the docks so they cater to the spacers who don't care what they drink as long as they can drink fast and cheap."

"That was mean, Mr. Bentley," I said.

"It was. I'm sorry, Tom." He shrugged. "But everything the captain has said is true. Dark Knight is almost always our first stop out of Venitz and almost always our last stop before going back."

Mr. Hoag looked back and forth between us a couple of times. "I'll take your word for it, Captain. I'm sure we'll learn for ourselves eventually."

"Is it a common belief that we're hazing you?" I asked.

"Not everybody has said as much, but I think so. A few of the others have tried to convince us that it's not hazing."

"What would it take to convince you?" I asked. "Besides docking at Dark Knight?"

"Captain, I've seen the charts of the Western Annex. I've never seen anything like what we've been told is out there."

"Fair enough." I stood and crossed to the astrogation console, flicking the switch to wake it up. "Look at this, if you would, Mr. Hoag."

He crossed the bridge and looked into the display.

"You recognize this?" I asked, zooming the chart out to show the sectors immediately around our current position in Newmar.

"Yes, sar. It's part of the Western Annex."

"Can you find the Venitz sector?"

"Yes, sar. This one." He pointed to it.

"New Caledonia?"

"No, sar. It's far to the south side and the view isn't big enough."

"Sigler?"

"Here, sar." He pointed.

I pointed to an unlabeled portion of the screen. "Here?"

"Unclaimed territory, Captain. Deep Dark."

I toggled the view to display the Toe-Holds. The new icons washed across the screen in flood of amber.

He frowned and leaned in to look at the screen.

"The standard CPJCT chart only shows the Confederated Planets systems, Mr. Hoag. It suppresses the Toe-Holds." I pointed to Dark Knight Station. "This is where we're going." I zoomed the display in and overlaid the course from Newmar to Dark Knight. I gave him a moment to look at it before zooming out to show the whole Annex. "Every one of those amber dots is a station. Still think we're hazing you, Mr. Hoag?"

He straightened up, still staring at the console's screen. He looked at me. "There must be a thousand stations. That's a lot of work to go to for a prank, sar."

"Altogether it's more than four thousand and it's growing. It's no prank, Mr. Hoag. You're here to learn what it's like to crew a freighter. Your future lies among those amber dots."

"I'm not sure what to say, sar. This is not what I expected."

I grinned. "Don't feel alone. A lot of officers currently working in the fleet don't believe this is real. I was a captain before I found out. Mr. Carstairs introduced me to it when we bought the Chernyakova."

"Skipper, I'm showing an eddy in the flow," Mr. Bentley said.

I crossed to the helm and looked at his instruments. "Take it off auto and correct manually for a bit, Mr. Bentley. Reef up a few percent if you need to."

"Off auto. Reef on need. Aye, Cap." His hands spidered over the controls for a few moments before he grabbed the stick and nudged it around.

The green spot on the tell-tale came back to center and steadied.

"We're on course, Captain. Strain gauges still show some irregularities in the flow. Nothing major."

"Herd us along for a bit, Mr. Bentley. Let me know when the flow flattens out."

"Herding, aye, sar."

I took my seat at the console and made a notation in the log before noticing that Mr. Hoag still stood beside the astrogation console. "Thrilling, eh, Mr. Hoag?" I grinned at him.

"Sar? Can I ask? What was that about?"

"Of course. You can always ask. We may be too busy to answer at the moment, but you won't learn, if you don't ask. Mr. Bentley, can you talk and sail at the same time?"

"Yes, sar. We've passed through the eddy. Just riding the outer fringes."

"Care to explain to Mr. Hoag?"

"My pleasure, Skipper." He glanced at Mr. Hoag. "The ionized flow out of the star isn't smooth. It has eddies and ripples just like water. The autopilot does a good job of riding the smooth flow and taking us through the smaller ripples and eddies, but sometimes we need to hold the ship's hand and nudge it to keep it on course." He nodded at the joystick. "This is how I steer." He pointed to the console with his free hand. "Come see. These are the strain gauge readings from the sail emitters. When they're all the same, we have a smooth flow across the field. When the field ripples or eddies, they begin fluctuating. That puts an imbalance in the field and shifts us off the course. My job at helm is to put us back on course and keep it there."

Mr. Hoag frowned as he stared down at the screen. "I've seen those when I relieve the watch for head call but never knew what they meant."

"Now you know, Mr. Hoag. In theory, the autopilot should be able to handle it. It's faster and can recognize the patterns even better than I can."

"In theory," Mr. Hoag said.

Mr. Bentley looked up at him. "In practice, I think I can do better. Sometimes the computer rules don't work as well as human brains."

"How often do you have to do that?"

"Not very often. We're not even halfway to the limit, but we already need to intervene less. There's generally more variation in the flow when we're deeper in the well. By the time the wind gets out here, it's had a chance to flatten out a bit."

Mr. Hoag nodded and stepped back. "Thank you, Virgil."

"My pleasure, Tom. Any time."

"Still think we're hazing you, Mr. Hoag?" I asked.

"No, sar." He shrugged. "I mean you could be, but I don't see what the point of it would be."

"Well, there's never a point to hazing. Too many people see it as an initiation rite." I shrugged. "Especially at the Academy."

Mr. Bentley glanced up from his helm. "This isn't the Academy, Tom. We might pull the occasional prank, but the Toe-Holds are real. You'll see when we get there."

"Streets paved with gold and beer in the fountains?" he asked, a crooked grin twisting his lips to the side.

We laughed.

"No, Tom, but you're going to love the shares."

"Don't oversell it, Mr. Bentley."

He glanced over at me. "Am I wrong, Skipper?"

He made me chuckle. "This is our first run with a mixed-freight hauler. We don't know what this is going to look like yet."

"Fair enough." He looked back at his console. "We seem to be out of the eddy, Captain."

"Set auto, Mr. Bentley."

"Set auto, aye, sar." He flicked a couple of keys and took his hand off the stick. "Auto set. We're on the beam, sar."

"Thank you, Helm." I made the log entry before turning back to Mr. Hoag. "Think about what you'd like training to look like. I'd like you to be at least half share by the time we return. You could be full, even specialist rated in a stanyer."

"Now, he's lying, Tom." Mr. Bentley shot me a grin. "Full share, maybe. Spec/3 is a bugger and it helps if you've got some time in the job."

"I did say 'could,' Mr. Bentley."

"Yes, he did," Mr. Hoag said.

Mr. Bentley nodded. "All right. It's possible, but just making full share, able spacer for us deck apes, would be a significant achievement."

"Anything else, Mr. Hoag?" I asked.

Hoag shook his head and collected his tray. "Sar, no, sar." He grimaced.

"It's a hard habit to break, Mr. Hoag. Relearning it when you go back may be just as painful."

"I can see that, sar. Perhaps by then I'll learn to think before I speak." He gave me a broad smile. "Thanks for your time, Skipper."

"Spread the word among your peers," I said. "Dark Knight Station is real."

"I will, sar. I surely will." He glanced at the astrogation console before ducking down the ladder.

"Think he believes it, sar?" Mr. Bentley glanced over at me.

"I think so. Do they really think we made it up?"

"To be fair, Captain, we still send the new kids to the forward locker for two fathoms of water line."

"Still? We don't even have a forward locker."

"We do have water line, though, Skipper." His grin looked positively evil. "That's what makes it so effective."

"I'll grant you that, Mr. Bentley. I guess I was lucky."

"Lucky how, Skipper?"

"I started as a steward on the mess deck."

"What did they have stewards do, sar?"

I laughed. "I had Mr. Carstairs as a coworker. What didn't he do?"

"I'm impressed, Skipper."

"That we still work together after all this time?"

He glanced at me again, his evil grin back. "I was thinking more like 'you survived' but sure, we can do 'still work together.'"

"You think he's dangerous?" I asked, unable to keep the smile off my face.

He stared at his console.

"Mr. Bentley?"

"I'm thinking, Captain."

I laughed. "He wasn't that bad."

"If you say so, sar."

"What do you have against Mr. Carstairs? Or have on him?"

Mr. Bentley laughed. "Nothing, Captain. He seems a decent sort. Always has a kind word for the brow watch in port. I hardly ever see him underway."

"He's mellowed in his old age."

"Has he?" Mr. Bentley turned to look at me. "He must have been a hellion."

"He had his moments."

Mr. Bentley turned back to his console and shrugged. "If you say so, sar. All I know is that he's got a reputation among the crew as the officer most likely to."

After a moment, I asked, "Most likely to what?"

"Anything you care to name, Skipper. Anything at all."

"Is that good or bad, Mr. Bentley?"

"Yes, sar. It is."

I laughed and turned back to tend my own knitting. Only a month underway and my reporting queue had already backed up. As awkward as the morning watches felt, they gave me time to know more of the crew and hack away at the expanding pile of reports.

Chapter Eight
Newmar System: July 17, 2379

It didn't take long for our instructional designer to show up at the cabin door again. "Come in, Mr. MacBradaigh. Have a seat."

"Sorry to bother you, Captain, but it's about the training."

"What about it?"

"The crew isn't attending my sessions."

"Do you know why, Mr. MacBradaigh?"

"The word is that you said they don't have to."

I nodded. "That's probably an overstatement. I don't remember making such an announcement, but training isn't mandatory. It's what we all do between watches. Even captains. Is there something wrong?"

"They're not taking it seriously, Captain."

"What's your evidence, Mr. MacBradaigh?"

He blew out a breath laden with exasperation. "They're not attending the training sessions."

"You keep saying that like there's some relationship between their interest in advancing their skills and the sessions you run on the mess deck, Mr. MacBradaigh." I let that sink in for a moment. "What evidence do you have that the crew is not taking their training seriously, besides their unwillingness to have you lead it?"

He pressed his lips together and squinted at me. "Unwillingness?"

"What else would you call it? They are studying. I don't know who or how much, but we'll be coming up on a testing day before we make the jumps into Dark Knight. We'll see then."

He scowled at me. "When are they studying? Because they're certainly not doing it on the mess deck in the mornings or afternoons."

"Have you checked to see if they're doing it somewhere else? Like in their berthing areas? Or perhaps at a different time? Like the evenings?"

His frown morphed into surprise. "Why would they do that?"

"And now we're back to my original thought, Mr. MacBradaigh. They're unwilling to have you lead the sessions."

"Preposterous. They're cadets—" He wisely clamped his mouth shut on whatever he might have been about to say.

"Have you had much experience in the classroom, Mr. MacBradaigh? As a teacher?"

"Mostly I design courses for other teachers to use."

"What process do you use? I assume there's some kind of process for this?"

He nodded. "Of course. Every art has a core of science."

"So what's the first step? Walk me through it."

He frowned. "Why do you want to know?"

"Consider me a captain in search of education."

His frown relaxed but he still carried visible tension in his shoulders. "It depends. What's the scope of the work? Is it a full program? Like the deck officer major at the Academy? Is it a course? A particular lesson?"

"Those sound like iterations of scope to me, Mr. MacBradaigh, but take a course. Say the Academy wanted a semester-long course in adult development."

"Psychology? They have one."

"I know. I took it a long time ago. Assume they don't have it. Pick a generic topic. Automated Widget Assembly. What's the first thing you need to do?"

"We need to figure out what the need is."

"So, if there's not a need, where did the determination that the course needed to be developed come from?"

He blinked a few times. "Well, obviously there's a need. Otherwise, there's no impetus to design instruction for it. We need to determine what we want the student to know when the teaching ends."

"Then what?" I asked.

"Know the goal and scope. How much material. How to sequence it. That will determine whether it's a day's lesson or a week-long unit in a larger structure. Perhaps a series of seminars. Up to a full semester-long course."

"Is that it?"

He shrugged. "We try to assess where the student is coming from. There's no need to teach the student to read, usually, but we may need to teach them nomenclature before we use that language in the instruction, for example. In more advanced classes, they're expected to know foundational knowledge. That's why some courses have prerequisites."

"Let's use the crew problem, Mr. MacBradaigh. What need are you acting on?"

"The one you gave me, Captain. The crew needs to advance in rank."

I held back the sigh fighting to escape. "If I gave you that as a need, then I apologize."

His eyes shot open and he stiffened in his chair. "What?"

"The crew does not need to advance in rank. If I said that, I misspoke." I took a moment to let that sink in. "It benefits the ship if they advance, if they learn more about how the ship operates. It benefits them by giving them more pay. They don't need to advance for the ship to operate safely and efficiently and are under no obligation to do so. If it were required, we'd just hire the people who had those skills already."

"Then why do it?" He frowned, obviously perplexed. "Isn't it a waste of their time?"

"For one thing, on this ship they get paid more. For another, it improves their opportunities for advancement and employment on their next ship, should they grow tired of us."

"But they're going back to the Academy," he said. "There's no 'next ship' for them."

"I'm relatively certain only those crew members who came from the Academy will return to it, Mr. MacBradaigh."

He shook his head. "You're talking about the senior ratings?"

"I'm talking about the crew. There is only one crew, Mr. MacBradaigh. It's composed of the senior ratings and the quarter and half shares who came from the Academy. Right now, those senior ratings are carrying the training load." He opened his mouth, but I plowed over him. "And before you get too far along that course, it's what they've always done. It's what they'd be doing even if those crew members weren't going back to the Academy in a few months."

His frown came back, deeper than before. "I thought you said that too many crew members don't pursue training. That they don't advance beyond one or two levels. That it was a problem."

I nodded. "Those statements are all true. What I'd like is for every one of the former and future cadets to leave here with full share ratings in their divisions. Ideally, I'd love it if they'd leave with full share ratings in multiple divisions."

"Why? Isn't that working at cross-purposes?"

I looked up at the overhead to try to find an answer that might make sense to him. After a moment, I looked back at him. "Because, Mr. MacBradaigh, they're going back to the Academy to finish their programs and become officers. Officers who would benefit from understanding what the other divisions do and how those crew members work. Having an appreciation for the deck division makes the engineering officers work better with their counterparts and vice versa. Same with cargo. Same with steward. The cross-pollination means those new third officers will be less likely to trip on their own feet when they get jobs in the fleet."

"Then why did you put them in their original divisions?" he asked. "Wouldn't it make more sense to put them in a different one?"

"Arguably, yes, if our only goal was to cross-train them. The primary goal is to give them a feel for what the people they'll be managing do. What those lives are like. Anything beyond that is a bonus, but since we have a full stanyer, I'm not above hoping that at least a few of them will cross-train into divisions beyond their own."

"Does that really help?"

"I believe so. It helped me and I can't help but think it would help any officer."

"You cross-trained?"

"I sailed with Alys Giggone on the Lois McKendrick before I went to the Academy. I thought that was common knowledge."

"Well, yes, but weren't you a steward?"

"I started as a steward, moved to engineering, and ended in deck. When I left the Lois, I had full share ratings in all four divisions. Cargo was the only division I didn't personally work in."

"Is that common among crew members?" he asked. "What's the incentive?"

"It's not terribly common, no. My incentive was job security. If I hadn't gone to the Academy, I'd have found myself beached at Dunsany Roads. Federation Freight policies would have bumped me off and I'd have had to find a new berth. Being qualified to take any full share berth on the ship made me a lot more employable than if I only had rating in one division."

"Because there are more full share job openings?" he asked. "I'm sorry. I don't really know how the crew hiring process works."

"Because any rating is qualified for every job below theirs. Anybody is qualified for any quarter share as long as they're physically able do the work. Half shares get a leg up and better pay. Full shares get another boost. Any full share in the deck division can take any lower-rated job in deck. That opens up three potential jobs instead of the one that quarter shares have. Take that across the other divisions? It multiplies the opportunities, particularly in engineering because they're the largest division in terms of crew numbers. For every rating in the deck division, there are usually two or three in engineering. From a crew member's standpoint, even getting a half share rating in engineering opens more doors than moving from half to a full share rating in deck. Cargo is the hardest because it's the smallest division on every ship. Even steward is better because there's almost always two steward berths, where a solo cargo berth is usually a cargo officer."

"You're talking about the crew member's perspective," he said.

"Yes. Of course. What other perspective would I take?"

"At the Academy we approach coursework based on what CPJCT needs their future officers to know."

"I think we're talking about the same thing, just at a different level."

He raised his eyebrows at that. "I'm not following, Captain."

"Turn it around to the cadet's perspective. What do they need to know in order to earn their third officer's ticket? What do they need to know to graduate with their bachelor's degree?"

"Those two things are not the same, Captain."

"I'm aware, Mr. MacBradaigh. You're missing my point. Talk to me about this needs assessment from the perspective of the student, not the teacher. What does the student need?"

He shook his head. "Big picture at the Academy?"

"Sure. We can start there."

"It breaks down to skills, knowledge, and attitude. The Academy's mission is to teach the proper skills, provide the necessary knowledge, and imbue the proper attitudes. At the highest level we break down what each graduate should know, what they should be able to do, and how they should behave. Many of the requirements feed directly into the CPJCT third officer certification. We have a lot of general knowledge courses that provide the foundations for those requirements."

"I agree. They can't run until they can walk. Now bring that idea to the ratings here."

"That's where I'm confused, Captain. I thought you had a need for them to advance."

"They have a need to advance, Mr. MacBradaigh. Whether they know it or not, their future well-being depends on it. The ship benefits from it as well, but the need is theirs."

He slumped back in his chair and pulled at his lower lip. "And everything they need to learn is in the Handbook?"

"Yes. The early lessons are simple, mostly nomenclature and procedure, which is why getting them studying early is important. Senior ratings generally push quarters to half share so they don't have to point and explain everything all the time. If they can pass half share, they're much easier to work with."

"That sounds like a ship's need to me, Captain."

"It's a ship's benefit, Mr. MacBradaigh. Of course, I want them to move up so the ship has that benefit, but if they can't see a benefit to themselves, why would they pursue it?"

He nodded, his head sinking and rising slowly as if he were rolling mental marbles into his brain holes. "Two things. You said 'whether they know it or not.' Don't they understand this employability logic?"

He caught me sideways with that. "I don't know. It seems so obvious that I can't imagine they don't."

"You also said that it's not a common strategy among ratings, cross-training in another division."

"It isn't, no, but that's really a secondary issue. The main issue is that too many of them get to full share and stop without moving up to a specialization."

"My understanding is that wasn't the case on the Chernyakova," he said. "You had a lot of specialists who moved up into senior ratings positions here."

"True, but, remember, we give them an incentive to move up the skill tree by paying them for their skill level instead of their position."

"So the problem isn't a training problem, is it?" he asked. "It's a management problem."

I laughed. "All right. I'll grant you that."

"You don't actually have this problem on your ships, do you."

"No—at least we didn't on the Chernyakova. It's too soon to say what will happen here."

"What about before?"

"It was a problem on the William Tinker. Less so on the Agamemnon, but we only had three ratings there."

"So what is it you think I should be teaching?"

"I'm not convinced you should be teaching anything. You don't have the background for it."

He gave me a slow blink, his eyes closing for a long moment before opening again to stare at me. "I thought that's what you asked me to do."

"I thought what I asked you to do was come up with a program that supported the crew's self-directed study. These quarter and half shares are motivated to move up right now because they're looking at the extra credits for tuition. Once they see their share payouts, moving up from quarter to half to full will make good economic sense. It still benefits them to advance their skills and knowledge, and to cross-train in other divisions. That's a program that can work for future cohorts, if it's well-designed." Yes, I made a blatant appeal to his vanity, but it seemed a handy lever to pull. "Anybody who makes half share early will be better positioned to go up to full share. The extra time should give them the opportunity to do that cross-training even in the absence of additional credits."

He frowned. "Why would they? What's their motivation?"

"To be better officers? Self-fulfillment?" I shrugged. "Many, perhaps most, will not. The path I'd like to see them take is have every one of them at full share by the time we've been underway six months, and be cross-trained to at least half share in one other division by the time we dock at Newmar again."

"Is that even feasible?" he asked.

"It will be tight. We already have a few stepped up to half share in engineering. They took the test on the orbital before we left. After the next testing period in a couple of weeks, we should have more. Alys wants us to show the flag around the Western Annex, so we'll be hitting at least one more orbital before heading back. Maybe two, although I'm not happy with the amount of time it would take."

"Aren't they all the same?"

"Toe-Holds are usually closer to the Burleson limit. None of the major ones are very deep in the gravity wells. It's taking us nine weeks to get out of Newmar. It'll take less than ten hours to get out of Dark Knight."

"Ten days?" he asked.

"Ten hours. Dark Knight Station is practically at the Burleson limit. It's a shallow well to begin with and depending on the position of the major bodies, we can sometimes jump within an hour or two. That cuts down the transit times between Toe-Holds. It's why this trade is so lucrative. We still have jump errors and it takes time to rendezvous with the stations, but we don't have to spend weeks getting out to the limit as a rule."

"But you do in CPJCT space?"

"All but Margary, yes. There may be others, but I've led a sheltered life." I grinned at him.

"Why?"

"A good question. I suspect it's because the CPJCT gets the most revenue from systems with planets in the liquid water zone. Those are the systems that they deem most 'commercially viable' because they're the ones with planets that can be terraformed economically. They're the systems that companies most want to lease. Unfortunately, that zone is deep in the gravity well. We need to get in and get out. It all takes time."

He sat there staring into the middle distance for so long, I began to wonder if he'd checked out altogether. Eventually he focused back on me. "Why does anybody trade at CPJCT ports?"

I grinned at him. "The point of this exercise is that most people don't."

His eyebrows flew up. "Really?"

I shrugged. "I've only been trading in the Toe-Holds for a few stanyers. Prior to taking the Chernyakova into Mel's Place, I didn't know any more about the Toe-Holds than you did. Neither did Captain Case nor most of her officers. I'm coming to believe that the only people who carry freight in the High Line are those who don't know any better or who have some reason other than profit to maintain a presence there."

"What kind of reason?"

"CPJCT is still the largest organized market in the Annex. Highly regulated and only marginally profitable, but it's reliable. Very low risk. Everything is organized, sanitized, and regulated. It's the 'safe bet.' You won't get fat, but you won't go broke unless you're stupid or careless. If you're too stupid or careless, TIC steps in so you learn the error of your ways."

"And the Toe-Holds are the high risk, high payout ports?" he asked.

"In a sense. What they aren't is centrally regulated or located deep in gravity wells. We can get cargo from Dark Knight to Mel's Place and back again with a return cargo in less time than it takes us to just get out of Newmar with one."

He pursed his lips. "And you think that most of the freight in the Annex is handled by these Toe-Holds."

"I do. It's only a feeling, but I've seen the numbers on what we've carried on the Chernyakova and it beggars the amount we hauled on the William Tinker. Both Barbells. Both profitable. Tinker only worked in the High Line and turned a modest profit. The Chernyakova, mostly in the Toe-Holds. We really only ran cargo up to the High Line when we wanted to get back to Port Newmar. The profits turned our lowest ratings into millionaires."

"I've heard that noised about," he said. "It's true?"

"Well, they earned that much over a few stanyers. Whether any of them still have it? I don't know. About eighteen months ago they started up an investment pool. Everybody buys a share, and they invest the money.

"We also had a few significant windfalls that boosted us early on. The point is that I am convinced there are more opportunities to trade in the Toe-Holds. Faster transit times between systems. More stations than orbitals. Fewer restrictions on production. Fewer stations that specialize at the cost of self-sufficiency."

Mr. MacBradaigh gave a short nod. "Anecdotal evidence at best, but better than nothing. Will these crews replicate that success?"

"Hard telling. The cohort on the Chernyakova will almost certainly earn enough to pay for their third year. Probably their fourth." I looked around the cabin but seeing the ship in my mind's eye. "Here? I don't know. Mixed freight should have as good a chance to earn a similar amount. The strategies differ because we can't carry a big pile of anything. The other side of the coin is that the Chernyakova generally won't get a full can of a very high value commodity. Nobody keeps high value commodities sitting around long enough to fill a large can."

"So we can take smaller amounts that are worth more in aggregate?" he asked.

"Yes. We've got eighty-eight cans to move around. Some will move at every station, but no station is likely to take them all, unless the Toe-Holds are vastly different from the High Line in that regard. As long as we can clear as much on a few of our smaller cans as the Chernyakova can clear on her single one, then we'll earn the same amount. It's one of the things that Pip wants to test out."

"Test out?"

"He has some mathematical modeling that predicts that bulk cargo and mixed freight should perform at similar levels based on the mass-value ratios, regardless of the ship configuration."

"Why wouldn't they?" he asked.

"Historically, bulk haulers have been considered the bread and butter of freight. They really are the backbone for raw materials processing and even some low-level processed commodities like refined metals and some liquids. If you only make a fractional credit per unit, moving a few million units can give you a good sized pile of credits. Maybe more than you could earn on a smaller pile of units where you earn multiple credits each."

"But Mr. Carstairs thinks otherwise?"

"He thinks they're on par. One's not better than the other over the long run. He believes that the long-standing belief comes from the way freight gets managed in the High Line. It's quite true that a mixed-freight hauler is not as profitable, but 'not as profitable' isn't the same as 'not profitable.' There are some cargoes that need those smaller cans. Tractors bridge the gap between the small cans we carry on the

Collins and the big cans that the Chernyakova uses. Tractors are interesting in that regard because they're small, fast, and cheap to run."

He shook his head. "You're using terms that I'm not familiar with, Captain. I'm sorry."

I laughed. "Sorry, Mr. MacBradaigh. I got a little carried away. Back to the issue. The crew is not attending your training sessions. Have you asked them why?"

"Should I?"

"Seems like the most likely source of information."

"If they'll talk to me." He said that almost to himself.

"Why wouldn't they, Mr. MacBradaigh?"

"Because I'm the Academy in their eyes. Why would they criticize the Academy knowing they've got to go back to it?"

"Ask the senior ratings. They're not going back and they're not attending either, are they?"

He frowned and shook his head. "Why would they?"

"Why, indeed, Mr. MacBradaigh? They used to use the mess deck all the time on the afternoon watch. They still use it in the evenings when Chief Bashar isn't running a movie. It wouldn't surprise me to find some of them there in the morning watch as well, but I'm on the bridge then so I don't see it."

He pulled on his bottom lip again, staring into the middle distance. "One of my problems is that I have no context. No frame for this effort. It's too amorphous."

"Whenever I've got a problem, I have a few things I do first." I said.

He dropped his hand and looked over at me. "Care to share, Captain?"

I shrugged. "I don't know how much they'll help but my first principle is 'feed the crew.' Usually that's literal. It means get the galley going. Brew the coffee. Literally feed the crew."

"But it's also a metaphor, right?" he asked.

"It is. With any project, I need a place to start. Once started, I can usually figure out the next step toward solving the problem or achieving the goal."

MacBradaigh repeated the words. "Feed the crew."

"Who's your crew, Mr. MacBradaigh?"

"What's my project?" He shook his head.

"Another of my first principles is figuring out what the problem is. When things get ugly, it's easy to focus on the thing in front of you instead of the situation that put it there in the first place."

He chuckled and shook his head. "I should be recording this."

I laughed with him. "No, you don't need that right now. Alys gave you a mission to learn all you can about the Toe-Holds and to design a curriculum to replace the badly flawed propaganda the Academy currently uses. That's your main mission. Like mine is turning a profit on cargo."

"Isn't that Mr. Carstairs's mission? I thought you were just the bus driver." He grinned at me.

"Pip is just the guy doing the buying and selling. He's the sharp edge on our chisel, but he's not the one responsible for all the expenses. He's not the one incurring the cost of doing business. That's me. Yes, I'm the bus driver, but we can't turn a profit if the bus doesn't go anywhere, and that costs credits. My mission, my goal, is to do it profitably."

"Isn't that at odds with paying the crew for their rank instead of their jobs?"

"My mother used to say 'penny wise and pound foolish.' I'm not going to chase fractions of a credit but lose hundreds in the process. Paying the crew for their ranks buys loyalty. It's recognition that they're performing above and beyond the requirements of their current jobs. When it comes to crew, we control turnover by giving them no reason to leave and by giving them reasons to stay, too. In the High Line? I honestly don't know if we could afford it. A really good share there is equal to your salary. Out here? We haul more freight in shorter periods of time. The ship can get paid two, maybe three times, before we have to pay the crew once. In the High Line, we'd have to pay them two or three times before the ship landed a single shipment." I let him digest that for a moment. "So? What's your goal? What's your mission? What's the problem you're trying to solve?"

He sighed. "It's not teaching the crew. You seem to have that working in spite of me." He shot me a wry smile. "The problem you gave me, getting more of the crew working on their ratings, seems to be well in hand here."

"It is and it isn't," I said. "Right now, we only have a rough idea of who's paying attention. The senior ratings can help those who are studying, but can't do much for those who aren't. Who won't. I'd guess that fewer than half of the quarters are working on half yet. The few we have in the deck division are, but the majority of quarter shares are in engineering. Natalya has her finger on that pulse. She'll know."

"I can ask her. Will she tell me?"

"Oh, yes. She's even more fanatical about it than I am. She can't order them to study and it frustrates the hell out of her when she gets crew who aren't working on their next rating."

"Does that happen often?"

"It usually only takes one share payout for the quarters and halfs to realize that they'd have gotten twice as much share if they'd just taken the test. Moving them from full share to specialist ranks is harder."

"Isn't the work more satisfying?"

I laughed. "It's all boring after the first hundred days. Boring is good. We like boring. The opposite of boring isn't interesting. It's terrifying, and that's not where we want to be." I shook my head. "The net present value of study is entertainment. Something to engage your mind. A bulwark against the tedium."

He kind of squinted at me. "Entertainment? Studying is entertaining?"

"Of course." I shrugged. "What do you call it? Work?" I very purposefully punched that button.

He grimaced. "Touché." He settled himself in his chair again, a disgruntled pigeon smoothing his feathers. "What I'm gathering here is that my efforts at providing structure to this process are failing. Until we get to the Toe-Holds and I can begin to see for myself, I'm not going to be of much use."

"You've got two or three weeks before we have a testing period. Why don't you walk the walk before you try to talk the talk?"

He frowned. "What do you mean?"

"You can take the half share exam. Pick a division. Deck, if you like."

"Don't I have to be a member of the crew?"

"Anybody can take the test. You could even try the full share. Able Spacer for Deck Division is pretty straightforward. A bit more esoteric knowledge, but if you run through the half share, take a couple of the practice tests, you should be able to move right ahead to full share."

"Is there time?"

"You don't have any pressing duties. You're used to the academic regimen. See how the other half lives."

"And it'll keep me busy until we get out of Venitz." He raised an eyebrow in challenge.

I shrugged. "We each have to provide our own entertainments."

"Are you challenging me?"

"I'm relatively certain you can pass it. I don't see it as any kind of challenge."

"Do I have to do anything special?"

"You have a copy of the Spacer's Handbook, right?"

He nodded.

"Just follow the lessons. Do the exercises. Take the unit tests. At the end, take the practice tests until you can score 95 percent on at least three consecutive tries. Five would be a more reliable measure."

"Any division?"

"Any division. None is easier or harder. That's my first-hand experience. I've taken them all. The off-division ones can seem harder if you're not immersed in the day-to-day tasks of that work. For you, that will be any of them, but the difference is small. Easily overcome by study. All the answers are in the book. You just have to copy them into your mind."

He laughed. "Isn't that true of all learning?"

"I'm not sure it applies to physical skills to that degree, but the Handbook can't test you on manipulating a wrench safely. It can only ask you how you'd do it. You have to tell it. You can't show it."

He shook his head. "Assessments are the devil's work. They never measure learning. They're just proxies, but proxies are better than nothing."

"Maybe, but we have the actual performance aspect in the day-to-day work."

He bit his lips together and nodded. "Thank you, Captain. You've given me a lot to think about."

"Once you've studied the half share materials and tried taking the tests yourself, see what you think of the design. It's been largely unchanged for as long as I've been in space. Perhaps you can design something better."

He stood. "I will. I'll let you know what I find out." He left the cabin, almost running into Zoya in the passageway. "Oh, excuse me, Ms. Usoko. I wasn't watching where I was going."

She nodded and he disappeared in the direction of his stateroom. She stepped into the cabin and looked at me, eyebrows raised.

I shook my head. "Long story. I suggested that he take the half share exam with the crew."

"Instead of trying to tell them how to study?" she asked.

"Well, the crew has been skipping his sessions on the mess deck. He's distressed that they're not taking study seriously."

She snickered and leaned her shoulders against the bulkhead beside the open door. "Sorry I missed that conversation."

"How's your section coming along?"

"I expect Josh will take the spec/3 for ship handling. I wanted him to take it before we left Newmar, but he wanted a few more weeks to practice. Being on helm watches will dial him in, I think."

"Any doubts about him sitting at helm?"

"None. He's got the touch. I think he took lessons from Mary Torkelson." She grinned. "Ms. Freano is going for able spacer in a single jump."

"Will she make it?"

Nathan Lowell

"I think so. She studies on the bridge with us instead of sitting on the mess deck."

"Hm. She doesn't during the morning watch."

"You're the captain, Captain." She lifted one shoulder in a half shrug and dropped it again. "Captains aren't usually seen as approachable. Especially to the junior crew."

I nodded. "I'll invite her when second section comes around again."

Zoya smiled and I lost my train of thought for a moment. "Good idea. Anything else?"

"Any problems that you don't want to bring to my attention?"

She laughed. "You just had him in the cabin. I think you're aware of it."

"Has he been a larger problem than I know?"

She shook her head. "No, I don't think so. His biggest problem is claiming the mess deck for instruction. If you've got him to stop doing that, things should smooth out nicely."

"Ripple effect?"

"Yeah. The study groups retreated to the berthing areas where they made more noise than usual." She shrugged.

"Got it," I said. "I think I'd rather they didn't study if the cost is having sleep-deprived watchstanders."

"I'm with you there, Skipper."

"Thanks for tipping me off about Ms. Freano."

"Just doin' muh job, Cap'n." She gave me a rakish grin and a jaunty two-fingered salute. "I better get back to it."

She left me sitting there in the empty cabin. The echoes of my conversation with MacBradaigh sounded loud against the background noises of a ship underway—the whoosh of the fans in the vents, the faint vibrations in the hull from the generators all the way aft, and the occasional voices and footsteps of the crew going about their business.

I looked at my console but didn't wake it up. Talking to Mr. MacBradaigh about study, about entertainment, awakened something in me. I couldn't remember the last time I studied something beyond the latest specs on various pieces of equipment. I couldn't remember the last thing I'd done for fun. The last time I'd challenged myself.

111

On a whim, I went to my grav trunks and started pawing through the odds and ends that never got unpacked. Buried in the bottom of one, I found my running shoes and a pair of shorts. I pulled them out and nodded.

This ship had a gym with a running track. I grinned.

The shoes felt a bit stiff but they still fit. The shorts seemed a bit snug around the waist. A ship's tee over the top hid most of the damage. The middle-aged man in the mirror in the cabin waved at me and I headed down the ladder, collecting odd looks from the few crew that I passed.

Kim saw me pass and grinned. "Yer out of uniform, spacer."

I laughed and kept going.

I dropped down the ladder to the boat deck and managed to say "As you were" before anybody noticed the captain on deck. I blended in with the others in workout clothing. I crossed to the track and did some stretches to limber up a little before going up the few steps to the track surface and starting along at a slow jog.

I'd only gone halfway around before somebody came up behind me. I heard their footsteps and slid to one side, looking over my shoulder and seeing Mr. Jacobs hoofing along. I waved him ahead. "No ceremony required on the track, Mr. Jacobs."

He kicked a bit harder and passed me. "Thanks, Skipper." He pulled away and had nearly come around again before I got back to the beginning. I ducked down the ladder to the main deck, and he stopped at the ladder. "Giving up already, sar?" He gave me a cocky grin.

I grinned up at him. "I'm out of shape. I don't want to be crippled tomorrow. I've got time and nothing to prove."

He nodded and kicked off on another lap.

I watched him go for a moment, seeing in my mind's eye a younger me on a track not unlike this one. I looked around at the crew working the stations. Listening to the metallic clanks and ratchets. The low voices and occasional laughter.

Nathan Lowell

They'd forgotten I was there. I accepted that gift, taking it as the reminder that it was.

I smiled to myself and headed back to the cabin and a shower. It hadn't been a long workout, or a hard one, but my tee stuck to my sweaty back. A few days of one lap would help. Maybe two after a week.

Mr. MacBradaigh wasn't the only one with a lot of work to do. I found myself looking forward to doing it.

CHAPTER NINE
NEWMAR SYSTEM: JULY 29, 2379

The testing period hit a few days before we were due to jump out of Venitz. Mr. Cartwright had settled into the shipboard routine nicely. Kim helped him organize the testing, matching engineering with stewards on the first day and deck with cargo on the second. The ship had been abuzz for a couple of days beforehand. Mr. MacBradaigh had stayed in his stateroom except for meals. I presumed he was studying. His name appeared on the half share exam schedule for all four divisions.

The ship's office became the center of attention as the big day approached. Between them, Kim and Mr. Cartwright, with a little assist from Natalya, installed two extra consoles to supplement the normal pair.

I braced Mr. Cartwright at breakfast on the first day. "Are you ready?"

"I think so, Captain. Ms. Fortuner practiced with me yesterday." He shot her a nod and a smile. "Thanks for your help."

She grinned and nudged him with her elbow. "Pay it forward, shippie. You'll get the chance before too long."

"Everybody's got a chance who wants it?" I asked.

"I still have a couple of open seats, so I assume so." Cartwright shrugged. "Not like people aren't aware it's happening."

"How's the watch roster holding up, Kim?"

She took a sip of coffee, nodding at Natalya. "She's got the worst of it."

"We've scheduled morning watch for afternoon testing and vice versa," Natalya said. "We'll have to do some patchwork and a couple of temporary reliefs, but it's covered."

"Deck was easy," Ms. Fortuner said. "We're tomorrow with the cargo crew."

"How many are taking a test?" I asked, looking around the table.

"All of mine are going up at least one," Natalya said. "The two enginemen that bumped up in Newmar will be taking machinist. Two of the wipers are trying for machinist as well."

"Will they make it?" I asked.

She shrugged. "They should. Schulties and Go have been drilling them. I think they all know they need to be able to pass the practice on a regular basis."

"They're cadets," Mr. MacBradaigh said. "They're used to test taking."

I raised an eyebrow in his direction.

"They were cadets," he said, with a little shrug. "Habits, Captain."

"I saw your name on the testing schedule, Mr. MacBradaigh," I said.

"You did, Captain. I took your words to heart." He finished off his breakfast, laying his utensils across the plate.

"What did you think of the materials?"

"It's probably some of the best designed self-directed study I've ever seen, the limitations of the media notwithstanding. I saw what you meant about the difference between talking about it and doing it."

"Think you'll pass?" Kim asked, smiling at him across the table.

He gave a short laugh. "I don't know. I'm following the same advice all the other quarter shares got. Passing the practice tests at the 95 percent or higher level. I don't have the advantage of application that they do, but I've aced the practice tests."

"Why all four?" I asked.

"Something you said, Captain. I saw what you meant when you told me that the half shares all had a lot of duplication. All the material about watchstanding, shipboard routine, expectations. It's all the same with some minor variations based on the division."

"Watchstanding is watchstanding," Mr. Cartwright said.

Mr. MacBradaigh nodded. "The steward division is the most different. I assume it's because they're day workers?"

"Largely," I said. "They're busy through the day in various levels of intensity. Meal times are only the parts we see. There's a lot of work that goes on behind the scenes."

"I noticed," he said.

"Pip? Your cargo fledglings?" I asked.

"They're ready. I've pushed them to take the full share test because I want them to run up to spec/2 before we get back."

Mr. MacBradaigh looked at him. "That's ambitious. You have a reason, I assume."

Pip grinned. "Always. In this case, it's because spec/2 is about 90 percent of what they'd need to get their cargo third officer ticket. Even spec/3 would give them a leg up on graduation."

"Any problems with either of them?" I asked.

"No. King has some background in orbital cargo ops. Jenkins worked for a cargo broker in Tellicheri before going to Newmar. They'll have no problem getting full share."

"Why not push them straight up to spec/3?" Natalya asked.

"I want them at full share by the time we pay out after Dark Knight. Full share will give them the credits, and I'm sure they'll both make it. I'm not sure they could jump straight to spec/3 without a little more experience and another couple of months of study."

"What do you do between ports?" Mr. MacBradaigh asked.

Pip chuckled. "On a Barbell, it's mostly market analysis. You can't even inspect the cargo once the can's tied on. Here? It's never-ending. We've got daily checks on each of the eighty-eight cans. The market analysis is a monster because we've got analysis on every single market sector from raw materials to finished goods. On a Barbell, there are only so many things you can ship in bulk. We've taken cans of machine parts on the Chernyakova before but those are pretty rare. Mostly the analysis is 'who's moving big piles of stuff?' and 'where is it going?' Here? We're looking more at underlying market forces. Where is there a spike in manufacturing of computer chips? Where is the demand for those chips? How does the material flow between stations? We're going to Dark Knight next, so what do they export and who are their market partners?"

Kim looked at him wide-eyed, but it was Natalya's expression that struck home with me. Pip might have been talking to Mr. MacBradaigh, but Natalya's smile said that he'd spoken to her as well.

She caught me looking at her. She gave me a crooked grin and a quick shrug before paying extra attention to her coffee cup.

"Are the stewards up, too?" I asked.

Mr. Cartwright nodded. "Mr. Franklin is up for chef. The rest are going for half shares."

"So nobody in the quarter share ranks are sitting this one out?" I asked.

"I think everybody's on the schedule, Skipper," Ms. Fortuner said.

"Anybody who's dragging their feet?" I asked.

"As far as I know, the only people not testing are the higher level specialists," Natalya said. "I know all of mine are at least studying."

"I know Mr. Jenson is working on spec/1 astrogation," Ms. Fortuner said. "Mr. Bentley? I'm not sure. He just made spec/3 recently. Ms. Heath is working on helm. Mr. Keen is on the fence on astrogation but he only made able spacer on the last cycle."

I nodded. "Thanks. I appreciate everybody pushing the training." I glanced at the chrono. "I better get my hustle on. I've got to relieve Zoya in a bit." I stood and left the wardroom, heading for the cabin. I had to admit to myself that I hadn't expected the new cohort to be pursuing training as enthusiastically as they appeared to be. I wondered if I would have been as diligent had the opportunity come to me after my second year.

I stopped by the cabin and freshened up, making sure I didn't have breakfast stuck on my face or anything.

Mr. MacBradaigh's embrace of the training materials surprised me. He hadn't been back to the cabin once since the conversation that sent him down the path. Even if he was only going through the motions, I had the sense he was engaged on two levels. First, studying the materials to take the tests—the surface level. Second, studying the materials through the lens of somebody who designed such things for a living. Funny how a simple thing can change one's outlook.

I noticed my running shoes lying on the deck where I'd toed them off the night before. After only a couple of weeks, I was up to three laps. My muscles still weren't up to snuff. I'd been neglecting them too long, but I could already feel the difference. The meditative effect of running had helped center me, and my legs felt stronger just climbing the ladders over the course of the day. On a whim, I dropped to the deck and did a dozen pushups. Clambering back to my feet, I realized that my legs weren't the only parts that needed some attention.

Well, not like I didn't have the time. I glanced at the chrono and then at the mirror, using my reflection to settle my uniform back into place. I had a standard to maintain.

That thought made me laugh as I left the cabin and trotted up the ladder to the bridge.

One of the practices I'd brought to the Collins was my nightly prowl around the ship. After talking with Mr. Bentley, I made it a point to do more than stick my head into the compartment and nod at the crew. Hindsight is always so much easier than foresight, but I still kicked myself. I knew some of the new people still thought they were being hazed, but to have it continue so long gave me more than a few concerns.

I headed for the mess deck. Helping myself to the coffee there was a mostly symbolic gesture, but I did it anyway. It was the same exact coffee we drank in the wardroom. Ours just came out of a carafe that one of the stewards filled from the urns. The crew had no reason to know that, so I always grabbed a cup when I started my tour.

Ms. Martinez had messenger duty and jumped up to attention when she saw me enter. "Captain, on deck."

"As you were." I tried to be as fast as possible, but it still gave time for the messenger to announce me. The old crew never flinched, knowing my habit and preferences, but the new ones all scrambled to stand. "Just here for the coffee."

Mr. Schulties looked up from his tablet long enough to chuckle. "You say that every night, Skipper."

"It's true every night, Mr. Schulties."

He laughed again and went back to his reading.

I looked around, noticing that the new people all watched me while the old crew just went about their business. "How many people think that Dark Knight Station is some kind of prank?" I asked, addressing the room in general.

Mr. Schulties looked up again. "You asking me, sar?"

"I was mostly asking the room, but do you have an answer, Mr. Schulties?"

He scanned the room before shrugging. "About half of them, I suspect, Skipper."

Ms. Martinez looked down at her tablet and I noticed three or four of the other quarter shares looking anywhere but at me.

"What do you think, Mr. Schulties? Is it a prank?"

He laughed. "I might have thought so once upon a time, but I know too many people who live there now."

The gazes all fixed on him.

"What do you think of Molly Malone's, Mr. Schulties?"

"The pub?" He frowned and shook his head. "Handy to the docks, but weak beer. Too many idiots taking up space and substituting volume for potency on their course to drunken revelry."

"Captain?" one of the engineering crew sitting at Mr. Schulties's table raised his hand.

He was close enough I could read his tag. "Mr. Healey?"

"This isn't a joke?"

"No, Mr. Healey. It's not a joke. It was never a joke. I'm sorry that it's gone on this long. I can't prove it absolutely for a couple more weeks, but Dark Knight, Mel's Place, The Ranch. All real. All older than any orbital you care to name because the Toe-Holds were here first."

"Then why have we never heard about them?"

"I have." A voice came from the back corner where a young woman in a steward's white smock looked up. "My mother was born on High Tortuga. She worked for a company at Mel's Place and met my father at The Ranch. It's all true. I tried to tell you, but you wouldn't believe me. I gave up two weeks ago. You'll see for yourselves soon enough."

Mr. Healey's jaw swung down.

"Thank you, Ms. Huber." I looked at Mr. Healey. "Do you believe her now?"

"How do I know she's not in on the gag, sar?"

"Do you think I'm in on the gag, Mr. Healey?"

He paused, glancing at Schulties who simply stared back at him. "It's possible, Captain."

I toasted him with my cup. "I'll grant you that, but ask yourself, why would I?"

Mr. Healey shrugged. "Why do I need to know how many windows are in Hutchin's Gym, sar?"

I laughed. "I have no idea. Is it still Twenty-seven to the outside, six ticket, and twelve boxes for real people, not cadets?"

"No, sar. Thirty-two to the outside, six ticket, two in the doors and twelve boxes for real people, not cadets, sar. They put on an addition in 2370."

I shrugged. "I'll take your word for it. My point is that the answer can be easily proven. We're going to dock there. It's our next port of call."

"I thought we were heading to Lesiter in New Caledonia, sar," Mr. Healey said.

"You know how far away that is, Mr. Healey?"

"No, Captain. Only that it's more than a few jumps from Newmar."

"I don't know either, Mr. Healey. I'd have to check but 'more than a few jumps' is pretty accurate." I looked around at the crew. "Dark Knight Station is one jump from Newmar, at least on the Chernyakova. We'll be doing a double because this ship isn't really configured for Toe-Hold space. It'll work fine, but we'll be taking two steps for every one our sister ship will make. They got underway before we did, but we'll jump sooner, jump twice, and may still make it to Dark Knight Station ahead of them." I glanced down at Mr. Schulties. "Have I said anything that isn't true, Mr. Schulties?"

"Not that I know of, Skipper."

CHAPTER TEN
DARK KNIGHT: AUGUST 3, 2379

The double jump to Dark Knight kept us well ahead of the Chernyakova. The first leg jump error put us off by half a day, which gave the capacitor enough time to charge. Since we jumped from Venitz three full days before the Chernyakova could, we arrived in Dark Knight a couple of days before them.

"Navigation confirms. Welcome to Dark Knight, Captain," Zoya said, looking up from her console.

"Do we have a plot to the station, Ms. Fortuner?"

"We do, Captain. Passing to helm now."

"Helm confirms course. Course set. Ship answers to helm, Captain." Mr. Bentley looked up from his position.

"ETA, Ms. Fortuner?" I asked.

"Two weeks and change, Skipper. We got a lucky break on jump error."

"Thank you, Ms. Fortuner. Secure from navigation stations, Ms. Usoko. Set normal watch throughout the ship."

"Secure from navigation stations, set normal watch, aye, Captain." She made the announcements and I stood up from my chair, in preparation for finishing the morning watch rotation.

"I relieve you, Ms. Usoko."

She smiled and made the changeover note in the log. "You have the watch, Captain. Don't break it."

I laughed and slid into the seat, making my own notation in the log as the rest of the crew flowed off the bridge. We'd jumped in the middle of the morning watch, so I was really only taking the watch back from her. Since the third section had the duty, Mr. Bentley never had to move.

As the last of the navigation crew left the bridge, Mr. Hoag climbed the ladder with the morning coffee and cookies. "Here you go, sar." He handed off the coffees and looked forward. "Are we here?"

"Yes, Mr. Hoag. We're here. Still a couple of weeks out. Not much to see yet."

He crossed to the helm. "Need a break, Virgil?"

Mr. Bentley looked to me and I nodded. "Thanks, Tom." He released his seat belt and stood after making the notation in his log.

They swapped seats and Mr. Bentley dropped down the ladder.

"I don't think I mentioned it before, Mr. Hoag. Congratulations on your new rating."

"Thank you, Captain. In hindsight I should have gone for able spacer."

"There's time. Have you thought about making a run at spec/3?"

He looked over at me. "Seriously, Captain? Would I even get a chance to work that rank?"

"Probably not, but you'd get paid for it anyway."

"The share is the same, isn't it, sar?"

"It is. Once you make full share the only way to make more share is to take the path you're already on."

He grinned at me. "I have to say, I've got a new appreciation for the work, sar." He paused and checked the helm. "I mean, I always thought being an officer on a freighter would be a great job."

"Second thoughts now?" I asked, teasing him a little.

He laughed. "No. Nothing like that, Captain. It's just I never thought about what the crew's life must be. At all."

"Officers are part of the crew," I said.

"But you can't run a ship with just officers, sar. Can you?"

"Well, yes. You can if the ship is small enough. Most of the fast packets only have a captain and an engineering officer. If you carry passengers, you can get by if the captain has a steward endorsement, but then you have to figure out how to feed the passengers."

"You ran a fast packet for a while, didn't you, Captain?"

"I did. I have the endorsement and hired a couple of spacers and a chef to keep things moving." I shrugged. "I wasn't qualified in the engine room so I hired a chief engineer, too."

"What was that like?" he asked.

I rummaged around in my mental baggage trying to find an answer. "It was my first try at being an owner. It was a successful venture, but when the time came to sell the company, I did."

"What's your favorite class of ship, sar?"

"Hard to say. My first post as an officer was on a Barbell like the Chernyakova. They're a nice berth. Not a lot of fooling around with cargo. Just the one can to worry about. Enough crew to keep things interesting. Not so many that I couldn't know them all."

"Any downsides, Captain?"

"Well, the one can has its ups and downs. You roll the dice on it every time and have no way to diversify the risks. Not so risky in the High Line where you know there's always going to be an outbound can when you get there. In the Toe-Holds? We have to be careful to go to stations that support Barbell traffic."

He glanced over at me. "Is that a serious risk, sar?"

"No, not really. There are plenty of stations where we know we can get cans. Between The Ranch, Mel's, here at Dark Knight, and Ice Rock, there's always something outbound, generally to one of those same four stations. Even so, we leave a lot of cargo at the dock because we can't go to the smaller places where a full Barbell can is too much—coming in or going out."

"Why is that a problem, sar?"

"Mostly because there are so many of them. For every Dark Knight Station, there are a hundred smaller ones that produce maybe a couple of large cans a stanyer. They can't afford to buy any kind of material in Barbell-sized quantities, so there's no bulk cargo going there and rarely any leaving."

"How do they survive, sar?"

"Just smaller units of scale. I believe Ms. Regyri's company just bought a tractor to service those stations. It's a market that looks ripe for profits, and the tractors are the right ships for it." I paused for a moment. "Tractors might be my favorite ships. My first job as captain was a tractor."

"Yes, sar. The Agamemnon. You left to start your own company after that, didn't you, sar?"

I looked at him. "You seem to know a lot about me, Mr. Hoag."

He glanced at me before focusing on his console again. "I looked up your public jacket, Captain. I wanted to know more about all the officers."

"I did the same thing when I first signed the articles. What did you learn?"

"You're very highly rated, Captain. After your first stanyer on the William Tinker, you had excellent performance reviews." He glanced at me again. "Can I ask what happened in that first stanyer?"

"Why do you want to know?"

"Well, is there something about being a freshly minted third mate I need to watch out for, sar?"

I chuckled. "I didn't get along with my first skipper. Let's leave it at that."

"Is that something I need to watch out for, Captain?"

"First thing to remember, and the thing I forgot, is that every ship has a culture. Going into any crew with the perspective from the last one? You can find yourself an outcast pretty quickly."

"So? Keep my head down and my nose clean until I learn the lay of the land, sar?"

"That's a good way to look at it. Every time you change ships, you're joining an established culture. Learning how they do things, and why they do them, will help you mesh with them faster."

"Thank you, Captain."

Mr. Bentley came back up the ladder and took the watch back. "Thanks, Tom."

Mr. Hoag nodded, collected his tray, and left the bridge.

After a few moments, Mr. Bentley glanced over at me. "He seemed interested in your past, Skipper."

I shrugged. "How long were you listening?"

"A tick or two. I heard you talking and didn't want to interrupt, sar."

"Learn anything interesting?"

He made a note in his log before answering. "I learned that you have a public jacket, sar." He shot me a grin. "Any skeletons I can leverage there?"

I laughed. "Everyone has a public jacket, Mr. Bentley. Even you. There's nothing there you can leverage because anybody can see it at any time."

"Good point, sar."

"Why, Mr. Bentley? Do you think you need leverage?"

"Not at the moment, no, Skipper. Just wondering if it might come in handy later."

"Speaking of later, Mr. Bentley, have you given any thought to your future?"

He glanced at me with a faint frown. "Should I be worried about that question, Captain?"

I shook my head. "Not at all. I just wondered if you planned to work up to spec/1 on helm, or retire, or what."

He shook his head. "Retire? Not any time soon."

"You're just going to ride along with us?"

"Until you kick me off or stop paying big shares, sar."

Alys Giggone's admonishment about recommendations flashed through my head. "Have you ever considered the Academy, Mr. Bentley?"

"I often consider the Academy, Captain." He shrugged. "More favorably since I joined your crew, sar."

"More favorably? In what way?"

"Well, sar, it might just have been bad luck, but most of the officers I worked for in the past weren't exactly the brightest stars in the sky."

"And you considered that an artifact of their Academy backgrounds?"

He shrugged. "It was the only thing they all had in common, sar."

"Not exactly the kind of consideration I had in mind, Mr. Bentley."

He looked over at me. "What kind of consideration were you thinking of, Captain?"

"More like have you considered attending?"

His eyebrows shot up and his eyes widened. "Me? No."

"Why not you?"

"I'm just a rating."

"That's not exactly a disqualifying condition, Mr. Bentley."

His frown returned and he straightened in his chair, looking forward.

"Mr. Bentley?"

"Sar?"

"Have I offended you?"

He didn't answer for a long moment. "No, Captain. I'm wrestling with the question of 'Why would you ask me that?' and not finding any good answers."

"I'm asking because I think you might make a good officer. Having the degree won't impede your career in any way. You can always come back to helm duty, if you like."

He glanced at me. "After telling you about the officers I had before this crew? You thought I should become one of them, sar?"

"Ah. Sorry. Yes, bad timing on my part. I only bring it up because we need more good ones to balance the scales. I don't believe the Academy teaches how to be stupid."

He sighed. "No offense, Skipper, but a lot of them seem to learn it anyway."

"True enough." I pondered his observation for some time. "I wonder if it's just human nature."

"Stupidity?" he asked, looking over at me.

"Yes. There's a myth that some of the best leaders in business and industry are high-functioning sociopaths."

He stared at me. "Myth?"

"It's largely because business leaders tend to be seen as heartless and often unconcerned about their own well-being. They put their business first and everything else second."

"You're using a lot of weasely words, Skipper."

"Weaselly?"

"'Tend to be seen' and 'myth,' sar."

"That's fair," I said. "My personal opinion is that most people don't understand the label of 'sociopath.' There's a reason for that 'path' at the end."

"Why myth, Captain? Wouldn't a high-functioning sociopath be the ideal captain? Avoiding the tendencies for criminality and being unable to make long-term plans, they'd still be able to use people without remorse, make decisions that might be counter to their own self-interest."

I shook my head. "That's a good question. I don't have any good answers. From my seat, I don't think you can lead effectively without empathy. Without understanding what you're asking people to do. Sometimes you still have to ask them to do it, but understanding what you're asking, what it will cost them? That seems like a solid prerequisite for a good leader. A good officer."

He continued to stare at me. "And you think I'd be a good officer."

"I think you'd be a good candidate, yes, Mr. Bentley. You're young enough to have a full career. You've been in space since you were old enough to sign the articles. You've a sharp eye and a quick wit, but I've never seen you being cruel. You'd still have to buckle down and do the work. It's not all fun and games."

He laughed and straightened to face front. "Just seeing these quarter shares makes me think there's not any fun and games, Skipper. I'm not sure I'm cut out for that."

"You've got one advantage almost none of them have."

"What's that, sar?"

I grinned at him. "You can afford it."

He laughed and nodded. "Probably so, but why would I want to spend my hard-earned shares on that?"

"What else would you do with them? Invest the credits in a business? Start one of your own? Settle down and open a sandwich shop?"

He shrugged without looking over. "I'd thought about opening a bar."

"Seriously or just in passing?"

"I looked into what it would take in terms of licensing, staff, codes. All that."

"Have you rejected the idea?"

He nodded. "I'll be twenty-three by the time we get back to Port Newmar. I don't want to settle down just yet. I'm earning credits hand over fist right now and it feels like I should hold onto the position I have. Every trip just adds to my credit balance." He did look over at me then. "I didn't like being broke, Captain. Didn't like not having a home. I've got both a home and a steady income here. That counts a lot in my book."

"I can relate. I may be a big-shot captain now, but remember I started as a mess deck attendant under Alys Giggone when I was only eighteen."

"And she pushed you to the Academy?"

"She did." I let that sink in for a moment. "I won't push you. If you want to go, I'll help you get in, but you have to want it."

"What would I have to do?" he asked, still not looking in my direction.

"Fill out the application. Get the required recommendations from officers. Pay the fees."

He glanced at me. "You're not pushing, sar?"

"Simply pointing out that I know plenty of officers who'd sign off on your application, Mr. Bentley."

He nodded. "I need to think about it, Captain."

"Take your time, but consider we'll be back in Newmar just about in time for the new class to start."

He shot me a look. "But no pressure, sar?"

"None at all. I'm happy to have you on my bridge, Mr. Bentley. You've still got a ways to go before spec/1 in ship handling. And you can always cross-train on astrogation."

He chuckled and fiddled with his console but otherwise offered no response. Over the course of the watch, I caught him staring off into the distance straight ahead a couple of times.

After the watch change, he caught me at the foot of the ladder to the bridge. "I'll think about it, Captain."

"All I can ask."

He nodded and dropped down toward crew berthing.

The aromas coming up the ladder promised a delightful lunch. My stomach grumbled a little in anticipation so I wasted no time getting cleaned up and heading for the wardroom.

By the time we'd gotten within a couple of days of docking, the station itself had resolved from a faint dot in space to a sprawling conglomeration of empty cargo cans welded together with assorted beams and girders. The station's marshaling yard showed on the screens, but the cargo stacked up there wasn't visible to the naked eye. Compared to an orbital, which looked like a giant soup can, the station looked more like some fantastical city adrift in space.

"What do you think, Ms. Vincent?" I asked when she came up to bring our morning coffee.

She stood beside the helm and looked at the glittering array. "It looks so small, but so big at the same time." She shook her head. "I'm saying it badly."

"The scale is hard to deal with from this distance," Mr. Jenson said. "By this time tomorrow it'll be easier to look at."

"Those are freighters?" she asked. "Lined up along that long straight stretch?"

"They are, Ms. Vincent," I said. "They look like toys, don't they?"

"No atmosphere," Mr. Jenson said. "You're not used to being able to see that far, so your eyes are making you think it's closer than it is. We'll be docked alongside them within two days."

She shook her head. "It's huge. It has to be huge."

"It is," I said. "I don't know the actual numbers but probably at least twice the population of Newmar's orbital. Certainly some multiple of the volume. Where the orbital gets deck space from the levels, the station just keeps spreading out horizontally."

"Wait till you see Mel's Place," Mr. Jenson said, grinning up at her. "It's one of the biggest."

"Still think it's a ghost town?" I asked.

She shook her head, not taking her gaze from the glittering edifice out in the dark. "No place that has that many freighters docked can be a ghost town, Captain."

I laughed.

She looked at me. "What? Did I say something, sar?"

"No, you're absolutely right. The direction your thinking took just struck me funny in the best possible way."

"What way is that, Captain?"

"Most people look at the size of the place and think about how many people it would take to run it. It takes some amazing engineering to keep it alive. A few might look at all the lights. Or all the shapes in the structure. None of them would be as valid as your observation about the number of ships docked, Ms. Vincent."

Her smile flashed white in the dimness of the bridge. "Thank you, Captain." She gathered her tray and headed for the ladder. "I've got to get back. Thanks for letting me look, Captain."

"You're welcome, Ms. Vincent."

"Wait until tomorrow," Mr. Jenson said. "We'll be so close you can't see it all."

She laughed as she dropped down the ladder.

"I'm not sure she believed me, Captain."

"Doesn't matter, Mr. Jenson. We've shown her the truth in some small part. It's a much different perspective from here than it is inside the docking gallery."

He nodded. "True, sar. Maybe we should give tours."

I chuckled but he gave me a good idea. I sent a note to ask Mr. MacBradaigh to join me on the bridge. It only took a couple of ticks for him to come up the ladder.

"Yes, Captain?" His head swiveled as he tried to look at everything at once.

"First time on the bridge, Mr. MacBradaigh?"

"Yes. It's not what I expected."

"What did you expect?"

"I thought there would be more screens and fewer windows."

I caught Mr. Jenson biting his lips together and paying very close attention to his helm. "Well, the windows are armorglass. They're stronger than the metal of the hull, but they have a bad strength to mass ratio so we don't build the whole ship out of them."

He nodded, paused at the top of the ladder. "Is there something you needed, Captain?"

I stood up from the console and walked toward the bow. "Something to show you. I thought you might appreciate this view."

He followed me forward, not like he couldn't have seen from where he was, but standing close to the armorglass made the ship all but disappear, almost like you floated in space.

"That's Dark Knight Station," I said, pointing it out.

He squinted a bit as he peered out. "How far away are we?"

"We'll dock day after tomorrow. We're just matching vectors now."

"I don't know what I'm seeing," he said, shooting me a quick sideways glance. "I know you said it's a station but what scale is this?"

I pointed to the docking gallery. "See that straight line along the bottom edge?"

"The one with the sort of uneven fringe?"

"That's the one. It's one of the docking galleries. The fringe is made up of ships. Freighters like this one."

He looked at me as if I'd told him the hull was made of blue cheese for a moment before looking back at the station. "How many ships is that?"

"A dozen, at least," I said.

"That's huge." His words came out almost in a whisper. "That's bigger than an orbital, isn't it."

"Yes, Mr. MacBradaigh. It's not even the biggest one. You're also only seeing the main construction. The system is filled with mining outposts, grinders, smelters. They're scattered all around the belts. They keep some of the products, but use the revenue from selling most of it to buy what they can't make themselves."

"How many people live there?"

"I don't know. A lot. They have a large hydroponics section for food, use a lot of plants to supplement the mechanical scrubbers. Anything you can think of that people might want or need, it's probably there."

"Anything?" he asked, raising his eyebrows in challenge.

"Well, no large bodies of water. No sailboats. Anything you could find on an orbital, though. And a lot of things you couldn't."

He looked back at the station, his head tilting this way and that a few times. "I'm going to have my work cut out for me, I think."

"Designing a course to explain this?"

"No, Captain. Trying to understand it myself. Everything I know says this is not possible. That it's a trick. I'm having trouble wrapping my mind around the idea that a man-made city of this scale is floating in the void. That it not only exists, but appears to be thriving." He looked around, turning in place to look out in all directions. "Are there planets in this system?"

"A gas giant that's currently on the other side of the system and a small rocky cinder in close to the primary."

He turned to look toward the primary. "We're a long way out, aren't we?"

"We are. Very close to the Burleson limit here. We've been maneuvering for the last couple of weeks to shed the velocity we carried in from Newmar so we can dock."

He looked back at the station. "Even looking at it. Seeing it with my own eyes. I'm having trouble accepting it."

"Wait until you get inside. By this time tomorrow we'll have started our approach, so much of it will be obscured. I wanted you to see what an actual Toe-Hold station looked like. This is a large one, sure. It's not the largest. A lot of the smaller ones hope to grow to be this size someday."

He thrust his hands into the pockets of his shipsuit and stared out at the station for several moments. "Thank you, Captain. I'm beginning to understand what Alys wants now."

"Skipper, we're getting final approach instructions from Dark Knight," Mr. Jenson said.

"Thank you, Mr. Jenson. I'll be right there."

The interruption nudged Mr. MacBradaigh from his reverie. "I'll get out of your way, Captain. Let you get on with business." He turned and headed for the ladder, stopping for a moment at the top, his hand on the railing, looking back at the station once more before dropping out of sight.

I returned to my console and routed the approach vectors to the helm. We still had stans before we'd be in position to make that course change, but the autopilot would take us along when we got there. I logged the pending course change notice and settled back in my seat.

"Think it'll help, Skipper?"

"What's that, Mr. Jenson?"

"Showing him the station?"

I shrugged. "I don't know. We've just rocked his universe. It's not easy finding out everything you knew about a subject was wrong."

He glanced at me. "How did you take it, sar? When you found out."

I chuckled a little. "You were there, weren't you, Mr. Jenson? Mr. Carstairs had me pretty well prepared. Something about jumping into the Deep Dark with two hundred metric kilotons of black malt made me think that we weren't taking it into a ghost town. Even if it went to a wholesaler, that's still a hell of a lot of beer."

He laughed. "That's true, I suppose, sar."

"What about you, Mr. Jenson? That was your first jump into a Toe-Hold, wasn't it?"

"Personally, yes, but I knew about them. My uncle worked engineering for Allied and they made Toe-Hold runs all the time. I knew it wasn't what everybody thought."

"I wonder if that's the problem," I said.

"Which, sar? That everybody thinks they're ghost towns?"

"No, Mr. Jenson. That most people don't think of them at all. They're not just ghost towns. They're invisible."

He shrugged. "If you don't know to look for them, you surely won't see them, sar."

I turned back to my logs, flipping the page to review the latest departmental reports. The thought had occurred to me in the past. Had I just not seen them because I didn't know to look? Odin's Outpost, now that I saw it in context, should have been a flashing light in my eyes instead of a curiosity in the dark. How many less obvious signs had I not even noticed?

Mr. MacBradaigh was right on that score. He had his work cut out for him.

I hoped Alys Giggone had thought it through, because I felt certain that Zoya was right. The CPJCT would not take kindly to having the blinders removed from the public's eyes. I suspected that we'd all need to step carefully over the next few months.

We docked just before lunch mess. It gave us a chance to meet with the station authorities and establish the ship as a first-time visitor. As I stepped off the ramp, the dock official smiled at me. "Captain Wang. It is you. What are you doing on this ship? The Chernyakova's coming in behind you. I thought the forms got mixed up."

I held out a hand. "Good to see, Steph. We're sailing as a fleet these days. Captain Case has the Chernyakova and I've got the Collins."

"How'd you get one of the new Eighty-Eights?" She glanced down at her table before shaking my hand. "We don't see many of those."

"It's her maiden voyage. We picked up a charter from the Academy at Port Newmar. It's a longish story but the bottom line is that Phoenix hired some new officers to run the Chernyakova. Most of us moved here. You got the rosters? All in order?"

She nodded. "Of course. Full visa for your crew. You and Mr. Carstairs are still residential, as are Ms. Usoko and Chief Regyri."

"Has Captain Case arranged for the Chernyakova visas?"

She flipped a screen and consulted it. "Full visas. Applied inbound. Cosigned by Mr. Carstairs."

"He'll be at the dock to meet them, I'm sure. It's the first time for Captain Case, so he'll want to be on hand to help out."

"That's all I have for you, Skipper. Welcome back."

"Thanks, Steph. Good to be back."

She looked at the lock as if she could see through it to the ship beyond. "Maiden voyage, eh? And you brought her here first?"

"Best place, isn't it?" I asked, grinning at her.

"We like it, but we're biased." She grinned back. "How's she go?"

"Short legs. I got spoiled by the Chernyakova, but we can do short jumps and still get where we're going."

"Never thought you'd leave her, personally."

"Who? The Chernyakova?" I asked.

"Yeah. That's one dialed-in Barbell."

"The Madoka ever dock here?" I asked.

"Occasionally, yeah."

"That's a dialed-in ship. Designed from the engine room forward to work in the Toe-Holds." I glanced back into the Collins. "Manchester intended this one for short-hauling around the High Line with a bunch of cadets."

Her eyes widened. "From the Academy? How'd you get it?"

"The commandant of the Academy chairs the Phoenix Freight board of directors. She hired us."

"Cadets?"

"Who do you think are filling the quarter and half share berths?"

She blinked, looking down at her tablet again. "I thought you had a lot of green hands." She frowned and flipped back a couple of screens. "So does the Chernyakova. They're all cadets?"

"Not at the moment, no. A couple of months ago, they were. Right now they're all trying to move up the rank table to get better shares." I shrugged. "I have to give them back eventually and pick up new ones."

She frowned and her mouth moved like she might be trying to say something but wasn't exactly sure what it was she wanted to say.

"It's not as bad as it sounds," I said with a laugh. "Port Newmar is deep in the well there so we had a long time to get them into the jobs. We brought over some senior ratings from the Chernyakova to help. They've been doing a great job getting the new people up to speed. We had our testing period just before we jumped. A couple of them managed to make it to full shares. Some made it to half."

"That's still a lot of quarters."

"Perennial problem. I don't know if they didn't study, didn't master the material, or just assumed they'd be able to pass it. It was their first try. They'll have another chance in a few weeks."

"It's not a big deal out here," she said with a shrug. "I imagine the Joint Committee on Everything has more to say about it."

I laughed. "Yeah. Well, these junior ratings will go back to the Academy when we finish this cruise. We'll see what happens after that."

Her tablet bipped. "Duty calls." She stuck out her hand again. "Good luck, Captain."

"Thanks. I'll take all the help I can get."

She laughed and headed down the docking gallery.

I climbed the ramp back into the ship where Ms. Heath had set up at the brow.

"We all good, Skipper?" she asked. "She had a lot to talk about."

"We're good. She was confused by having the Chernyakova inbound but me listed as captain here. It took some explaining."

She laughed. "I imagine it did."

"We'll declare liberty after lunch mess. Feel free to pass the word."

"Thanks, Captain."

I headed deeper into the ship and pondered the testing again. Going into the test period, I'd felt confident that we'd have a lot more people passing, but even Mr. MacBradaigh only snagged two of the four half share tests, missing the other two by only a couple of points according to Mr. Cartwright's test records. The new cadre had never seen that kind of testing before. I hadn't talked to Mr. MacBradaigh about it. He hadn't brought it up, but perhaps I should have.

CHAPTER ELEVEN
DARK KNIGHT STATION: AUGUST 17, 2379

The next morning, Louisa Oscella pinged me with a dinner invite. It raised my eyebrows. I hadn't heard from her since our hijacking.

"What does she want?" Pip asked, when I told him I had a dinner date.

"Just catching up with old friends?" I asked.

He snorted. "How many times have we been here since then?"

I shook my head. "A few."

"Watch yourself," he said.

"You want me back by midnight, Dad?"

He grinned. "Eleven-thirty or I'm sending station security."

"She is station security. What good would that do?"

He laughed. "All right." He frowned but headed for the cabin door. "You're a big boy. Don't do anything I wouldn't do."

He left the cabin, headed down the passageway toward his stateroom before I could ask what he wouldn't do.

———

She met me at the lock at 1900 with a smile and a brief hug. "Ishmael. It's so good to see you again."

"Good evening, Louisa. Nice to see you, too."

She hooked her arm in mine and we strolled along the docking gallery toward Main Street. She looked good in a pair of trim black slacks, a turquoise blouse, and a silver bolero with tab collar. Her clothes set off her darker complexion to good effect. "You have a preference as to food?" she asked, looking up over at me. "Steak? Italian?"

"You're the resident expert. Where don't spacers eat that I haven't heard of?"

"I know just the place. It opened a couple of months back. I keep hearing about the great food but haven't had a reason to try it until now. Feeling adventurous?"

"I'm game," I said, still trying to find my way with the whole situation, but willing to play along until she filled me in.

She led me into the station and over to Main Street, the business district at Dark Knight. Main Street never closed, but evening always found it a veritable hive of activity with day-work locals mixing with watchstanders and spacers. A few station security people nodded to Oscella as we passed, but none spoke to her. We didn't find much to say to each other along the way, but I didn't feel any pressure to do more than walk along with her on my arm. It felt good in a way that I hadn't felt in a while. Eventually we ended up at Jake's Chop Shop with only a short wait for a table.

The waiter took our drink orders and left us to peruse the menu.

Louisa placed her menu flat on the table and leaned forward. "You're probably wondering why."

I glanced at her over the top of my own menu, giving her a smile. "I don't get asked out by beautiful women that much anymore. Particularly women who are head of station security." I shrugged. "I figured you had a reason and you'd tell me about it when you got the chance. I take it this place is secure enough?"

She laughed and shook her head. "It's nothing like that." She bit her lower lip and picked up her menu again. "I've heard the prime rib is excellent."

I scanned down the offerings. Nothing jumped out at me so I closed it and placed it on the edge of the table. "Fine by me."

She kept glancing over at me above the top of her menu.

The waiter brought our drinks, red wine for her and coffee for me. "Are you ready to order?"

I looked at Louisa. "I am if you are."

She nodded. "I'll have the prime rib, medium, mashed potatoes, steamed vegetables."

"Salad?" he asked. "We have a nice house salad. Local source. Very fresh."

"Sounds lovely," she said.

"Dressing?"

"Always a good choice," she said, pausing a beat. "Italian on the side?"

He smiled at her. "Of course." He looked at me. "Sir?"

"Same."

"You're making my job very easy tonight, folks. Can I bring you an appetizer while you're waiting? It'll be a few minutes."

"Just the salad for me," Louisa said. "Ishmael?"

"Salad sounds good."

The waiter nodded. "I'll get those right out for you." He took the menus and headed off.

She pressed her palms on the table in front of her, one hand over the other, before straightening in her seat. "I'm not head of security anymore."

"Was that your choice?" I asked, not sure what the appropriate response might be.

"Yes. In a way. I was tired of the job. I worked up from patrol. I'd been at it three decades. It was time to do something else." She stared at me across the table, almost as if daring me to argue. I saw something tired behind the challenge.

"In a way?"

She sighed and took a sip from her wineglass. "I've been struggling ever since, well, ever since." She shrugged. "When all that went down—" She looked off to the side, shaking her head. "I don't know what I'd have done if not for you and your people."

"Ever think that it might not have happened at all if we hadn't been stirring the pot?"

"They built a nuke on the station. Right under my nose. They kidnapped Kondur and could have kept him if your people hadn't found him for me."

I took a sip of coffee and shook my head. "Not the way I remember it."

She sighed and shook her head again, this time looking straight at me. "I've lost my edge, Ishmael. As much as I love the job—and I do. Or did." She shook her head again. "I have to be honest and admit there are people on the station that can do it better. People already in the department."

"You're feeling superfluous? What are you going to do instead?"

She sighed and took a solid slug of wine, seeming to shrink inwards a little. "I don't know. Something. Something different."

The waiter brought our salads and a basket of bread. "Your dinners will be right up. Anything else you need?" He glanced at Louisa's wineglass. "Another?"

She shook her head. "Not yet, thank you."

The waiter nodded and slipped away.

"What are you doing now? Are you still employed?"

She shrugged. "I do consulting work with security. Kondur has projects he wants to get done but the normal staff hasn't the time. It was always that way. Now I'm off the firing line and shepherding some of these lost sheep into the fold."

"Not enough, though, is it?"

She grimaced and shook her head. "No. It's not."

The salad was good and the dressing had just the right mix of spices to bring out the flavors.

"What do you want to do?" I asked.

"I don't know. That's the hell of it." She cut up some of the greens and sopped a forkful of them in the dressing before tucking them into her mouth. She chewed and swallowed. "I thought I had things all scoped out, you know?"

I grabbed a slice of the bread and used it to corral the fiddly bits of salad. "Been there."

She raised her eyebrows at that. "Really?"

"You're talking about having everything you want, only to have it all come crashing down? Or worse, that you don't remember why you wanted it but have the sneaking suspicion that it's not enough now that you have it?" I don't know where the words came from. They just bubbled out of me. "Enough isn't the right word." I shook my head and looked down at my salad plate, nearly devoid of vegetation.

"Yeah. That," she said, her voice barely making it across the table. "You know that, too, huh?"

I nodded. "Oh, yeah."

The waiter swooped in with our dinners and swapped the empty dishes for the full ones in a few deft motions. "How's that look?"

"This looks great," I said.

Louisa nodded. "I'll take that refill now."

I still had half a cup of coffee so waved the waiter along before digging into the rich beef and creamy potatoes.

Louisa followed my lead. We'd made small dents in our meals before the waiter returned with her wine, swapping the glasses before moving on.

The beef practically melted in my mouth. I must have sighed in satisfaction because she looked over at me with a little grin. "Good, huh?"

I nodded. "How's yours?"

She held up a morsel on her fork, considering it for a moment before nodding. "Oh, yes." She popped it into her mouth and smiled.

We didn't say much more until our plates were nearly empty. I sat back in my chair and sipped the last of the coffee. It wasn't bad coffee, but not as good as we had on the ship. Then again, little was.

"What did you do?" she asked, putting her utensils on the plate and picking up her wine glass, lounging back in her seat.

"I started over."

"Started over, how?"

I pondered my response for a few heartbeats before stepping back from the brink. "I sold my business. Took the credits and went back to my roots. Carstairs found me and convinced me to go along with his harebrained scheme to buy a derelict freighter."

She laughed. "Just like that?"

I shrugged and pushed my plate away. "There might have been therapy involved. I spent a lot of time in limbo."

"I lost my partner," she said.

"I'm sorry for your loss," I said. "Was it sudden?"

Her brittle laugh drew the attention of one of our neighbors. "Sorry." She shook her head and held her napkin in front of her lips. "Yes. Very sudden. He decided I was too old for him and took off for parts unknown with one of Kondur's accountants." She shrugged. "A younger accountant."

"Oh. That kind of loss."

She shook her head and finished off her wine. "Honestly, good riddance." Her expression belied the words. She sighed and shook her head. "That's not fair. We'd been drifting apart for a while. I don't know that I ever thought of him as the one. You know?"

I nodded.

"I guess we just grew apart." She looked into her empty glass. "I didn't have the nads to end it. He did." She put the glass back on the table and looked across at me again.

"You have anybody to talk to?" I asked.

"At the moment, you." She grinned at me. "You mean professional?"

"Yes. It's not an easy road under the best of circumstances. Having a coach helping you along the path? It helped me."

"Are you over it?"

I looked around the restaurant and thought about my answer. Was I? "No," I said at last, looking back at her. "I'm better. I can see colors again. I'm pretty sure there's a road ahead. Over it?" I sighed. "I'm not sure that's the result I want."

She frowned. "What do you want?"

"I want to remember the good. I want to find a new path. I don't want to get over it as much as grow from it. Learn from what I've been through. Embrace it, in a weird way. The idea of getting over it implies a kind of excision. I don't want to have the scar removed. I earned it." I sighed and looked down at my hand fiddling with my coffee cup. "I think my goal is to find a way to live with it without feeling like a failure for doing so."

"A failure?"

I looked across the table. She sat with her head tilted to the side and a frown on her face. "Like the whole situation was somehow my fault. That the wounds were self-inflicted."

"Isn't that counterproductive? I'd think you'd want to remove the evidence." Her smile made me smile back.

I pondered the idea. Something in the way she asked the questions, like she really wanted to understand, made me dig in to find the words to explain it to her. "I think it's so I don't make the same mistakes again."

"But if it wasn't your fault to begin with? How can you take the blame for it? What lesson do you take from it?"

The waiter came back to collect the plates. "Can I get you a dessert menu?"

I shook my head. "None for me. Louisa?"

"No. I need to walk this off a little before there's room. It was delicious, by the way."

The waiter nodded. "I'll tell the chef."

"Just the tab then, I guess," I said, flexing my thumb.

He pulled a tablet from the pocket of his apron and offered it to me. I added the tip and accepted the charge.

"You didn't have to do that, Ishmael. I asked you out."

I grinned. "I'm still employed. Shall we go?"

She nodded and we stood, winding our way back through the dining room to the exit and out into the passageway beyond.

"I'm still employed, too," she said, linking her arm in mine again and pulling me along toward Main Street. "But thanks."

"Thank you. I haven't been back to see my therapist for a while." I grinned at her. "Hope my maundering helped. At least a little."

She shrugged and pulled me to a window display of potted plants. She looked at my reflection in the glass. "I think it did. I kept thinking about putting it behind me, getting rid of it so I'm not reminded all the time by the little things."

I nodded.

"I felt pretty bad that I couldn't just pack it up and stow it away. Everything reminds me. Death by a thousand paper cuts."

I chuckled at the image but waited her out. I knew the feeling, her words finding a truth in me.

She resumed our stroll, once more pulling me along the sidewalk as people flowed around us going in the opposite direction. "You've given me a different perspective." She looked over. "One I like better."

"I'm not sure it's the right answer. Even for me. It's a work in progress."

She shook her head. "We're all works in progress, aren't we?"

"I guess we are." My tablet bipped. "Excuse me."

She nodded. "Captains and doctors. Always on call."

I pulled up the message and sighed. "I'm needed."

Something like regret passed over her face before a somewhat forced smile took its place. She released my arm. "I understand. Go. Thanks for the evening. Perhaps we can do it again before you leave."

"I'd like that," I said.

She put a hand on my shoulder and reached over to peck my cheek. "Take care, Ishmael."

I saw something in her face that made me pause. "You, too. Good luck with the consulting thing."

She gave me a quick shrug and a rueful grin. "Yeah. Well. It'll be what it'll be."

I headed back toward the ship carrying the sense that she'd been disappointed. Like she'd been hoping for something more than dinner. It took me a moment to realize that she'd been leading me deeper into the residential sections of the station. I dodged through the pedestrian traffic, lengthening my stride and picking up the pace. As much as I liked Louisa Oscella, I felt like I might have dodged, if not a bullet, at least an uncomfortable situation. While the conversation triggered something in me, I felt certain that being her rebound squeeze wouldn't have worked out for either of us. I'd played the spacer–stationer game before and learned my lesson.

I realized the face I wanted to see in the morning wasn't hers. Not that she wasn't easy on the eyes, but that I felt a tidal attraction in a different direction. The realization made my heart beat a little faster, but I wasn't sure if it was from the positive possibilities or the fear that the rising tide might drown me.

I pushed the thoughts aside and picked up my pace.

Natalya met me at the brow, a frown pushing her eyes almost closed.

I checked in with the watchstander and led her into the wardroom. "Status?" I asked.

"Station security has four of the new cohort locked up. Bar fight. Jacobs, Powell, Lindner, and Brooke."

I raised my eyebrows. "There's more to it than that, isn't there?"

"Jacobs pulled a knife. Cut one guy pretty bad. He's in the autodoc at one of the substations now."

I sighed and shook my head. I had one of those sinking feelings that cascades down the back of your neck and settles in your gut. "Charges?"

"Jacobs is in the worst shape legally. They'll put him in front of the local judiciary in the morning."

"What do I need to do? Is the station threatening visa?"

"Not for us. They've all had their visas revoked for the length of the port stay. Restricted to the ship until we leave, basically. Zoya's down there bailing out Powell, Lindner, and Brooke."

"What about Jacobs?"

"They won't release him until the local courts have had their say." She paused. "If then."

I shook my head and perched on the edge of the wardroom table. "It's only the second night."

She sighed. "First time Jacobs has been ashore. He had the duty last night."

"What is it with this guy? He's had a stick up his butt since the first day."

Natalya shook her head. "I interviewed him at Port Newmar. He fit the profile we wanted. No significant spacer background. Lower half of the class. Good marks but struggling, according to his fitness reports. Was polite enough in the interview."

"What about the other three? Any insight?"

"All three tried for engineman and dropped the ball on the exam." She shook her head. "I don't know what the story is. These guys should have been able to walk right up to machinist and dunk it."

"Jacobs?"

"I'm coming to believe he's just biding his time until he can get back to the Academy. He does the minimum required for every job. Didn't even bother with the exam."

"I thought everybody was signed up."

She grimaced. "He just ditched it."

Natalya's tablet bipped. "Zoya's on the way back with the three of them now."

"How do you want to handle it?" I asked.

"Me? You're the captain."

"Do you want to bring this to a mast? A simple but thorough dressing down? Do you want to keep it out of my sight until you've had a chance to deal with it yourself? Some combination?"

She pondered for a moment. "I think you're going to have to be involved. Their visa revocation will reflect on the ship. Jacobs is going to be the stickier situation."

"Agreed. I'm going to have to discipline him. Your choice?"

"Well, confined to the ship as a start. Without visa, he can't go ashore even if we do nothing."

"Agreed. He's already a wiper. I can't bust him down."

"Garnish his share and wages," Natalya said. "You fine him. I'll work him. I can find lots of things he can be doing instead of going ashore to raise hell."

"We'll see what the adjudicator says. Bring him up for a mast after that. We can see what he has to say."

She nodded. "You want to address the crew?"

"I will. Tomorrow. I'll cancel liberty at 0600 and keep everybody aboard until after breakfast. Most of them won't notice. I'll have Ms. Fortuner send out a recall so everybody gets back before the expiration."

"You hope," she said.

I chuckled. "Yes, I hope."

She sighed and looked at the deck. "Sorry to spoil your evening, Skipper."

"Not your fault."

"How was it?" She gave me a sly look from under her eyebrows without lifting her head. "Pip said you were out with the head of security?"

"Ex-head of security. She was in charge when we found the nuke, but that was a couple of stanyers ago now."

"So, you two an item? Pip seemed to think she was kinda sweet on you."

"You're spending a lot of time with him."

She shrugged. "Neighbors. He thinks the world of you."

"So I'm the subject of gossip?" I asked, a little bubble of mirth popping in my chest. "Really?"

She laughed with me. "He worries about you." She looked to the side for a moment. "We all do."

"It's my job to worry. Not yours."

She looked over at me and grinned. "Keep telling yourself that, Skipper." She straightened up and headed for the door. "I want to meet them at the brow. Shall I bring them up when they arrive?"

I nodded. "I'll go put on my captain suit. Bring them to the cabin."

CHAPTER TWELVE
DARK KNIGHT STATION: AUGUST 17, 2739

Natalya brought them up to officer country with Zoya right behind. "Here they are, Captain."

"Thank you, Ms. Regyri." I eyed the trio of once and future cadets. They had the grace to look embarrassed, maybe a little nervous. They looked at the deck. The bulkhead. Anywhere but at me. "Atten-hut." They snapped to attention and I stood up from behind the console to stand in front of them. "You're not in uniform but respect the forms. Does anyone need medical attention?"

They chanted in unison. "Sar, no, sar."

I let them stew in their own juices for a few moments. "Ms. Usoko? What's station security's position on these three?"

"Revoked their visas for this stay, Captain. I promised they'd be confined to the ship."

"Fines? Fees?" I scanned their faces. One had the beginnings of a shiner on his left eye. Another had a bruise growing on his cheek. "Damages?"

"None charged against them, Captain. It would have been a simple drunk and disorderly slap but for Jacobs."

I nodded. "We'll get to him. The question in front of me is what to do with these three."

"Bread and water, Captain?" Zoya asked.

"Well, they're Ms. Regyri's crew, Ms. Usoko. I hesitate to come between her and her crew." I looked at Natalya. "Ms. Regyri?"

"I can find extra duty for anybody confined to the ship, Captain."

The one with the black eye twitched and lifted his chin a few degrees. "Sar, permission to speak, sar."

"Mr. Lindner, is it?" I asked.

He barely flinched when I called him by name. "Sar, yes, sar."

"Speak, Mr. Lindner."

"Sar, the cadet wishes to apologize for his inexcusable actions in this matter, sar."

I stood in front of him, just a little bit too close, and stared into his face. "Ms. Regyri? Do you have cadets on your roster?"

"No, Captain."

"What is Mr. Lindner's rank and position, Ms. Regyri?"

"Mr. Lindner is a wiper in the power section, Captain."

"Thank you, Ms. Regyri. Mr. Lindner, you have spoken for a cadet in a manner that indicates that you believe yourself to be a cadet. Clearly you are mistaken in that. Are you also mistaken in your apology?"

He was a good cadet. He'd been broken in by professionals and barely flinched. "Sar, no, sar."

"Anybody else have anything to say?" I looked to the left. "Mr. Powell?"

"Sar, no, sar."

I looked to the right. "Mr. Brooke?"

"No, Captain. We screwed up. No excuses, sar."

"Will you accept summary judgment on this matter?" I asked. "Or would you prefer me to convene a full court?"

"Sar?" Mr. Lindner broke attention to look me in the eye. "Is this a captain's mast, sar?"

"It is, Mr. Lindner. They're the usual result of having to bail crew out of jail."

"Sar, I accept summary judgment, sar," Mr. Brooke said, staring straight ahead.

"Thank you, Mr. Brooke. Mr. Lindner?"

"Sar, may I make a statement, sar?"

"You may."

"Sar, I really am sorry. This got way out of hand so fast. No excuses, but sincere regret, sar."

"Is that all, Mr. Lindner?"

"Sar, yes, sar."

"Do you accept summary judgment, Mr. Lindner?"

"Sar, yes, sar. I accept the summary judgment."

"Mr. Powell?"

"Sar, yes, sar. I accept summary judgment."

"Very well. Ms. Usoko, Ms. Regyri, these three have accepted my summary judgment. Do you agree?"

"I do, Captain," Zoya said.

"I do, Captain," Natalya said.

"Then in light of their misconduct, they shall be restricted to the ship for the duration of our stay. Given that they are no longer welcome on the station, that seems insufficient. Therefore, they shall forfeit their shares for this leg of our voyage, and they shall report to Ms. Regyri for any additional remediation she might deem necessary and appropriate." I looked down the line of them. "Any questions? Comments? Second thoughts about accepting summary judgment?"

Mr. Powell lifted his chin. "Sar, permission to speak, sar."

"Mr. Powell?"

"What of Mr. Jacobs, Captain? They still have him locked up, sar."

"I appreciate your concern for your shipmate, Mr. Powell. Unfortunately, his fate rests in the hands of the local adjudicators at the moment. And whether or not the person he stabbed survives, I should think."

"Survives, Captain?" Powell broke and turned to me.

"I don't know where you think you are, Mr. Powell, but even the CPJCT frowns on sticking knives in people. Would you expect it to be any different here?"

He straightened back to attention. "Sar, no, sar."

"In that case, dismissed. Go get into uniform and get cleaned up. You'd be well advised to get some sleep tonight. I'm confident you'll have a few busy days in your futures."

They did a parade ground about-face and marched out of the cabin, disappearing down the ladder toward engineering berthing.

Natalya and Zoya shared a look.

"What?" I asked.

"Survived?" Zoya asked, grinning at me. "Really, Skipper?"

"All I heard was the victim was in an autodoc." I shrugged. "One presumes he'll survive but they don't need to know that."

"I'd give him about a 7.5, Zee," Natalya said. "Good tone. Nicely controlled rage. What do you think?"

Zoya nodded. "I'd go with a solid eight. I liked the part about you having cadets on your roster. That was a nice touch right out of the box. Set the tone."

"Comedians. I thought Pip was bad. He's corrupting you two."

They laughed.

I looked at Zoya. "What'd security have to say?"

"Mr. Jacobs is going to adjudication in the morning."

"Any damages we need to pay?"

She shook her head. "Not in the normal sense. Apparently the 'bar fight' was more in the nature of 'alley outside the bar fight.'"

"We'll see what tomorrow brings." I looked at Natalya. "In the meantime, see if you can get stories out of the three musketeers individually."

"Will do, Skipper. You thinking they've cooked up a good one already?"

"I don't know. Pip would have talked us out of the problem by now so I never get much practice in covering my own butt."

Natalya laughed and headed for the cabin door. "Lemme go see what I can shake loose."

"I've got a copy of the official report," Zoya said. "We can see if they match."

Natalya nodded and waved as she left.

"Sorry about your date, Skipper," Zoya said.

I shook my head and took a seat behind the console. "Nothing to be sorry for. Just dinner with a friend who needed an ear." I shrugged. "It's been a couple of stanyers since we worked together."

Zoya nodded and headed for the cabin door. "We planning to stay until the Chernyakova gets in?"

"That's Pip's plan, yeah. He's got some kind of exercise with his section running, trying to fill up the cans for a run to Mel's next." I paused. "Alys wants us to visit some other High Line sectors while we're out, too."

Zoya grimaced. "She say why?"

"Officially, show the flag. Recruit new cadets. Unofficially? I think she wants to give us cover for spending time in the Toe-Holds."

Zoya nodded. "Makes a bit of sense, I suppose." She paused at the door and looked back as though she wanted to make some other comment, but she just nodded and smiled. "Night, Skipper."

"Night."

As she ducked out of the cabin I thought about why Louisa Oscella hadn't really grabbed me and why I wasn't disappointed that the night had ended sooner than it might have otherwise. I blew out a breath and went to work on the log. I needed to record a summary of the mast. I could wait a day to update their jackets, but perhaps doing them right away would distract me from that smile.

We got the call from security just after 0930, and I reported to the appropriate security station. The officer on duty gave me a sympathetic smile. "He was a good boy overnight but he's in it deep, Captain."

"I read the report. What's the status on Mr. Reddy?"

"He's still in the autodoc, but made a statement. He's pressing charges." The officer shrugged. "The station would have anyway because of the weapon involved."

"Something special about it?"

"Knives are tools. Most of us carry one. Station reg says no concealed blade longer than twelve centimeters. In your pocket counts as concealed." He shrugged.

"Likely outcome?"

He shrugged again. "Reddy's claiming your boy and his buddies started it. Fists? Yeah. A small fine and a kick in the ass. Everybody goes home." He grimaced. "You've been around docks long enough, I suspect."

I nodded. "Oh, yeah. Not my first trip to bail out a crewman. Pay the fine. Pay the damages. Make their lives hell for a few weeks and hope they don't repeat it."

"First strike for the Marva Collins," he said. "Won't count against the ship, as far as I know."

"I've been here before on the Chernyakova. My crews generally know. These are all greenies on their first port visit."

He rolled his eyes. "Claimed he's really a cadet at the Academy at Port Newmar."

I snorted. "I can imagine just how much mass that shifted."

He laughed. "Yeah. Is he?"

"At the moment he's a quarter share in the engineering division. He was a cadet a few weeks ago. I have to give him back at the end of the stanyer."

"I don't envy you."

"It's not so bad. Expectations for quarter shares are pretty low. It's unusual to get a whole bunch of them at once. We had plenty of time to get them up to speed on their duties before we jumped out of Newmar." I shook my head. "I didn't think we'd need to housebreak them, too. My apologies."

He smiled. "Save it for the judge. The hearing's at 1000." He glanced at the clock. "If you'd head down that passageway, Captain?" He pointed to the right. "Room Five. An officer will accompany him to the hearing, but you're free to talk to him before and after. Expect the judge to ask you questions."

"Thank you, officer. Appreciate the info."

He smiled and nodded. "Thank me by making sure he stays out of trouble in the future."

"Well, his visa's been revoked, so he'll be confined to the ship until we dock someplace else." I grinned. "Our chief engineer will be having him painting bilges until he questions his life choices."

The officer laughed.

I headed down the passageway and found room five. The door stood open and showed a standard hearing room. A single table with three chairs faced the raised platform where the adjudicator would sit. The floors gleamed in the overhead lights. A door opened to the side and an officer brought in Jacobs. She sat him down in one of the chairs and stood behind him before turning to me. "You his captain?"

"I am."

"Judge Jessica Modzelewski will run the hearing. You can sit with your crew if you like."

"I'll stand, if that's all right?"

She nodded. "The judge will have questions for you." She glanced at the chrono on the bulkhead above my head, before turning and facing the bench.

At the stroke of 1000 a slender woman with distinguished streaks of gray in her brown hair came in and took a seat. She settled her black robe over her shoulders and clicked a switch on the podium in front of her. "This hearing is being recorded. August 18, 2379, 1000 hours. Judge Jessica Modzelewski presiding. Docket 9234. Paul Jacobs charged with aggravated assault, battery, possession of a prohibited weapon, use of same." She looked up from the tablet to Jacobs. "You're Paul Jacobs?"

"Yes, sar."

"Your Honor is the approved honorific, but simple answers to simple questions will work the best." She looked at me. "You're his captain?"

"I am, Your Honor. Captain Ishmael Wang. Clipper Marva Collins."

"Thank you, Captain." She looked down at her tablet. "Mr. Jacobs, you stand accused of attacking Mr. Manfred Reddy in the passageway behind the Rusted Thruster. Did you?"

"No, your honor. He attacked me and my friends."

The judges eyebrows rose. "That's your story?"

"It is, Your Honor."

The judge glanced up at me, before spearing Jacobs with a stern look. "Are you aware that lying to the court is itself an additional offense?"

"Are you saying I'm lying, Your Honor?"

The officer placed a hand on Mr. Jacobs's shoulder, and he looked up at her.

"Just so we understand each other, Mr. Jacobs," the judge said. "Two simple rules. I ask the questions. You answer the questions. Answer the question, Mr. Jacobs. Are you aware that lying to the court is itself an additional offense?"

"No, Your Honor."

"In that light, I'll let you revisit your earlier statement. Did you attack Mr. Reddy?"

"No, Your Honor."

The judge sighed. "Perhaps we have a language problem here." She flipped a switch on her desk and a screen flipped open on one side of the room. She pressed some keys on her tablet and the screen showed a passageway, viewed from above and looking along the passageway. Several people walked along the passage, three walking away from the camera, two toward it until they were out of frame. "Do you recognize this place, Mr. Jacobs?"

"No, Your Honor."

The judge shrugged. "I suspect all of the passageways look alike to you, Mr. Jacobs. The indicator on the bottom of the frame gives the location and view as well as a date-time stamp. This is the passageway where you and three of your associates met Mr. Reddy last evening." She paused. "Anything you'd like to say, Mr. Jacobs?"

Mr. Jacobs shook his head. "No, Your Honor."

Judge Modzelewski lifted her chin in my direction. "Captain? Would you care to counsel your crew before I play this security footage?"

"Mr. Jacobs. How many windows in Hutchins Gym?" I asked.

He twisted in his chair to look back at me and grinned. "Thirty-two to the outside, six ticket, two in the doors and twelve boxes for real people, not cadets, sar."

"If you'd like to be able to answer that question on the campus again, I suggest you rethink your response to the judge."

"What, sar?"

I nodded at the screen. "That video is about to show exactly what happened last night. Judge Modzelewski has given you three chances to come clean. You're still going to be restricted to the ship, but what you say next will determine whether or not you get to go back the Academy when we're done here."

"What? For a bar fight that's not even in TIC jurisdiction?" His jaw hung open, disbelief pouring off his face.

I sighed. "Honesty. Integrity. Duty. Do those words seem even remotely familiar to you, Mr. Jacobs?"

He blinked. "Of course, Captain."

"Do you think you should choose between them? Or should you display all of them?"

"Well, all of them, of course, sar."

"How does location come into play then, Mr. Jacobs?"

"Captain?"

I sighed again and looked to the judge. "I'm sorry, Your Honor. Mr. Jacobs seems to be under the misguided notion that he only needs to uphold the tenets of his profession under certain circumstances and in specific locations."

The judge nodded. "I appreciate your efforts, Captain. Should I assume you'd have no problem if I were to sentence him to, say, an extended stay in one of our comfortable jail cells?"

"None at all, Your Honor. He's a quarter share crew who can be easily replaced."

"Captain!" Mr. Jacobs's jaw hung open, his eyes wide in shock.

The officer pressed her hand harder on his shoulder.

"Mr. Jacobs, I will have order in this proceeding," the judge said.

"But, Your Honor, I have to get back to the Academy."

"And I'm sure you'll be able to purchase passage when your sentence has been served, Mr. Jacobs." The judge shrugged. "Assuming I find you guilty as charged and assess a jail term."

Jacobs sank back against his chair and swallowed.

"Now, Mr. Jacobs. Did you and your associates attack Mr. Reddy?"

He slouched in his seat and crossed his arms. "Why bother? You've already made up your mind, Your Honor."

I winced.

The judge sighed and pressed the Play button. The video started up again and showed Mr. Jacobs leading his pack coming toward the camera from the passageway beyond. Another person entered the frame from the bottom, back to the lens. Mr. Jacobs crowded the man, bumping into him as they passed and pushing the man against the bulkhead.

"Watch where you're going," Jacobs said, confronting the man he'd bumped and pushing a hand into his chest to hold him against the bulkhead.

"Hey, you bumped me, asshole. Why don't you find your way back to your little hidey-hole before somebody takes offense?"

"Like you? You?" Mr. Jacobs shoved the guy in the shoulder, knocking him back against the bulkhead again.

Mr. Reddy came off the bulkhead with a solid right-cross that Mr. Jacobs blocked. The other crewmen hung back for a few seconds before trying to pull Mr. Jacobs back. I saw where Mr. Powell got hit in the cheek and Mr. Lindner got the shiner for his trouble. Mr. Reddy seemed to be gaining the advantage until a blade flashed in Mr. Jacobs's hand and Mr. Reddy fell back against the bulkhead holding his side.

In the resulting shocked pause, Mr. Lindner and Mr. Brooke finally pulled Mr. Jacobs off. A half second later, two security officers ran in from the bottom of the screen and corralled my crew against the opposite bulkhead. One of them saw Mr. Reddy sliding down the opposite bulkhead and reached for his comms unit.

The judge stopped the playback. "Care to explain yourself, Mr. Jacobs?"

Mr. Jacobs shook his head. "No excuses, Your Honor."

"Did you attack, Mr. Reddy?"

"Yes, Your Honor."

"Why, Mr. Jacobs?"

Mr. Jacobs sighed. "I don't know. He was there." He shook his head and looked down at his hands. "I don't know."

"I know why," the judge said, her voice growing hard. "You're a bully, Mr. Jacobs. With your shipmates at your back, you thought you could abuse one of the station's residents. Somebody who'd done nothing to you. Somebody whom you'd never seen before and thought never to see again. Isn't that right, Mr. Jacobs?"

"I didn't give it that much thought, Your Honor."

"Yet you entered the station carrying a weapon?" the judge asked. "You were expecting trouble, even though you've never been here before."

"Yes, Your Honor."

"You didn't find it, so you made it, Mr. Jacobs." The judge shook her head and looked at me. "What's the ship's position on this?"

"He will be confined to the ship. His quarter shares are forfeit for the entire voyage. I've already rescinded the shares for his friends. Mr. Jacobs's actions have called his character into question, Your Honor. It will go on his record, which will go back to the Academy when we return. It's the kind of error that ends careers before they begin." I watched Mr. Jacobs's shoulders slump.

The judge nodded. "How much would a quarter share in the engineering division earn over the course of a stanyer, Captain?"

"The company rate is fifty credits a day for a quarter share, Your Honor."

"The ship will be responsible for his fines and assessments?" the judge asked.

"Of course, Your Honor. The Marva Collins pays her debts."

The judge nodded. "Thank you, Captain. Mr. Jacobs, stand."

Mr. Jacobs stood, facing the judge.

"In the matter of Docket 9234. Paul Jacobs charged with assault, battery, possession of a prohibited weapon, use of same. How do you plead, Mr. Jacobs?"

"Guilty, Your Honor."

"I find you guilty, Mr. Jacobs. You are hereby fined nine thousand credits and billed for an additional nine thousand in damages to Mr. Manfred Reddy. You may take him away, officer. This hearing is at an end." She clicked the button to stop the recording.

The officer took him by the upper arm and led him out, back through the door they had entered.

When they'd gone, the judge nodded to me. "Thank you, Captain. Not everyone who comes to my court understands the nature of the business."

"I'm sorry he's been a problem, Your Honor."

"You were the skipper from the Chernyakova, weren't you? The one who got mixed up in that nasty business a few stanyers ago?"

"Guilty as charged, Your Honor."

She grinned. "Thank you. I have no idea as to the details, but I know something of what you did and I'm personally grateful. As to young Mr. Jacobs, do you think he's learned anything?"

"I honestly don't know, Your Honor. I'm appalled. If he'd pulled a stunt like that on the Newmar Orbital, he'd have been on a fast packet to somewhere else by day's end."

"But he thought he could get away with it because it's just a Toe-Hold," the judge said, her lips turned down in a grimace.

"Yes." I sighed. "One of the goals in bringing them out here is to disabuse them of the idea that Toe-Hold space is less than."

Her eyebrows rose at that. "Is that a common perception in the High Line?"

I pondered that question for a few heartbeats. "I really don't know how common, Your Honor. I can't speak for all the people in the High Line. I know the curriculum at the Academy portrays Toe-Holds as only one step removed from ghost towns."

Her eyebrows rose even higher at that. "What's your opinion, Captain?"

I laughed. "The Toe-Holds are the future of the Western Annex. The Academy needs to change its curriculum to prepare future officers to deal with it."

"Will they?" she asked. "My impression of the Academy at Port Newmar is that it's pretty hidebound in its outlook."

"I've brought one of their instructional designers with me. His job is to prepare the curriculum that will replace the current one."

The judge's eyebrows came back down and she stared off into the middle distance for a moment. "Well, it's a step. Having the curriculum and teaching it are two different things."

"Agreed, and I'm glad I don't have to fight that battle, Your Honor."

She chuckled. "As a personal aside, Captain, if Mr. Jacobs has learned his lesson, would you make sure that this little peccadillo doesn't kill his career?"

"I can't promise that, Your Honor. I can promise that he'll have every chance to redeem himself, but thank you for not charging him with lying to the court. That will help."

"You caught that, did you?" She grinned at me.

"I get paid to pay attention to the details, Your Honor." I smiled back at her.

She nodded a few times. "In that case, court dismissed." She stood. "Safe travels, Captain."

"Thank you, Your Honor."

We each left by our respective doors and I found my way back to the front desk to collect a somewhat subdued Mr. Jacobs.

"If you'd thumb the tab, Captain?" the desk officer said, holding it out.

I checked the total and thumbed it.

He checked it and nodded. "He's all yours."

"Thank you, officer." I led Jacobs out of the station and back to the ship. We didn't speak until we got to the lock.

"Get cleaned up and get into uniform. Report to the cabin in half a stan."

"Aye, aye, Captain."

I keyed the lock open and checked us both back aboard, adding Mr. Jacobs's name to the list of personnel restricted to the ship. He headed toward engineering berthing, and I went to the mess deck for a cup of coffee.

Natalya joined me in the cabin almost as soon as I settled my butt in the chair.

"How bad was it?" she asked, taking one of the visitors' chairs.

"Bad enough. Apparently he didn't understand the entire station is wired for sound and pictures. Caught him center frame losing a fight against one of the stationers."

"What about the others?"

"They didn't contribute and tried to pull Mr. Jacobs off. I think Mr. Lindner's black eye was friendly fire. None of them contributed to the fight, but nobody got in the way of it until it was too late."

"Could they have stopped it?"

I shrugged and sipped my coffee. "It's possible, but the video clearly showed Mr. Jacobs bumping into the stationer, a Mr. Manfred Reddy, on purpose and then pushing him against the bulkhead."

"Fines?"

"Half his annual pay in fines. Other half in damages to Mr. Reddy. He probably could have gotten off with a slap on the wrist, but he tried to smart-mouth the judge, played stupid, and then tried to lie to her. "

She winced. "What do you want to do about him?"

"I was hoping you'd have some guidance, to be honest. My gut reaction is send him packing. Alys would expel him."

She pursed her lips and nodded. "She might still. This will go on the record we pass back to them when we're done." She gave me one of those sideways looks. "What are you thinking?"

"I'm wondering if he learned anything from the experience."

She sighed and leaned back in her chair, staring at the overhead. "I thought that might be the case."

"Is he worth keeping?"

Zoya knocked on the door jamb. "Sorry I'm late."

"Come in. We've got about a quarter stan before our black sheep gets here. We're just discussing the options."

"What are the damages?" she asked, taking her usual standing position against the bulkhead just inside the cabin door.

"Mr. Reddy survived and is pressing charges. I didn't hear more than that. Mr. Jacobs started it. The other three didn't interfere until it was too late. Judge levied his annual salary. Half fine. Half damages to the victim. Along the way, Mr. Jacobs thought he could lie his way out of it."

Zoya drew in a sharp breath through her nose and blew it out slowly through her lips.

"Yeah. My thought exactly," Natalya said.

"What're our choices?" I asked.

"Keep him or toss him," Natalya said. "Some variations on those two."

Zoya sighed. "He's not in my division."

"If he were?" I asked.

"I'd need to know more about him before I'd recommend rehabilitation."

Natalya leaned forward, turning slightly. "You think he can be?"

She shrugged. "Just from what I know, he's young, stupid, and male. I realize some of those are redundant." She looked at me. "If it had only been the scuffle, I'd be inclined to give him a chance."

I nodded. "For what it's worth, the judge didn't charge him with the lie. Even after catching him in it."

Zoya raised her eyebrows at that.

"She took me aside after the hearing and asked me to give him a chance."

Natalya's head came up. "The judge?"

"Yeah. Thought that maybe getting him booted from the Academy might not be in anybody's best interest."

"If he'd pulled this crap in Port Newmar, he'd have already been chucked off campus," Natalya said.

Zoya sighed. "Agreed, but we're not in the High Line. How much of this can we lay at the CPJCT's door?"

Natalya looked at her, frowning a little. "What?"

"The whole reason we're running this drill is to reshape the curriculum. To educate the eventual officers, and by extension their crews," she said. "How much of Jacobs's attitude and actions flow from that 'less than' indoctrination?"

"You're thinking we can change it?" Natalya asked.

Zoya shrugged. "I don't know. He's your crew. Is he trainable?"

Natalya sighed and shook her head. "I really don't know. He's been kind of an asshole the whole time."

Zoya shrugged again. "Is this going to be a big enough wake-up call?"

Natalya stared at the deck for a couple of heartbeats. "I'm choking on trying to lie."

"Me, too," Zoya said.

They both looked over at me.

"Well, let's see what he has to say for himself," I said. "My choices are put him on a packet home or keep him working for a credit a day until we get back."

"His share?" Natalya asked.

"Forfeit."

Zoya nodded. "And you can't make him work for nothing."

"Correct. The judge's levy was eighteen thousand in total. That leaves him a few credits. The ship paid it, so his work would pay the ship back. His share is up to me."

"I hate this crap," Natalya said. "Remind me again why we took this job?"

"Because it's attitudes like Mr. Jacobs's that need to be changed," I said.

Zoya gave me a calculating look. "We aren't going to change his if we send him packing."

I nodded. We waited there in silence for a few moments before I heard footsteps coming up the ladder.

Mr. Jacobs braced himself in the open door frame and knocked on the jamb. "Sar, Cadet Paul Jacobs reporting as ordered, sar."

Natalya and Zoya both stood and took up positions to witness.

"Come in, Mr. Jacobs. Close the door."

He did his best cadet-on-the-carpet moves, eventually standing at attention in front of my console.

I stood. "Mr. Jacobs, you've consistently characterized yourself as a cadet. Your friends did as well. Let me assure you that you are not a cadet. You are a quarter share crew on a vessel I command. Nothing less, but nothing more. Is that clear?"

"Sar, yes." He practically strangled himself but managed to chop off the final "sar."

"You've put me in a position that I find uncomfortable, Mr. Jacobs. It's not good to make your commanding officer uncomfortable." I walked around the console to stand in front of him, not quite in parade ground confrontation distance but closer than social norms might call appropriate. "Do you have anything to say in your defense, Mr. Jacobs?"

"Sar. I have no defense. I was wrong."

"They say recognizing the problem is the first step to correcting it, Mr. Jacobs. Why did you decide it would be a good idea to attack Mr. Reddy?"

He paused. His Academy training kept him staring straight ahead, focused on the bulkhead, but I could practically hear the gears turning in his head. "I don't know, Captain."

I nodded. "He was just there. Alone. One guy against the four of you? Something like that?"

He licked his lips. "Something like that, Captain. I just saw him and reacted. I didn't think."

"The crux of the problem, Mr. Jacobs. You didn't think. You haven't been thinking since you came up early, got lost on the orbital, and I had to come find you. Maybe before." I let that sink in a moment. "Ms. Regyri, how would you characterize Mr. Jacobs's performance in his duties since coming aboard?" I didn't look at her. Just kept staring at him.

"Lackluster, at best, Captain."

"How did he do during the testing period, Ms. Regyri?"

"Didn't even try, Captain."

I raised my eyebrows at that, still staring at him. "You didn't even try, Mr. Jacobs. Why is that?"

"It seemed pointless, Captain."

"Pointless? Why is that?"

"Because I'm going back to the Academy and I'll lose those credentials in the end, sar."

"I see. What of the knowledge, Mr. Jacobs?"

"The knowledge, Captain?"

"Yes, the knowledge. The things you'd learn by earning the credential? To say nothing of the incremental credit value, but what of the knowledge?"

"I'd never have to do those jobs, Captain."

"No, Mr. Jacobs, but you'll have wise ass crew who think they know better than you doing them. If you don't know how to do them, how will you know if they're doing them correctly? How will you know how to correct them if they're not? How can you manage them if you don't know what they are, in fact, supposed to be doing?" I paused to take a breath. "Did that never occur to you, Mr. Jacobs?"

His strict attention-face crinkled at the forehead. "None of the cadets who didn't come on this cruise will know either, Captain."

"So, you're saying that you'll give up an advantage to those people who graduate higher in the class?"

"Advantage, Captain?"

"Yes, Mr. Jacobs, advantage. You have the opportunity to learn more than they do. You have the chance to become a more effective third officer right out of the Academy, but you're turning your back on that advantage because why? Mr. Jacobs? You think the work is beneath you? You think it's silly to have clean water or drives that work?"

"No, sar."

"Then why, Mr. Jacobs? Even ignoring the credits you've given up by not doing the simplest thing to double your share amount, why would you turn up your nose at the opportunity to be a better officer?"

"I didn't understand that, Captain."

"Ms. Regyri?" I asked.

"You can give a spacer the wrench, Captain, but you can't make them think. I told all of them why it was important on numerous occasions. Specifically to Mr. Jacobs and his cronies."

"Did she tell you, Mr. Jacobs? That the importance of taking the tests was so that you'd understand the job you'd be overseeing?"

"Yes, sar." His tone carried defeat.

"What am I going to do with you, Mr. Jacobs?"

His eyes widened. "Do, Captain?"

"Yes. You've forfeited your quarter share pay and shares. You've embarrassed the ship on our very first voyage and in only the second night in port. You've injured an innocent man. Spurned your duty. Basically made a complete ass of yourself here in only a few short weeks since leaving the Academy. You must expect that your actions will have some kind of accountability."

He swallowed, his eyes fixing on the far bulkhead again. Just a little wider this time. "Yes, sar."

"Which would you prefer, Mr. Jacobs? A quick trip back to the Academy in disgrace, or working for a credit a day until we complete our voyage?"

He blinked several times. "A quick trip back to the Academy, Captain?"

"Yes." I stepped back and perched my haunches on the edge of my desk. "I'm prepared to buy your ticket to ship you back so Commandant Giggone can show you the error of your ways. Frankly, a large part of me feels that to be unfair to Commandant Giggone. You have earned a quick trip, a fast expulsion, and the rest of your life to consider the choices you've made, but I'm not sure the commandant deserves the insult."

He swallowed again, harder this time. "A credit a day?"

"Well, the judge levied almost all your pay. Your quarter share is forfeit, not just this leg but until we dock at Port Newmar. I can't make you work for nothing, but I can pay you one credit a day." I let that sink in. "Even then, I can't guarantee that the commandant will let you resume your coursework, given your criminal record."

"Criminal record, sar?"

"You perhaps remember being arrested? Charged? Convicted? You pleaded guilty. It happened just this morning, Mr. Jacobs."

"But this is the Toe-Holds, Captain."

"What's your point, Mr. Jacobs? You believe that the records won't follow you back to the High Line? You believe that our logs will be, somehow, expunged?" I gave him a beat to think about it. "You think that you can do any damn thing you want here because it's outside some arbitrary line in space? TIC versus not?"

"No, sar."

"Yes, Mr. Jacobs. That's exactly what you thought. Would you have pulled this crap on the orbital at Port Newmar? Or maybe in some company system like Darbat?"

"No, sar."

"But you did here, Mr. Jacobs. I submit that you did it because you thought you could get away with it. You thought that the Toe-Holds are somehow less than the High Line. You thought that integrity only mattered when people are watching."

"Sar, I—"

"I didn't ask you a question, Mr. Jacobs." I paused to take a breath. "The question I have to answer is whether or not I think those are permanent traits or simply learned behaviors." I let that sink in for a few heartbeats. "I'm willing to give you the benefit of the doubt, Mr. Jacobs. Ms. Regyri assures me you can learn. Will you, Mr. Jacobs? Will you take this lesson and learn from it, if I keep you on as crew?"

He opened his mouth but closed it again, his gaze boring holes in the far bulkhead. "I will give it my best effort, Captain."

I snorted. "Well, that's at least a more honest answer than 'sar, yes, sar.' I suppose it will have to do. Your quarter share salary and payout excepting the last credit are both forfeit for the remainder of the voyage. You're confined to the ship until further notice. While I appreciate you don't really want to leave while we're underway, you might find it significantly more onerous to be stuck aboard when we get to Mel's Place or beyond. Dismissed."

He did his best parade ground about-face and marched out of the cabin, closing the door behind him as he left.

I took a deep breath and blew it out before looking at Natalya and Zoya. "Nats?"

She shrugged. "I don't know. Are we doing him a favor? Are we letting this poison into the system?"

"Yeah. Both those. Zee?"

She smiled at me. "You've given him a gift. It'll be interesting to see how he receives it."

"A gift?" Natalya asked.

I nodded. "I took his quarter share pay and share. I didn't say anything about future earnings. If he gets half or full, he can have the difference plus one credit."

Her eyes widened and she laughed. "I didn't catch that."

"He'll have to earn it. Don't tell him. Let's see if he figures it out himself and does the work to move up before the next testing period."

She nodded. "Even if he doesn't make it, just taking the test would be a big improvement on his performance."

"I'm hoping we can adjust his attitude as much as his performance. The kid I saw in the hearing this morning is not somebody I'd want serving as an officer on my ship."

"That bad?" she asked.

I nodded. "But the judge saw something in him, even while Mr. Jacobs was being stupid. I'm willing to give that opinion some weight."

"I'd have given him the ticket home," she said.

Zoya looked at her. "No, you wouldn't. I've seen you work harder than that to replace an antique flow valve."

Natalya laughed. "Speaking of flow valves, I need to check the tankage. We should be topping off by noon." She left the cabin, propping the door open on the way out.

"Now that it's just us chickens?" I asked, glancing at Zoya.

"I think that was well done. You're right about it being career-ending. At least potentially. His future performance will provide either a nail in his coffin or a fig leaf for Alys Giggone."

"Thanks. I'm still not convinced that it's the right move, but if I'm calling him a quarter share, I need to hold him to that standard. If he were just some guy off the docks, I wouldn't be able to threaten him with being sent home. I'd just beach him and replace him."

"But you wouldn't without giving him a chance to redeem himself."

"You sound pretty sure of that."

She nodded and gave me a rueful smile. "Yeah. I am." Her tablet bipped. "Brow needs me."

"I'll take the night watch," I said. "Let Mr. Cartwright have the night off."

She nodded as she left. "I'll let him know, Skipper."

She left me with my thoughts. I still wasn't sure I'd made the right choice, but it was made. The dice tumbled. It would be some months before I'd know how they fell.

CHAPTER THIRTEEN
DARK KNIGHT STATION: AUGUST 21, 2379

We waited a few days for the Chernyakova to dock. It gave Pip extra time to line up cargoes for us, and he coordinated with Abe Kotawalla on the way in, so they had a can waiting for them. He went to the dock to make sure their check-in went all right. I never heard anything more about it, so I assumed he walked Beth through the rather odd ritual of establishing visa. I didn't always have to do the visa authorization in person, but I'd always made it a point to stay on good terms with the various dock officials in the Toe-Holds. They had long memories and often passed along good tips.

When the Chernyakova docked, Pip arranged for a senior staff meeting at DiPietro's, one of the nicer eateries just off Main Street. We left Mr. Cartwright in charge of the ship while Pip, Natalya, Zoya, Chief Bashar, and I met our counterparts in one of their private dining rooms. We arrived a few ticks early to give Pip a chance to make sure the room was set up the way he wanted. Before long, Beth arrived with her cadre.

Pip got us all seated where he wanted us; I was between Beth and her first mate, Julie Southern. We alternated around the table with Chief Bashar the odd man out, sitting between Pip and Abe Kotawalla. The serving staff circulated, taking drink orders, and Pip placed an order for some appetizers.

I took advantage of the action to lean over to Beth. "How are you holding up?"

She chuckled and shook her head. "The leg out of New-mar was a bit shaky at first, but the ratings you left got my ducklings quacking correctly within the first week."

"How many took the tests?"

"Not as many as I'd hoped. Too many seem to think it's wasted effort."

"They'll change their tunes when they see the share pay-outs." I took a sip from my water glass.

"You want me to tell you that I'm shocked and pleasantly surprised to find this station to be as large and active as it is?" she asked.

I chuckled. "No. That would be too close to 'I told ya so' and I don't want to be that guy."

She smoothed her napkin on her lap, looking down at the table in front of her. "You told me it was more than a ghost town. I believed you, eventually." She shot me a glance out of the corners of her eyes. "I wasn't expecting this much more."

"Rumor is you already have a can ready to go. Any prob-lems?"

"Pip explained the visa thing. That's weird, but I suppose it makes sense."

"You should have unlimited visa on the ship," I said. "The Chernyakova is a known quantity with a good reputation."

"The dock people wanted to know where you were. I had to point them down the docking bay."

The servers brought drinks and nibbles, interrupting us for a few moments.

"You've been here a long time," Beth said. "Aren't you ready to move on?"

"It's been a long week. We had a bit of a problem with some of the junior ratings. One got arrested. He picked a fight with one of the residents. Didn't realize all the public areas are wired."

Her eyebrows shot up and she started looking around the room.

"Not here," I said. "At least I don't think so. Passage-ways. Docks. I suspect the entries for all the commercial establishments."

"You know a lot about the Toe-Holds for only learning about them a few stanyers ago."

"I know more about this one, but that's a story for another day." I tilted my head to listen to Zoya and Ms. Southern's conversation. They were talking about Mr. Jacobs, too. I turned back to Beth.

"You're standing watches, I hear," she said.

"Day watch underway. It made sense in the abstract. In practice?" I shrugged. "I got to meet and work with all the watch sections but the constant shuffling of the watches?" I sighed. "Not ideal."

She nodded. "I know what you mean. What problem were you trying to solve?"

"Spreading the knowledge faster in the junior ratings. It was an interesting idea, but the messenger is the only junior rating I see."

"You'd rather rotate?" she asked.

"I think so. It's not like I don't know the senior ratings already, and I've been introduced to all the quarter and half shares."

She took a sip of her wine. "Speaking of half shares, how did your people do on the tests?"

I shook my head. "For students at an elite institution of higher education, they really had a problem with the tests."

Ms. Southern nodded, joining the conversation. "Ours, too. Only one of the deck people moved up to half."

"How did engineering do?" Natalya asked from the other side of the table.

Mr. Reynolds snorted. "About half took the test. Fewer than half of those passed the engineman test. None of the people trying for machinist did."

"Speaking of testing, where's Mr. MacBradaigh?" Beth asked.

"Mr. MacBradaigh wasn't invited," Pip said. "He's not command staff." He paused, looking around the table. "And now that I have your attention. As CEO of both companies, let me thank you all." He raised a glass in a toast. "Congratulations on taking the first step. Next stop is Mel's

Place. We're loaded and ready to go, but I understand the Chernyakova will need a few days in port."

"We'll be ready in two," Captain Case said, glancing at Mr. Reynolds who nodded. "But we'll need to take the whole four days."

Pip nodded. "As expected. We won't have as much of a difference in arrival times at Mel's. The Collins will wait until you're ready and we can head out together. We'll only need about a day to clear the local traffic, so we'll be able to jump at almost the same time. You'll be able to make it in one shot. We'll need a double to make it, but that will give you a leg up on getting to dock, barring any jump errors."

The servers returned with our meals and the conversation lapsed for a few ticks while we each dug into the food.

I glanced at Pip after making a dent in the pile of linguine on my plate. "You want to talk about the junior ratings?"

Pip shrugged. "We had a problem with a few. Starting fights is a bad idea. Something I'd have expected our newest crew to understand. One didn't and it cost him. It might cost him his place at the Academy when we return." He looked at Beth. "Impressing the importance of best behavior falls to us all."

"All right," Reynolds said. "Put it on the table. What happened?"

"One of the cadets took an illegal weapon onto the station. A knife with too long a blade," Natalya said. "He started a fight with a resident in an alley. Three of his buddies got involved when the resident, quite rightly, took umbrage. Our genius pulled the knife and stabbed the resident just in time for station security to show up. They characterized the scuffle as a bar fight, but the security cams showed our boy pulling the 'bump into you on purpose and then complain' thing. All four are restricted to the ship. It's been a long week for them but the decks in engineering have never looked better."

"They're brand new, aren't they? The decks?" Mr. Reynolds asked.

"Yes, but now they're clean. They'll get cleaned again tomorrow." She shrugged and took a sip of her beer.

"That brings up an important point," Pip said. "Security cams are everywhere. You think there's a lot of security on the orbitals? They learned it from the Toe-Holds. There are private spaces, like this room, like hotel rooms and the stalls in public facilities. Assume every other place on the station is wired, sight and sound. Usually multiple views. Impress on your people that if they so much as spit on the deck, somebody will see it. Ours have learned the hard way."

"How limited are these visas?" Ms. Southern asked.

"You're unlikely to run into the limits," Pip said. "There are residential areas where transient personnel aren't allowed. It's nothing personal. It's protecting their neighborhoods. Limited visas mean you'll be asked to leave if you're found there. Unlimited means you can go anywhere that a resident can. Residential visas mean you can live here. There are still places that will need security access, but that's understandable. They don't want any old moke poking into the power plants and environmental stations."

"Residential?" Abe asked, leaning forward to look around Chief Bashar. "Who would live here?"

Pip laughed. "All the people who do live here. It's not a bad place if you're looking to settle down. Maybe open a shop. Start a restaurant. Cost of living is reasonable. The station management encourages immigration as long as you bring something with you besides a need. Some of us here have residential visas. I'm not ready to retire yet, but I could see moving here and setting up a cargo brokerage in my old age."

Chief Bashar looked at Pip. "I could open a restaurant here but I'd need a residential visa?"

"More like, apply to open a restaurant. If it's granted, you'd get the residential visa."

"How did you get yours?" the chief asked.

"We stopped a group of terrorists from blowing up the station with a nuke," Pip said.

The room went silent.

"You can't just lay that out on the table and expect us to just accept it," Beth said.

"It's a long story. Sometime over adult beverages in another setting."

"You said this place is safe. How common is this terrorist bomb thing?"

"It's not common at all," I said. "I have reason to believe that it was a unique circumstance."

Pip gave me a quizzical look but I just gave him a little head shake.

Beth looked at me. "You're certain?"

"I'm risking my own life and the lives of my crew. I believe it to be safe. Yes. Certain?" I shrugged. "Nothing is certain but I'm certain enough to stake my own life on it."

She frowned at me for a moment before a smile touched her lips and spread to her eyes. "That's fair."

Zoya leaned forward to look at Beth. "We believe that a single bad actor operated in the Toe-Holds for some time. That operation has been removed from consideration."

Natalya leaned in, too. "It's a hell of a story and I'm willing to let you buy me drinks sometime to tell you the whole thing."

Mr. Reynolds looked at her. "Were you aboard for that?"

"We joined just after," she said. "But we heard all about it."

"The thing to remember," Pip said, drawing everybody's attention, "is the key difference between Toe-Hold space and the High Line is regulation. The High Line is a single entity. It's helpful to look at it like a hotel chain. A lot of rooms where people stay, but only one management at the top. There's a staff of security professionals to make sure that the residents don't get disturbed. That's not the same thing as keeping them safe, although the concepts are related. If enough people get disturbed, it disrupts their business, and that's something that can't be allowed."

"You make it sound so draconian," Beth said.

"I'm probably understating it. The CPJCT intercepts every transmission through their terminals in order to put a surcharge on it. They also slow down commercial message traffic. Out here, we can get a message to Port Newmar in a couple of days. To Mel's Place, which is the same distance, in a day. Getting a message out of Port Newmar to someplace in the same sector like Blanchard takes at least three days if the comms run through the CPJCT network, but only a day if you tap into the High Tortuga network directly. You already know about the issues with trying to enter or leave the High Line. The Trade Investigation Commission certifies cargoes while turning a blind eye to the backdoors. They only catch the smugglers who don't follow their rules."

"It still makes no sense to me," Ms. Southern said.

Mr. Kotawalla shook his head. "It does make sense, but only if you accept that the CPJCT exists for the benefit of its members, not the people who live there. The Toe-Holds exist to benefit each individual station. I've been reading up." He addressed that last to Pip. "Did you know there's a station run by a bunch of religious people that's studying cosmology? Something about celebrating their god by trying to understand his power or something. There's no place for that kind of effort in the High Line."

"Remember that no stable system is irrational," Pip said. "It may seem irrational, but that's only because you don't know all the rules."

Ms. Southern frowned. "I know you can't change a stable system. But irrational?"

"Irrational, as in makes no sense. Like the relationship between the Toe-Holds and the High Line. If you see a stable system and think 'that can't work' but the system continues to exist, then the conclusion is that you don't know something key to the system. You can change a stable system. You just have to destabilize it first." He grinned. "That's the real challenge, because a stable system will fight you."

"Is that what we're doing with the Academy?" Beth took a sip of her wine.

Pip shrugged. "I don't know. Are we destabilizing a system? Or are we correcting an imbalance that has grown too large for the system to accommodate?"

She frowned. "What imbalance?"

"Toe-Hold growth," Mr. Kotawalla said. "When the High Line was growing, when the companies there were finding markets for their goods, the system was stable enough to continue. That's changed. It's happened in the last few decades, if my reading of the history is correct."

"Nat and I saw the beginning of it right after we graduated from the Academy," Zoya said. "We did some work with the High Tortuga Holding Company to expand their network capacity. Even then, the growth was almost all in the Toe-Holds. Small startups but some of them succeeded. It concerned High Tortuga even then. I've not seen anything that says that growth has subsided."

"My family operates extensively in the Toe-Holds," Pip said. "Our data says the rate of growth has increased. Not just new stations but station expansions and populations. That new growth has gotten to the point where the High Line needs the Toe-Holds more than the Toe-Holds need the High Line. That was always true, but now the High Line doesn't just need the materials that the Toe-Holds provided. They need the markets that the Toe-Holds represent. The balance in the system has shifted to the point that what was a nicely balanced machine is becoming more and more unbalanced."

Beth frowned and fiddled with the knife beside her plate. "I see what you're saying. You think that's why Alys Giggone is pushing this?"

Pip nodded. "I do. Once you get outside of the bubble and realize that the High Line is only part of a larger machine, the Western Annex looks very different."

We addressed our food again, conversation falling into a lull as we digested the information while continuing to ingest dinner.

After a few ticks, I turned to Beth again. "How's your second mate doing?"

She nodded and swallowed before answering. "Once we got underway, he settled in. Or maybe I don't see him enough to notice. I haven't heard any rumblings and he seems pleasant enough in the wardroom. Whatever chip he had on his shoulder seems to be gone. Or maybe just hidden in his grav trunk."

"What's he think of Dark Knight Station?"

She laughed, drawing attention from around the table. "Sorry. It's just being told that there's a whole massive city in space, not connected to any planet, just orbiting the system primary? That's a tough image to sell. Seeing it? That was a brand new experience. For those of us who hadn't seen it before, anyway." She shrugged. "I'm looking forward to exploring a little myself."

"Main Street is the shopping district," Pip said. "The bars closest to the docking gallery will have the cheapest beer, but the places like this, just off Main Street? Those will have the best value. Every time we come here, I find a new place to try out."

"And you come here every time you enter or leave Venitz?" she asked.

"Almost. We've taken a different route maybe once or twice. Dark Knight is a good gateway from this side of the Annex," I said.

"What are the others?" Ms. Southern asked.

"Coming in from Diurnia, we usually hit Mel's Place first, but The Ranch is the same distance. Ice Rock if you're coming in from the southeastern side. It's the right distance coming out of New Caledonia or Gretna."

I took a sip of coffee. "Speaking of that end of the Annex, we should wave the flag down in in New Caledonia. Maybe the confederation port in Chiba."

Pip nodded. "I'll check my charts and see if we can do something." He turned to Mr. Kotawalla. "You up for an adventure in cargo picking, Abe?"

Mr. Kotawalla's eye narrowed a bit. "What kind of adventure?"

Natalya laughed. "He's got your number already, Pip."

Pip grinned and shrugged. "Nothing serious. The southeast corner of the Annex isn't an area I've worked in much. Any new territory is an adventure."

"Cargo's cargo," Mr. Kotawalla said with a shrug. "You're the CEO. I think we go where you say, don't we?"

"See, Ishmael? This is the attitude I wish you'd adopt."

I made a rude noise with my lips. "You pick our cargoes based on where they pay the most. I go where you tell me they belong. Don't know how else we'd do it."

"Yes," Pip said. "But I'm talking about the deference due my position as CEO."

"You calling me a kiss-ass?" Mr. Kotawalla asked, his eyebrows high on his forehead and a grin on his lips.

Pip chuckled. "Admiring your skill and tact, Abe. Skill and tact."

We shared a laugh as the servers came back to clear the table of the empty dishes and offer desserts. We lingered over cake and coffee for a while but by 2100, we'd all had about as much food as we could handle. The party broke up while Pip thumbed the tab.

Beth tarried for a bit, and I stood with her.

"How comfortable are you on the station?" I asked.

"Any place I should look out for?"

"Stay in the commercial district. It's the station's bread and butter and has the best level of security. Probably better than the docks."

Zoya came over and spoke to her. "What did you have in mind?"

"I'd kind of like to get the lay of the land, but I don't know where to start."

"You want company?" Zoya asked. "I'll go with you."

Ms. Southern joined us. "Oh, me, too, please? I saw some places that looked interesting as we were walking over."

Zoya looked around. "Anybody else for an after-dinner stroll?"

Natalya grinned at us from the other side of the room and shook her head, but Chief Bashar raised a hand. "I'm in."

"Who's up for a pub crawl?" Pip asked, raising his voice to cover the room.

Mr. Reynolds nodded. "Now you're talking."

Abe Kotawalla grinned and walked over to stand with Pip. "I just have to be back by morning to thumb for the new can."

I shook my head. "I'm heading back to the ship."

"Oh, come on, Skipper," Natalya said. "You're not pooping out so early, are you?"

I laughed. "I've been here before. I've seen the sights."

Zoya turned to look at me. "Come with us, Skipper. We'll do a slow stroll around Main Street. Stretch your legs a little."

Something in her voice changed my mind. Before I knew it, I'd joined their party and followed them out.

Pip peeled off with his people outside the restaurant, Natalya and Patrick Reynolds already deep in the weeds about the Chernyakova's capacitors as they walked away.

Zoya, good to her word, headed toward Main Street and the shops and bistros that lined the wide promenade. Beth walked alongside her with Julie Southern walking beside Chief Bashar. The dynamics of the group fascinated me. Zoya and the captain walking in front seemed all but oblivious to the pair behind them. Along the way, the captain paused to look in display windows or gaze out at the space. With the street lights lining the path and the darkness far above, it felt like any street on any planet.

We looped around after a quarter stan or so and started down the other side. I saw Beth do a double take when we walked by a pleasure palace, the attractive people in the window smiling at us as they lounged on divans. It made me wonder which side of the glass was the display. Chief Bashar looked over his shoulder at me. "You still there, Skipper?"

"Hanging on. Enjoying the floor show."

His laugh rumbled a little and he nodded before returning his full attention to Ms. Southern.

We shared the broad sidewalks with a variety of people. A lot of spacers mixed in with the residents. Most people wore civvies, but I caught sight of a couple of men in station livery walking hand in hand and a number of uniformed security officers keeping an eye on the foot traffic.

"Why is this so big?" Beth asked.

Zoya looked back at me. "Skipper? Any insight?"

"Main Street is actually a supply route. It's big enough for the large haulers to supply the shops without getting tied up in alleys."

Ms. Southern's eyes widened. "How big are those haulers? You could fit a shuttlecraft in here."

I shrugged. "Never seen them myself. Just one of the stories I heard."

"Why not big?" Chief Bashar said.

Zoya had stopped on the next intersection and we stood in a rough circle on the corner.

"What do you mean, Chief?" Beth asked.

"Volume has no mass, other than the gas filling it. The station doesn't need to navigate, so the overall mass is negligible. Having a tall overhead? What's the cost? Just the amount of material needed to put it up there and, unless I miss my guess, those end caps are old Barbell cans." He nodded to the nearer end of the street.

"Is it always night time?" Ms. Southern asked.

"They have lights in the overhead. Turns this place into day from 0600 to 2000," Zoya said. "Natalya and I lived here for a time when we graduated from the Academy."

Ms. Southern tilted her head a little to the left. "You and Natalya? Are you a couple?"

Zoya laughed. "No more than the captain and Pip are. We just teamed up and neither of us found a reason to wander off on our own." She gave me a quick glance. "At least not yet."

Beth saw the look and frowned. "You think that's likely?"

"Short answer, yes, of course. Eventually, it seems almost inevitable, doesn't it? We roomed together at the Academy, got thrown together on graduation day, and we've been wingmen ever since." She shrugged. "We've both seen shipmates come and go. Nobody ever stays forever on the same ship."

"Your core team has been together a long time, though," Chief Bashar said. "Thinking of breaking up the band?"

"Not that long. Nats is at the top of her org chart now. So are Pip and the skipper." She gave a wry smile and a quick shrug. "I'll have time in grade eventually, and then we'll see what happens." She gave me another of her glances.

"One stanyer and a few months," I said.

Beth smiled at me. "That's when she'll have the time?"

I nodded. "I haven't filled out the forms yet, but I have a tickler in my calendar."

"I've got stanyers yet," Ms. Southern said. "I'm not even sure I want it."

"Really?" Beth asked.

"Yes, Captain. Really. I mean if you're all set to put me up for the boards, then by all means." She laughed. "But I'm doing what I love right now. I'd take the boards if you want to put me in when the time comes, but I doubt that I'd hang up a master's ticket anywhere."

"I was the same way," I said.

Zoya's head snapped around, her eyes wide. "Really, Skipper?"

"I never expected it. I thought I'd be first mate forever." I gave Ms. Southern a grin. "Life happens when you're busy planning something else."

Zoya looked around at the people flowing past us for a moment, then nodded at the intersection. "Well, that's the passageway back to the docking gallery. The question on the floor is whether to walk some more or head back to the ship."

"I'd like to see a little more," Ms. Southern said. "It seems safe enough."

"I'll go with you," Chief Bashar said.

Beth nodded. "I'm up for it. It feels good to walk where the nearest bulkhead isn't two steps away."

I took a step toward the gallery. "I'm for the ship. I've got the day watch tomorrow."

"You have the day watch every day, Skipper." Zoya grinned at me. "I'll go with you."

Beth grinned. "We'll see you later then." She started across the alleyway heading further into the station with Ms. Southern and Chief Bashar in tow.

Zoya fell into step with me as we strolled along.

"That was well done, Zee."

"Thanks, Skipper. I thought they only needed a little push to get them going. Captain Case seems to be adjusting to the new reality pretty well."

"What of Ms. Southern?"

"I think she'll be fine. Chief Bashar seems to have taken a shine to her."

"You think?" I asked.

She grinned at me. "You saw it, too. Don't give me that."

"What's the skinny on the steward division?"

"We're talking shop now?" she asked.

"You have another topic?" I glanced at her.

"You didn't want to be a captain?"

"Ah. Yes. Well. I didn't think I'd be allowed to be a captain." I shrugged. "Captain is something other people do. Not for land rats like me." I saw her give me a long look. "What? A lot of people never make captain."

"Like Al?" she asked.

"Like Al. I should have—"

Zoya shook her head, cutting me off. "Alberta Ross wasn't ever going to be a captain without selling her soul. She's too strong a woman to do that for so little."

I raised my eyebrows in her direction. "You know her?"

She chuckled. "I've known of her for a long time. Never expected to meet her, let alone take her place."

"I met her before I went to the Academy," I said. "Just in passing. At least, that's what I thought."

"Something change your mind?"

"She signed off on my Academy application."

"Really? How'd that happen?"

"Not sure. Alys Giggone gave me the form all filled out. I just had to thumb it and send it in. Al's signature was already there along with a lot of others."

She glanced at me and snickered. "I can see that. You must have been something else as a rating."

"What?"

"You got full share in all four divisions, right?"

"Yeah."

"How'd that happen?" She gave me a long look as we strolled out of the alley and into the docking gallery. "It's hard enough to get crew to grow in the one they're in."

"Job security. I thought the best thing I could do was to have as many openings as possible in case I got fired."

"That's not a bad reason, but I'm not buying that it's the only one." She shook her head. "No, something else."

"Alys Giggone had all four before she went to the Academy," I said. "I looked her up early on."

Zoya laughed and the humor sparked in her eyes. "I knew it."

"You know her grandmother was the original Lois McKendrick?"

"Really? The woman who took on the corporations and won?"

"Yeah. That Lois McKendrick." I shook my head. "I don't even know how Alys got the job as skipper on the ship named for her grandmother, but it doesn't surprise me."

"You know she married Benjamin Maxwell, right?" Zoya asked.

"Yeah. You ever meet him?" I asked.

"No. Just knew he was her first mate for a long time and followed her to Newmar when she took over from her father."

"That whole thing strike you as just a bit too much?" I asked.

"What? Marrying her first mate?"

"No, that Alys got the commandant's job."

She shrugged. "Not really. From what I understand about the politics of it, her father told the board that he'd die in the post unless they gave it to her. Refused to retire."

"They could have fired him."

She looked at me like I'd sprouted a second head. "Technically, yes. Politically?" She shook her head. "Robert Giggone was the Academy's second commandant. Pinkney might have gotten it started, but Giggone made it the crown jewel of the Western Annex in CPJCT's eyes. They couldn't fire him. Besides, Alys knows where the bodies are buried."

"Which bodies?"

"I don't know. Whatever bodies there are. I guarantee she found out from her father and she wanted that position."

"She seems to be doing a good job," I said. "From what I've seen in my visits, things seem to be moving in the right direction."

Zoya gave me another side-eyed look. "Even this deal?"

I nodded. "This deal may break her, but it's the thing that the Academy needs to do."

"Agreed."

A weird thought punched my brain. "I wonder if Margaret Stevens had anything to do with it?"

Zoya laughed. "Now that would not surprise me in the least."

CHAPTER FOURTEEN
DARK KNIGHT STATION: AUGUST 23, 2379

After the Chernyakova docked, our routine felt more normal. We had a departure date; the end of the long portside watches was in sight. I really didn't mind taking the day watches, but the more I thought of it, the more I second-guessed the idea of always taking the day watch. We did adjust from the twelve-hour portside watches, downsized to eights so they weren't quite so onerous. I could leave the ship pretty much any time I wanted after 1600 so long as I was back by 0800. I'd become a day worker, and something about that irked me.

My concern was with the watchstanders who almost never had the same officer of the day twice in a row. The day before our pullout from Dark Knight, I had Zoya change the watch rosters so I rotated with my section starting when we got underway.

She pulled out her tablet and propped her shoulders against the bulkhead beside the cabin's door. "You sure you want to do that, Skipper?"

"You could sit down, you know?"

She just grinned at me.

"I'm sure. How well do you know your watch section?"

She grimaced. "Do I even have a watch section?"

"That's my point. We had a few weeks where everybody rotated through. We all got to meet everybody in the division, but it's all in-and-out. Especially with the messengers."

"The messengers are the only quarter shares," she said. "We already knew the helms."

"Yeah, and only two of them went up a grade, Ms. Martinez and Ms. Vincent."

"Think that's related?"

I shrugged. "I don't know. I don't know Ms. Freano or Mr. Hoag well enough to say."

"Wanna have a little division meeting with them before we get underway again?" she asked.

"I really want to have a sit-down with Mr. MacBradaigh. Have you seen him lately?"

She frowned. "Now that you mention it, no." She flipped through a couple of screens. "He leaves early and comes back late. He's ashore now."

"Well, his job is to learn all he can about the Toe-Holds." I shrugged. "He's going to learn a lot by firsthand observation."

Zoya grimaced. "As long as he's not pissing them off in the process."

I laughed. "He has that talent. I want to know what happened with the tests. He claimed he was clearing all the practice exams. Somehow that conversation has never happened."

"I wonder why." Zoya's voice carried a certain level of sarcasm. "Not like he's particularly shy or retiring when it comes to his accomplishments."

"You still thinking about the 'educational credentials' crack when we first met?"

"You didn't have to be quite so protective, Skipper." She holstered her tablet and folded her arms. "I'm not some fainting flower."

"Sorry. He just pissed me off. He was so mindlessly dismissive." I sighed. "I should have let you eviscerate him."

She laughed and shook her head. "I appreciated your support at the time. I still do. He wasn't listening to me. He'd already made up his mind about Nats and me. We were just young officers who didn't understand the wider implications of his difficult task."

"He didn't understand them either," I said.

Zoya grinned. "That's what made it so funny."

"What time does he come back aboard?"

"Varies. 2200 to midnight. He leaves every morning at 0800. He must be getting breakfast ashore, or skipping it altogether. I haven't seen him in the wardroom."

"Me either." I pulled up my console and sent a note to the brow asking them to send Mr. MacBradaigh to me on his return. "Let's see what he has to say for himself."

"You gonna wait up for him, Dad?" She gave me a smirk.

I laughed. She had the most amazing ability to puncture me in the most interesting ways. "If need be. I want to touch base with Captain Case again. See how she's doing with the ship."

"She seemed to be taking to it like cherries on ice cream. You have concerns?"

"Mr. Skaggs. She said he'd calmed down, but she also said she hadn't seen that much of him underway."

"Think it's just a matter of changes? Some people just don't deal with change well. We don't know why he left New Caledonia, do we?"

"Not exactly. Just he lost his job and Alys tapped him for the post."

Zoya pursed her lips and frowned into the distance. "That's a long way for a stranger."

"Meaning Alys has cause to know him?"

She focused on me and nodded. "Stands to reason. They graduate a couple of hundred fresh thirds every stanyer. She can't keep track of them all, but she definitely tags a few for one reason or another."

"She didn't mention it, but that doesn't mean anything."

"Want some advice, Skipper?"

"Always."

"Sic Ms. Fortuner on him, second mate to second mate. The seconds and thirds have been excluded from our little confabs. Maybe do something nice for them. Get Pip to take them to dinner."

"I like this idea." I paged Pip on my console. "What's your take on Cartwright?"

She shrugged. "Hard worker. Did a great job on the testing even if we didn't get the kind of responses we wanted from the junior ratings."

I sighed. "Liberty expires at 0600 tomorrow. Pass the word I want an all-hands meeting on the mess deck at 0700, would you?"

She nodded and tapped a few keys on her tablet.

Pip showed up at the cabin door. "You rang?"

"I did. What do you think of setting up a dinner for the junior officers, both ours and the Chernyakova's?"

"Good idea. Any particular reason?"

"I want to do something nice for them. They missed our dinners."

"That's on me," he said, grimacing. "I should have included them."

"Hard to do with the watch schedules," I said. "All the more reason to get them a table at DiPietro's and treat them."

He frowned at me, then looked at Zoya. "Something else is going on."

"I want to make sure Mr. Skaggs is settling in."

"That's not your circus, Ishmael." His frown turned more to a scowl. "You wouldn't appreciate it if Beth started interviewing your clowns."

"You're the CEO and I'm the largest shareholder. You saw him."

"And I also talked to Beth. She says he's settled in nicely." He arched an eyebrow at me. "You second-guessing a senior captain?"

I winced. "Yeah. That's not what I meant, but it's what I seem to be doing."

Zoya gave me a wry grin. "It's what you are doing."

I sighed and nodded. "I still think it would be a nice thing to do. Let them cross-pollinate a little."

Pip nodded. "It's already on. They're having dinner on me at DiPietro's at 1900 tonight."

I laughed. "Thank you, Mr. Carstairs."

"You're welcome, Captain Wang." He tilted his head to the side. "Is there anything else you need, or can I get back to work?"

"That's it."

He grinned and headed back down the passageway.

"Why didn't you stop me?" I asked, looking at Zoya.

"What? Skaggs?"

"Yeah."

"I take his point. You are worried about somebody who's not your responsibility. Captain Case has been a captain for at least a decade longer than you and probably has had to deal with much worse problems than Richard Skaggs." She shrugged. "But she also asked you about him back at Newmar, didn't she?"

"Yes."

"You did your duty then."

"It still makes me nervous that we've got officers in charge of the Chernyakova who aren't familiar with the Toe-Holds."

"She's your baby." Her warm smile brightened my day. "It's only natural, but she's just a ship. Alys didn't tap fools to take it over from us."

"I guess Mr. Jacobs set off my alarm bells."

"He still sets mine off." She shook her head. "Natalya will deal with him. If he doesn't straighten out, she'll sink him. An unfavorable review coupled with his conviction will end his Academy career."

"Will it?" I asked. "Should it?"

She sighed. "A good officer is flexible. Rigid people break. Furtner always told me that. I didn't really understand it until much later. I had to learn to be flexible right after graduating from the most rigid experience of my life." She grinned. "I had Nats as a guide, but it was still a struggle."

"That doesn't answer the question."

"He's like most of them. No idea about the Toe-Holds. They challenge his world view. They're not supposed to exist. Not supposed to matter. Yet they do, and they're going to be more important going forward. Should we take his action as evidence of a flawed character, or as a human response to being thrust into an unfamiliar and antithetical position?"

It still irked me. "So, we treat him like any other quarter share. First offense. Slap him hard and see if he learns from it?"

She nodded. "That's what you've set in motion. I agree with you, for whatever that matters."

I was surprised by how much it did matter. "I hope it's the right choice."

She shrugged. "You seem to do best when you don't over-think things. Your instincts are almost always better than your reasoning."

I laughed. "Thanks, I think."

"You're welcome."

"You're going to make a great captain."

She shrugged. "I'll have to convince a board of that, but thank you. I thank my future stars that Maggie brought Natalya and me over to work with you." She bit her lips between her teeth and looked down at her hands, appearing flustered for the first time since I'd met her.

"Me, too. Thanks for taking the job even though you couldn't stand Pip."

She laughed. "He's gotten a lot better. Thank Natalya for that."

I raised an eyebrow. "Natalya?"

"You can't say you haven't noticed."

She had me dead to rights on that. I nodded. "I noticed."

"Natalya keeps him busy and thinking about business. They've got a lot in common."

"Both from the Toe-Holds," I said. "Both from Toe-Hold families, even."

"Yeah. You ever meet her father, Demetri?"

"No. Never did."

"He's the living cliché of three cans and a head. Was working on starting his own station when we hired him to run Zvezda Moya. I think he's still chipping away at his own on the side. Brilliant engineer. I know where Natalya gets it. And Pip's family is Carstairs. His sister Rachel? One of Maggie Stevens's protégés. I'm not sure what position she carries, but she's in Maggie's pocket."

"I met Pip's aunt and uncle. They turn up in some of the oddest places."

She shrugged. "Probably best not to see them when they show up."

I took her meaning and nodded.

"My point was that between Pip and Natalya? That's a lot of Toe-Hold," she said. "It's no wonder they gravitated toward each other."

I took a deep breath and tried not to think about gravitational attraction as I pushed myself back into my chair. "Good insight."

"You have a problem with it, Skipper?"

"No. None. Good for them."

"Natalya's never managed to keep a relationship going," Zoya said, looking down at my console with a pensive frown. "It's kind of odd to see her that way."

"Pip's always been a will-o-the-wisp. I don't know what he did for the stanyers between graduation and our reunion at Port Newmar, but he seems a lot more solid now. Even Alys Giggone mentioned it."

She nodded. "That's Natalya's doing, I bet."

"I'll have to thank her."

"Eh. People change. Maybe he just hadn't found the right person," she said.

"How about you?" I asked.

"You asking if I've ever found the right person?" Her eyebrows rose.

"No." I answered too quickly and backtracked. "I mean maintained a relationship."

She shook her head. "No. Clearly not. I'm here, aren't I?" She smiled. "That's the thing. Nats and I have been running from one thing to the next since graduation day. We stayed on the Madoka the longest. Hard not to when you own the ship and the company."

"Yet you moved when Maggie Stevens called."

"It was time." She shrugged. "That was something else Furtner used to say. 'Nothing is forever except dying.' Maggie knew what we both wanted. Nats wanted a chief engineer's billet. She still feels a little cheated over that."

"Cheated? How?"

"Maggie just gave it to her."

I laughed. "Maggie gave her nothing she didn't earn. Does she think she has to pass an exam?"

"I've told her that." She shrugged. "Something about the anticlimax, I think. We worked for so long toward our various goals. To meet them without a final showdown seemed liked cheating."

"You still haven't reached yours. What did you gain by coming here?"

She laughed and looked to the side. "You'll laugh."

"That's possible, but not at you." Never at you, but I swallowed those words.

She looked at me square on. "You. I got you."

If she'd hit me with a pipe wrench, I would have been less surprised.

"You're famous, Skipper. At least among those of us who pay attention to who's making a difference." She chuckled a little. "I sound like a stalker, but there are only few names active in the Western Annex that keep popping up again and again. Yours is one of them."

"And Maggie Stevens's name isn't," I said.

She laughed at that. "Yes, well. I think we both know why that is. I knew about the Chernyakova. It was all over the trade press when DST found it. I kept watching the auctions fail, and Natalya considered adding it to her fleet for a short time. Before that? Icarus? You're not the youngest captain, but you might have been the youngest owner. What you did with Icarus and the Iris? That was staggering. Since you sold it to DST, Christine Maloney has single-handedly brought the Higbee yards back into the fast packet game with her orders out of Diurnia. You can get passage almost anywhere in the Western Annex on ships based on the Iris design."

"That's her doing. All I did was sell it to her."

She snorted.

"I'm willing to bet you credits to crullers she'd never have looked twice at that ship until you and the crew turned it into a luxury cruiser. Then you and Carstairs started Phoenix. That showed up in the trades, too, winning the bid on the Chernyakova, no less. You dropped out of sight for a while. Then I find out it's because you've been tearing up the Toe-Holds." She fiddled with her fingers and examined them for a moment before looking back at me. "Maggie knew I needed a different captain if I was going to be the kind of skipper I wanted to be. So did I. I never in a million stanyers would have believed it could be you." She shrugged. "She and I have a lot of history. I've always owed her more than she owed me. This berth is just icing on a really big cake."

I shook my head. "I'm just trying to do the best I can. Nothing fancy. Frederica deGrut was my role model. Perhaps more than Alys Giggone, because I didn't see Alys unless I was in some kind of scrape."

She laughed at that. "You and Pip as ratings? I can only imagine."

"I'm just waiting for Mr. Bentley to find his sidekick," I said. "Pip always had me. Mr. Bentley's been a solo act for as long as he's been aboard."

She raised her eyebrows at that. "Really? You see yourself as Pip's sidekick?"

The question caught me sideways and I laughed. "Of course. He's always been in the pilot's chair. I'm just along for the ride."

She laughed and shook her head. "Didn't you say you hadn't seen Pip for over a decade? Not until he conned you into going into business with him?"

"He didn't con me."

She just shook her head.

"He didn't. I needed something to do. He needed my credits." I looked around at the ship. "Not where I expected to end up, but here we are."

"The mark never thinks he's being conned." She gave me a small grin and the lights danced in her dark eyes.

I snorted. "What do you think about splitting up the band?"

She blinked and shook her head. "You need to give me a signal when you turn the conversation that sharply, Skipper. What band?"

"Sailing with the Chernyakova. We've been docked for a week. It's making me twitchy."

"Something to consider for later. The big problem was always that jump out of Newmar. You said it yourself. We'll be more in sync from here on out."

"True."

"Have you been hitting the track?" she asked.

I nodded. "Haven't today yet."

She pushed off the bulkhead and stood straight. "Then I'll let you get on with it, Skipper." She grinned. "You're sure you want to rotate with the crew?"

"I'm sure. We can swap messengers around as we go if you think it'll help round them out."

"I'd be more interested in trading quarter shares with engineering or stewards," she said.

I raised my eyebrows at that. "Think it's a good idea?"

"Never hurts to learn how the other half lives." She smiled at me again. "It didn't hurt you, did it?"

I laughed and shook my head. "Fair enough. See what Nats has to say."

"Of course, Skipper. Anything else?"

"We've probably done enough damage for now. I've got another stan before handing off to Mr. Cartwright. Time enough to catch up on my reports."

"You staying aboard for dinner?" she asked.

"I don't know. Pip hasn't told me yet."

She snickered. "I'll leave you to it, then. Have fun." She turned and left the cabin.

I couldn't keep myself from watching her walk away. I sighed before opening the console and working through the various approvals and notations that seemed to fill my days. Having a rotating watch would be better. More comfortable. I hoped everybody else would think so, too.

Mr. MacBradaigh came back earlier than expected and knocked on the cabin door frame at 1700. "You wanted to see me, Captain."

"Yes. Thank you, Mr. MacBradaigh. Come in. I wanted to talk to you about the testing, but maybe you can fill me in on what you've learned about the Toe-Holds so far."

He took a seat and laced his fingers together over his stomach. "What can I tell you about the testing?"

"Before you took them you seemed pretty confident. Well done on the two you passed."

"Thanks. I'm not sure what happened on the other two. Engineering and cargo? The content across all four divisions was so similar, but the tests for engineering and cargo seemed to pull more questions from the specific areas than deck and steward did." He shrugged. "Mr. Cartwright said I only missed by a couple of points on each."

"What's your opinion of the study materials?"

He blew out a breath. "I said before I think they're good. Very good. The randomization in the practice tests seemed to balance well from test to test. The pools of questions have to be pretty large for that to happen."

"What advice do you have for how to help more people pass?"

He frowned and looked down. "I suspect the number of practice tests is a good predictor. Getting them to take and pass more of those would be a good step."

"How so?"

"It's a mistake to generalize from a single experience, but I did the most practices in deck and steward. I did fewest on cargo. Engineering seemed to be just 'more of the same' and I only did a few of them. Same with cargo by the time I got to it." He shrugged and looked over at me. "Test fatigue, I suppose."

"It's a common pattern." I shrugged. "We encourage ratings to take at least ten practice tests."

He nodded. "My experience would indicate that's good advice. Advice which I believe you gave me, but which I failed to follow."

"Will you try again?" I asked.

"No." He shook his head. "I learned a great deal from that experience, but the last week has shown me where I need to focus."

"On the Toe-Holds?"

"Yes. I can see why you and your crew are convinced that the Toe-Holds are the future."

"Are you convinced yet, Mr. MacBradaigh?"

He sighed and shook his head. "Not convinced yet, but I'm forced to admit that my preconceived notions about what I'd find here have been thoroughly shattered."

"Welcome to my world." I grinned at him. "I didn't have much by way of preconceptions, but what I expected went out the airlock as soon as I saw my first station."

"I want to thank you for letting me up on the bridge to see it on the way in, Captain."

"You're very welcome." I paused, unsure if I wanted to open a new can of worms. "Have you learned anything from your forays onto the station?"

He raised his eyebrows. "You know about that?"

"Logs show you leaving and returning pretty regularly. I have no idea what you're doing there, but I have to admit I am curious." I shrugged. "I was prepared to wait up for your return this evening if need be."

He chuckled. "Yes, I'm afraid I may have gone a bit overboard, pardon the expression. There's just so much to see."

"What's the most interesting thing you've found?"

"Interesting? That's hard to say. Everybody here knows the Chernyakova. I found that fascinating." He gave me a considering glance from under his bushy eyebrows. "With all the ships that dock here, only the Chernyakova got a lot of attention in the local newsies and among the stationers when it docked."

A flush of surprise rolled through me. "I'm not sure how I feel about that."

"It's all good, Captain. Something happened a few stanyers ago? Is that the hijacking you mentioned?"

"Yes, but we've been here a lot in the intervening stanyers."

"Your luster has not worn off. Mr. Carstairs seems to have a solid reputation here as well."

"Which Mr. Carstairs?" I asked.

He frowned. "Is there more than one?"

"Carstairs is a shipping company with their headquarters here. They run Port Lumineux. We'll probably visit there at least once. Pip's family goes back to the beginning of the Western Annex."

"That's not a name I'm familiar with. Were they contemporaries of Oswald Newmar?"

"At least. I don't know the full extent of it, but I know for certain that Port Lumineux is older than the oldest CPJCT orbital. His family is huge. They run fast packets exclusively and pop up everywhere."

He frowned and pursed his lips. "I'll have to review my notes. Perhaps all the references to Carstairs weren't actually about our own Mr. Carstairs."

I chuckled a little at that. "Don't rule that out until you've had a chance to digest it. You could ask Pip about his family and the history of the Annex as well."

"That would be most useful. Reconstructing the history of the Annex and CPJCT's place in that timeline is my current focus. Once I have the history right, I'll have a framework to put together a curriculum."

"There are resources here, I suspect," I said.

"Oh, yes. Some fascinating resources. Say what you will about the sensationalism that newsies seem to thrive on, they keep archives. I've been working forward from their earliest surviving records. You know that the station changed hands about a half a century ago?"

"I've heard reference," I said. "Verkol Kondur took over from the previous owners, but I don't know much about it."

"The place was failing. The earliest records were clearly censored by management but enough got through. The station was originally Vagrant Station. Edgar Vagrant ran it like a private fiefdom until his death. His younger son took it over for a time but ultimately sold its assets to a company that Verkol Kondur runs to this day."

"Have you met him?" I asked.

"Who? Kondur?"

"Yeah. Did you go talk to him?"

Mr. MacBradaigh's eyes widened. "Merciful Maude, no."

"Would you like to?" I asked.

He blinked several times. "I wouldn't know what to say."

I laughed. "I've never known you to be short of words, Mr. MacBradaigh."

He blew out a short laugh. "I guess I had that coming, Captain."

"You know he went to the Academy?" I asked.

"Verkol Kondur is an Academy grad?"

"One of the early classes, if my calculations are right. I was told he owned the station before he went to the academy, but the math is wrong on it. He must have gone to the Academy first."

"According to the records, he was a mining barge captain until the incident where he wound up with the station. I saw no mention of the Academy."

I shrugged. "It's all hearsay to me. I may be mistaken. Zoya and Natalya worked for him for a time."

"Did they?"

"This was their first stop after graduation. You should ask them."

He pulled his lips into a line and stared at the corner of my console for a moment. "Will they talk to me?"

"I'm pretty sure they will. Just remember that Natalya runs a shipping line remotely from the engine room of this ship, and Zoya still chairs the board of the Western Annex's largest companies. Neither of them is as young or inexperienced as they look."

"Where does Phoenix Freight fit in there?" he asked. "Commandant Giggone seems to think you hung the stars."

I laughed. "She's just happy at the dividends, I think. Phoenix is small. Just the one ship. Just us running it until Alys pulled us out to set up the Collins. We're not hauling anything like the big freight lines yet."

"Is Ms. Regyri's company hauling a lot?"

"I'm not in that loop. You'd have to ask her. I'm just impressed that she's running a company by wire from wherever she happens to be in the Western Annex."

"And Mr. Carstairs is running two, now," he said. "Am I correct on that?"

I laughed. "Two that I know about. I wouldn't bet he hasn't got more than that and I just haven't heard about it."

He nodded. "Is there anything else, Captain? I'd like to get my notes from today taken care of."

"Why are you back so early? It's our last night in port. I'd have thought you'd want to spend as much time as you could."

He shrugged and looked to the side. "I ran out of funds."

I felt myself goggling at him. "Ran out of funds? What? Credits?"

"Is there some other kind, Captain?"

"What will you do for the rest of the stanyer?"

"I've sent word to the Academy to send me more."

"How do you normally get paid?"

"My salary is automatically deposited to my bank account at Port Newmar. I can submit expense reports and have them reimbursed." He shrugged.

I looked at him for a long moment. "You know that you can access your bank account from here, right?"

"How's that even possible? We're not even in the CPCJT, let alone Port Newmar."

I laughed. "How'd you like to go to dinner with me, Mr. MacBradaigh? My treat."

Pip breezed in at that point. "Oh, good. You're making dinner plans?"

"I am. What are you planning?"

He shrugged. "Nats and I are hitting up one of the new bistros before hitting a concert later. Jazz at the Razz at 2100." He paused a moment. "You wanna come with us?"

Something in the way he asked made me think twice before answering. "No. I'll pass. I want to talk to Mr. MacBradaigh here about what he's learning about the Toe-Holds."

"The captain tells me that the Carstairs family has been here longer than some of the Toe-Holds. Is that true?"

Pip shrugged. "That's the story I got growing up. I've no reason to doubt it."

"Nobody's written a definitive history of the Toe-Holds, have they?"

"That I couldn't tell you. If anybody has, Maggie Stevens would know about it."

"Isn't her specialty engineering?"

Pip glanced at me and nodded. "Yes. That's her specialty but she has a lot of outside interests. You might be surprised."

Mr. MacBradaigh shook his head. "I've used up my annual quota of being surprised, I think. I'll just take your word for it and see what I can uncover."

Pip chuckled at that. "I like that plan."

Natalya showed up at the door dressed in civvies. "We ready?"

Pip waved. "We're off. Don't wait up."

They clattered down the ladder, heading for the lock.

Mr. MacBradaigh turned back to face me. "If you'd give me half a stan to stow my notes and get cleaned up, I'd welcome a chance to have dinner with you."

"See you in half a stan," I said.

He left me sitting there thinking about Natalya and Pip out on a date. It was an unsettling experience.

Mr. MacBradaigh and I made an odd-looking pair strolling through the station. I wore my favorite jeans and a pullover under a light gray jacket with a lot of pockets. He sported his usual khaki shipsuit under a baggy brown coat. That in itself didn't matter as much as the feeling that I walked along beside a shambling bear of a man. He was taller than I, a reality that seldom struck me since we most often sat when talking. In truth, many people are taller and I almost never notice. More than that, Mr. MacBradaigh was big—broad in the shoulders, deep in the chest. He lumbered along beside me, his head turning this way and that, seeming fascinated by every shop front, every sign.

I felt like a small dog trotting along beside him.

I stopped us at the first banking terminal, pointing it out to him. "You recognize this?"

He frowned. "It looks like a standard banking terminal. I've seen them all over the station."

"Did you know you can access your account from here?"

"What? My account on Port Newmar?"

"Your account isn't in Port Newmar. The data gets stored somewhere in the Far Shores. High Tortuga runs the banking system. You can access your account from anywhere in the Western Annex."

"You mentioned that before, back in Newmar. That wasn't hyperbole?"

I shook my head. "Try it."

He stepped up to the terminal and keyed in. The screen refreshed with some data that I did my best not to see. He frowned. "This looks like my account."

"It is your account. How have you been paying for things?"

He pulled a credit chip from his pocket. "Alys gave me this. Told me to use it when I didn't want to wait for reimbursement." He looked at it, twisting it in his fingers. "It's all but empty now."

"Have you put in any expense reports?"

"No. I haven't thumbed anything here."

"Well, you can recharge that chip here, or just use your thumb and send the requests for reimbursement to Alys from the ship. It'll take a few days for the report to get to her."

He pursed his lips. "It'll take a month for it to clear the Academy finance office."

"So? Is that different from your normal process?"

"No. That's the normal process, but I don't use it very often as a matter of course. I just requisition what I need from the Academy."

"We'll be in space for at least a week between ports here in the Toe-Holds." I nodded at the chip. "How much was on that?"

"A thousand credits."

I raised an eyebrow. "You went through a thousand credits here?"

He shrugged, looking somewhat abashed. "A couple of meals a day, plus bar tabs."

"You buying drinks for the bar?" I fought to keep the amusement out of my voice. I'm not sure I succeeded.

He shook his head. "No. Nothing like that. I was amazed at what I learned just by sitting at a bar and observing. You know there are different places here for different workers?"

"I'm certain of it." I held out my hand. "Let me see that chip?"

He dropped it onto my palm and I stepped up to the terminal. It took almost no time for me to top it up to ten thousand credits and hand it back to him. "This should hold you for a while. Just do me a favor and send me a write-up of what you find."

"You didn't have to do that, Captain."

I shrugged and nudged him along. "No skin off my back, and I'm paying to see your research. That's a pretty fair deal in my book. Let's go find some dinner."

He wrapped his beefy fingers around the chip and nodded. "I'll send you a full report once we're underway. You have my word."

I grinned at him. "I know where you sleep, Mr. MacBradaigh."

He chuckled. "That's fair enough, I suppose."

I stretched out my pace a little to get us moving. "What do you fancy for dinner?"

"I've tried most of the restaurants along Main Street," he said. "They seem remarkably similar."

"You have to get off Main Street. The side passages hold some of the more interesting places." I glanced up at him. "You have any dietary restrictions?"

He shook his head. "Nothing I'm aware of."

"You feeling adventurous?"

"You're the man who knows the way here, Captain. I've just been bumbling along in the dark."

"I know just the place." We walked along for a bit, heading deeper into the station. "You said different places for different workers?"

He nodded.

"Tell me about them."

"I started at the diner at the end of the docking gallery. I expected to find a lot of spacers there, but it's mostly dock workers. Spacers walk right by it."

"You know why?" I asked.

He frowned. "I have no evidence, but I suspect it's because it's not what spacers look for."

"What do you think they look for?"

"It's something of a cliché, but alcoholic beverages seem to be very high on the list. It's something they share with cadets." He grinned at me. "And faculty, if I'm going to be honest. That diner caters to the working person, not the person who's looking for a good time." He frowned. "I'm saying that badly."

"Seems fine to me. I frequently eat there myself when we're docked, but you're right about my motivations. I eat there to get a solid meal at times of the day when the galley isn't serving. You'll find those places on every station. Reasonably priced. The food is usually good-to-great."

He nodded, his brow furrowed in thought. "Makes sense. I may have underestimated the number of spacers by paying too much attention to their clothing."

"We still look like spacers," I said. "Most spacers keep their hair very short. Stationers don't. There are exceptions but even in civilian clothing, spacers tend to look different."

He lifted his head and looked around. "We're still close to the docks. There are a lot of spacers."

"The mix evens out once you get to Main Street. The street beyond it, Second Street, that's mostly stationers."

"Are we allowed there? I thought we had a limited visa."

"You probably never ventured over the boundary. It's a big place." I glanced at him. "What else did you find?"

"There's a pub for miners. If you walk through the chandlery and around the corner, there are separate docks for the barges. I call it a pub because it serves alcohol and food. It's almost always got somebody eating breakfast beside somebody eating dinner. They apparently brew their own beer."

"Did you sample it?"

He glanced at me like he wanted to see if I would judge him. "I might have had a pint or two."

"How was it?"

He laughed. "Really good."

"Did you feel out of place?"

He thrust his hands into his pockets and frowned at the deck as we walked. "A bit. They didn't make me feel unwelcome in any way. It was just clear that I wasn't part of the community." He pursed his lips. "I'm trying to put my finger on the cause."

"They recognize their own," I said. "Some of those barge crews are probably second or third generation. They grew up together on the station and in the belts. They probably know each other's parents and children."

He nodded. "That's it. I should have figured that."

I shrugged. "You and I live in transient cultures. You know the faculty better than the students. You know the admin best of all, I suspect."

"You're not wrong there. I hardly see the cadets except at a distance."

"The cadets see the most of each other, followed by faculty. It's the same with crews. When we dock, we go ashore as visitors. After a few days, we get back in our ships and sail away. With the Chernyakova, we visited the same places often enough that we became known and came to know the people and places we visited. That's not the same as growing up there and seeing the same faces very single day."

"No, I suppose not." He looked over at me. "You're quite the philosopher, Captain."

His comment made me uncomfortable for some reason. "I don't know about that. I just go by what I see."

He shrugged. "You see more than some. Probably more than most." He grinned at me. "You see more than I do."

"Maybe here. On campus? I doubt it." I looked around. "I may see more here because I'm familiar enough with what's normal to spot what's not."

"Everything is novel to me. I can't pick out the unique parts, other than the way society has formed the culture."

"You think it's different?" I asked.

"Don't you?"

I nodded. "I do. I'm willing to be persuaded that the differences are cosmetic."

"Cosmetic how?"

"Take the café at the docking gallery. They exist on all the stations in some form, but they also exist on the orbitals."

He raised his eyebrows. "I never spent enough time on the orbital to notice."

"The social strata are different on orbitals. Spacers tend to stay on the docks and the oh-two deck. Most of the ship-related business happens on the oh-one deck. Docks are the main deck. Anything above is more mixed use. The higher you get, the fewer spacers."

"I didn't realize that."

"There's something here that you don't see on the orbitals," I said. "Have you noticed what it is?"

He eyebrows almost met each other over his nose as he pondered, head down. He almost walked into a planter at the edge of the sidewalk, sidestepping at the last minute. "I haven't seen everything."

"I'll let you ponder it. It's pretty subtle here. I didn't notice it myself right away. When we get to Mel's Place, it'll stare you in the face."

He grinned. "That sounds like a challenge."

I shrugged and smelled the distinctive aroma I'd been looking forward to. I lifted my face and pulled in a deep whiff. "Smell that?"

He lifted his nose and took a few sniffs. "Is that smoke?"

"Pip introduced me to this place. They have a barbecue here. I have no idea how they deal with the environmental issues, but they do and I'm grateful."

He frowned. "Barbecue? I have a feeling that you mean something different than what I think that term means."

"If you're not thinking 'delicious' and 'primal,' then you're not thinking the same thing." I grinned at him. "Come on. I think you're in for a treat."

We ducked into the alley and walked up to one of the tall, clean tables with its cluster of napkin dispensers and condiments in the center.

He frowned, looking around at the other diners standing around the tables and eating with their fingers. "No chairs?"

I shook my head. "No. I had the same reaction." I nodded to the board on the bulkhead. "Menu over there."

He lifted his gaze and pursed his lips. "Just meat?"

"There are a few vegetarian options. The style of cooking with slow heat and smoke doesn't work as well with vegetables."

"Mouta?" he asked. "Where do they get mouta?"

"Farm it, I suspect. I never asked."

He turned to me with the most incredulous look on his face. "Mouta in space?"

"Why not? Water. Gravity. Food. Probably some amount of light." I shrugged.

"Doesn't it have to be flowing water?"

"We have these things called pumps, Mr. MacBradaigh. Perhaps you've heard of them."

He stared at me for a moment before laughing loudly enough to attract the attention of our neighbors. "Fair enough. I need to broaden my horizons, I see."

A server on roller skates zipped up to the table. "Know what you want?"

"Pulled pork sandwich. You still have that red ale?" I asked.

"Yeah. It's a favorite. Full or half on the sandwich?"

"Full. I'm hungry and we're leaving tomorrow. A pint of the ale."

She grinned and looked up at Mr. MacBradaigh. "For you?"

"Same."

She gave a single nod and zipped away, slaloming between the tables and diners.

"I have no idea what I just ordered," he said, looking around at the busy alley. He leaned over the table and lowered his voice. "This is a restaurant?"

"Depends on your definition, I suppose. If you're thinking of a dining room with chairs? No. If you're thinking of a staff who'll cook your food for you and deliver it to you and having a place to put your plate? Yes."

He straightened up and pursed his lips. The slightest frown creased his forehead. "You think like an academic."

"My mother was an ancient lit professor. I grew up with people who couldn't say 'good morning' without defining the terms first."

He laughed again and the server skated up, depositing a pair of pints. "Food in a couple of ticks. Need anything else?"

"Not yet," I said.

She nodded and skated on.

"Roller skates?" Mr. MacBradaigh asked.

"Why not?"

"What if they collide with somebody?"

"You see any collisions?"

He shook his head. "Absence of evidence is not evidence of absence."

Hearing my own words come back to me made me laugh and I toasted him with my glass before taking a sip of the delicious bitter brew.

His head tilted to one side. "You find that funny?" He took a sip of his own beer and gave it an appreciative glance after.

"Not funny. Fun to hear somebody say it besides me." I took another sip, letting the faint caramel and coffee notes wash across my tongue and down my throat. "It's something my mother used to say all the time."

"A lit professor? Where?"

"University of Neris. Over in Dunsany Roads."

"You're a long way from home."

I shrugged. "I suppose. I would have been deported when she died, if I hadn't found Alys Giggone. Home's been a ship for a long time now."

A pair of plated sandwiches with some potato chips on the side hit the table almost before I realized our server had come back. "There ya go, folks. Need anything extra?"

I shook my head and snagged a couple of napkins from the holder in the middle of the table. "This looks great."

"Enjoy." She grinned and pushed off from the table, doing a pirouette before dashing away.

Mr. MacBradaigh shook his head, watching her go. "She's really good."

"When you do something a lot, you tend to get better." I lifted half the sandwich, leaning forward over the plate to catch any drips. "Or you stop, I guess." I took a big bite and savored the smokey flavor of tender pork. The chef hadn't done anything except use a terrific, solid bread and slather it with a generous serving of seasoned meat and sauce. I chewed it slowly, feeling myself relax a little. Enjoying the moment.

"What is this?" Mr. MacBradaigh said, lifting the top bread to peek under it.

"A sandwich," I said. "Why?"

"No. What's in it?"

"Barbecued pork with some barbecue sauce. Why? Don't you like pork?"

He shrugged. "I've never had it cooked this way."

"Try it. If you don't like it, you can try something else. They do a killer sausage, ribs to die for, and the chicken is excellent."

He shrugged and picked up half his sandwich, holding it gingerly in both hands.

"Lean over the plate. It can be a little juicy."

He hunched forward a little and took a small bite from one corner. I watched as he chewed, frowned, and went back for a bigger sample. "Wow," he said, talking through the mouthful. "It's delicious."

I took a big bite of my own and nodded in agreement. It didn't take long for either of us to demolish the first half. I took a break for beer and a few of the chips. "How about you? You always wanted to work at the Academy?"

He used one of the paper napkins to wipe his mouth and fingers before answering. "Just one thing led to another. I hated school, those first few stanyers trying to learn to read and deal with the numbers." He shook his head. "I was a slow reader and numbers wouldn't stick in my head. At all. Torturous." He lifted his beer and shook his head. "Luckily I was pissy enough to think there had to be a better way, so I set out to try to find it." He grinned and took a belt off the top of his beer, sighing in satisfaction. "This is really good, too." He looked around, taking in the surroundings in general and looking up at the overhead. "Is this what you meant by finding things that don't exist in the High Lands?"

"High Line." I took a sip of beer and crunched another chip. "Sort of. Can you imagine this on Newmar Orbital?"

He shook his head. "Health and Safety would shut it down."

"Why is that?" I asked.

"It's not exactly sanitary, is it? And the servers on roller skates?"

"Why isn't it sanitary?"

"It's out in the open, for one thing."

"It's in a station orbiting a system primary in a vacuum. It's not exactly 'the open,' is it?"

"You know what I mean," he said, grinning at me while he dug into the other half of his sandwich.

"I do know, but I'm trying to get you to question why the rules exist in the High Line and why you think they don't apply here." I followed his lead and went to work on my own meal.

He chewed for a few moments before washing it down with a slug of beer. He turned his head off axis a few degrees and frowned into the distance. "It's right next to Main Street. Everybody going by contributes to the problem."

"Would you say the same thing if we had chairs? If this were a sidewalk dining place like Oswald's in Port Newmar?"

"Well, there's a dining room there. You don't get to the tables without being seated."

"And that makes them more sanitary? The tables there really are right out in the open. Birds could poop on the tables. Bugs could land in the food." I took another large bite of the spicy pork, already regretting how fast it was disappearing but unwilling to order another, even assuming I'd have room for it.

He frowned and shook his head a little, like shaking off a pesky fly. "You're making me question basic assumptions, aren't you."

"I hope so. That's kind of the point."

"What about the skaters?"

"What about them?" I asked.

"They're moving really fast and they're on roller skates."

"We've been here, what? Not quite half a stan?"

He nodded.

"Have any of them fallen? Dropped a tray? Bumped a customer? Run into a table? Or a bulkhead?"

He shook his head. "Just because I haven't noticed, doesn't mean it didn't happen. Or that it hasn't happened before. Or won't happen after we leave."

I nodded to grant him the point and took another bite.

He finished off his sandwich one bite before I finished mine, and took a swig from his pint.

214

As if summoned by radar, our server skidded to a stop beside the table. "How'd that work out, folks?"

"Delicious, as always. It was my friend's first taste of barbecue." I nodded at Mr. MacBradaigh.

She grinned at him, her teeth flashing white in the ambient lighting. "What'd you think?"

"I'm sorry I didn't find this place earlier." He smiled back. "We've been here almost a week and I regret not having more opportunity to sample the menu."

"You'll be back." She nodded her head in my direction. "He's in here often enough. He'll bring ya."

His eyebrows rose. "You recognize him?"

"Captain Wang?" She glanced at me and shrugged. "Of course."

"You know all the ship captains?"

"No. I know the regulars." She shot me a grin. "You and Mr. Carstairs are as regular as any of the spacers."

"He has a question about the skates," I said. "I've never seen any of you fall or drop anything. Does it ever happen?"

She shrugged. "I used to work at Vagrant's place. We don't drop things any more often here than there. Comes with the turf, if you know what I mean."

"But on wheels?" Mr. MacBradaigh asked. "Isn't that particularly challenging?"

She laughed. "Job security. Not everybody has the skills. They really help cut down the legwork and it's fun."

"I would think any kind of spill on the deck would be a hazard," he said.

"You'd be right. We're really careful about that, but that's true everywhere people walk. You ever think about what happens to the sidewalks?" She shuddered. "People do all kinds of nasty things on them."

Her infectious optimism got to him and he laughed. "I'm having to question all my assumptions on this voyage."

She nodded and motioned to the plates. "It's good for ya. Keeps ya limber. You done with these dishes? Want some dessert?"

"We're done and I'm gonna pass on dessert," I said.

She pulled the empties into a neat pile and jerked her chin at the empty glass. "'Nother beer?"

"I think I need to walk that one off a bit," I said. I looked at Mr. MacBradaigh. "You?"

He shook his head and patted his stomach. "Nothing more."

I flexed my thumb at her and she pulled a tab from her apron one-handed and held it down on the table for me to thumb. I added a good tip and authorized it.

"Thanks, Skipper."

"Thank you."

She nodded and rolled off toward the back with the pile of dirty dishes in one hand.

We headed back to the sidewalk and he shook his head. "It still feels off, somehow."

"It's not exactly fine dining, but it's darn good food and it makes business sense." I nodded back at our table. Two of the staff on skates had just finished wiping the surface down and sweeping up around the table. "That table's ready for the next customer. How long were we there?"

He stopped beside me on the sidewalk. "Maybe half a stan? If that."

"They make money when they sell food, not when we eat it."

His eyebrows rose and the credit registered. "Faster turnover, better revenues." He scanned the alleyway with a new understanding. "There are still empty tables."

"That's just because we're not at peak time. Around lunch time? Later after the evening entertainments let out?" I shook my head. "People will be standing in line to eat here."

"Huh." He gave me a glance. "You're not what I expected."

I laughed and headed along Main Street. He fell into step with me. "What were you expecting?"

He shrugged, looking around at the other passersby. "My exposure to captains led me to believe you're a singularly focused lot. Captain Case seems very focused on her ship and her crew."

"You think I'm not?"

He chuckled, a bass rumble. "No. It's just that it's not your only focus. You've clearly thought about that barbecue place and its relationship to the station as a whole."

"I can't believe you hadn't found it on your own. You had the run of the station for days."

He pressed his lips together and stuck his hands in his pockets again, frowning at the sidewalk as we went. "It never occurred to me to look." He paused and snorted. "I'm not sure I would have found it without your guidance."

We stopped in front of Kondur's pub. The two guards gave us the once-over but didn't shift from their posts.

"What's this place?" Mr. MacBradaigh asked. "I've walked by it a couple of times but those people look like guards rather than bouncers."

"That's Verkol Kondur's place. They're security."

"What? He lives there?"

"It's a pub. His office is in a booth." I grinned.

He stared at me.

I shrugged. "Wanna go in?"

"Can we?"

I walked over to the front. "Evening. Is he in?"

The smaller guy on the left side of the door shook his head. "Gone for the evening, Skipper. I can call him for you if you need."

"Not necessary. Just looking for a good cup of coffee."

They both smiled. "You know the way," the larger guy said.

I pushed through into the dimly lit interior and led Mr. MacBradaigh to the bar, taking a couple of empty seats near the end.

The barkeep, an attractive woman with a few streaks of silver in her hair, tossed a couple of coasters in front of us with a nod of greeting. "Evenin', folks. What'll ya have?"

"Got a pot of coffee going?" I asked.

"Always."

"The good stuff?" I asked, nodding at the corner where Kondur normally held court.

"He only left a stan ago. There might be a couple of cups left." She grinned.

"I'll take one. Black." I looked at Mr. MacBradaigh. "Don't feel obligated."

He nodded. "Same."

She nodded and drifted down the length of the bar to the other end before pulling a pot from under the counter and pouring two heavy mugs full.

Mr. MacBradaigh looked around at the other patrons. "This is his office?"

"As much as he has one. This is where you come if you want to talk to him. For all I know, he has a fully staffed office suite tucked away somewhere."

"He does," the barkeep said, returning with our coffees. "He's still the station owner. That needs more support than we can give him here."

"Figured," I said, taking a sip of the coffee before flexing my thumb.

She shook her head. "On the house for you, Skipper."

"You know him?" Mr. MacBradaigh asked.

She snorted. "What? Don't you?"

"Well, yes, but I'm on the ship with him."

She chuckled a little, glancing down the length of the bar. "Captain Wang here saved our asses. Dark Knight doesn't forget our friends."

"I've been looking into the history of the station," Mr. MacBradaigh said. "It used to be called Vagrant?"

"Yeah. I was a toddler when the old man kicked it. My da used to tell me about the old days. It was grim here." She shrugged. "He works for Kondur now in one of the big smelters out in the belt."

"Are all the facilities owned by Mr. Kondur?"

She laughed and shook her head. "Hell, no. He doesn't even own this place. We just let him camp here because he brings in customers."

"Why the security if he's not here?" Mr. MacBradaigh lifted his cup to take a sip. "Shouldn't they be with him?"

"The crew out front? They're the bouncers."

He took a sip of his coffee and did a double take on it. "This is really good."

"Private stock. You only got it because you're with him."
She nodded at me.

"According to my reading, the station has changed quite
a lot."

"Kondur's got the touch," she said, casting an eye down
the bar. "He's added smelters out in the rocks so the barges
can unload and resupply without coming all the way back.
Every few stanyers he adds a new one. He's got a couple
of fabrication plants turning some of the metal into building
materials. The station is still growing. Some of the residential
sections are getting a mite crowded." She grinned.

"If he can build the platforms locally, he only needs to
bring in the smelting hardware," I said.

"Like I said. He's got the touch."

"What's with all the plants?" Mr. MacBradaigh asked.

"Plants help clear the air. More plants growing means less
power to the environmental systems."

He took another sip of coffee. "That makes sense. Thank
you."

She shrugged. "You're welcome. You two need anything
else?" We both shook our heads and she drifted away down
the bar.

I glanced at Mr. MacBradaigh and took a slug of coffee.
"Anything strike you about that conversation?"

He squinted his eyes a little, staring into the distance.
"She claimed they're just bouncers."

"Is that a problem?"

"You asked them if he was here. Mr. Kondur, I presume?"

"Yeah."

"They knew he wasn't but offered to call him for you."

"How is that unusual?"

"I wouldn't have expected a bouncer to know whether he
was in the building or how to reach him."

"Why not? He's the station owner."

"This isn't his establishment. He's not their boss." He
frowned at me. "They recognized you, too."

I nodded. "It's both a blessing and a curse. Everybody
knows my face here. Pip's, too. A lot of them know Maggie
Stevens, when it comes to that."

"The rank and file?"

"Key players know Maggie. She's got a ton of history here that must go back to before I was even born." I took another sip and thought about it. "I'm sure there are some people who don't know me or Pip, or wouldn't recognize me in civvies. We both tend to revisit places like the barbecue spot. A couple of the pubs around. This isn't the first time we've needed a space like DiPietro's. I don't think every server or cook knows us, but the management did once Pip flashed his ID to secure the meeting room."

"His ID?"

"If I were renting out space, I'd do a credit check on the person renting." I glanced at him. "Phillip Carstairs has excellent credit."

He grunted and buried his face in his mug for a moment. "I've missed so much that's been right in front of me all this time."

"We'll be back. Probably more than once. I hope you're not going to have more than a few days to poke around next time, but it's not like you won't have another opportunity."

He nodded. "Good point. It might be better that way. I'll have time between port visits to reflect and digest some of my observations."

"You've got a good start here. As far as major stations go, this is the only one I know of that has had a change of management."

"Really? I would have thought it would happen more frequently."

"Only one I know of. There could be any number of them but it's not something I've spent much time looking at. Remember, I didn't find out about the Toe-Holds until Pip brought me out here with the Chernyakova." I finished my coffee and put the mug back on the coaster. "Natalya might have some insight. You've already button-holed Pip?"

"I tried." He shook his head. "He doesn't seem to have much background on the history, although his take on current events in the Western Annex feels encyclopedic." He finished his coffee just as the barkeep returned.

"Anything else?" she asked.

I looked at Mr. MacBradaigh who shook his head. "We're good. Thanks."

She nodded and collected our empties.

I fished in my pocket for a couple of small chips and dropped them on the bar.

She frowned. "It's on the house, Cap."

"Tips aren't." I grinned at her and left the chips on the bar.

We left, nodding to the bouncers on the way to the sidewalk.

"You didn't look at those chips. How do you know what's on them?" Mr. MacBradaigh asked.

"They were five credits."

"How do you know?"

I reached into the same pocket and pulled out half a dozen chips. "All fives. I keep them for tips."

"You only carry small chips?"

"No, but I don't carry multiples of large denominations. I don't carry them in the same pockets, either."

"Never thought of it." MacBradaigh shook his head. "Never thought of a lot of things, it seems."

"It's all new to you now. By the time we get back to Port Newmar, you'll be an old hand."

He frowned and thrust his hands in his pockets again as we shambled along, avoiding the passersby as we headed back to the ship.

"What are you thinking so hard about?" I asked, as we reached the alley leading back to the docking gallery.

He shook his head. "It's all spinning around. Even after all this time wandering the station, I find myself struggling to sort out just the new information I've learned in our brief foray this evening."

"You'll have plenty of time to think on our way to Mel's Place. Write it down so you can see it."

"Yes." He let the word hang there alone before glancing at me. "You left a ten-credit tip for five credits' worth of coffee?"

"Yes. It was probably more like ten credits' worth of coffee. The good stuff isn't cheap."

He raised his eyebrows. "Is over-tipping considered de rigeur here?"

I shook my head and grinned at him. "What have you been tipping?"

"Ten to twenty percent. Same as I would on the orbital."

I nodded. "Funny thing that. Something for you to consider."

He lifted his chin in question.

"How some of the social fabric remains constant across the Western Annex while other pieces vary widely." I paused to let that sink in. "High Line. Toe-Holds. We all tip about the same rates. We all say please and thank you. We generally ask permission and say 'excuse me' under the same kinds of circumstances. Prices and services vary, but we all treat each other in similar ways even if we organize our lives differently."

He sighed. His frown deepened and he shook his head, pushing his hands deeper into his pockets. "It wouldn't have occurred to me to even notice." We walked in silence until we got to the long docking gallery. "Alys sent the wrong person."

"Why do you say that?"

He looked at me. "This needs an ethnographer, at the very least. A historian, perhaps. My expertise is making instructional materials logical. Accessible. Useful. I rely on subject matter experts to develop the knowledge. To define the goals. To help establish the parameters." He sighed and shook his head again. "I'm surrounded by the source material but have no guide for how it should be organized."

"You see that as a disadvantage, Mr. MacBradaigh?"

He bit his lips into a line between his teeth and looked at me. "Don't you?"

I shrugged. "I don't know. Maybe. Maybe not. You're in the rather unusual position of being where I would expect the majority of cadets taking the course would be, aren't you?"

"If you mean facing a subject matter domain that I thought I knew something about, only to learn that everything I thought I knew isn't true?" He nodded. "Yes. That is correct."

"Is that an unusual position for you? As an instructional designer? Do you often have to design courses where what you know is false from the start?"

He barked a short laugh. "No. My usual position is not knowing anything about the subject matter." He shrugged. "Over the stanyers, I've picked up some of the jargon, some of the Academy-specific knowledge, but I rely on the experts to give me the outline, provide a frame, as it were. I'm then able to organize and sequence the content."

"I see what you mean." We'd reached the lock and I keyed it open. "In the absence of those experts, you have nothing to organize or sequence."

"Precisely."

"Step back one step," I said.

He did.

"No, mentally. You need to acquire the knowledge for yourself. You must know enough by now to have some questions."

He laughed. "I have a lot of questions. Mostly about what I'm missing because my preconceptions are blinders. I'm focusing on what I think I know and missing everything else."

"How do you solve that problem, then?" I asked. "Normally you'd have an expert to guide you, right?"

"Yes."

"Well, find an expert."

He raised his eyebrows. "I've found one, Captain, but I can't very well have you trailing me around all the time."

"I'm not sure I'm that much of an expert. Perhaps ask around the senior ratings? See if any of them have a history in the Toe-Holds? Most of them have spent at least as much time as I have. Some maybe more."

"I'll do that."

"You can always bring it up in the wardroom. That's perfectly acceptable dinner conversation. Natalya and Zoya have lived and worked out here for quite a while. Zoya has the outsider's perspective. Natalya grew up in and around the Toe-Holds. Pip spent most of his childhood on a fast packet that I can only assume spent a great deal of time in the Toe-Holds, given the Carstairs's base."

He nodded. "I hesitate to distract the crew."

"You've spent enough time with us to know distraction isn't as big a problem as boredom." I grinned at him and waved him up the ramp. "After you."

He nodded and lumbered up the ramp into the ship. "Good points, Captain. Thank you."

I followed him in and wondered why Alys hadn't sent somebody with more of a background in either the history of the Toe-Holds or the research needed to establish it.

The idea intrigued me. Made me wonder how I would study it.

CHAPTER SIXTEEN
DARK KNIGHT: AUGUST 24, 2379

We pulled out of Dark Knight Station right on time. The morning wardroom round table uncovered no obstacles or surprises. A meeting with the crew revealed no major surprises. The biggest takeaway was learning that they had not, in fact, realized that the difference between quarter and half shares amounted to a sum equal to their salaries.

Mr. Hoag had said it best. "Are you kidding? I thought it was going to be something like an extra 2 percent." The look of shock on his face made me smile, even as I looked over my shoulder at the tug.

"Something amusing, Skipper?" Zoya asked, looking over from her station.

"Nothing serious. Just recalling our morning meeting with the crew."

"Mr. Hoag?" she asked with a wry grin.

"Yeah."

"I told him how much to expect. He didn't believe me."

"It's a theme," I said. "We're showing them a world that cannot exist because it's not compatible with the one they live in."

"You're beginning to sound like Mr. MacBradaigh."

I settled back in my chair and smiled at her. "Is that good or bad?"

"Bad," Ms. Fortuner said, not looking up from her console.

Mr. Bentley snickered a little and even Mr. Cartwright seemed amused.

"I'll be more careful," I said. "He's looking for a guide to help him navigate the Toe-Holds. Any of you jokers want to be his wingman at Mel's?"

Everybody paid very close attention to their duty after that. Perhaps fearing to raise their heads. I chuckled to myself. I didn't blame them.

"Where's the Chernyakova, Ms. Fortuner?"

"About three stans ahead of us, Skipper."

"What's our schedule look like?"

"Tug will drop us in the next few ticks. I make it about eighteen stans until the Burleson limit, but we can put our sails up as soon as the tug is clear." She flipped a screen. "The Chernyakova should be jumping at about the same time. They'll be able to jump directly into Mel's."

"What's our first jump look like?"

"We're taking the longer leg first, Skipper. There's a nice spot not too far out of Mel's. We'll have the larger jump error in the Deep Dark and a more accurate placement when we get there."

"Thank you, Ms. Fortuner."

"Tug is already signaling, Captain," Mr. Cartwright said. "Release in five ticks."

"Thank you, Mr. Cartwright."

The tug kicked us around in pitch and yaw, pointing us in the direction we needed to exit the system. We felt nothing of the vector change in the ship. The stars looked like they moved around us.

"That never gets old," Mr. Bentley said.

"You like that view, Mr. Bentley?"

He nodded without looking back at me. "I do, sar. The jump is nice, too, but it feels like we're really moving when the tug moves us."

I laughed and had to agree with him. Most of the time we didn't appear to be moving at all. Once we got out of sight of the station, we had no visual referents close enough to measure our progress against. We could have been suspended in space, for all we could tell by looking out the ports. Even the jump gave us only the smallest sense of movement. The only change was the bright spot of the star we jumped toward suddenly appearing ahead of us, where before there had been only the Deep Dark. Occasionally our destination might appear as a faint star against the black, but it blended in with all the others.

"Tug signals release, Captain."

"Thank you, Mr. Cartwright. Signal my thanks." I turned to watch the small tug fall away astern. The tug captain blinked their running lights twice in farewell.

He tapped a few keys. "Done, Captain."

"Do we have sails, Ms. Usoko?"

"Raising the generators now, Skipper."

I heard the faint vibrations through the hull as the sail and keel generators came online.

"Sails are deployed, Captain."

"Thank you, Ms. Usoko. Helm?"

Mr. Bentley put his hands on the controls and stared at his console. "Helm has sail, Captain. Ship responds to sail. Course locked."

"Thank you, Mr. Bentley. Secure from navigation stations, Ms. Usoko. Set normal watch throughout the ship."

"Secure from navigation stations. Set normal watch. Aye, sar." She made the announcement, then turned to me. "I'm ready to be relieved, Captain. First section has the watch."

I grinned and remembered to unbuckle my seatbelt before standing. "I relieve you, Ms. Usoko."

A bad jump into the Deep Dark put us two days behind the Chernyakova at the docking gallery at Mel's Place. According to Pip, they navigated the visa process without a problem. I was surprised when Beth showed up at our lock, waiting behind the station officials when I signed off on the visas for the Collins.

"You know," she said. "A couple of months ago, I called you crazy."

I chuckled. "I didn't take it personally."

"I don't want to interrupt your docking routine, but I wanted to catch you before you got busy." She paused. "Dinner tonight? It's my turn to buy."

"I've got the watch at 1800." I shrugged. "Down side of joining the rotation. I have to rotate with the rest."

She chuckled. "Done it enough myself."

"Wanna join me in the wardroom?"

She shook her head. "No. I wanted to thank you for not giving up on me."

I felt my eyebrows rising. "Shouldn't you be thanking Pip? He's the one who hired you."

"Yes. Probably." She shrugged. "He's not the one who took me aside to make sure I'd found my feet again. Is he laying on a senior officers' dinner again here?"

"He hasn't mentioned it to me, but I'm not sure that means much."

Zoya joined us at the foot of the ramp and grinned at Beth. "Fancy meeting you here."

"Ms. Usoko. Good to see you."

"Sorry to interrupt, Skipper. Liberty?"

"Fourth section as the watch until 1800. It's what? Just after 1500 now?"

"Yeah."

"Spread the word for liberty at 1800. Notify Chief Bashar that dinner may be sparsely attended."

She nodded. "Liberty at 1800, aye, Captain. I'll go see the chief now." She nodded to Captain Case and trotted back up the ramp.

"I'll let you get back to work, Captain. Perhaps we can have dinner tomorrow night?"

"If nothing breaks between now and then, I'd love to."

She smiled and nodded before turning away, heading down the docking gallery toward the Chernyakova's dock.

I went back aboard and met Zoya in the passageway just off the mess deck.

"I've notified Chief Bashar, Skipper. I think he was expecting it."

"He's been around long enough to know," I said, continuing on to the ladder up to officer country with Zoya close behind.

She stopped at the cabin door when I entered. "Was that odd, Captain? Captain Case?"

I stopped halfway to my console and looked back at her. "Meeting us at the dock?"

She nodded.

"I'm not sure why she didn't just send me a message, but other than that? I don't know." I paused. "Why? Something I'm not aware of?"

She shrugged. "Just me being nosy."

"You getting any rumbles from our replacements?"

"No," she said. "Nothing."

I shrugged. "Well, Pip said it. Not our circus. Any bets on what happens here?"

She grinned. "Depends. How long we staying?"

"My plan is four days."

"Is the Chernyakova staying that long, too?"

I shrugged again and took a seat at my console. "Pip hasn't said. If they keep the normal rotation, they'll be out day after tomorrow."

She leaned a shoulder against the door jamb and crossed her arms. "Are they ready?"

"When it comes down to it, it's not that much different from the High Line in terms of navigation. They've been through the visa process twice. That's the same from station to station. I'm pretty sure Pip is holding Abe's hand in terms of cargoes."

She nodded at that. "Pip said they had a can lined up before they even docked. His fingers were all over it." She smiled "He can't let go."

"Given that, maybe it's time they took the lead. Maybe go their own way for a while. Captain Case seems to have settled in fairly well."

"Agreed."

When she didn't move on, I asked, "Something else?"

She shook her head and straightened up. "Anything you need from me before I go ashore?"

"Nothing I can think of. You have plans?"

She sighed. "No. I'll probably go wander down Artist's Row. Head over to see if that ramen stall is still there off the main plaza."

"Taking Natalya with you?"

"I asked, but she begged off. She and Pip are heading out to a gallery opening. She asked if I wanted to come along but ..." Her words trailed off and she shrugged. "It felt weird."

"Take Mr. MacBradaigh with you?"

She blinked. "What?"

"You know the Toe-Holds better than I do. Maybe better than Natalya. I'm sure he'd welcome any insights."

She laughed. "Better than Natalya? I don't think so."

"Sometimes the outsider sees things the insider doesn't."

She squinted at me and tilted her head. "You believe that?"

"I do, but I try not to only look at things from the outside."

After a long moment, she asked, "You think he'd listen to me?"

"Yes."

"Why? He didn't seem to put much stock in what I had to say back in Newmar."

"That was his mistake. I think he may realize that, now that he's had a chance to see you work."

"Now that he's seen the actual Toe-Holds, you mean?" She laughed at me with her eyes.

"That helped."

"I never did hear what happened with you two on Dark Knight." She crossed her arms and leaned against the door jamb again.

"You can come in and sit if you want."

She shook her head. "Don't want to get comfy."

The way she said it made me pause. "I took him to that barbecue place. The one in the alley between Main Street and Second?"

She nodded.

"Afterwards we had coffee in Kondur's pub."

"Not bad for a first date," she said, her lips twitching like she was trying not to grin.

I laughed. "He found some interesting places that I wouldn't have expected him to."

"Like what?"

"He found the miner bar down off the barge docking gallery."

"I didn't know there was one."

"He spent some time puzzling out why the diner at the docks didn't have a lot of spacers in it."

"What did he decide?"

I shrugged. "He came to the conclusion that it didn't sell what spacers wanted to buy."

She chuckled. "I sometimes think I should go for an advanced degree. Then I hear stories like this and say 'nah.'"

"I'm doing him a disservice. He realized that most of the people there are dockworkers who use it more as a break room than anything else. That spacers don't go there because they aren't the clientele it caters to." I shrugged. "I'm not sure he recognizes spacers if they're not in shipsuits."

She blinked at that. "Really?"

"To be fair, he hasn't got the background for it, does he?"

She pursed her lips. "No, I suppose he doesn't."

"You lived on Dark Knight for a time."

"Yeah. Nats and I rented a tiny place. Not far from the long-term docks, actually. We told you that, didn't we?"

I nodded. "Has it changed much?"

She narrowed her eyes and bit her upper lip, staring into the past. "It's grown. I wouldn't say 'changed.' There are a lot more people there. Transient quarters and long-term docks used to be the back side of the station when we were here. They still are, but there's like a whole extra station between where that was and where it is now." She snorted. "Kondur finally figured out he needed to keep his Barbell running full time. Hired a crew and everything."

"That's new?"

"Yeah. It used to stay docked up between runs to the High Line when we were here. Never could figure out why."

"Maybe he just couldn't keep the crews."

"I think it was more that he only had one skipper who didn't really want the job but did it on an as-needed basis."

I grinned at her. "You angling for that berth?"

She laughed, a sound that filled me with joy. "No. I'm not even thinking of my next berth. It's still too far away." She gave me a long look. "Never know what's going to happen in the meantime."

"Pip would buy you a ship, I think."

She laughed. "Nats would, too. Like I need somebody to buy one for me." She shook her head. "Money makes things a lot easier, but listening to Pip talk about helping others has me thinking about how to do it best."

"Really?"

"Yeah. The four of us have as many surplus credits as some of the orbitals and most of the stations. People fall through the cracks in society all the time. How do we help?" She shrugged. "Is the problem credits? Is it jobs? Is it something else, like mismanagement or mental health? All of the above?" She shook her head. "I don't know how to parse out the problem, so I'm damn sure I don't know how to solve it."

"Does anybody?" I asked.

She frowned and tipped her head like she was listening to something I couldn't hear. "I don't know. I should look into that." Her tablet bipped and she pulled up the message. "Interesting discussion, Skipper. I need to get back to work." She holstered her tablet and threw me a wave before heading down the ladder.

The cabin felt emptier without her, even if she had only been standing in the doorway. I sighed and went to take a nap. I'd be up most of the night. I could do my reports then.

Pip and Natalya stopped by the cabin when they came back aboard at 0100. I waved them in and they plunked down in the visitor's chairs. I caught a faint whiff of beer from them, but they didn't seem overly drunk.

"How was the show?"

"You'd have been bored," Pip said. "I found it fascinating."

"Al was there," Natalya said.

"Really? Did you talk to her?"

They both shook their heads.

Natalya said, "She has a couple of pieces there. She was surrounded by people. I'm not even sure she saw us."

"She looked happy," Pip said. "Very much at home."

"Anything new and exciting?"

They looked at each other before shaking their heads in unison.

Natalya shrugged. "I didn't see anything."

"Me, either," Pip said. "We haven't been gone that long."

Natalya chuckled. "Just seems that way."

"Anything shaking here?" Pip asked.

"Beth Case met me at the lock when we docked. We're going to dinner tomorrow night." I glanced at the chrono. "Well, later tonight."

Pip's eyebrows rose. "Captains' meeting?"

I laughed. "Well, we're both captains, so I suppose so."

Natalya flicked her eyebrows up and down a couple of times. "Something going on there?"

"Not on my part," I said. "Familiar face in an ocean of strangeness."

"Funny, she didn't ask me," Pip said, frowning.

"Did you miss the part where he said 'ocean of strangeness?'" Natalya asked, giving him a little dig.

"I'm not strange."

She laughed. "Keep telling yourself that, Carstairs."

He gave her a "harumph" and folded his arms, looking at me. "You wanna talk business?"

"If you want. I'm here until Zoya relieves me at 0400."

"We got cans. We should be buttoned back up by day after tomorrow."

"Are you going to keep the Chernyakova in port until we're ready?"

He pursed his lips and tilted his head back and forth a couple of times. "I'm on the fence. Your opinion?"

"Move 'em out. It'll take them a bit to get their mass out to the limit. I assume we're going to the same place again."

He nodded. "Ranch next. We've picked up about thirty cans of assorted parts and pieces. We've got a few cans of feed supplements for them."

"Then where?"

"I don't know," he said, stifling a yawn. "Alys wants us to show the flag. We could hit Diurnia. Give Beth's crew a chance to see the back doors there."

"You could cut her loose," Natalya said. Her tone said it was a subject they'd already discussed.

He sighed. "Yeah. We could. It's only been a few weeks. She'll beat us to The Ranch and I'll talk to her about it then, all right?"

Natalya gave him a smile. "See? Not so hard, is it?"

He chuckled and yawned again. "I'm done. I think it's time I hit the rack." He stood, starting for the door. "See ya in the morning."

"Night," Natalya said, glancing over her shoulder for a moment before looking back at me. She lounged back in the chair, stretching her legs straight out, heels together. "So how are you?"

"Still captain." I grinned at her. "Being back on the watch rotation feels pretty comfortable, but a little like cheating."

"Cheating?"

"I don't see as much of the crew as I used to when I'm riding the merry-go-round. Feels like I'm shirking the captain part a little."

"Is it because you're not spending your days in the cabin?"

"I think it's because I'm not getting my nightly walk around the ship."

"You're still getting your running in, though, aren't you?"

"Yeah. Usually after watch. Having four sections really spreads out the demand on my time."

She paused for a moment, looking at me with an odd expression. "How are you with me and Pip?"

"I have no problems with it. Neither of you is on the same chain of command."

"You're talking like a captain, Skipper." She grinned. "We're all on his chain of command. Even you."

I thought about that for a moment and sighed. "Yeah. I suppose I'm being a bit myopic on that front. He's not your boss when the ship's underway and not directly your boss when we're docked."

"You're still talking like a captain. How do you feel about it, Ishmael?" She stared at me, something like sympathy in her eyes.

I shrugged. "He's a lucky guy. You've got a handful with him."

"Has he changed that much since we've joined the crew?"

"You and Zoya?"

She nodded.

"Yes. Unquestionably. He had a bad case of Zoya-worship in the beginning." I couldn't blame him for that, but I wasn't about to say it out loud.

She chuckled. "Yeah. I think we all noticed that. Even him."

"Alys noticed the change in him back in Port Newmar. It's that obvious."

"Be fair. She knew both of you before he went to the Academy. I've heard some of his stories. He was a hellion."

I wrinkled my nose in a grimace. "That's probably overstating it. He wasn't evil. At least not on purpose, I don't think. I really don't know much of what he did between graduation and finding me again."

"I think he wanted to be a con man." She looked down at the toes of her boots. "He's got a competitive streak two kilometers wide. Doing deals is good. Doing great deals feeds his ego."

I smiled at her. "You're good for him."

She looked over at me, eyebrows raised. "You think so?"

"I do."

"He thinks the world of you, you know."

I thought about that. "He and I make a good team. He's got the drive and connections that I lack. He's got the personality for it."

She laughed. "Personality. Yes. He has that in diamonds and spades, but he's still the joker in the deck." She gave me a long look. "What about you?"

"What about me?"

"He couldn't do what he's doing now without you."

I shook my head. "I'm nothing special. Just the—"

"Oh, cut it out with the bus driver bullshit." She grinned. "He couldn't have done this with Beth Case." She looked around at the ship.

I snorted. "He is doing it with Beth Case and me at the same time." I frowned as I heard the words coming out of my mouth. "That didn't sound right."

She laughed. "I know what you meant, but you're being dense. If it had been Beth Case in Port Newmar back in the beginning, would he have been able to even start Phoenix?"

"Not unless she'd just sold a company and had a few million spare credits laying around."

"Still being dense."

"I don't know where you're going with this."

"You and Pip are Romulus and Remus." She raised her eyebrows.

"Raised by wolves?" I asked.

She laughed. "Not what I was thinking, but as a metaphor? Not bad."

"What then?"

"You're Romulus. He's Remus. You're really the dominant one who's founded a city."

"You realize Romulus killed Remus."

"Alys Giggone is the shepherd and don't get literal on me." She shook her head. "Be that as it may. Pip couldn't do this without you at the helm."

"I couldn't do it without Pip's management." I shrugged. "We make a good team. Where are you going with this?"

"What do you want, Ishmael?"

"What do you mean?"

"By any rational measure, I'm rich beyond reason. I do this because I love it." She looked down at her boots again. "I thought the credits and the job would be enough."

"But it's not," I said.

"It was." She sighed. "Making the final step up to chief. Getting off the Madoka. Changed my perspective."

"What do you do when you've done it all?" I asked, knowing where she was coming from finally.

She gave me a wan smile. "Yeah. That."

"You think Pip's the answer?"

She pursed her lips. "I don't know." She sounded amused by the question. "I don't know if there's just one answer."

I waited her out.

"It's been a long road. Zoya's been on the journey with me since the Academy." She shook her head and grinned. "So many people think we're a couple. Like we can't just be friends."

"Yeah. I don't ever want to sleep with Pip."

I surprised a short laugh out of her and she stared at her boots for a few moments, tapping the toes together, the smile on her face telling the story her words probably couldn't. She glanced up at me without lifting her head. "Who do you want to sleep with, Skipper? Anybody?"

I sighed. "Yeah. That's the question, isn't it?" I don't know what made me answer her.

She lifted her head at that and looked at me, eyebrows raised. "You've thought about this already."

"Yeah." I sighed, deciding to level with her. "Back on Port Newmar, when I had more credits than I could have imagined. When I had already been a captain and an owner but had lost the woman I thought was my one. The one." I shook my head, memories dredging up the hollowness I'd felt then. "What could I do? Why would I do anything?" I shrugged. "So when Pip came to me, I threw in with him. It was something to do."

"What's stopping you from doing what you want to do now?"

I frowned at her. "I don't know what I want to do."

"Why get up in the morning, then?"

"How drunk are you?"

She laughed. "Not that drunk." She closed one eye and looked around. "The room's not spinning. That's a good sign. Why? Am I being obnoxious?"

"You're being pretty free with your words. That's not like you."

She shrugged. "Maybe. Maybe not. Maybe I'm just feeling like I can talk to you like I'd talk to Zoya now. We haven't been through the same things together, but it's pretty clear the four of us have gone through a lot of similar things. We've all been hurt. We've all carried on. We've all buried ourselves in our work to the extent that we've mostly cut off anything other than 'professional' relationships." After a moment she said, "I'm too young for a midlife crisis, but I'm not happy with just professional anymore." She paused and sent some glances around the cabin out of the corners of her eyes. "Maybe I'm a little drunk."

"I get it."

Her eyebrows rose at that. "Do you?"

"I think so."

She nodded. "I think you do."

"Where are you going with this? Do you know?"

She drew in a deep breath and frowned at me for a moment. "I'm wondering how you feel about me coming between you and Pip."

"We're not a couple."

"Dense again." She shook her head. "You're a team. I'm a complication to that team. Just like Pip is a complication between me and Zoya."

"Is she feeling left out?"

"She's happy for me."

"So am I." I let that float in the air between us for a moment. "I'm happy for Pip. Everybody deserves the somebody they need."

She looked at me for a long, long moment. "What about you, Captain?"

I shrugged. "I haven't found them yet."

Her lips pressed into a line but her eyes danced. "Liar."

I pulled a deep breath in through my nose and bit down on the inside of my lower lip for a moment. "You think so?"

She nodded. "I know it. The question is, what will you do about it?"

I sighed, feeling the coldness gathering around my heart. "One lesson I learned since losing love once. There's always tomorrow. I don't expect anything today. I just try to keep myself open to tomorrow."

She shook her head.

"What?"

"I know what happened in Greenfield. Maggie told me."

I felt the stirrings of anger coiling in my gut. "And she set you in my path?"

"No, idiot. She told both of us so we'd know you were still healing but that you'd be the captain we needed to sail with." She sighed and shook her head. "All right. Maybe I am drunk."

"What?"

She rolled her eyes to the overhead and sighed. "Look, Captain. I'm sorry. I shouldn't have called you an idiot. You're very much not an idiot."

"Not that. I am an idiot. Thank you for calling me on it. The other part."

She brought her gaze down to me again. "What? The healing thing? Or the captain we needed to sail with?"

"Either. Both."

"She knew I wanted to be chief engineer and was just waiting until I could get the board together. The Madoka's skipper had it in but the CPJCT works in mysterious ways. Mostly slowly."

"Can't argue that." I grinned at her. "And you wouldn't leave without Zoya?"

She frowned. "Are you out of your mind? Zoya would have kicked my ass out the lock to take the job. She's my friend, not my keeper or anchor or whatever it would be." She reached up and rubbed a finger on the tip of her nose. "I seem to be sobering up a little. It's not as numb as it was."

"I'm not following. She told you and Zoya that you both needed to sail with me?"

Her frown deepened. "Isn't that what I just said? What did you think? She could have waved her fairy-godmother wand over me on the Madoka at any time." She shrugged. "Well, as soon as I had time in grace—er—grade. It wouldn't have done me any good there because I wasn't going to bump the chief out."

"Right. Why did Zoya come over?" I don't know why I pressed on this, but it seemed important and I didn't know why.

"Well, mostly because you needed a first mate, I suspect."

"Why did Chief Stevens say she needed to come here?"

She blinked and stretched her face a little as if settling it back into place. "I just told you. You needed a first mate."

I took a deep breath and started again. "That's what I needed. She already had a first mate berth. What did she need?"

"She needed more challenge or she was going to get stale before she even had a shot at the board. She'd already out-grown the Madoka."

"And I'm a challenge?"

Natalya gave a series of almost silent laughs. "Oh, yes. Indeed you are, Skipper. I mean that in only the most positive of ways."

"So, Maggie Stevens pulled you two out of the Toe-Holds, dragged you to Port Newmar, and told you that you needed to sail with me. Specifically."

"No. Don't be silly. She told us at Mel's and convinced us that we needed to get to Port Newmar to meet you. The rest was just mechanics. We crossed paths at Dark Knight. I had no idea who you were at the time." She shook her head. "We've gone over this before, haven't we?"

I sighed. "Probably. I remembered you from the tea shop when I saw you returning Sifu Newmar's tea cup."

"Zoya remembered you as soon as we walked past." Natalya's eyes focused somewhere else. "She nudged me after we passed you on the path and mentioned it. She wondered if you were a stalker."

"I might have wondered myself."

She shook herself, and sat up straight in the chair before pushing herself up with her hands on the arms. "Well, it's been a great little chat, Skipper. I need to sleep the rest of this buzz off. Don't expect me at breakfast." She managed to navigate between the chairs and get to the cabin door where she stopped and looked back. "Whatever you think, I think Maggie Stevens was right. You are the right skipper. Zoya and I both needed to sail with you. Not just because we needed you." She paused for a moment. "Don't take this the wrong way, but you needed us. Not just another first mate and engineering officer. You needed Zoya and me. I'm sure of it."

I nodded. "Thank you."

She blinked. "You're welcome?"

"For joining the crew. For being here."

She grinned. "You know I'm not that drunk, right?"

"I know you'll remember this conversation, if that's what you're asking."

She gave a little shrug. "It's not, but close enough. G'night, Ishmael."

With that she headed off down the passageway, leaving me stewing over the conversation. I didn't know if I should curse Maggie Stevens or bless her. I turned in my chair and looked at the blank bulkhead where the screen would have been on the Chernyakova. I stared at it for a long time.

CHAPTER SEVENTEEN
MEL'S PLACE: SEPTEMBER 4, 2379

After Zoya relieved me, I crawled into my bunk and slept until noon. I might have slept longer but for somebody knocking on the cabin door. It took only a moment to slip into a shipsuit and call out, "Come in."

Mr. MacBradaigh opened the door a crack and peeked in. "Sorry, Captain. I should have realized you'd be sleeping."

"Come in, Mr. MacBradaigh. I needed to get up anyway. Take a seat and let me wash my face. I'll be right with you."

He nodded and came in, leaving the door open while I went back through my sleeping quarters and into the head. A quick visit to flush out my bladder and splash some soap and warm water on my face made me feel better. I'd slept well, considering. I finished up, wiping my hands and face before returning.

"How can I help you, Mr. MacBradaigh?" I took a seat behind the console.

"We've only got three more days in port this time, as I understand it."

"Correct."

"I'd prefer not to waste it by wandering around aimlessly. What areas should I pay attention to? Are there any things I could make it a point to observe?"

I shrugged. "I think you're right in your own approach. The newsie office here probably has an archive you can access to learn about the history. You could also check with the station administrator's office. They probably have, or know where you can find, any official history of the station."

"I looked in my copy of the Traveler's Guide to Toe-Hold Space." He pulled out his tablet and consulted it. "It's quite interesting. I had some idea about the convention at Delta Pavonis IV in 2152. It's part of the common history. I didn't know about the Board of Exploration or that it formed the basis for the Confederated Planets Joint Committee on Trade." He looked over at me. "Apparently it's part of our historical canon but not part of our curriculum."

"Mel's is one of the oldest stations in the Annex, I think. Their archives would be valuable. Have you checked the station net to see if any of it is publicly available?"

He raised his eyebrows. "Really? I have access to the station's networks?"

"Only the public side, but they may have historical information. The Traveler's Guide is just a condensed version of the official story."

He frowned down at his tablet. He flipped a screen and poked at the window. His eyebrows flashed up and he blew out a breath. He looked over at me. "I'm a victim of my experience. It never occurred to me that I might have access to the network here. I have access to the planet net when I'm in Port Newmar and the orbital network when I'm on the orbital. Being on the ship, I guess I didn't think that our net would interface with theirs."

"It's how we manage our communications. It's how we know what's happening on the station. The station likes us to know about things like restaurants, art galleries, and public events. They encourage us to spend our credits here."

He sighed and nodded. "My bias is showing."

"You didn't think they'd have a station net?"

"I don't know that I even gave it that much thought, Captain. I just assumed they didn't."

"Even after Dark Knight?"

He looked down at his screen again and bit his lips between his teeth. "I never looked."

"You're still operating with the idea that the Toe-Holds are nothing more than ghost towns? After all you've seen?"

He scratched at the angle of his jaw with the index finger on his free hand, staring into the middle distance. "This is useful."

"In what way?"

He focused on me. "I'm going to need to make a case that challenges the known universe for the students."

"Only for some of them." I grinned at him. "Some of them will know, but that's not going to be the biggest challenge."

He chuckled and holstered his tablet. "True. I'm here and seeing it with my own eyes and I still see the place like some kind of backwater in my mind. What I think I know about the Toe-Holds makes me discount the notion that they may be as advanced as the High Line."

"You might find that the High Line has a lot of catching up to do," I said.

He blinked and looked to his right, staring into space again. "Oh. Mercy. Mel's has been here longer than the oldest orbital. Mel Colby discovered systems the High Line later colonized." He looked back at me and shook his head. "You're right, as always. Propaganda is insidious."

"My mother used to say something about controlling the rhetoric. If you can define the terms, you're halfway to winning the argument."

He chuckled. "I've heard that myself, but I always thought it meant establishing the terms in advance. I'm facing a problem of redefining the terms currently in use."

"Co-opt them?" I asked.

He worried his lower lip with his teeth for a moment. "I think I need to replace the term. Toe-Holds makes them sound tenuous. Like barely able to maintain a position."

"Can you? They're pretty set on using the term here."

"I don't need to change it here. The term I need to change here is High Line."

"Why?"

"It sets the CPJCT above."

"Only for one definition of high." I shrugged.

He chuckled again and stood. "Thank you, Captain. History is the right framework. We're at the center of that history here. Sorry to wake you. I've got a lot to look into." He headed for the cabin door.

"When you go ashore, look at the plazas. See how the space is organized. Pay attention to the shopping district."

He paused and looked back. "The shopping district?"

"Yes."

"That's it? No hints?"

I laughed. "No. Go in with your eyes and ears open. The cognitive dissonance will let you know when you've seen something you didn't expect."

He tilted his head. "You're using my terminology now, Captain. Are you trying to control the rhetoric?"

"Remember, my mother was an ancient lit professor, Mr. MacBradaigh. I teethed on cognitive dissonance."

He grinned at me. "Thanks for the warning, Captain." He chuckled as he left the cabin.

Zoya swung by in his wake. "He got you up?"

"It was time. Anything break this morning?"

"Nothing that needs the captain's attention." She grinned and crossed her arms, leaning against the door jamb, in her usual position. "What'd you say to Natalya last night?"

"Not very much. She had several words for me."

Her lips curled into a grin. "She giving you advice now?"

"She's having a midlife crisis."

Zoya snorted. "Aren't we all?"

"Why? What'd she say this morning?"

"Only that she bent your ear around 0200. Something about Maggie Stevens and needing to ship out with you and Pip. She didn't make a lot of sense, but she was feeling the effect of her excesses."

"It was the 'what do you do when you fulfill your dream and find it isn't enough' talk."

She pursed her lips and shrugged. "It's a good question. Did you give her an answer?"

"I don't know if she was looking for one. She mostly wanted to make sure that I didn't have any problem with her and Pip."

"You don't, do you?"

I shook my head. "No. Technically, he's not on her chain of command since they both report to me. The chain of command is bent pretty badly because Pip works for me but he's the CEO of the company that owns the ship."

"Bent is a good word for it." She smiled.

"Who's got the watch? Ms. Fortuner?"

"Yeah. She just relieved me. Mr. Cartwright has the overnight tonight. I'm thinking about getting some lunch ashore."

"Tired of Chief Bashar's cooking already?"

She laughed. "No, but I can eat here when we're underway."

"Want some company?" I asked.

"If you want to go, sure. Gimme a couple ticks to change into civvies."

"Deal."

I went back to my sleeping quarters and pulled on some jeans and a navy blue polo, stashing my uniform in the closet and straightening the bedding on my bunk. It wouldn't pass inspection at the Academy, but it would feel better when I got back to it.

I grabbed a jacket from the hook and shrugged into it as I walked through the main cabin.

Zoya met me at the door and laughed. "Uniform of the day, apparently." She wore almost the same outfit except for the color of her pullover, burgundy to my navy. We even had similar cuts in our jackets.

"Only so many ways to take it," I said. "It's a good color for you."

She grinned. "Thanks. Nat gives me crap for being too fleet, but I just can't get the hang of the clothing here."

"You haven't seen my purple suit, have you?"

She raised her eyebrows. "Purple? How purple? Like royal purple?"

I chuckled and pulled the cabin door closed behind me before heading down the ladder. "More like electric purple with a paisley brocade."

She laughed. "I'm sorry but I can't imagine you wearing something like that."

"It came with a hat." I stuck my head in the ship's office. "Ms. Fortuner, Zoya and I are going ashore for lunch. Anything I need to be aware of?"

She looked up from her console and shook her head. "All quiet here at the moment, Skipper. I got the astrogation updates loaded. Pip says The Ranch next?"

"That's what he told me, too. Must be true." I grinned.

She chuckled. "Enjoy your lunch, Skipper."

We checked out of the ship and Zoya looked over at me as we walked down the ramp. "Really? Purple."

"Really."

"Was it the hat that sold you on it?" She gave me a little grin.

I shrugged and struck off for the main passage into Mel's. "Maggie Stevens sold me on it. You've seen her wear civvies in the Toe-Holds, haven't you?"

She nodded. "She's got a flair for it. So's Nat, for that matter."

I nodded. "Pip does, too. Something else they have in common."

"That bother you?"

"What? That they have so much in common? Isn't that what relationships are based on?"

She shook her head. "I don't know. Maybe."

I caught her giving me little side-eyed glances. "What?"

"Purple?"

I laughed. "I was having a rough time, all right? Don't give me crap about it. I wasn't myself, so it was easy to think I might be somebody else."

She laughed along with me.

It felt really good. Perhaps better than was wise. I dodged around a party of spacers coming the other way. "Where are we going?"

She shrugged. "Don't ask me. I'm following you."

"I thought you had someplace in mind when you said you were coming ashore for lunch."

"I do. Not the ship." She gave me a comical grimace. "That's as far as I got."

"So? Restaurant row and see what appeals?"

"You're the captain, Captain."

"You lead for a change," I said. "Good practice."

She laughed again, the overhead lights dancing in her eyes. "You willing to follow me?"

"Of course." I bit off the rest of the sentence and swallowed the "anywhere" that wanted to come out.

"All right, then." She picked up her pace a notch. "Let's go commit some foodery."

"Foodery?"

She shrugged. "I'm not up for felony at the moment."

"Are you ever?"

"Not so far. No." She grinned at me again. "I wouldn't rule it out under the right circumstances."

"You're making me question your judgment, Ms. Usoko. You sure you're fleet through and through?"

Her smile flashed. "I was at one time. Natalya might have corrupted me. A little."

"It looks good on you," I said, before I could think about my words.

She gave me a shy smile, a quick glance out of the corners of her eyes. "Purple, huh?"

I sighed. "I'm going to regret telling you that, aren't I."

She laughed.

We decided on a hole in the wall place called Tagaytay just past the main plaza, heading toward the theater district. The menu in the window displayed an eclectic mix of dishes. The scents that wafted down the alley—something spicy, something sweet, and a lot of yeasty bread—drew us both to it. I held the door and waved her in.

A host looked up from her podium and gave us a smile. "Two for lunch?"

"Yes, please."

She waved us on through an open arch. The whole dining room was about as wide as the wardroom on the ship, but four times as long with booths along both long walls and tables set in a line down the empty floor. She showed us to a booth along the bulkhead, about half way down, and settled us with menus.

"Ivan will be right over to take your orders. Enjoy."

"You haven't eaten here before?" I asked.

"No. Walked by a couple of times but never stopped." She pulled open the menu and scanned down.

I followed her lead and my eye got caught on the chicken adobo. The description sounded great and my gut seemed to be making rumbling noises in approval.

"Inasal chicken for me," Zoya said.

"You're familiar with this cuisine? I have no idea what some of this is."

"There used to be a place in Port Newmar. Good, cheap, filling, and didn't serve beer."

I raised my eyebrows. "That was a selling point?"

She snickered and kept reading the menu. "You were never accosted by a drunk cadet in town, I take it?"

I sighed. "No. I take your point."

She closed the menu, laid it on the end of the table, and folded her hands together at the table's edge. "It was a good place to go to grab some food that wasn't made bland enough that everybody could eat it, even if nobody really wanted to."

"I didn't think the food was that bad at the Academy."

She shrugged. "It wasn't bad. It just wasn't great. Plentiful and boring, but not bad."

"I didn't spend much time off campus. Pip made forays out into the world at least once a week, but I stayed pretty close to the dorms."

"You worked with Sifu Newmar a lot, too, I bet."

"Guilty." I folded my own menu shut and laid it on top of hers. "The first summer was the worst."

"Didn't they keep the dorms open?"

"Yes, but we had to move out for the summer while they renovated. They gave us Baird for the summer. The mess hall stayed open, of course, but Pip and I both thought we'd move back into the newly renovated Martin Hall when it was ready."

She snickered. "Lemme guess. Upperclassmen?"

"They got the renovations done in mid-August and the new fourth-years moved into it."

"Did you have to stay in Baird?"

"We got Swanson." I shrugged. "The next summer they redid Baird."

"We had Reine the whole time. I liked it because it was handy to the library."

The server came over. "Sorry for the wait. Can I get you something to drink?"

"Coffee?" I asked.

"Of course. For the lady?"

"You have tanglad iced tea?"

"We do. With milk?"

She shook her head. "Not needed."

He smiled, taking notes on his handheld. "Appetizers? You know what you want?"

"Inasal chicken for me," Zoya said. "Rice?"

He nodded. "You want just steamed or adobo fried rice?"

Her face lit up. "Adobo, please."

"Vegetable? Sautéed green beans or water spinach?"

"Kangkong?" she asked.

He smiled. "Adobong kangkong."

"I'll have that."

He nodded and made a note. "For you, sir?"

"Adobo chicken."

He nodded. "That comes with steamed rice. Your vegetable?"

"What's water spinach?" I asked.

"It's spinach that grows on the water," he said, his grin broadening. "The stems and leaves float."

"It's basically spinach, Skipper. The stalks are larger, but basically it's spinach spiced up with garlic."

I nodded. "I'll try it. I can get green beans anywhere."

He made a note. "No appetizers?"

Zoya and I looked at each other and shook our heads simultaneously.

"We're good," she said.

He nodded and collected the menus. "I'll be right back with your drinks." He scooted off into the back.

"You know your way around this pretty well," I said.

"Only the most common stuff. The tea is made with ginger, sweetened, and flavored with a stalk of lemongrass."

"Sounds good."

"I haven't had it in forever. I'd forgotten all about it until just now."

"What do you think about Pip and Nats?" I asked after the silence had grown too long.

"Good for them." She shrugged. "I haven't heard of any of the rest of the crew pairing off."

"I never encouraged bunk bunnies on the Chernyakova. Didn't discourage it, either."

She snorted. "Really? Bunk bunnies?"

I laughed. "I don't know. Is there another term I'm not aware of?"

Our waiter brought the drinks. "Your lunch will be right up."

We thanked him and he stepped over to the next table.

I eyed Zoya's tea and watched her take a sip. "How is it?"

She closed her eyes and sighed. "Delightful. Quite refreshing." She held the glass out to me. "Wanna sip?"

I shook my head. "I'll stick with the coffee." I picked up the heavy china mug. The first sip made me take notice. "This is pretty good." I took another sip. "This isn't the normal bean. Reminds me of the coffee Chief Bashar has."

"Wonder if it's from the same source," she said, taking another sip of her tea.

"Could be, but it wouldn't surprise me if it's locally grown."

"Don't you need a planet for that?" she asked.

"I don't know. It's a tropical plant, but I can't imagine why the plant would care as long as it has what it needs to grow."

"Here he comes with the food. Ask him."

The waiter set a tray beside the table and doled out our dishes. The aromas shot right to my nose. My mouth watered and I forgot all about the coffee.

"The coffee?" Zoya asked, looking up at the him. "Where do you get it?"

"The owner's cousin grows it. He has a plantation over in Consort. Something about the light from the system primary."

"On a station, though, right?" she asked.

"Of course."

"Thanks."

He nodded. "Anything else I can get you?"

I shook my head and Zoya followed suit.

"We're good, I think," she said.

He nodded and took his tray away, heading for the kitchen.

Zoya picked up her fork and dug in. I didn't know where to start so I picked up a piece of the chicken and just kept going.

It was heavenly. Spicy where it needed to be. Savory. The spinach had a good texture and the flavors just exploded in my mouth. About halfway through the plate I stopped and sat back in my seat.

Zoya grinned over at me. Her plate was half empty as well. "Good, huh?"

I chuckled and gave a little contented sigh. "I never knew this was what I needed."

She took a sip of tea. "What? The food? Some time off the ship?"

I nodded. "All of it."

"You don't take enough time for yourself," she said, forking another morsel of chicken from her plate.

"You think?"

"You have any hobbies?" she asked. "Things you do that aren't work or sleep?"

"Everybody's asking that lately." I shrugged. "Mostly just wander around the ship when I'm not doing the reports."

"Well, yes, but that's work. What about your running? What are you up to?"

"Five kilometers, I think. Twenty laps on the track."

"What do you do for fun?"

I shook my head. "Look forward to the next port visit. Pip always has some kind of thing happening."

She sighed and gave me an exasperated look, her eyes wide and her lips pressed together. "And now that happening thing is Natalya. You thought about that?"

"No. I haven't." I had, but I wasn't about to tell her.

"Even Pip reads. He has his math and his model. Something to keep his brain from atrophying between ports."

"What do you do?" I asked.

She shrugged. "I have my music."

I felt my eyebrows climbing up my forehead. "You listen or play?"

She speared another bundle of the water spinach. "Both, if you must know." She thrust fork into her mouth and began chewing.

"You play in your stateroom? I've never heard it."

She shrugged and swallowed. "Keyboard. It's electronic. I listen with headphones."

I found the subject delightful and I didn't understand why. I took another bite of rice and pondered my plate.

"Does it matter?" she asked.

"No." I shook my head. "I'm just surprised. I had no idea."

"I picked it up when I got my first mate ticket. I've always been drawn to music, even as a kid. I promised myself that when I made first, I'd learn to play."

"You have a large music collection?"

She grinned. "Digital music doesn't use much mass. The keyboard takes a bit, but my allotment covers it easily enough."

"What do you play?"

"Whatever I feel like." She shook her head. "I play for me. That's all. Sometimes jazz. One whole stanyer back on the Madoka, I worked on classical music. The really old stuff. Chopin. Bach." She speared some more spinach and grinned. "I prefer jazz."

"Why?" I asked, mixing some of the rice into the sauce from the chicken and scooping up a forkful.

She sighed and looked up a little above my head. "I don't know. It's certainly not easier. Some of it has fewer notes." She grinned. "Mostly it's the feeling."

"The feeling?"

She nodded. "You can take any tune, any music, and make it jazz. It's less about the song than the style."

"So you could take stuffy like Chopin and make it jazzy?"

She laughed. "Yes, I suppose." She looked to the side as if considering the question. "Yeah, I know it's been done. There are a lot of takes on it." She paused, chasing a bit of spinach around on her plate with her fork. "The question is, could I do it." She shrugged and looked across the table at me. "I don't know. Maybe. I'd have to know the music better than I do."

We both realized we'd finished lunch when the waiter returned. "Can I interest you in some dessert?"

I shook my head. "I'm good."

Zoya nodded and placed her cutlery across her plate. "I'm done. No, on dessert for me, but this was wonderful."

He grinned, his face lighting up. "It's not every day we get customers who know tanglad tea and kangkong. I hope you'll come visit again. You must try the rendang. It will make you sweat and love every bite."

Zoya laughed. "Sounds lovely."

"It's only on the dinner menu," he said. "Bring your boyfriend back for dinner some night." He winked at me.

I opened my mouth to correct him but she beat me to the punch. "I'll do my best." She leaned toward him and lowered her voice. "He doesn't take direction well."

The waiter gave me a mock frown. "Tsk. He seems like a good man otherwise."

I sighed and flexed my thumb. "Come on. I'm not that bad."

She gave me a quick shrug and a smile I wished I could keep in a jar so I could look at it as often as I wanted. "All right. You're not that bad."

Everybody laughed and I thumbed the tab, leaving him a good tip. He took the first load of dirty dishes back to the kitchen, and we made good our escape.

"Not that bad?" I asked when we got to the sidewalk.

"What? You think you're that bad?" Her lips pressed together and her eyes sparkled as she teased me.

"You could have at least said 'You're not that bad, Skipper.' Now that guy thinks we're a couple."

She gave me that little shrug again and flickered her eyebrows a couple of times. "Well. If you think about it, Captain—" She really laid on the title. "We are in a long-term relationship. Have been for some time now. I don't know about you, but I expect it to continue for the foreseeable future. Don't you?"

I laughed, but I honestly wasn't sure if it was because the idea tickled me or frightened me. "I'm not planning on firing you, if that's the question, Ms. Usoko." I returned the favor by leaning into her name. "But the day's not too far away when you'll be Captain Usoko, is it?"

We strolled along for a bit while she pursed her lips and looked at the sidewalk. "There is that, isn't there." She didn't seem as excited by the prospect as I might have thought she'd be.

"Mr. MacBradaigh came to see me. Worried that he didn't know enough about the Toe-Holds to be able to know what he was supposed to look for."

"So you said. You think I should be his guide?"

I shrugged. "You've got a unique perspective on it. Not quite as much a native as Pip or even Natalya. Certainly not as much an outsider as I am."

"What did you tell him?" she asked.

"Hit the newsie archives to reconstruct the history of the early days."

"Creating a structure for the current events?" she asked.

"Exactly. The Academy presents the history of the Western Annex as largely nonexistent until the CPJCT established the first orbital in Gretna. The Toe-Holds that allowed that to happen and supported CPJCT's expansion get footnotes at best."

"High Tortuga," she said.

"What about it?"

"That's where the real history is."

"Because of the banking?"

She nodded. "For all that it's a central bank, they know their bread is buttered by taking a microscopic fraction of every transaction. I have to wonder how hard the CPJCT is working to cut them out of the loop."

"Interesting question, isn't it? I'm not surprised they haven't been able to."

She glanced at me. "Why?"

"They need trade from the Toe-Holds. In the beginning it was to prop up the corporate economies. They needed the raw materials and finished goods to support development. Now it's to prop up CPJCT itself, because they need the markets to sell to."

"I'd bet on trust," she said.

"Trust? You implying that the CPJCT doesn't trust itself?"

"Do you trust them?" She looked over at me while we waited on the corner for a cargo hauler to rumble by in the passageway. "I mean trust them to do what's right instead of what's in their best interest."

I let that question stew a moment. "I don't know. You would think that doing what's right is in their best interest, wouldn't you?"

"I used to think that." She shook her head. "I'm not sure now."

"You think I'm naive?"

"No. I think you're isolated." We crossed the passageway and ducked down an alley that led back to the docking gallery. "Being on the ship all the time puts us in a world that we control. You and Pip talk about the conditions on Breakall when you got the Chernyakova. Al was beached there. Al, of all people, should never have been stuck on Breakall Orbital. Was that the right thing?"

"Was she stuck or just didn't have a place to go?"

Zoya sighed. "I don't know. Good question, but all those other spacers? You can't tell me Ms. Sharps wasn't stuck there. Woman with her skills? She should have been able to ship out whenever she wanted to."

"We're back to economics," I said. "Does the Western Annex have too many spacers? Not enough ships?"

She grimaced. "Or the wrong skills in the wrong places? I don't know, but I'm pretty sure it's systemic."

I sighed and nodded my agreement. "How do you see it in relation to the Toe-Holds?"

She pursed her lips and looked around as if searching for the answer. "I don't know. The Toe-Holds I've seen don't appear to have an excess labor problem. It's not as obvious as it is on the orbitals, if they do. I know if we ask for a quarter share here, we're going to get a few people here. If we ask on an orbital?" She raised an eyebrow in my direction. "You've seen it firsthand."

"True." We turned down the gallery toward our lock.

"It might be that the successful stations find jobs for everybody," she said. "It could be that I don't see it because we only visit the same few stations and those stations can support Barbell levels of trade. It might be different if we were running a tractor."

I grinned at her. "It's a shame you haven't given this much thought."

She laughed and shrugged. "Well. A bit. Yeah."

"How does Usoko Mining see it, if you put on your corporate hat?"

"We have jobs empty all the time. High Line and Toe-Holds both." She shook her head. "Trained barge crews to untrained labor. Management to line. I haven't checked lately, but historically a couple of percent of our jobs are empty."

"Expansion?"

"Between expanding the operation and turnover, a lot of which happens because we hire from within. Somebody moves up and it takes a while for the new person to come in and fill the slot." She stopped at the lock and keyed it. "Something between 3 and 8 percent of our employees leave Usoko in the course of a stanyer. Move on to greener pastures or to be with significant others. It's highest among the lowest tiers, smallest among the highest. About what you'd expect in a ship's crew, actually."

I thought about that as the lock finished opening. "We haven't lost anybody from the Chernyakova in a while."

She raised her eyebrow at me again. "No. Just your chief engineer and first mate. Out of a crew of twenty-eight? What's that? Seven percent?"

"That was a couple of stanyers ago."

She grinned. "Yes, and you knew Maggie Stevens was temporary and that Al should have had a ship of her own. My point still stands. Mr. Cartwright will want to move up but can't as long as Ms. Fortuner doesn't move. She can't unless I make way for her or she leaves. At some point, I'm hoping to get a master's ticket and then we'll see what happens."

"Would you leave?" The question popped out of my mouth before I could put the brakes on it. It felt vitally important while I was asking but I regretted it as soon as question left my lips.

She shrugged. "It depends. A lot of first mates have a master's ticket in their trunks. Cargo and engineering firsts, too."

"Fredi deGrut did," I said. "She didn't want the headaches. She took over when Rossett got canned."

We stood there at the foot of the ramp looking at each other for a long moment.

"I'm going to hate to lose you when the time comes," I said, swallowing back anything more.

"There's a lot of cargo to move between now and then, Skipper. Let's not borrow trouble." She turned and climbed the ramp into the ship.

Cargo, yes. And a fair amount of baggage.

I followed her into the ship and wondered what Mal Gaines would suggest.

CHAPTER EIGHTEEN
MEL'S PLACE: SEPTEMBER 4, 2379

I spent the rest of the day wandering around the Collins and thinking about what Zoya had said. We saw the CPJCT in the same light, even if not in the exact same way. To be honest, I thought as much about Zoya herself as about what she said. I'd be able to put her in for her captain's board in a little over a stanyer. A lot could happen, a lot could change, in a stanyer. Around 1700 I'd stopped wandering and put on my running shoes, clocking in twenty laps before hitting the shower and getting ready for dinner with my counterpart.

Beth met me at the foot of the Chernyakova's ramp with a smile. Slacks and jackets appeared to be the uniform of the day. Her outfit mirrored Zoya's from earlier in the day with a charcoal pullover under a navy blue jacket. "Thank you for joining me, Ishmael."

"My pleasure. I always feel the need to get off the ship whenever I can. So much of our time is spent in places where 'stepping outside' isn't really an option."

She laughed a little. "So true. What's your dining pleasure this evening?"

"I'm adventurous. Any place you want."

"I need a steak," she said. "Any recommendations?"

"I know just the place." I headed toward the main plaza and she fell into step. "Pip showed me. His family owns it. Great steak."

"I've wandered around the station a bit, but it's surreal. Unless you look up and notice there's no sky, it could be anywhere."

I glanced around. "Not anywhere. We're clearly not out-doors, even without looking up."

She pursed her lips. "Explain."

"No wind. No birds. Sure there's the sound of vehicle traffic, but the sounds are all wrong."

"Well, there are trees and gardens and plantings every-where," she said. "You can even stop and smell the flowers, if you're so inclined."

I laughed. "True, but they don't have weather. No fog. No rain. No storms."

She pursed her lips and nodded. "Is that a bad thing?"

"Not at all. Just I have a hard time forgetting that I stepped out of one artificial environment and into another."

"Yet you still look forward to it."

"Like you said. A chance to walk in a straight line without running into a bulkhead." I grinned.

"You've spent some time here. What's with all the shops?"

"What about them?"

"On Dark Knight I saw a few specialty shops and the like, but here? Artists row? The theater district? There are whole shops of furniture and furnishings. Kitchen supply stores."

"You didn't see them on Dark Knight but they're there. Back in the residential sections."

"I'm just—why?"

"Well, it's not like you can shuttle down to the surface. The only significant planet is the gas giant. In a lot of ways, Mel's is the cultural hub of the Western Annex. Christine Maloney's art galleries can't match the scope of what's here." We came out of the passageway and started across the main plaza. "I'm pretty sure this is where she got the inspiration for opening her galleries. There are only a few galleries in all of the High Line. I suspect there are more than that, just here on Mel's."

She frowned and studied the deck as we walked. "This is really challenging my conception of the Toe-Holds."

"Mr. MacBradaigh is struggling with it, too."

She chuckled and looked over at me. "I suspect he is. How's he taking it?"

"He's doing better than I would have expected back on the orbital in Newmar."

"Well, that first view of Dark Knight told me how wrong I'd been. Spending a few days there just rubbed my face in it." She looked around. "This? The planters. The air quality. Hell, the trees? Do you know the story of the Wizard of Oz?"

"Oh, yes. Mother was an ancient lit professor. I know a lot of the old stories. You think this is Oz?"

She chuckled. "Let's just say I'm a lot more sympathetic to the idea that travel broadens the mind."

"We should have invited him along. He's looking for guidance in his research."

"I'd have thought he'd have a framework already built." She looked at me. "He doesn't?"

"I think he did, but it went poof as soon as he stepped foot on Dark Knight." I turned down the alley that led to the restaurant. "I'll give him credit. He discovered a lot of places I wouldn't have expected him to. Drew some useful conclusions even."

"Like what?"

"He found the miner's hangout and noted that the diner off the docking gallery didn't cater to spacers."

She raised her eyebrows. "That was a surprise to him?"

"Let's just say he brought a bit of baggage with him. He bemoaned the fact we didn't bring an ethnographer along. Somebody trained in studying cultures and the people in them."

"I can't blame him for that. Did Alys know what a job she'd set for him?"

"I'm pretty sure. She couldn't send more. At least not yet."

"Politically, you mean?"

I nodded and stopped in front of the door. "This is it."

She looked around. "This is what?"

I pointed to the door. "The restaurant."

"You're kidding. It's in a maintenance closet? Where are the signs? Where's the menu? Where are the people?"

I pointed up to the sign above the door. It had changed since the last time I saw it. "That's the sign."

She looked up at a flickering neon tube formed in the letter Q. "What's that mean?"

"It means that Pip's Uncle Quentin owns it, I think. You ready to go over the rainbow?"

She blinked at me a couple of times. "Sure. Long as there's steak there, I'll take on the wanton witch of the wizard."

"Wicked Witch of the West," I said.

She laughed. "I knew it had W's in it."

I stepped up to the door and rapped a knuckle in the approved pattern, hoping it hadn't changed since we'd been there last.

The shutter opened with a startlingly loud snap. "Yeah? Whadda ya want?"

"Mel sent me," I said.

"Mel's dead."

"What's your point?" I asked.

He slammed the shutter closed and the door opened. "Welcome back, Captain Wang. Good to see you again."

Beth looked at me with the strangest expression but didn't say anything.

"Thank you, Milton. Two for dinner?"

He nodded. "Right this way, sir." He led us through the dim labyrinth of tables and dividers. He stopped beside a cozy booth. "Will this be satisfactory?"

"Perfectly. Thank you."

He waited for us to slide in on opposite sides of the table before placing the menus in front of us. "Satine will be with you shortly. Enjoy your meal." He nodded and disappeared toward the front of the house.

"What is this place?" she asked.

"This is a recreation of an ancient, well, I suppose you could call it a bar. They also have the best steaks outside of The Ranch and pride themselves on being discreet."

"Why the theater at the front door? Don't they want people to eat here?"

I chuckled and scanned through the menu. "At one time, way back on Earth, alcohol was banned. I don't know the full story but there's a lot of literature about the time period and location. People found ways to make money off selling it anyway. You just had to know where to go and the pass phrase to get in." I grinned at her. "Anybody who knows about this place knows the password."

"What was it?" she asked, looking around the dining room. "I might want to come back here. It's so quiet."

"They've got white noise generators running. It's not actually quiet but your ears think it is."

"How do I get back in?"

"You remember the knock?" I tapped it out on the table. "That pattern. Then Milton, or whoever has door duty, will open the hatch and ask something like 'What do you want.' The answer has been 'Mel sent me' for some time now." I shrugged. "I don't know what to do if it changes. Ask Pip, probably."

"He said something back to you. What was that? Something about Mel?"

"'Mel's dead.' Then you ask him 'What's your point?' and he opens the door."

She shook her head and started reading the menu. "Crazy, but it must work." She cast a meaningful glance around the busy dining room. "All these people know the secret."

"Well, maybe not all of them. Only one person in the party needs to."

She glanced up at me. "Would he really keep you out if you didn't know?"

I laughed. "The first time Pip brought me here, he didn't know it. The doorman wouldn't open the door. Pip went back into the plaza and asked one of the locals."

She chuckled. "Well, it can't be that big a secret if a random local knew it."

"True." I picked my favorites off the menu, marking them mentally before closing it up and putting it where Satine could get it.

"You already know?"

"I've been here before. I try to get dinner here at least once a trip."

A curvy brunette in a black dress sashayed up to the table. "Evening, folks. I'm Satine and I'll be happy to take care of you this evening. Can I start you out with a drink?"

"What's on tap? Last time I had a porter. It was quite good but I've forgotten the name," I said.

"Blind Tiger?"

"That's it. Is it available?"

She nodded. "It's a staple now." She looked at Beth. "And for you?"

"Something in a dry red?"

"We've a nice house syrah. It's one of the favorites among both the staff and customers. Good body. Excellent nose and works well with the beef."

"I'll have a glass of that."

She nodded. "Appetizers?"

"Let us look a bit," I said. "It's her first time here."

"Of course." She gave us a smile. "I'll just get your drinks and we'll see how you're doing when I get back."

She swayed off between the tables.

"She's something," Beth said without looking up.

"She knows her product and her clientele. Every person here does, I bet. Well, the staff anyway."

She glanced up at me over the top of her menu. "I should hope so." Her amusement reached all the way to eyes. "I'll be here all night looking at this menu. What do you recommend?"

"There's a rib-eye steak about halfway down the list of 'Prime Cuts.' Usual sides are baked potato and some kind of steamed or roasted vegetable. Comes with a salad first course. She'll bring a dessert menu to tempt us with when we finish."

She scanned down, nodding. "That what you're having?"

"Yup. It's not the biggest cut but very satisfying. I hate walking away feeling stuffed."

She nodded and folded her menu up, placing it on top of mine. "Sounds about right to me. Ms. Sharps is an excellent chef, by the way."

"I know." I grinned at her. "I hired her, remember? Chief Bashar has risen to the occasion. We're the lucky recipients of some fancy cooking that most spacers don't even get in port." I shrugged. "I still eat somewhere else when I have a choice. Nothing against home cooking, but I can eat there when we're underway."

Satine returned with our drinks and a smile. "Know what you want?"

I gave her my order and Beth nodded. "I'll have the same."

"I'll get that order right in. Would you like your salads now?"

Beth nodded again.

I said, "Yes, please."

"Be right back." She took the menus with her when she left.

I lifted my beer in a toast. "Cheers."

She tapped her glass against mine. "To adventure."

I laughed and took a sip of the porter. It was just as good as I remembered, and a happy sigh bubbled out of my chest.

"That good?" she asked.

"You know how it is when you remember something was really good? But you go back to it later and the actual experience doesn't live up to the memory?"

"I do indeed."

"This lives up to the memory, and that makes me happy."

She grinned and took a sip of her wine, nodded and took another. "This is excellent, too." She shook her head. "Where do they get wine out here?"

"I'm pretty sure they get it the same place everybody does. Fermented crushed grapes."

"It can't be that simple. Growing grapes in space?"

"Why not? There's a coffee plantation in one of the neighboring systems. I had some of their coffee at lunch. It was superb."

"I didn't think there were terraformed planets in the Toe-Holds. Isn't that why they're Toe-Holds and not part of the Confederated Planets?"

"Who said there was a planet?"

She sat back a little and blinked a couple of times. "You said plantation and I immediately jumped to the conclusion. No, huh?"

"I was told a station. Whoever set it up had the right idea. Getting the correct soil is apparently the major hurdle."

She took another appreciative of the wine. "Whatever they're doing, they're doing it right. This is quite good."

Satine showed up with our salads and a small basket of rolls. "Here you go. We'll have your steaks up by the time you're ready for them."

"Thank you. Can you tell us where the wine came from?" I asked.

She smiled. "The source?"

I nodded.

"Mel's youngest son, Ernest Colby, started a vineyard over in Consort only a few stanyers after Mel got this place up and running. He's got quite an operation now with several grapes. Our cabernet and pinot noir both come from there as well. I think the syrah is the best of them, although he's got some riesling that is really coming along nicely."

"How does he manage the terroir on a station?" Beth asked.

"I'm sure I have no idea." Satine grinned. "I just enjoy the wine."

Beth chuckled. "Thank you."

"My pleasure, Captain. Enjoy your salad. I'll go check on your dinners." She sailed off toward the next table.

I drizzled a bit of the oil and vinegar over the greens and dug in. The mix was equal parts soothing crunch and peppery accent with the occasional fruity cherry tomato. I looked over to see an almost beatific expression on Beth's face as she chewed. "Good, huh?"

She smiled and nodded, finishing her bite before answering. "If the steak is as good, you may need to find a new skipper for the Chernyakova. I'm staying here."

"I'm in trouble then. Or maybe Pip is. The steak is at least as good."

She laughed and took a sip of wine. "He's a piece of work, isn't he?"

"Oh, yes." I took another forkful of greens. "He's mellowed some in his old age."

"Really?" Her eyebrows climbed up and then fell back down. "What was he like? He comes across as almost manic now."

"Oh, he's always been that way. He's focused a lot more in the last couple of stanyers. Bringing Zoya and Natalya on board was a big change in the command structure. The only major crew shakeup we've had."

"There's a story there?" she asked, reaching for one of the rolls and breaking it open over the remains of her salad.

"Yeah." I finished the last of the lettuce and placed my fork across the plate. "I don't know how much I should say."

"Trade secrets?" She tilted her head to the side. "I don't mean to pry."

"He's the CEO in both our companies. I've known him for decades. I don't want to color your perceptions of him by showing you his baby pictures."

Her eyes went wide. "You don't mean that literally, I hope."

I chuckled. "No. I don't have his baby pictures, although I've met his father and some of his extended family. I know his Uncle Quentin and Aunt P." My mind blanked for a moment. "Penelope, if I remember." I shrugged. "We always refer to them as Aunt P and Uncle Q. They run a fast packet called the Bad Penny. Or used to. It's been a while."

"That's how you know Quentin Carstairs owns this place?"

"Yeah."

"You two got together as ratings under Alys Giggone?"

"Yeah. I lucked into a quarter share berth when my mother died and I had to leave Neris."

She winced. "That had to have been tough."

I nodded. "You don't get to pick your tragedies, but everybody has them."

Satine interrupted the blue mood with two plates of steak and the aroma of seared beef and onions. She put a plate in front of each of us and took the empty salad plates away in a few deft movements.

"Merciful Maude, this smells amazing," Beth said.

"Is there anything else I can get you?"

"Nothing for me," Beth said.

"For you, Captain?" Satine asked.

"I'm good. I've been here before and know how good this is." I nodded across the table. "She said she wanted a steak. I knew it had to be here."

"Well, enjoy. I'll be around in a bit to check on you." With that, she moved away, heading back toward the kitchen with our empty plates.

I carved off a bit of steak and let the flavors explode in my mouth. Savory beef. A sweet hint of grilled onion. Black pepper. Even a little garlic. It melted in my mouth and I melted a little myself, just enjoying the food for a moment.

I paid homage to my dinner for a few ticks, letting the peaceful almost-quiet surround me and the good food settle. Feeling the first blush of enjoyment moving toward satiation, I took a sip of my porter. "Did you always want to be a captain?"

She looked over at me and shrugged, chewing and swallowing before answering. "You mean when I was a kid?"

"Yeah. Did you see yourself growing up and sitting in the big chair?"

She chuckled and took a sip of her wine. "No. I never expected to make it to the Academy, let alone graduate and move up the ladder."

"Why's that?"

"My parents wanted me to be a lawyer."

"That's a good profession. Didn't appeal to you?"

"Too many hoops." She grimaced. "Bigger fool me for thinking becoming an officer would be easier, I suppose." She shook her head, taking up knife and fork again. "For a time, I thought I might have liked to be a teacher."

"What happened?"

She picked up the last piece of steak on her plate and shrugged. "I turned ten and didn't have to go to school anymore." She grinned and tucked the steak into her mouth.

I laughed and finished off my own steak, clearing my plate of the baked potato in the process.

"What about you?" she asked. "Aspirations toward space?"

I placed my utensils on my plate and pushed it back from the edge of the table. "No. I didn't know it was possible until I needed to get off Neris. I didn't know what I wanted to do. My mother wanted me to attend the university there. I'd just given in to her when she was killed in a vehicle accident."

"What would you have studied?"

"Biology, probably. Maybe botany. That was their premier program, because of the granapple crops."

"What was it like, living on a corporate planet?"

I sipped my porter and tried to remember. "We lived in the university enclave. I didn't see much of the planet outside of the campus. I was forced to leave at eighteen, so I never really got the chance to explore it on my own."

"You ever wonder why they do that?" she asked, sliding her own plate back and leaning forward over her nearly empty wineglass.

"What? Restrict residency?"

She nodded.

"It does seem odd, but it's common in the corporate leased systems. At least the ones I'm aware of."

"Same way over in Ciroda. Made me wonder if it's some kind of corporate agreement with the Confederated Planets. Maybe a rule in their leases that requires them to do it."

I pondered that for a few heartbeats, feeling my eyes narrowing as I thought. "What advantage would that give the CPCJT?"

She shook her head. "I don't know, but it just seems weird that the surplus populations in all those systems gets shuffled off planet, if they can't get jobs." She took the last sip from her glass. "Why would you think it gave the CPJCT an advantage?"

"I'm just that cynical, I guess. They don't do anything that's not in their favor, one way or another."

"Including turning a blind eye to the Toe-Holds?"

"Yeah. I wonder if Alys realizes just what kind of response she's going to get to her curriculum changes."

She placed the empty glass beside her plate and shrugged. "She's never struck me as being either overly cautious or overly oblivious. You don't think it's going to change the official stance, do you?"

I thought about that for a bit. "Probably not. It wouldn't be too hard to maintain the fiction to the public at large. It's going to change the Academy, though."

She frowned at that. "You think? How?"

"Just the awareness among the cadets will cause the faculty to have to shift their thinking. If they start teaching doctrine that's counter to the official dogma, it will make some of them ask some pointed questions. If only of themselves."

She grinned. "You think they have that much awareness?"

I laughed. "Maybe not all. Some do, certainly. It'll spread to other departments."

"You think cadets will question the authorities?"

I shook my head. "That's not what they teach, but those who think for themselves will see the dichotomy. They'll graduate knowing the truth, or as much of it as the faculty review process will allow."

She frowned. "You think they'll try to squelch it?"

"Almost certainly."

Satine showed up with the dessert menus. "Everything good here?"

"Delicious," Beth said. "The wine, superb. Great recommendation."

"Thank you. Did you save room for dessert?" She waved the menus in the air. "Lots of choices."

I shrugged and looked to Beth. "Your call."

She looked at her empty plate and glass before shaking her head. "I think I'm done. It was terrific and I'll definitely be back."

"Same here." I flexed my thumb but Beth shook her head. "My treat this time."

Satine smiled and tucked the menus under her arm as she gathered the plates at the side of the table before handing the tab to Beth. "Sorry, Skipper. You asked first, but seniority rules here, Captain."

Beth's eyebrows rose a fraction, but she smiled as she left a tip and pressed her thumb against the sensor. "You calling me old?"

"Not at all. I'm acknowledging your greater wisdom." Satine grinned back at her.

Beth laughed and thumbed the tab.

"Thanks for coming in this evening. Hope to see you again." Satine gave us a little bow and headed off to the next table even as a couple of bus people approached with a tray.

We made good our escape, leaving them room to work. Background noise came back when we stepped out into the alley.

"That's astonishing," she said, tugging on her earlobe. "It didn't feel strange inside. Everything seems so loud now."

I nodded and headed for the main plaza. "It'll pass soon, but you're right. They have the white noise generators turned up all the way in there."

She glanced at me. "Is there a reason for that?"

I shrugged. "I can guess it's to attract business customers. It would be a great place to have a meeting that you didn't want to risk somebody overhearing."

"Wouldn't you rent a private room for that?"

"I would. Pip would. Would everybody?" I shrugged again. "I suspect a lot of business happens as a result of 'Hey, let's grab a bite and chat' kinds of interactions."

She nodded and we strolled along. "Interesting observation."

"What's your pleasure now?"

"Can we just stroll about a bit? I need to get back to the ship pretty soon. We're getting underway tomorrow afternoon."

"Sure. I've got the early morning watch tomorrow, but it's not that late yet."

She glanced at me. "You're on the rotation? I thought you were just doing days."

"I was, but I didn't like what it did to the sections, having a different officer in charge but only during the day watch. I asked Zoya to put me back in the rotation. It's working out, I think."

We strolled around the plaza for half a stan until she angled us back toward the docking gallery.

"Where are you on fraternization?" she asked, after a long pause in the small talk.

I looked at her, surprised at the question. "How do you mean?"

She glanced at me. My expression must have given away my consternation. "In the crew. Chain of command stuff."

"It's not something we encourage, but it's not forbidden. We have enough crew and enough posts that nobody needs to work with somebody they have a personal problem with."

"What about in officer country?"

I sighed. "That's a smaller cadre, but my policy has been to take it on a case by case basis. Why? You have a problem?"

"No." Her answer was too quick but I didn't call her on it. "I just figured that Mr. Carstairs would be consistent across his companies. If you had a policy, I could expect he'd want me to follow the same one."

"Good bet, but Pip's really good at not bumping my elbow. Crew management is definitely my problem and he's never offered to influence it." I gave her a side-eyed glance that she caught.

She shrugged and I thought she might have colored slightly, but the dim evening lighting made it difficult to tell. "Good to know."

"Anything you want to share?" I asked. "Captain to captain?"

She shook her head, looking down and biting her lips together. "No. Just wondered how the company looked at it." She glanced over at me. "I'm not used to having quite this much latitude."

"Big companies have big bureaucracies to support them. They can't be as nimble as we can."

She nodded. "I spent all of my career at Saltzman. Except for that first stanyer as third mate." We got almost to the docking gallery before she spoke again. "Saltzman cut me loose when my wife left me. I guess I'm still processing that a little."

"Had to have been hard. Double whammy."

She glanced at me and nodded. "That's why I went back to Port Newmar. Lick my wounds. After a couple of months,

Alys's offer sounded really good. Skipper of an established ship with a good track record with a small company." She grinned. "You and Mr. Carstairs threw me for a loop and kicked me down the stairs with this Toe-Hold thing." She sighed. "Sorry I took it so badly."

"That jump's behind us."

We stopped at the docking gallery and waited for a troop of boisterous spacers to stride past.

"What do you think is going to happen to the ships after our tour is up?" she asked.

I drew in a deep breath and blew it out. "That's the big question, isn't it."

"You know the Chernyakova's your ship, right? I'm just keeping the seat warm."

I chuckled and shook my head as we stepped out in the foot traffic, heading for our locks. "Don't bet on it."

She gave me a long look. "What are you thinking?"

"It's too early to say. We're not even halfway through this."

"But there's the real possibility that the Academy will shut down the program once they learn what we're doing out here."

I nodded. "That's a possibility. There are a lot of possibilities with various levels of probability attached. With a little careful timing, we could easily get a second load of cadets and be gone before the trustees discover just how subversive we're being."

"That's just kicking the ball down the field, isn't it?"

"Yeah, but it's a big field." I grinned at her. "Why? You thinking of hanging it up?"

Her eyes looked tired for a moment. "No. I've thought about it, but this is all I know. It's going to take a while for me to put together the kinds of funds I'd need to retire."

"You're in a good place to make that happen. I should know."

She chuckled a little and we stopped at her lock. "You're a good man. Thanks for the pep talk."

I studied her face. She looked tired. Maybe scared. "Here's what I believe. It's not what I know, but what I think will happen."

She nodded.

"Sooner or later, the Academy will shut down this project. They may sell the ship to add to their endowment. We'll have two full crews, most of whom will have specialist ratings or at least be advanced juniors."

"That's my fear," she said.

"Why? What do you think Pip will do?"

She shook her head. "I don't know him well enough to predict."

"Well, Pip's not going to put anybody ashore. Natalya's already talked about adding another Barbell to her company. Zoya has the funds to buy a ship of her own when she gets her ticket. So could I, for that matter."

She blinked. "Would you?"

"What? Buy my own ship? Be an owner again?"

She nodded.

I looked down the gallery, letting my mind catch up with my mouth. "Maybe. Depends on the circumstances. Tractors are going to be game-changers in the Toe-Holds over the next couple of decades."

"You like those ships, don't you." A faint smile curved her lips. "You talk about them a lot."

"My first command was a tractor. I know they get short shrift in the fleet, but they're credit mills. They're overengineered, run with a short crew, and can turn a profit in stations that a Barbell can't afford to dock at."

"But you didn't come out to the Toe-Holds in a tractor, did you?"

"No." I shrugged. "I still made out pretty well with a captain's share in the High Line."

"Interesting perspective, Ishmael. Thanks for that."

"Us captains have to stick together," I said with a smile. "Safe voyage, Skipper."

"Same to you. You're only going to be a couple of days behind us."

"Jump error is always the wild card. We might dock at The Ranch before you, depending on how it shakes out."

"I'm not used to this time table. We're carrying twice as many cans out here."

"Yeah. And the costs are about the same on an annual basis. The killer is having to get into and out of the deep gravity wells in the High Line."

She sighed and shook her head. "No wonder they don't want people to know about this."

I raised my eyebrows.

"Who'd voluntarily run cargo there when it's so much more profitable here?"

"That's the question, all right." I shook my head. "I suspect it's why the CPJCT is so coy about it. The only times we took the Chernyakova out of the Toe-Holds was to meet the board at Port Newmar."

She chuckled and keyed her lock open. "Thanks for keeping me company, Ishmael. You've given me a lot to think about."

"You're welcome. My treat on The Ranch."

"I'll be ready for another steak by then." She gave me a grin and climbed the ramp.

I headed down the gallery toward the Collins's berth. I may have given her some food for thought, but our dinner made me realize just how much I depended on Pip to keep me entertained. Taken in juxtaposition with lunch with Zoya, I found I greatly preferred the latter.

I glanced back at the closing lock and wondered what her question about fraternization was all about.

CHAPTER NINETEEN
MEL'S PLACE: SEPTEMBER 4, 2379

I got to the Collins in time to meet orbital security pressing the lock call button. The officer looked up as I approached. "Problem?" I asked.

"You are?" she asked, as the lock levered up.

"Captain Ishmael Wang."

She nodded and Mr. Jenson came down the ramp.

"How can we help you?" he asked.

"This is your skipper?" she asked.

Mr. Jenson nodded. "Evenin', Cap."

"Mr. Jenson." I nodded back.

The officer pulled out her tablet and flipped open a screen, holding it up for me to see. "This one of yours?"

The image showed a battered face framed by an autodoc pod. Her eyes were closed. "Looks like Nunnelee," Mr. Jenson said.

I nodded in agreement. "Wiper Jennifer Nunnelee. What happened?"

"Bar fight. By the time we got there, it was all over but the bleeding." She flipped her tablet back around. "She was unconscious so we took her to medical." She punched a few keys on her tablet and my tablet bipped. "I've sent you the report including her location."

I pulled up the message. "No other of our crew was involved?"

The officer shook her head. "According to the witnesses, she was alone."

279

I frowned as I read down through the report. "Wait. This says she started the fight."

The officer gave me a wry grin. "Yeah. We checked that pretty thoroughly. Surveillance footage showed it pretty clearly and corroborated all the witness accounts."

"What the—?" Mr. Jenson said.

"That's the question we'd like answered," the officer said. "Unfortunately, I suspect the answer is a common one."

"Which is?" I asked.

The officer shrugged. "She's a mean drunk."

I blinked a couple of times processing the answer. "So she got liquored up and started swinging?"

"Pretty much."

I sighed. "So many questions. So little time."

The officer chuckled. "It happens. More often than you think."

I finished scanning down the report. "You're not kicking her off the station?"

"No, so long as the damages get paid, nobody's pressing charges. No charges, no problem." She shrugged. "First time's free. Second time's a lot more expensive."

I nodded. "Thanks. Any word on when she'll be out of the pod?"

"Medics will keep her until 0800. You might want to send somebody to collect her. She took quite a beating."

I nodded. "Thanks, again."

She gave me a jaunty, two-fingered salute before heading back down the gallery.

I forwarded the report to Pip and holstered my tablet.

Mr. Jenson shook his head. "That doesn't add up."

"Does seem odd that she'd be alone, drunk, and pick a fight."

"She didn't leave alone. She left with Healey and Brooke?"

"Good question. They're still out?"

Mr. Jenson frowned. "Let me check the log. They might have come in while I was taking a head break."

I followed him up the ramp and waited while he checked the rosters.

"They're still out," he said after a half a tick.

"Mr. Carstairs?"

"He's out, sar. So's Ms. Regyri."

"When Mr. Carstairs returns, would you tell him I'd like to see him before he hits the rack?"

"Aye, aye, sar."

"Thank you, Mr. Jenson. Mr. Cartwright has the OD?"

"Yes, sar. He's in the office."

"Thanks."

He grinned. "All part of the service, Skipper."

I stuck my head into the office on the way by and Mr. Cartwright looked up from his console.

"Evening, Captain. How was dinner?"

"Good steak. Good company. Coming back, I intercepted station security at the lock." I pulled out my tablet. "I'm sending you a report for the log. Ms. Nunnelee is in medical. We'll need to send somebody to collect her in the morning. If you'd make the log entry, I'll have the watch by then and will take it from there."

His eyes widened as his console bipped. "Ms. Nunnelee? What happened?"

"It's in the report. She was on the losing end of a bar fight."

"What? Somebody jumped her? Was she alone?"

"Apparently she started it."

His jaw dropped. "Another one?"

"Another one?" I asked. "Has she been in other fights?"

"No. I mean we had Jacobs on Dark Knight. Now Nunnelee here. Do all these people have anger management issues?"

In spite of the seriousness, his response started a chuckle out of me. "A question we'll be asking when Ms. Nunnelee gets back."

He eyed the chrono. "You crashing now, Skipper?"

"I'm going to get changed and wait up for Mr. Carstairs. I've already sent him the report so I don't expect him to be too late."

"Mr. Carstairs?"

"He's not just the cargo master."

The credit apparently registered and he nodded. "CEO. Got it." He shook his head. "Sorry, Skipper."

"No worries. He's really good at compartmentalizing this stuff. It's easy to overlook the fact that he's actually in charge of the company that owns the ship they let me be the captain of."

"I'll make the log entry," he said.

"I'll be in the cabin."

He nodded.

I swung by the mess deck and waved to Ms. Vincent as I drew a mug of coffee from the urn.

She looked up at me from her tablet, a little bleary-eyed but awake. "Evening, Skipper."

"Studying for able spacer, Ms. Vincent?"

"I am, Skipper, and also looking at engineman."

I took a fortifying sip. "Cross-training?"

She nodded. "I'm focused on able spacer because credits." She shrugged and grinned. "Full share is twice as good as half."

"A sound assessment."

She nodded. "But there's not a lot of new material in the engineman exam. Some extra hazards and dangers stuff. Basic watchstanding doesn't change much between deck and engineering at our level. May as well give it a try."

I thought of Ms. Nunnelee in the doc pod and nodded. "Never know when those skills might come in handy. Carry on, Ms. Vincent."

"Good night, Skipper."

I made my way up to the cabin and traded my civvies for a uniform. I had just about settled at my console when Pip hit the door.

"What the hell?" he asked by way of greeting, breezing in and plopping in his usual chair.

"I don't know more than was in the report," I said. "Where's Natalya?"

"She went to medical to check on Nunnelee. How do you want to handle the damages?"

"Ship will pay them. In fact . . ." I fired up the console and made the payments against my personal account. "There.

That way they're settled and less likely to grow. We can figure out whether to dock Ms. Nunnelee's pay when she gets back."

"Will you confine her to the ship?"

"Probably. I want to talk to her before I make a decision. I'm not sure what the liberty schedule is, but she'll have at least one more watch before we pull out of here so that'll take a chunk out of the possible time in any event."

He nodded. "Based on the images, she'll need some recuperation time as well."

Natalya breezed in and took a seat. "She'll be out of the pod in the morning. Medic says she's got a lot of bruising, some cuts. No broken bones, but she's gonna hurt."

"Are you as surprised by this as I am?"

Natalya pursed her lips and sighed. "I probably should be."

Pip's head ratcheted around and he stared at her. "But?"

"She's got a hair trigger. She's never come to blows on the ship, at least not that I know of. But she has a temper and it has gotten away from her."

"You'd think that would have come up at the Academy, wouldn't you?" I asked.

She blew out a breath, her lips making a buzzing sound. "You'd think, but I can see where the rigid rules of discipline might bottle up the explosion."

Pip shook his head. "What are you saying?"

She glanced at him. "I'm saying that being at the Academy is designed to be maddening, and the only thing keeping it in check is exhaustion and the fear of expulsion."

Pip's jaw dropped.

"She's not wrong," I said.

He looked at me like I'd grown a second head. "What?"

"Think about it. College is hard enough. Add in the military trappings. Inspections, marching drills, enforced exercise, and restrictions on movement? That's on purpose. Part of it is to get cadets used to being in positions of command. Part of it is just pressure-cooking them to see if anybody pops a cork."

He frowned. "What do you base that on?"

"Seems logical. I may be wrong on that, but it makes a certain amount of sense."

He sighed and shook his head. "That seems overly manipulative."

Natalya grinned at him. "I think the phrase you're looking for is 'overtly manipulative.'"

He shot her a grumpy look, eyebrows pulled down and his lips pressed together.

"Don't look at me like that. It's not like they hide it. It's in the catalog. They spell it out in writing. They tell you what's involved. They just don't call it manipulation."

He harumphed.

She shrugged. "Call it like I see it."

"What do you need from me?" Pip asked, looking across the console at me.

"Just wanted to keep you in the loop as CEO. It's a crew problem so I'll deal with it."

"She's my crew," Natalya said. "Can I have first crack?"

"You bet. I was going to suggest you go pick her up in the morning, anyway."

She frowned and glanced at the chrono. "Don't you have the duty in a few hours?"

"Yeah. Thanks for coming back so fast." I grinned. "I was worried I'd be up half the night."

She looked at the time again and stood. "Come on, Pip. Let the skipper get in a few stans before he goes on duty."

He rose and followed her out, stopping at the door. "What is it with these people?"

I snorted. "I'm not sure. First trips are fraught with peril for everybody. We just happen to have a larger contingent of first-timers."

He paused, looking off into the distance for a moment. "That's true. Something to consider if we do this again."

"What, take fewer people on as quarter shares?"

"No, but knowing the propensity for quarter shares to get into mischief, we might be able to guard against some of it."

"We still have a few months and plenty of people who haven't gotten into trouble yet," I said. "I'm open to suggestions for when we get to The Ranch."

He chuckled and waved as he left.

Mr. MacBradaigh joined Zoya and me for breakfast in the wardroom. "Good morning. Is this a private party?"

I laughed and waved him in. "Join us. We've just settled in."

"You're pretty chipper for somebody who got as little sleep as you did," he said, coming in and helping himself to the buffet on the sideboard.

"Lots of practice." I took a sip of coffee and dug into Chief Bashar's egg bake casserole. "You were up late yourself?"

He collected a cup of coffee on the way by and took his usual seat near the foot of the table. "I came back early last evening. I had a lot of work to do that didn't entail meandering around a strange station at night."

"Oh?" Zoya asked. "Anything interesting?"

He fortified himself with a sip of coffee and nodded. "The newsie archives here go back to the first months. Melisande Colby featured prominently in the earliest articles. Understandably."

"What is that? Two centuries?" Zoya asked, lifting her own mug and cupping it between her palms. "Two and a half?"

"Something like that, yes." Mr. MacBradaigh grinned as he dug into his food. "The first iteration of the station really was little more than an airlock on an empty cargo can. Older design than the Barbell uses now, but something very similar."

"Mark fours, probably," Zoya said.

He looked up, surprised, his fork halfway to his mouth. "Yes. Precisely. Mark fours. I don't know what that means, but that's what I read. I assume they were large, obviously empty shells for transporting large volumes of materials."

She nodded. "Exactly. They're a bit smaller than the current Barbell cans but still big enough to make you feel tiny if you're standing in one."

Mr. MacBradaigh's eyes widened. "You're familiar with them?"

"They were common in the belts for transferring raw ore to the smelters. A lot of the early mining outpost stations used the empty cans as a foundation. They're airtight, ruggedly built, and have a considerable volume. Toss in a small environmental section to manage the air and water. The power requirements were minuscule. The hard part was keeping them positioned. Every time somebody docked a little too hard, it would bump the station off a bit." She sipped her coffee. "How long before they grew out of the single can?"

He took a couple of bites of his breakfast, chewing and swallowing quickly before washing it down with a slug of coffee. "Five stanyers. An article commemorating the opening of the new station inside one of the larger asteroids and the mass migration from the cans to the permanent station. By then there were multiple cans in the mix. They stripped the cans down to metal and then melted them for the first expansions. There are supposed to be plaques around the station showing where the additions were built, marking the edge of the old rock. I'm hoping to find some and collect digital images of them."

"There's one on the far side of the main plaza just past Artists' Row," Zoya said. "I think there's another halfway down the small ship docks on the other side of the station. It's really just a chunk of the original rock that's been cut and polished with a bronze plaque on it."

"Thank you for the tip. That will be my priority this morning."

"Did you find anything else interesting?" I asked.

He inhaled and blew out a sharp breath. "I've barely scratched the surface. Did you know that the Colby family split up very soon after the station proper got established?"

"I knew her son, one of them anyway, left to establish his own station over in Consort." I took a sip of my coffee. "He established a vineyard."

Zoya's eyebrows rose. "I thought you were going to mention the coffee plantation."

I laughed. "I thought that was the restaurant owner's cousin."

She nodded and scooped up the last of her breakfast from the plate, helping it along with a piece of toast. "You're right. Odd that they both chose Consort."

I shrugged. "Maybe not so odd. Maybe something with the light from the primary over there. If Mel's son had an established vineyard there, it would make for a handy neighbor."

She nodded and swallowed the last of her meal. "Good point."

Mr. MacBradaigh scraped his plate clean, his fork sounding loud in the quiet wardroom. "I've got an appointment to meet with the official historian later this morning. I'm looking forward to seeing what the station sees as historically significant about their own past. I'm hoping to get some insight into those early days beyond the overly sensationalized content from the newsie archives."

Zoya grinned at him. "Don't just leave it there. What's the skinny from the past?"

He chuckled. "Mel Colby wasn't universally admired. Or even liked. She was known for showing her workers the rough side of her tongue." He shrugged. "Yet, she allowed the newsies to operate freely on the station from the earliest days when getting enough water and air would have been less than easy."

"It's not as hard as you think," Zoya said. "The gas giant here has almost everything they needed. A smallish air processing plant, even two centuries ago, could have kept a good mix of gases with a couple of automated scoops out there." She nodded. "I take your point, though. It's interesting that she allowed the newsies to distribute unflattering stories."

"The Traveler's Guide mentioned that the Royalty group consists of more than just the one system. The similarities between this group and one of the High Line sectors are striking."

I grinned. "Do tell."

He chuckled at me. "Yes, you were right, Captain. This is so far away from the common perception of the Toe-Holds that I find myself wondering how that perception was formed to begin with."

"Propaganda is effective," Zoya said. "If you repeat it long enough, any lie can be made into a truth."

"There's an old saying about history being written by the victorious." He raised his eyebrows. "Makes you wonder who the CPJCT thinks they bested."

She grinned at him. "You're becoming something of a subversive, Mr. MacBradaigh."

"If so, I come late to the revolution, it seems."

"How are you going to deal with this when you get back to the Academy?" I asked.

He pulled a loud breath in through his nose and stared down at his empty plate. "The returning cadets? I don't see a problem. For those who know the Toe-Holds, it will be review. Perhaps a broadening of their understanding." He looked up at me. "The faculty? That's where the problems will occur."

"You have video equipment with you, don't you?" Zoya asked.

He frowned. "Yes. Why?"

"It would be easy to discount anything you say or write as being slanted or misleading." She shrugged. "Video evidence might be harder to dismiss."

He nodded. "True. Provenance would be the tricky issue."

"Proving that it shows what you claim it shows?" she asked.

He nodded again. "Precisely."

"Overwhelm them."

His head tilted a few degrees off vertical. "Overwhelm them with what?"

She shrugged. "Videos. Give them so many they can't ignore them."

"What? Walking through the stations?" He scratched the angle of his jaw. "Don't I need permission?"

"I'm not sure," she said and looked at me. "Would he?"

"Maybe. We could check with the station authorities. Maybe not show people's faces without their permission."

He pursed his lips and frowned down at his plate. "There's a standard release form in my kit."

"Do interviews. Set up in the plaza and ask people about life here at Mel's Place."

"What if they ask why?"

Zoya shrugged. "You're doing an instructional video for the school you work for. You could even tell them the school. It's not exactly a secret that we're a training vessel."

"I'd need some questions," he said, almost to himself. "A set I could use to springboard into a conversation."

The wardroom door opened and Pip breezed in, Natalya right behind him. "Good morning. Any new catastrophes?" He made his way to the sideboard without waiting for an answer.

"Nothing yet, but the day's still young," I said.

Mr. MacBradaigh looked at me. "With your permission, Captain? I've got some work to accomplish before I go ashore."

"Of course, Mr. MacBradaigh. Good luck with it."

He rose and nodded, sparing a smile for Zoya. "Thanks. Both of you. Some good ideas." He bustled himself out the door before Pip could even get around the table.

"Was it something I said?" Natalya asked.

Zoya grinned at her. "Mr. MacBradaigh is a man on a mission this morning."

Pip finished at the sideboard and took his seat while Natalya filled a plate. "Isn't he always?"

"He found the newsie archive and he's meeting with an expert on station history later," I said.

"He should video that," Zoya said. "It would make a good piece."

"Think he'll think of it?" I asked.

She shrugged and reached for the carafe to top off her coffee cup.

"What's the video for?" Natalya asked taking her seat.

"It's suddenly dawned on him that he may have a problem getting the faculty to believe him when he gets back with the new curriculum," I said.

Pip snorted. "Like it hasn't been a problem all along?"

"Yes, well, until he believed it himself, there was less of a problem," Zoya said.

Natalya toasted her with her coffee cup. "That's the truth."

"I suggested he do some video of the station and the people on it. It's easy enough to discount a written report. It's harder to ignore somebody talking to you on the screen."

"You think so?" Pip asked, spreading a little butter on his toast. "Won't they just think he faked it?"

Zoya pursed her lips and nodded. "Probably claim it's faked, yeah. If he does enough of it with enough different people in enough different places, it's going to be harder to discount it as manufactured."

"They've all got vested interests in disbelieving it," he said. "I don't think any logical argument will balance out the influence of their paychecks."

"That's why he needs to talk to people. It may be difficult to convince the Academy faculty, but the controversy would drive the videos into the public eye."

"There are plenty of people who don't have preconceived ideas. Seeing the videos won't be as jarring to them," Natalya said.

Zoya nodded.

Pip looked back and forth between the two of them. "You think it's going to get that much attention?"

"It could be a storm in the Academy, but I suspect it'll be more like a tempest in a teapot outside the hallowed halls," Zoya said.

"What about blowback?" he asked, looking at Zoya. "What's your thinking?"

She shook her head. "None of us can be hurt by it, I don't think." She paused, her mug halfway to her lips. "I'm not as certain about the cadets."

Natalya wiped her lips with a napkin. "If it comes to anything, they'll be told to shut up and forget the whole thing. Alys won't let them become collateral damage."

Zoya shrugged. "You're probably right."

Pip chased a bit of potato around his plate with his fork, frowning. "That's an aspect I hadn't considered."

"I hadn't either until just this moment," Zoya said.

"Alys has thought of it already," I said. "I'd bet on it."

Pip grinned at me. "You always were her favorite."

"You're going to pick up Ms. Nunnelee?" I asked, looking at Natalya.

She nodded and glanced at the chrono. "Medics said 0800. I've got a little time yet."

"Need backup?" Pip asked.

"I got it. We'll see what happens when we get back."

"You buying this bar fight story?" he asked.

Natalya shrugged and looked at me. "Healey and Brooke come back?"

I shook my head. "They hadn't when I relieved the watch at 0345. I asked the brow watch to bip me if and when they did."

"They're not on duty until noon," Natalya said. "It wouldn't surprise me if they scampered up the ramp at 1130."

"Still half in the bag?" Pip asked.

"They best not be, but I'll be interested to hear what they had to say about what happened last night."

"Is it just us?" Zoya asked, looking at Pip.

"What? Having trouble with the quarter shares?"

She nodded.

Pip pursed his lips for a moment. "I haven't heard anything from Beth. I'm not sure she'd notify me unless it interrupted their voyage."

"Would you check in with her?" I asked. "I had dinner with her last night. She didn't mention any issues, but then, neither did I."

"Given the number of inexperienced hands we've set loose on the station, I'd be surprised if it was just us," Zoya said.

"We have the lion's share of them, though." Pip took a sip of coffee. "I'll check with her." He pulled out his tablet and started mashing the screen.

"Might want to alert her to the issue," Natalya said. "Even if she hasn't had a problem yet, there's no guarantee she won't be the one with the problem at The Ranch."

Pip nodded and kept mashing his tablet.

"What do we have going on, other than that?" Zoya asked.

"Not a whole lot," I said, topping off my coffee to take with me. "Anybody need anything from me?" When nobody volunteered, I nodded. "In that case, I'll be working on the monthly reports."

Pip looked up. "Oh, good. It's going to be a slow quarter. Too much time in port."

"Yeah," I said, standing and heading for the door. "You'll know where to find me."

"I'll bring Ms. Nunnelee up to see you when we get back and I have a chance to talk to her," Natalya said.

I just nodded and headed for the cabin. My head felt full of cotton, even with the caffeine boost. The warm breakfast felt more like a warm lunch and it made me drowsy.

CHAPTER TWENTY
MEL'S PLACE: SEPTEMBER 5, 2379

Natalya returned with Ms. Nunnelee in tow at 0830. She parked Nunnelee outside with a curt "Wait here" and came into the cabin, closing the door behind her. She walked over and plopped into one of the chairs. "The autodoc took care of most of the hangover. She's still got some cuts and scrapes, a few bruises and residual pain, but no broken bones or sprains. She's fit for duty according to the medics."

"Is there a but?" I asked.

She shook her head but pursed her lips. "No. She doesn't appear to remember much about it. I can't tell if she was just blacked-out drunk or is playing coy."

"Tox screen show anything?"

"Alcohol." Natalya shrugged. "Nothing beyond that."

"What's your pleasure?" I asked.

She blew out a breath. "Restricted to the ship for the rest of our stay. How much were the damages?"

"Minor. A few hundred credits."

"Dock her pay for twice the amount," Natalya said. "It's not going to make a dent in her accumulated share, but it's a symbolic gesture."

"I can get behind that. Formal mast?"

"Can if you want. Do you?"

"No. Not for a bar fight. If she hadn't been injured, I'd be happy with 'beneath the captain's notice' myself." I grinned at her. "You're going to make her pay where it counts, so I'm fine letting you handle it."

She grinned. "Fair enough." She pushed herself up from the chair and crossed to open the door. "Ms. Nunnelee, front and center, if you please." She pointed into the cabin.

A rather bedraggled spacer stepped into the cabin, head high, not quite marching but close. She stood at attention in front of the console. "Sar, Wiper Jennifer Nunnelee reporting as ordered, sar."

"What do you have to say for yourself, Ms. Nunnelee?" I asked.

"Sar, I was out of line, sar."

"Yes, but that's not the question. Why did you start that fight?"

Her head twitched but she managed to refrain from shaking it. "Sar, I don't know, sar. One tick I was having a good time with Brooke and Healey, and the next thing I knew I was getting stuffed into the autodoc, sar."

"You don't know what happened to Brooke and Healey, then?" I asked.

"Sar, no, sar."

"Would it surprise you to learn that they've not returned to the ship?" I asked.

Her brow tensed for just a moment, making her eyebrows jump. "Sar, no, sar."

"Why is that, Ms. Nunnelee?"

Her response lagged for a moment. "Sar, I don't understand the question, sar."

"Very well, Ms. Nunnelee. I'm docking your pay for the amount of double the damages incurred by the ship. You're restricted to the ship for the remainder of our stay. Do you understand that?"

"Sar, yes, sar. Thank you, sar."

"At ease, Ms. Nunnelee."

She dropped the attention pose and went to at ease, looking at me.

"Do you have a problem with alcohol, Ms. Nunnelee?"

She took a breath and worried her lower lip with her teeth before answering. "Not that I know of, Captain."

"Do you drink much?"

"Very rarely, Captain." She bit at her lip again and shrugged. "You've no reason to believe that, I know."

"No reason not to, either, Ms. Nunnelee. I'm just trying to figure out what the hell happened last night."

She sighed. "I told Ms. Regyri. I have no idea, sar."

"You were with Brooke and Healey. Where did you go when you left the ship?" I asked.

"We went to a club just off the theater district. Dance club. We danced. Had a few beers." She paused and shrugged. "Probably more than a few. I don't know how many. More than three but I lost count. They kept refilling my glass even before it was empty, sar."

"Refilling?" I asked.

"We ordered by the pitcher, Captain." She shrugged.

Natalya winced and shook her head.

"How well do you know Mr. Brooke and Mr. Healey?" I asked.

She shrugged. "Classmates. We've had some classes together. We're all in the engineering division, sar." She shrugged again. "We've never dated or anything like that, Captain, if that's what you mean."

"Mr. Brooke got into a scrape on Dark Knight Station. Did you know that?"

"Yes, Captain. I think everybody on the ship knows. Mr. Jacobs complains that he's taking the fall for all of them."

I saw Natalya's eyebrows raise at that. "What do you think, Ms. Nunnelee?"

She sighed. "I think Mr. Jacobs has anger management issues, Captain."

"Do you, Ms. Nunnelee?"

"Do I what, sar? Have anger management issues?" She gave me a puzzled look.

"Yes."

"Not that I know of, Captain. No." I raised an eyebrow at Natalya, who gave me the tiniest of shrugs.

"According to the security report, you started the bar fight in which you were injured. The surveillance footage shows you striking the first blow. Does any of this ring a bell?"

Ms. Nunnelee's expression went from concerned to astonished. "I did what?" She blinked a couple of times before adding "sar."

"The report says you punched a patron and that triggered a brawl, Ms. Nunnelee."

She brought her hands out from behind her back and looked at them, front and back. "They don't hurt, sar. I'm not much of a fighter, but wouldn't I feel it?"

Natalya frowned and raised an eyebrow at me in question. I nodded and she came out from behind the young woman. "Show me your hands, Ms. Nunnelee?"

"Of course, sar." She held her hands out.

Natalya looked them over, front and back, her frown deepening. "Would you pull your sleeves up and show me your forearms?"

Ms. Nunnelee did so and Natalya looked over the bruising on Ms. Nunnelee's arms for several moments before nodded. "Thank you, Ms. Nunnelee. You can put your sleeves down now."

"Your conclusions, Ms. Regyri?" I asked.

She shook her head. "I'd really like to see the footage for myself, Captain."

"I'll see what I can do." I looked to Ms. Nunnelee. "Anything you'd like to add? Any questions?"

"No, Captain. I remember being at the dance club. Brooke and Healey were both there. Last thing I remember is sitting down after one of the dance sets ended and finding my drink full again. I was hot and sticky so I drank some more." She frowned, eyes blinking. "It's all jumbled. I was pretty loaded, I think, sar."

"Where, exactly, were Brooke and Healey?" I asked.

"They followed me back to the table from the dance floor, sar. I think Healey said something like 'Bottoms up' and picked up his glass. So I did, too." She shrugged.

"Thank you, Ms. Nunnelee. You're dismissed."

"Sar, yes, sar." She turned and left the cabin, dropping down the ladder toward engineering berthing.

Natalya stepped over and closed the door before coming back to sit down. "I know I said she has a hair trigger. She does. But if that girl threw a punch, I'll eat your hat. The purple one." She blew out a breath and leaned forward, bracing her elbows on her knees.

"No bruising?" I asked.

"Plenty of bruising. All of it on the outside of her forearms." She held up her arms in front of her face. "Block damage, not strike damage. Nothing on her knuckles. Not even an abrasion there." She ran through a few hand movements. "Even if she'd done something from one of the martial arts forms, done it for real against a live opponent, I'd have expected to see some bruising or swelling. She hasn't much meat on the side of her hand here." She held up the side of her hand to show me hers. "She's not a trained martial artist beyond what she's picked up at Port Newmar. That would leave a mark."

"Which is why you want to see the footage."

"Yes. The report says she threw the first punch. I'm not saying she didn't smack somebody with a beer glass, but that's not a punch. Something doesn't add up."

"I'll get Zoya to take the watch and head over to security."

"You want me to do it?" she asked. "I wasn't up all night like you were."

"It may take stars to get through the red tape."

"I appreciate it, Skipper."

"Comes with the job. Lemme notify Zoya and get cleaned up a little. Then I'll head out."

"Should we put out a recall on Brooke and Healey?" she asked, stopping at the door on her way out.

I paused. "Do we have any cause?"

"Only suspicion on my part," she said. "They've been off the ship a long time without even coming back for a change of clothes."

I glanced at the chrono. "It's not even 0930 yet. Checkout time's usually noon. When do they go on watch again?"

"Noon."

"I'll tell the brow to send them to you as soon as they get back aboard." I shrugged. "Even if we recalled them now, they wouldn't get here much before then. I should be back with a copy of the surveillance footage by that time."

She frowned. "You've got something?"

"No. Just a hunch."

"Spill."

"Either Brooke and Healey wound up with some company overnight and left Ms. Nunnelee to find her way home, or they didn't."

"Which? Didn't leave her to find her way home?" Her eyebrows rose. "Or found some overnight company?"

I shrugged and stifled a yawn. "Well, the concerning bit is leaving her to find her way home if she was that plastered."

"Agreed. Not a good way to treat a shipmate." She frowned and started to speak but shook her head.

"What?" I asked. "Don't do that to me."

"It's the 'Bottoms up' thing being the last solid memory."

I nodded. "I caught that, too."

She sighed. "I'll let you get on with it. I need to check on one of my crew."

I made it to the main security office just a few minutes before 1000. A desk officer waved me through to an interview room where a senior officer with gold hashmarks on his sleeve met me.

"Captain Wang. I'm the watch supervisor. Morris Pendleton. They said you want to see the footage on one of your crew?"

"Yes." I opened my tablet and showed him the report form. "I got this report last night and interviewed the crew in question this morning. I'm not saying the report is wrong, but something isn't adding up."

The supervisor sighed. "Well. I can't say you're the first one to ask. You realize the recordings almost always show the crew member is guilty?"

"I'd expect it," I said. "In this case, I'm looking for something else."

His eyebrows rose. "Mind telling me what?"

"Ms. Nunnelee left the ship with two others. Neither of them have come back. According to the report, she was alone.

According to her, the last thing she remembers is being in a dance club somewhere near the theater district."

The man frowned and nodded at the report. "This isn't a dance club."

"I didn't think it was. How close is this tavern to the theater district and a dance club?"

"Do you know the name of this dance club?"

"No. Quarter share on liberty. She didn't mention the name. I can ask if it matters."

The supervisor frowned and the tip of his tongue flicked to the corner of his mouth as he stared at the report still open on my tablet. "That pub is about halfway between the theater district and the passageway to the docking gallery. Without a name, it could be any of a half dozen places that cater to spacers." He looked up at me. "You're thinking what?"

"I'm thinking I may have a bigger problem than a quarter share who likes to swing her fists."

His eyebrows rose at that. "Well, let's see what's on the video." He typed in the report number on his tablet, and a screen on the bulkhead lit up. He fiddled with his tablet a bit; the images flickered as the time stamp rolled. "This is about a minute before the scuffle started. See your crew member? Bellied up to the bar, third one in."

"Yeah. From the back, it looks like her. That's the shirt she had on when she came back from medical this morning."

He pressed Play and the scene unfolded. Nothing happened for a few heartbeats, then a bulky man a few centimeters taller walked up to Ms. Nunnelee and leaned forward as if to speak to her. His body obscured her but in the next second the man's head jerked to the side, and he reeled back, falling to the floor. A couple of people standing nearby turned on Ms. Nunnelee and she went down hard. The scene froze.

"The barkeep got it under control real fast," the supervisor said. "Officers were on the scene in a matter of ticks. We took statements from the witnesses. They all said she swung first."

"How many is 'all?'"

"It was a quiet night. Not that many people paid attention to her." He shrugged. "Did you see what you wanted to see?"

"Can you back it up to where the guy falls down?"

He frowned but the video ran backwards a bit. "What are you looking for?"

"Watch his head turn and then look at Nunnelee's arm when he falls out of the way."

The video played out again but he froze it as soon as Nunnelee's arm showed up. He frowned. "I'm not seeing it."

"His head comes around to the left, like this." I twisted my head around so it was over my left shoulder. "Right?"

"Yeah. So."

"So, Nunnelee must have punched with her left hand, but that's her right hand reaching for her drink. She's not even turned toward him. Take it forward a bit. Her hips aren't even turned."

The supervisor frowned and punched a few keys on his tablet, zooming the image in. "Son of a ..."

"You have ID on all the people who said she hit first?"

He nodded. "Everybody thumbs their statement." He sighed. "Why would anyone do this? It makes no sense."

"Good question. There's no other video of the pub?"

"Only the entry cam. It faces the opposite direction."

"Do me a favor?"

"Depends."

"Do you have access to that cam? Can you see when she entered?"

He scowled at his tablet for a moment and then started flipping screens. He stopped for a moment and growled. "One tick, Skipper. I need to deal with bureaucracy."

"Thank you, Officer Pendleton."

He stood and nodded. "Now you've got me curious, too. It's not good for a lot of people when anybody in this department gets curious." He left me cooling my heels for about five ticks before returning and keying up his tablet again. "Sorry about that. I needed to bump it up the chain to reopen the closed case file so we can get access to supplemental evidence."

"Crossing t's and dotting i's," I said. "I know the drill."

He chuckled and turned to the screen. "Here's where we saw her before. I want the time stamp for when she came in." The video rolled backwards in high speed until she backed out of view. "That's when she arrived." He nodded and flicked the tablet, splitting the screen to show the entry cam on one side and the bar on the other for the identical time stamp. The videos rolled backwards for a tick. "That's odd. She didn't stagger in off the passageway and head for the bar." He glanced at me. "Sorry, but that's what I'd have expected to see."

"I understand. It wouldn't take that long to walk from the entrance, right?"

He nodded and hit a key on his tablet. The video kept rolling back. The timestamp reeled back almost ten ticks before Ms. Nunnelee appeared in the frame again. Officer Pendleton rolled it back a half a tick to catch her first coming into view. He started the playback but something caught my eye.

"Can you go back another half a tick?" I asked.

He glanced at me. "You saw something?"

"Maybe."

He rolled it back and the camera caught both Brooke and Healey leading her into the bar. "Freeze it there," I said.

The screen froze. "Something?"

"Those two are her missing shipmates."

"What are you thinking? They set her up?" His voice carried no surprise in it. His expression said he'd seen it before.

"I don't know. I intend to ask them when I find them again."

"You want us to watch for them?"

"Not yet. They're due back at the ship by 1130. If they don't show up, then yes."

He pulled his tablet around. "Go ahead and give me their full names. All the people who gave statements are from the station. Not a single spacer in the group." He pursed his lips and tilted his head. "Which might be odd, considering the location."

I shrugged. "It happened really fast, and if all you saw was from the back? That guy who faked the fall really sold it."

Officer Pendleton nodded. "Yes. He did, didn't he. We'll be talking to him about it. Anything else, Skipper?"

"Thank you, no. I've got lost wages to restore and an apology to make. If my lost sheep don't show up, I'll be back."

He nodded and stood, offering his hand.

I stood and shook his hand.

"Tell me. What made you curious?" he asked as he walked me back through the office.

"She didn't have bruised hands."

He stopped and looked back at me. "I thought she went to medical."

"She did. She's covered with bruises and contusions. Nothing broken but she was pretty heavily smacked around." I shrugged. "Nothing on her knuckles. Not even discoloration."

"Wouldn't the autodoc have cleared those up?"

I shrugged. "The pod can do a lot, but it didn't do much for the bruises on her arms and face beyond relieving some of the swelling."

He nodded. "My people didn't do their jobs. I'll see that they do better."

I snorted. "Don't feel too bad, Officer Pendleton. My people didn't do much better."

"Good luck, Skipper. Something tells me you're going to need it."

When I climbed the ramp back into the Collins, Mr. Keen stopped me at the watch station. "Ms. Regyri wants you to let her know when you're back aboard, Captain."

"Thank you, Mr. Keen. Would you notify her that I'm back and I'll meet her in the cabin?"

"Of course, Captain."

"Thank you, Mr. Keen." I stopped for a cup of coffee on my way past the mess deck. I could feel the grittiness in my eyes from not enough sleep. I somehow doubted that I'd be getting any very soon. Natalya met me in officer country and followed me into the cabin. "What's the scoop?"

She closed the door and took a seat as I flopped into my chair behind the console. "They came back about ten ticks after you left. Neither one of them is in great shape, but they're both sober."

"They say what they'd been up to all night?"

"Allegedly just wandering around the station. Neither of them smelled like anything but sweat and booze. They sobered up somewhere before they came back."

"Did they say anything about the fight?"

"They say they left Nunnelee in a bar. She wanted to stay and drink. They wanted to get laid."

"Well, at least they've got a rationale." I sighed.

"Uh oh. What's that sigh?"

"The fight was staged. Security has reopened the investigation."

Her eyebrows rocketed up her forehead. "What the hell? Staged?"

"The guy she's supposed to have slugged faked it. The angle of the security cam didn't show her swinging. It showed him taking a hit and falling from behind. His body blocked the view."

"How do you know he faked it?"

"It's hard to throw a left hook with your right hand. When he fell, the video showed her with an arm extended but it was her right arm, not the left. She was reaching for her drink and wasn't even turned to face him."

She snorted. "So the guy knew the camera would catch the fall but didn't count on somebody actually looking at her after?"

"He was right. Security saw what they expected to see. Big guy falling down. Helpful locals subduing the attacker."

"How many people are in on this and why in hell would they do it?"

"At least the bruiser who faked it. I don't know why he's doing it. I suspect the station security people will be having a serious word with him. The others could just be helpful citizens protecting one of their own from a vicious spacer."

She snorted. "Nunnelee?"

"You said she has a temper."

"She does, but she's maybe sixty kilos of raw fury and she's all flash. No bang. The only thing particularly sharp on her is her tongue."

I raised my eyebrows at that. "Really?"

"All right. She's not stupid. You can't be dumb and get into the Academy."

"I don't know. Mr. Jacobs isn't the brightest star in the sky."

She laughed. "No, but everybody's smart in different ways. Ms. Nunnelee is pretty good with the engineering. She doesn't have the corner on failing an easy test. Unlike some, she at least took it."

"How'd she take failing it?"

"As well as might be expected. She kicked herself once she saw the amount of the share payout." She grinned. "Nothing like waving a big pile of credits in their faces to really rub in the stupidity. We tried to tell them, but they didn't believe it. They do now."

"Think that's a factor?" I asked.

"How would some guy on the station know? What are you thinking?"

"I'm wondering if there's more to this than meets the eye. Did Healey or Brooke put the guy up to it?"

She stiffened in her seat. "That's a level of bad behavior we can't tolerate."

"Right now, it's only a suspicion. Brooke and Healey went into the bar. Nunnelee followed them in. Only Nunnelee appeared in the security footage from inside." I kicked myself mentally. "I should have had Officer Pendleton watch for them leaving on the door cam."

"Why?"

"Did they leave before or after Ms. Nunnelee was attacked?" I raised my eyebrows. "They didn't mention it?"

"No." She glanced at the chrono. "They'll be going on watch in a stan. You want to talk to them now?"

"I want to talk to them separately," I said. "You talked to them together, right?"

She nodded and frowned. "Yeah. Hindsight, I probably should have gotten them separately."

"That jump's passed. They could have agreed to some story, at least in broad terms, before coming back."

"True. What do you want to know? Whether they left Ms. Nunnelee alone in a strange bar?"

"That and whether they left a drunken shipmate to find her way back to the ship in a strange station."

Natalya sighed. "Or whether they paid some guy fifty credits to start a fight?"

"That, too."

I had Natalya page Mr. Brooke to the cabin at 1115. He arrived promptly and glanced at Natalya before saying anything. "You wanted to see me, Captain?"

"Come in, Mr. Brooke. Close the door, please."

He frowned but did as I asked. I waved him into a seat. "I know you're due on watch in a few ticks. This won't take long."

He nodded.

"Where were you when Ms. Nunnelee was attacked?"

"I'm not sure, Captain. I don't know when she was attacked, sar. I didn't know she was attacked until I got back to the ship this morning."

"Where did you go after you and Mr. Healey left her in the bar?"

He glanced at Natalya again. "We went looking for the red light district, sar."

"Did you find it?"

"No, sar. We didn't. We hit up a few more bars figuring maybe we could get lucky at closing time." He kept glancing at Natalya.

"You discovered the problem with that approach, didn't you?"

He nodded. "They don't close." He took a deep breath and blew it out his nose. "It was sometime after 0200 by the time we realized the problem, sar."

"What did you do then?"

"We just kept going, sar. We'd hit a bar. Work the room for a stan or so. Move on to the next. We gave up around

0900 and hit the diner at the head of the docks for breakfast before coming back to the ship."

"So you haven't slept?"

"No, sar."

"And you're going to sit a full watch?"

He shrugged. "That's the plan."

"Crappy plan," I said. "Ms. Regyri? What's your take on this?"

"Well, I got some sleep last night, Captain. I'm sure Mr. Brooke will manage to stay awake for his watch."

He gave her one last look, perhaps a little more alarmed than the others.

"Thank you, Mr. Brooke. If I were you, I'd swing by the mess deck for some coffee before heading aft. Dismissed."

He got up and left the cabin door open on the way out.

"Mr. Healey now?" Natalya asked.

"Yeah. I don't think it'll do any good."

She shook her head. "Me, either." She punched the key on her tablet.

Mr. Healey showed up almost immediately. He hadn't been very far away. He braced in the door frame. "Wiper Dayton Healey, reporting as ordered, Captain."

"Come in, Mr. Healey. Close the door. Have a seat."

He blinked a few times, perhaps struggling to process the break in his expected script. He nodded once then stepped in, closed the door, and sat on the edge of one of the chairs.

"How much did Mr. Brooke pay that guy?" I asked.

His jaw unhinged for a moment and his eyes went wide. "Captain?"

"The guy that started the fight in that bar. How much did Mr. Brooke pay him?" I paused. "I assume Mr. Brooke paid him. Unless you did? Did you?"

He clammed up. I saw the mental shields come down as if they were steel shutters. "I don't know what you're talking about, sar."

"Where were you when Ms. Nunnelee was attacked, Mr. Healey?"

"I don't know, sar. I didn't know she was attacked until I returned to the ship."

"What did you do after you left her in that bar?"

"We went looking for the red light district, sar."

"And you found it. Why did you pick that particular establishment?"

He shook his head. "No, sar. We didn't find it."

"Well, what did you do for nearly nine stans?"

"We went to a bunch of bars. We thought maybe we'd get lucky at closing time, but they don't close, sar."

"What did you do then?"

He shook his head. "We just kept hitting bars. One after another. Worked the room for a stan or so. Moved on to the next, sar."

"Persistence can pay dividends, Mr. Healey. Did it for you?"

He looked down, glancing at Natalya out of the corners of his eyes. "No, sar. We gave up around 0900 and went to the diner at the head of the docks for breakfast before coming back to the ship. That's when we found out about Ms. Nunnelee."

"So, neither of you got any sleep last night?"

"That's correct, sar."

"How are you planning to stay awake for your watch?"

He bit his lip and shrugged. "Probably a lot of coffee. A few jumping jacks at my station."

"Ms. Regyri? Your watchstander expects to do jumping jacks to stay awake."

"I hate to say it, Skipper, but that's probably a good strategy."

I nodded. "Fair enough. Thank you, Mr. Healey. You're dismissed. Grab some coffee and get aft to relieve the watch."

He stood and made good his escape.

I sat back down at the console and looked at Natalya. "What do you think?"

She came over and slumped in one of the chairs. "That was just too pat."

"That's my thinking too. I thought Mr. Healey might let something slip, but he's heard of the prisoner's dilemma."

"Yeah. He clammed up pretty tight." She raised an eyebrow. "Did you get what you needed?"

I shrugged. "I'm not sure. I know I need to contact Officer Pendleton and find out what they've learned."

She sighed. "It's possible they had nothing to do with it."

"Possible, but I'm choking on one key problem."

She raised an eyebrow.

"They couldn't find the red light district."

"Why is that significant?"

"All they needed to do was look it up on the station net. Same way they find the pubs and bars."

She nodded. "That's true, but there isn't a district. Sex shops are all over the place. If they were looking for a district, would they have recognized what they were looking at?"

"I know. I keep underestimating the level of stupidity."

"Theirs?" she asked.

"No. Mine." I shook my head. "I remember what it was like being a quarter share in the High Line."

She pursed her lips. "I've never been part of that High Line culture. How is it different?"

"The oh-two deck held all the pleasures for spacers. You can go up to the upper decks without a problem, but to scratch an itch? You went down to the pubs and bars on the oh-two."

"Officers, too?"

"I met some officers there. I met Al in a dance club."

"You met Al at a meat market?"

I chuckled. "Yeah. She was one of the most interesting people in the place."

Natalya chuckled. "I can only imagine." She shook her head. "What do we do about these two?"

"Keep them awake for the next watch. Wait to hear from security. If the beefcake who took the fall finds out that the neat story isn't playing, he'll rat out whoever paid him. Assuming somebody did."

She gave me a side-eyed look. "You think what? He did it for fun?"

"It's possible. It could be something as simple as sending a message to spacers to stay out of a station bar."

"Quite a message."

"I said 'could.' I want the facts before I draw any conclusions."

"You're an optimist."

"It's only one of my many flaws. It might be my largest, but I have others."

She laughed and pushed herself up out of her seat. "Speaking of sleep, shouldn't you be getting some?"

I eyed the chrono. "I've got the watch for another few ticks. Can I stay awake for lunch mess and then crash? Or just crash?"

"How hungry are you?"

A yawn caught me sideways and I had to turn my head away, covering my mouth. "Apparently not that hungry."

She snickered. "See you at dinner, Skipper." She closed the door on her way out.

CHAPTER TWENTY-ONE
MEL'S PLACE: SEPTEMBER 5, 2379

My tablet bipped me out of a sound sleep at 1615. I slapped the answer key before looking at the source. "Captain speaking."

"Captain Wang, Officer Pendleton. I thought I should let you know we found that guy who faked the fight last night."

"Fast work."

"Well, we had his thumbprint. That narrowed it down a lot."

"Yes, I suppose it would. What'd he have to say?"

He sighed. "We should have looked into him closer. When we went back to the case files and pulled his jacket? Well, let's just say he and his three buddies are known troublemakers. They won't be bothering anybody else any time soon."

"Seriously? Beating a young woman within an inch of her life was what? A prank?"

"No." He sighed again. "The helpful citizens were just looking for an excuse to get into a fight. They'll each be spending some rehabilitation time themselves. The pub will return your payment of damages, and the adjudicator has ordered them each to pay a fine for filing false reports in addition to funding a damage payment to Ms. Nunnelee for ten thousand credits. The credits should appear in her account in the next twenty-four to thirty-six hours."

"Thank you, Officer Pendleton."

"Don't thank me. Please. Really. Don't. If you hadn't been on the ball, they'd have gotten away with it. Again.

We'll be doing an internal affairs review of this incident. It's too early to say what the results might be. I'm not going to say somebody will lose a job over this, but there are going to be some pretty sorry officers before the dust settles."

I sighed, thinking of Brooke and Healey. "Well. I've got a few fences of my own to mend."

"Good luck, Captain. If there's anything Mel's Place Security can ever do, let me know. I owe you."

"I will."

"I'll let you get back to it then, Skipper. Safe voyage."

The connection went dead.

I sat up and padded to the head. I'd gotten just enough sleep to make me groggy but not enough to help. Duty called, but it would have to wait until I had a shower and a cup of coffee.

I started with Ms. Nunnelee. I had Natalya bring her to the cabin so I could fill her in on the investigation and the outcome.

She shook her head. "How does that even happen, sar?"

Natalya shook her head. "Happens everywhere. All the time. It's why we have wingmen."

"Are you saying it wouldn't have happened if Brooke and Healey hadn't left me there, sar?"

"No, but it didn't help you to be alone in there when the punches started flying," Natalya said. "Outsiders are often targets. It's part of the life you've signed up for."

"Have either of you ever been in a bar fight?" Ms. Nunnelee asked, looking from Natalya to me and back again.

"I never have, no." I shrugged. "But I don't get out much."

Ms. Nunnelee laughed.

"I haven't either," Natalya said. "I've lived in the Toe-Holds most of my life. I know bar fights happen. They tend to happen in the same places. Those are not places I go."

"How do you know, sar?" she asked.

Natalya shrugged. "Experience. Staying with more experienced crew. That's tough for you because so many of the people you know are just as inexperienced as you are."

I sighed. "We need to figure out a way to deal with this for future port visits and for future crews."

Ms. Nunnelee blinked. "What are you saying, sar?"

"We didn't take into account the reality of sailing with so many inexperienced quarter shares."

"I don't understand, sar. I thought quarter shares were common."

"They are and they aren't." I shook my head. "Almost nobody on my ships stays quarter share very long. This is the only time we've had more than one or two green hands joining the crew at the same time. The Chernyakova sailed with some quarter shares in the beginning, but most of them had experience in other vessels."

"That's the common pattern," Natalya said. "Most crews are well established. New hands join rarely, so they have a lot of support among the rest of the crew. Those established hands know how things work. They know which places are good and which places to stay away from." She shook her head. "But you came aboard as a cohort. All green and all knowing each other. It's no wonder you group up and go ashore that way."

"It's a dynamic we didn't anticipate," I said. "In that way, we failed you, Ms. Nunnelee. We've failed all of you."

"I thought captains were supposed to be infallible, sar," Ms. Nunnelee said, a little light dancing in her eyes.

"Captains are. Crews aren't. Any captain who doesn't recognize the distinction shouldn't wear the stars."

"It's the situation," Natalya said. "We're charting new courses. Some hazards appear obvious only in hindsight."

Ms. Nunnelee pursed her lips. "So what's that mean for me?"

"Nothing really, other than you'll be seeing an extra ten thousand credits in your account within the next couple of days," I said. "We'll be talking among the officers to see what we can do to help mitigate the issues. The one thing I want you to realize and be aware of is that it's not a function of the Toe-Holds."

Natalya nodded. "We have the same kinds of problems in the High Line as well. We've had worse. The problem is the system, and we need to figure out how to adjust to it."

She nodded. "Thank you for telling me, Captain."

"I'm sorry you've been through this trauma, Ms. Nunnelee. It shouldn't have happened. We will do everything in our power to make sure it doesn't happen again, short of restricting everybody to the ship for the duration."

She nodded again. "Is that all, Captain?"

"Yes, thank you, Ms. Nunnelee. You're dismissed."

She stood and left the cabin, dropping down the ladder toward crew berthing.

I sighed.

Natalya took the recently vacated chair. "What are you thinking?"

"I'm thinking we need Pip and Zoya."

"Pip's in his stateroom." She glanced at the chrono. "Zoya's still got the duty."

"You get Pip. I'll get Zoya. Let's meet in the wardroom."

She nodded and headed out the door with me right behind her.

In less than two ticks the four of us sat around the wardroom table.

"So, what do we do about it?" I asked, after bringing Pip and Zoya up to speed.

"Have you apologized to Brooke and Healey yet?" Natalya asked.

"No. It's on my agenda. They're on watch and I'll see them both as soon as they're off."

Pip sat back in his chair, arms folded over his chest. "Is it really that we have so many quarter shares?"

"No. It's because all our quarter shares are grassy green when it comes to getting along on the stations, and they bunch up together so they have no reliable guides."

Natalya nodded. "I agree with the captain. We'd have some of these same problems if we were docked at the orbital in Diurnia."

Zoya pursed her lips for a moment and then her head gave the smallest of shakes.

"What?" I asked.

"They know the High Line and they'd be less likely to act up. The oh-two deck isolates them pretty well, but if they get in trouble there, it would probably be worse."

"Why?" Natalya asked.

"Every one of the stations is wired for sight and sound. All the businesses. All the public spaces. Many of the private ones." She glanced at me and shrugged. "Orbitals are wired, too. I don't think they're wired to the same extent, but you'd never have gotten access to those video streams on an orbital. You'd need an administrative authorization to view them, and that would be tough to get."

I nodded. "Good points. Doesn't help us at the moment but it's something to consider." I looked at Pip. "What's our exposure from the business side? Do we have any culpability?"

He sighed. "We'd need a good lawyer to answer that. I can't see how we're negligent. We've followed all our procedures. We've treated these ratings the same way we'd treat any. The misstep happened because all of them are inexperienced."

I nodded. "I agree. We can't lock them up. What do we do?"

"Buddy system that's followed would help," Zoya said. "I don't know what their story is, but those two should never have left a drunk shipmate behind like that."

"Are they innocent in this?" Pip asked, looking to Natalya. "They're your crew."

Natalya shrugged. "I'd have bet credits to crullers that they'd done something to Nunnelee. That says more about my suspicious nature than anything."

"There's still the blackout period," I said. "The last thing she remembers was in the dance club. She followed them through the station for how long?"

"Head trauma," Zoya said. "She may remember more. It may stay a blank spot."

Natalya nodded. "The medics said they were concerned because she'd taken more than a few hits to the head."

I sighed. "Can we pull them all back to the ship at 0600 tomorrow?"

"We can," Zoya said. "You want everybody or just the juniors?"

"Everybody," I said, after thinking it over a moment. "We've got to break down the cohort and restructure it. We need the senior ratings to be part of the discussion, because they're going to have to be part of the solution."

Zoya nodded and pulled out her tablet. "Liberty suspended at 0600?"

"Yes, please."

"Liberty suspended, aye, Captain."

"Most of them will be back by then anyway," Natalya said.

"I'll go let Chief Bashar know he'll have a full crew for breakfast," I said. "Let's have an all-hands meeting at 0700."

Zoya tapped her screen a few more times. "On the shipnet, Captain."

"What are you going to talk about?" Pip asked.

"I'm going to let them all know what's going on and suggest that they need to be more cognizant of where their shipmates are and what they're doing."

"What would we do if this were the Lois?" he asked.

I snorted. "If this were the Lois, there'd only be one green hand aboard at a time."

"We always traveled as a pack," Pip said. "On the Chernyakova, we never had that kind of turnover. Even in the beginning we had experienced people as quarter shares."

Zoya nodded, her eyes narrowing. "That's really the problem, then, isn't it?"

Natalya nodded but Pip sighed. "I think it's not that simple, but it might suggest ways to deal with it."

"Have a crowd instead of a wingman?" Natalya asked.

He nodded. "Especially since the senior ratings are still leaving the ships in groups of three or four. We're the only ones going alone."

"Even we go out in pairs, usually," Zoya said.

"And we've all been here before," Natalya said. "Some more than others, but only Mr. Cartwright is new to Mel's."

"They aren't going to take kindly to being babysat," Pip said.

"Nor would I, but what do we tell them?" I asked. "Groups of at least three and one of them has to be an experienced hand?"

"If we can get the old hands to take a few new ones under their proverbial wings? That would go a long way to getting them in a better and safer mindset," Pip said. "I like that plan."

"Will our senior people go along with it?" Natalya asked.

"We can ask. It will make them very popular if the new people can't leave the ship without them," Zoya said.

My stomach chose that moment to grumble and everybody looked at me. "What? I've been busy. Dinner's in a few ticks."

As if on cue, the door to the pantry opened and Mr. Franklin led in Ms. Huber with a pile of cutlery and dishes. "Oh. Sorry, Captain. I didn't realize," he said.

I stood. "I think we're done here, Mr. Franklin. We'll just get out of your way."

He nodded. "Don't mean to chase you out, Skipper."

I grinned. "I'm more interested in getting dinner than standing on the ceremony, Mr. Franklin. Carry on."

I led the parade out of the wardroom and up to officer country. Pip and Natalya disappeared into their staterooms but Zoya stopped at the cabin door. "Think it'll help?"

"I don't know." I dropped into my chair behind the console. "If nothing else, we can make everyone aware of the issues. Maybe there are some better solutions."

"Maybe they'll be better if they come from the crew," she said, a half smile on her lips.

"I'm hoping for that," I said.

She nodded. "I'll see you at dinner, Skipper."

She was gone before I could answer. I sighed, remembering that I needed to go eat a little captain crow with Brooke and Headley.

The crew did not look happy. Some of them didn't look particularly wide awake, and at least one or two might have still been tipsy, but they all showed up. A couple of the junior ratings glared at me when I walked into the middle of the mess deck.

"Good morning. I'll make this short as I can. We have a problem with green crew. That means all of you who have never shipped out before signing on with the Marva Collins, in case you're wondering. The problem is not unique to you. It's not something unique to the Toe-Holds. The problem is that you've been thrown into the pool and are being expected to swim without having any of the support systems in place to make that actually possible." I gave them a moment to let that settle. "Usually we have one green quarter share at a time, and sometimes not even that. It doesn't take more than a voyage or two to learn the ropes. More importantly, a new crew member has a ship full of experienced, potential buddies to help them out. Unfortunately, the Collins is a bit short on the experienced part, and all of you came in with a buddy, or at least somebody you knew from the Academy. Somebody who's just as green as you are."

A hand went up in the back. I knew who it was without looking.

"Mr. Bentley."

"As resident smartass, I feel an obligation to point out that I'd be more than happy to act as experienced guide to as many of my junior shipmates who are willing to buy me a drink in return, Captain."

The remark drew a round of chuckles and a few laughs, mostly from the senior ratings.

"Thank you, Mr. Bentley. I'm sure your offer will be well received, but I'm more concerned with how to keep the crew safe. Part of that is understanding that every place has its share of bad actors. Of places where you shouldn't go." I paused. "So, tell me, Mr. Bentley, where would you not like to take a group of new shipmates here on Mel's Place?"

"What? Like a bar or restaurant or what, Skipper?" His grin lit up his face.

"Start with bar and why."

He paused and drew in a breath. "Arnold's On the Green. Beer's watery and costs too much. They charge you at the door and the floor show is never worth it. I'd stay away from Jolly Roger's Pub, too. It's where the stationers go to have bar fights."

"How do you know that, Mr. Bentley?" I asked.

He pulled out his tablet and flashed it in the air. "Look at the security calls. They're posted the station net."

"What about good places to eat?" I asked.

He shrugged again. "Too many to name. Depends on what you want. Good food. Cheap food. Fast food. Pick two."

"How do you know all this, Virgil?" Ms. Freano asked, craning her neck around to look at him.

"Port-o-call." He turned his tablet around to show the screen. "Every station lists the amenities especially geared to separate spacers from their credits."

I watched Ms. Freano's face screw up in a grimace. "You say that like it's an advantage."

Mr. Bentley shrugged. "It's actually good. There's a good feedback section. I've never gone to one of those places and been disappointed, but I've frequently been happily surprised."

Ms. Freano looked back at me. "Captain?"

I shrugged. "Sounds like one of them new-fangled things you kids have these days. Back when I was a rating we had to row between ports."

Ms. Freano stared at me for a moment and then burst out laughing.

"Seriously. Thank you, Mr. Bentley. All this time I've relied on Mr. Carstairs to lead me into temptation. I didn't realize there was an index."

Pip stood at the back of the mess deck with Natalya on one side and Ms. Fortuner on the other. Zoya and Mr. Cartwright stood on the other side of the passageway. "Have I ever steered you wrong, Skipper?" he asked, grinning.

"We can discuss that later," I said, getting another laugh from the crew. "Here's the message, people. We're all in the same boat. Literally, as it happens. Some of us know things the others don't. Sometimes those things are important. Like where to get a beer and where not to eat the salad. Each of us relies on all of us to help keep everybody safe. Not just when we're out there underway, but when we're here in port, too. A few of you have found out the hard way. I'd like to avoid having any more instances where a crew member winds up in the autodoc." I nodded to Ms. Nunnelee. "I'd also like to avoid being the scolding skipper who tells you who you can leave the ship with and under what circumstances."

"Actually, Captain, I think that's your actual job." Pip saluted me with his coffee cup.

When the chuckles died down, I shrugged. "All right. Yes. I just don't want to be a scold. We're all more or less adults here." I shot a meaningful glance at Pip who grinned back. "I'm going to strongly suggest that the junior ratings go out in groups of three and come back the same way. Ideally, ask one of your senior shipmates to be the guide."

Mr. Bentley held up his tablet and pointed to the screen, flashing it around in a dramatic flourish so everybody could see it.

"And use the guide," I said. I looked around until I spotted Mr. Brooke sitting beside Mr. Healey. "It can probably help you find the establishments you're looking for."

They glanced at each other and nodded to me. They'd been good sports about the inquisition I'd subjected them to. I'd probably broken at least two rules in the Captain's Secret Handbook, but I needed to make it right with them if I expected them to follow any order in the future.

I looked around the room again. "Any questions?"

Mr. Bentley raised his hand, a cheesy grin plastered on his face. "I have one, Captain."

"Anybody besides Mr. Bentley have a question?" I grinned back at him.

"Seeing no other questions. I think the answer is 0800, Mr. Bentley. What's the question?"

He lowered his hand. "Thank you, Skipper. That was the question."

"Ms. Usoko, announce liberty at 0800, if you would?"

"Liberty at 0800, aye, Captain."

"Thank you, Ms. Usoko." I looked over the crew once more. "Only one last word. If anybody has a problem, any kind of problem, don't sit on it. Small problems have a way of becoming a pain in the butt if you do." I grinned. "Bounce it up the chain of command. Chances are good we have a solution. That's all." I turned and left the mess deck followed by Pip and the others. I turned directly into the wardroom, leading the parade. I took my seat at the head of the table. "Well?"

Pip threw himself into his normal seat as everybody else took their places. "I thought it went well. I already sent word to Beth Case about the issue and I updated her on Port-o-Call." He shrugged. "One of those 'How can you not know this?' situations."

"I've never heard of it, but I'm used to the Toe-Holds," Natalya said.

"You wouldn't need it." Pip said. "It's been around for a while. It only started catching on in the last couple of stanyers. Not sure what happened, if anything. Fad today, gone tomorrow."

"You ever look at it?" Ms. Fortuner asked, looking down at her tablet.

"I've looked at it. You're pulling it up now?"

"Yeah. Us junior crew don't get all the privilege of rank yet." She grinned at me. "Helps to have some guidelines."

Pip pursed his lips and glanced at me. "Noted, Kim. That's on me."

She grimaced and shook her head. "Not where I was going, Pip. Sorry."

He shrugged. "Still on me. You reminded me of something I should have been doing all along and haven't."

"Cruise directing?" I asked.

"In a sense." He nodded at Mr. Cartwright. "You're the morale officer, aren't you?"

"Yeah. In theory."

"What do you need?" Pip asked.

"It's going pretty well, I think. Chief Bashar keeps the movie nights supplied. Fourth section has a tabletop gaming group that gets together at least once a week. Shipnet hosts a book club that meets asynchronously. We're reading Mandy Moon's latest book, When Darkness Sleeps."

Natalya leaned in to look down the table at him. "How'd you get that?"

"What? The book club? We just use shipnet. I set up a subforum for it."

"No, Mandy's book."

He glanced at Ms. Fortuner. "We picked it up at Dark Knight. Digital downloads don't count against mass allotment."

Pip looked at Natalya. "You behind on your reading?"

She shot him a look. "I didn't know it was out already."

I watched Ms. Fortuner playing with her water glass as if the conversation wasn't happening around her. It struck me as odd, but I shrugged it off.

"I have had one request, Skipper. I don't know if it's even possible," Mr. Cartwright said.

"What's that?"

"The cadets all play a networked computer game at the Academy. They've asked if we can set up a server."

Ms. Fortuner's eyes widened at that and she turned to him. "Really? You're the systems manager. How do you see that working?"

He shrugged and his lips twisted into a grimace. "Honestly, I have no idea. We can't run it on the ship's systems. That's just asking for trouble." He shrugged. "Is there another way?"

"Two problems," Natalya said. "Getting a server running is easy. It's accessing it that's hard. We can't use the ship's network and we can't interfere with the ship's wireless. That's first. Second, we can't play it on the ship's equipment. We'd need additional terminals set up somewhere."

"You sound like you've run into this before," I said.

She nodded and looked at Zoya.

Zoya shook her head and held up her hand, palm out. "Don't start this with me. I thought it was a bad idea even then."

Pip sat back and folded his arms. "Would you care to share your knowledge with the rest of the class?"

Ms. Fortuner snorted and turned her attention back to her water glass.

"The miners play a networked game in the belts," Zoya said. "It only works when the barges are relatively close together. Since they tend to work in clusters, they're usually within sight of each other, frequently on the same rock."

Pip sat forward again. "Lemme guess. You tried it on the Madoka."

Zoya nodded and sent a pointed look at Natalya with a jut of her chin. "She did."

"How'd it work?" Pip asked.

"Too well," Zoya said.

Natalya shrugged and didn't look up. "It became a problem. A morale problem. Technically, it worked fine. We set it up in the spine. Anybody who wanted to play had to go there. Near-field comms so nothing bled over into the ship."

Zoya pursed her lips, but I had a feeling she hid a grin behind that look of disapproval. "Nothing technical. The personal issues were a whole 'nother load of ore."

Natalya shrugged. "Some of the players became less than collegial with their shipmates. They were a pretty competitive group."

Zoya snorted. "Competitive? Is that what we're calling it?"

Natalya chuckled and shrugged. "What happened in the game didn't stay in the game. Crew started having yelling matches on the mess deck. Some shenanigans in the berthing areas. We had to pull the plug on it."

"You knew better than to put that game in there." Zoya shook her head. "How long did it take to go from 'This will be fine' to the captain yanking the plug?"

Natalya sighed and looked down at her coffee mug.

"How long, Nat?" Pip asked.

"Two weeks."

Mr. Cartwright leaned forward. "Two weeks?"

She sighed again. "Some of them weren't the best sports about losing."

Zoya laughed. Really tilted her head back and let it rip. She shook her head and looked around. "Sorry. It really wasn't funny. We lost crew over that game. Four people at the very next port. Three more quit when we docked at Zvezda Moya."

Pip frowned and leaned forward. "Over a game?"

"To be fair, it was a battlefield simulator," Natalya said. "It was pretty brutal."

"Is that the game they play in the belts?" Pip asked.

"No, that's the hell of it," Zoya said. "The game they play in the belts is a shipping and trade game."

Pip grinned. "Whew. At least it wasn't a mining game." He looked at Natalya. "Why did they pick that game? I assume they chose it?"

"Top-rated game. The equipment to run it wasn't onerous. It had a server we could buy instead of having to run it on one of theirs."

I raised a hand and got their attention. "All this is fun, but what's the game they play at the Academy? How is this organized? Is it something outside that they just tap into when they should be studying?"

"It's a trading game," Mr. Cartwright said. "Who can make the most money. I played a bit. You start out with a few credits and have to work up to owner. It runs on a server in the admin building."

"Is that the impetus for this request? They're afraid they're falling behind?"

"I suspect so, Captain. Junior cadets only play the practice games. They get ranked in their third year and can join the league officially."

Ms. Fortuner gave him a curious look. "Were you in the league?"

He scoffed. "Well, technically, yes, but I sucked bilges at it. My coursework ate me alive and I didn't have time to play that much."

I looked at Zoya. "What's your opinion on this?"

She shrugged. "I know of the game. Never played it. It does run on an Academy server, and network access means anybody on campus can play, students and teachers alike."

I looked at Mr. Cartwright. "Do any of the instructors play?"

"Not to my knowledge, Captain. If they do, they're not very good because the highest scorers at the end of the term are always cadets."

"What about you?" I looked at Natalya. "Is this something we should do?"

"No." She looked at Mr. Cartwright and shrugged. "The games out here are all real. Learn the trade. Take the tests. Earn more credits. Easy as that."

Pip gave her a hard frown. "That's harsh, isn't it?"

She took a breath before answering. "Maybe. Truth is, none of them have mastered their jobs yet. A couple have moved up to half share. Most didn't even bother, in spite of any claims they might have made to the contrary." She looked at Cartwright. "How many who took the tests only missed by a few points?"

He bit his lip and looked down. "Only a few. More than two, but one of them was Mr. MacBradaigh and he passed two of the four."

She shook her head. "Having done this drill before, I know what it will take to make it happen. We did it on the Madoka to reward a hard-working crew who all knew their jobs." She flexed her shoulders in a truncated shrug. "We don't have that here. At least not yet."

I looked at Zoya.

She shook her head. "I agree with her. This isn't something we should be considering right now. We've got a short hop over to The Ranch coming up and a new testing cycle coming pretty soon." She leaned over to look at Mr. Cartwright. "Next week?"

"Week after. I have the packets already. Just need to put up the schedule."

She looked back at me. "I'm all for keeping people entertained, within reason, but this costs too much in time, attention, and credits. We could do it, but I don't believe we should."

I looked at Pip. "You're being pretty quiet, Mr. CEO."

He shrugged. "I play games with real cargoes and real credits. I could see the training benefit to the Academy. I'm not seeing the benefit to somebody doing the actual work." He looked at Mr. Cartwright. "Propose that to them. Play the real game. We'll give a bonus to the crew member showing the most profit when we get back to Port Newmar. A thousand credits."

Mr. Cartwright frowned. "How would we know?"

Pip crossed his arms and stared at the overhead for a few moments. I figured he already knew, but he could never pass up a chance to put on a show. "Anybody who wants to play needs to register their current credit balance with me. I'll keep it confidential. Nobody will know. Not even him." He nodded in my direction. "The person with the highest balance increase gets an extra thousand on top. I'll even announce who so they have bragging rights when they get back."

Zoya started laughing and Natalya joined in.

Mr. Cartwright looked up the table at us, the question plain on his face.

Kim leaned over to him. "If they play the game, that thousand credits is going to be a pittance compared to what they'll earn in shares and salary."

Mr. Cartwright blinked at her. "You're serious?"

She nodded. "Oh, yes. At least I'm assuming that Pip hasn't lost his touch having to juggle so many cans." She shot him a sly look.

He harrumphed quite convincingly.

Mr. Cartwright frowned. "I can see a lot of ways this could be gamed."

Pip smiled. "Good. I'm hoping they do, too, because if they do, everybody's share goes up."

"Not if we're paying everybody full share it won't," he said. "Unless I misunderstand something. If we pay half the crew as quarter shares, that means four of them get one share. If those four move up to full, they take four shares. The total pool would be the same, we'd be giving out to the same number of people. They'd have to get smaller amounts."

"The people who already get full, or double, or even owners? Yes. Our shares will be less than if we had a crew of quarter shares," Pip said. "The difference to those quarter shares? They'll be getting four times what they'd normally get." He shrugged. "It's going to be a lot more than a thousand credits at the end of the voyage. The upside for us as officers and owners? We have a crew that's operating at peak efficiency. A crew that's focused on doing the job, doing it well, doing it efficiently, and looking for ways to make it even more so." He shook his head. "You can't buy that kind of performance, but you can certainly benefit from it."

"They'll also be looking for that bonus and the bragging rights that come with it. That means they'll be saving the credits they earn, which will let them pay for the rest of their program," I said.

Pip nodded at me. "There's more than one way to keep them out of trouble."

"Our galley budget will take a hit," Zoya said.

Pip grinned. "Got it covered. Chief Bashar has taken to my stores rotation scheme like he invented it. He's a relative stranger to the Toe-Holds, but the man knows how to stock a pantry."

"Maybe he did," Natalya said.

"Did what? Invent it?"

She nodded. "You're a brilliant trader, Pip, but you're not the only one in the Western Annex with a head on their shoulders and a need to play all the angles."

Zoya bit her lips together, but Ms. Fortuner snickered out loud.

Mr. Cartwright looked around the table at us. "So? I tell them that if they want to play the game they should see you, Mr. Carstairs?"

"You can call me Pip here at the table. And yes. I'll get them enrolled in the program."

Mr. Cartwright looked up at the clock. "If you'll excuse me, I want to catch a few people before 0800."

I waved him off. "Catch them before they spend it."

He laughed and nodded. "I think I'm going to like this game, even if I'm not playing it."

"I think we all will," Pip said, looking around the table as Mr. Cartwright left.

Natalya looked at him sideways. "What budget are you taking the prize money out of?"

"I'll take it out of my own pocket."

"Take it out of mine," I said. "As captain, mine's deeper and that's a brilliant solution. One we'll want to keep fresh for later crews."

Pip beamed a smile at me. "I know. It is, isn't it? I'm glad you're coming to appreciate my value."

We all laughed and I headed for the cabin. I still had reports to file. Even in the Toe-Holds.

Chapter Twenty-two
Mel's Place: September 8, 2379

We left Mel's a little more than two days after the Chernyakova. We'd catch up to them at The Ranch, but it was anybody's guess who'd dock there first. I'd called the crew to navigation stations shortly after lunch mess at 1330 so Chief Bashar had enough time to get the lunch cleanup started.

"Where are we on the course, Ms. Fortuner?"

"Locked and at the helm, Skipper."

"Thank you, Ms. Fortuner. Mr. Cartwright? The tug?"

"Just coming around now, Captain." He lifted his head and looked toward the starboard stern. "There she is."

I turned in time to see the familiar shape vector in to take us under tow. "Thank you, Mr. Cartwright. Ms. Usoko, do we have clearance to undock?"

"We do, Captain. Authorization on file and logged as of 1335."

"Thank you, Ms. Usoko."

"Tug is locked on, Captain. Ready on our signal."

"Thank you, Mr. Cartwright. Release the docking clamps, Ms. Usoko."

"Release docking clamps, aye, sar." The thud of the clamps releasing sounded up from the frame below our feet. "We are free in space, Captain."

"Thank you, Ms. Usoko. Mr. Cartwright, signal the tug that we are free in space."

"Signal the tug, aye, Captain." He tapped his keyboard a few times. "Signal sent. Tug reports affirmative. We'll have you out of there in a jiffy."

The station seemed to pull away from us as the tug took us back. It always felt disorienting when it happened. "Ms. Fortuner, where are we on the Burleson limit?"

She glanced at me. "Depending on when the tug lets go and our vector, maybe as little as two stans, Skipper."

"The planets are aligned in our favor, I take it?"

She shot me a smile over her shoulder. "At least physically, Skipper. I wouldn't want to invoke higher powers just yet."

Mr. Jenson chuckled at the helm.

"Tug reports yaw maneuver commencing, Captain."

"Thank you, Mr. Cartwright."

The station spun around, appearing to migrate to port and leaving us aimed into the Deep Dark.

"Ms. Usoko, signal to Chief Bashar, he can get back to lunch cleanup now if he needs to."

"Signal Chief Bashar, aye, Captain." She tapped her keys and nodded to herself. "Sent, Captain. Chief Bashar says 'Thanks.'"

"That shouldn't put him too far behind."

Her smile flashed in the dim lights of the bridge. "It's been less than a quarter stan since you called navigation stations, Captain. I'd be willing to bet Chief Bashar didn't actually sit down."

I chuckled. "No bet. If the captain sees it, he'd have to say something."

She laughed. "Noted, Captain."

We rode along like that with the tug giving us a good shove for half a stan.

"Tug reports they'll cut us loose in five, Captain."

"Thank you, Mr. Cartwright. How's our exit vector look, Ms. Fortuner?"

"Right on the beam, Skipper. Vector is good. A short burn after the tug lets go. We shouldn't need the sails until after we jump."

"Thank you, Ms. Fortuner."

The next five ticks counted down on the clock. The tug gave us a little extra boost for the last half tick.

"Tug releasing us now, Captain."

"Thank him for the ride, Mr. Cartwright."

He rattled his keys a little. "Message sent, Captain."

I turned in my chair to watch the tug fall away astern. He flashed his running lights a couple of times before rotating away and kicking his course back to the station.

"Helm, report?"

Mr. Jenson already had his hands on the helm controls and nodded. "Helm is responsive. Course is locked and we are on it, Captain."

"Thank you, Mr. Jenson. How long, Ms. Fortuner?"

"Programmed burn for twenty-six ticks, Skipper. We'll be free to jump in just over a stan."

"Initiate burn, Ms. Fortuner."

"Initiate burn, aye, Captain." The big kicker in the stern lit off and the low rumble carried through the ship's frame.

"Thank you, Ms. Fortuner. Ms. Usoko, patch me to the crew."

She clicked a few keys and nodded in my direction.

"Now hear this. This is the captain speaking. I'm going to release navigation stations for a stan. Take a break if you need it. Grab a coffee. We'll go back to navigation stations long enough to jump and then set normal watch throughout the ship. That is all."

I nodded to Zoya.

She clicked a key. "You're clear, Captain."

"Secure from navigation stations, Ms. Usoko. Set normal watch except for the bridge crew."

"Aye, aye, Captain. Secure from navigation stations." She made the announcement and tapped her keyboard. "Logged, Captain."

"Thank you." I stood up and flexed my back. "These Toe-Hold pullouts are always so grueling. Anybody need a break?"

Ms. Fortuner laughed and Mr. Cartwright smiled.

"I'm good, Captain," Mr. Jenson said.

"I'm going to get a coffee and stretch my legs. Can I bring anybody anything from the galley?"

"You waiting on us now, Skipper?" Ms. Fortuner asked.

"Well, I am keeping you here and I'm going down there. Seemed the least I can do."

She chucked. "I can wait, Skipper."

"Nobody?"

Everybody shook their heads and I dropped down the ladder. I didn't really need the break, but since I'd have the conn as soon as we jumped, I figured I'd better take advantage of it while I could.

I found Ms. Nunnelee standing outside the cabin door as I dropped down from the bridge. "Can I help you?"

"Sorry to bother you, Captain. I heard about the game? The one Mr. Carstairs is running?"

"Yes?"

"That's serious, sar?"

"It is. Why?"

"The winner is the person with the largest savings earned through the end of the voyage?"

"Register your balance now with Mr. Carstairs. You'll share your ending balance with him when we return to Port Newmar."

"My balance will be artificially inflated, Captain."

"The ten thousand from Mel's Place?" I shrugged. "If you make full share and start earning the full share payouts, that's going to overshadow that advantage, but you can also wait until the payment hits so you're starting with it already there if it makes you feel like you're being fairer to the other contenders."

She nodded. 'It does feel a little like cheating, sar."

"It's your call, Ms. Nunnelee. There are a lot of ways to game the system, especially on a ship like this one."

"Really, sar?"

"Yeah. Ask Mr. Carstairs for advice on how to maximize your value. I'm sure he has ideas, but the key one is to pass your full share test. I'm not sure of the timing relative to our docking at The Ranch, but the test will happen in about two weeks. My advice is skip half share and go for full. Take the practice tests until you can pass them at the 95 percent level every time and get a good night's sleep the night before the test."

She frowned. "Thank you, Captain. You've given me a lot to think about."

I grinned. "Fair warning. I'll give the same advice to anybody who asks."

She grinned back at me. "I like a good challenge, sar. If I'm hearing you correctly, I'll earn the share amount I'm eligible for when we dock?"

"Correct. Our policy has always been to pay the rate you've earned, not the rate your job pays. That will get pro-rated based on time, and it accrues every month. Shares accrue on docking. If you're full share when we dock, you'll earn a full share for the voyage."

She nodded. "Thank you, Captain. I'll get right on that."

"You're welcome, Ms. Nunnelee."

She headed for the ladder back down to the main deck.

"One other thing."

She stopped and looked back up at me.

"Depending on the jump error, we'll likely hit the testing period before we dock at The Ranch. A smart move would be to make sure you'd be able to take advantage of that."

"I figured that out already, sar." She grinned. "I also figured out that one winning strategy is keeping as many of the credits as I can."

I nodded. "Sometimes you have to spend credits to earn credits. Talk to Mr. Carstairs. There are no rules against getting advice."

She glanced at Pip's stateroom door just down the passageway. "When is a good time to catch him, Captain?"

"He's a day worker, so normal day worker hours."

She nodded, clearly realizing she needed to work that out on her own. "Thanks, Skipper. Most helpful."

"Carry on, Ms. Nunnelee." I went into the cabin and passed through to the head. I wondered what Pip would tell her. I finished up in the head and swung down through the mess deck to grab a cup of coffee to take back to the bridge. I spotted three of the engineering crew huddled around a table in the back, while Ms. Vincent seemed intent on her tablet at a corner seat near the coffee urns. The game was definitely under way.

I grabbed my coffee and started for the bridge when Chief Bashar stuck his head out of the galley. "Captain? Gotta tick?"

"Of course. I trust getting underway didn't discommode the galley operations very much?"

He shook his head. "No. Barely noticed. We got the trays in the machine and let them run for a bit while we kibitzed on the mess deck for a few ticks." He cast some meaningful glances around at the crew hanging around on the mess deck and nodded back into the galley. I followed him in and he led me to the back corner. "This game? Pip thinks it'll help?"

"I think it'll help. You know what led up to it?"

He shook his head.

"There's apparently a network game they play at the Academy. Some sort of trading game. Somebody in the crew approached Mr. Cartwright about it."

"To run it on the ship?" he asked, his eyebrows rising.

"You got it. Pip proposed playing the game with real stakes. Whoever keeps the most by the end of the voyage gets a little icing on their nest egg."

"Won't they all earn the same?" The chief frowned.

"That depends on how fast they climb the rank tree. Anybody who already made half share has a leg up when we dock at The Ranch. Their shares will be higher. They'll have earned more in salary."

"That gives those early birds a hell of a leg up, doesn't it?" he asked.

"It does, but it'll only be for one short voyage from Mel's to The Ranch. We've got another testing period coming right up. Anybody who manages to get to full share on that test will be leading the pack going home."

His eyebrows rose and a smile crept across his face. "The people who earn the most will run ahead of the pack, but that field will level out pretty fast, won't it?"

"It might. It depends on how seriously they take it. I'm betting the winner will not just earn the most. They'll keep the most." I grinned at him. "We'll probably see a lot higher attendance on the mess deck. You may want to adjust your stores to account for it."

"Yes. I'll do that." He grinned and shook his head. "There's a lot of mumbling and planning going on out there now. Think they'll keep going until we get back to Port Newmar?"

"Oh, I have no doubt that Pip will keep stoking the fire. He likes nothing better than a good scheme."

Chief Bashar chuckled, a low rumbling in his chest. "That man is twistier than a plate full of fusilli."

"Are you doing all right with him?" I took a sip of my coffee. "This is excellent, by the way."

"He's been great. I always traded stores a little on the side. It made no sense to carry all that stuff and not, you know, rotate the stock. Especially in the freezers." The chief shook his head. "But he's taken it to a whole other level. I've never run a galley as a profit center before, but I'll never run one any other way after this."

"Make sure your crew gets in on the game. Even Mr. Franklin. Maybe he can help the others along."

"He's going to have an edge since he's already full share, isn't he?"

"Maybe, but that's only going to last through the next testing cycle. There's no reason why they shouldn't all be full in the next couple of weeks."

The chief chewed on his bottom lip. "He could move up to spec/3."

I raised my eyebrows. "All of them could."

"And you'd pay them at that rate even though the billet maxes out at half share? Really?"

"Of course." I sipped again. "Now, how you use that expertise in the galley?" I shrugged. "How would you do things differently if you had four spec/3 chefs or food handlers? That's up to you."

He lifted a hand to his mouth and dragged it down over his chin, and his eyes lit up. "Oh. My, my, my."

"It's your galley, Chief. I'm just the bus driver."

He laughed and shook his head. "You drive the damnedest bus I've ever ridden on, Skipper. It's never dull. I'll give you that."

"Just keep pushing them. They may be going back to the Academy in a few months, but right now, they're yours to shape into the kind of people you'll be serving beside when they graduate." I looked around at the spotless galley and the smiling man standing in front of me. "I can't think of a better place for them. Or a better steward to guide them."

He swallowed and nodded. "Thank you, Captain. I'm looking forward to the challenge."

I toasted him with my mug. "I'd better get back to the bridge. Have fun, Chief."

He laughed. "This should be a riot."

We came back to navigation stations a few ticks before the jump. With the bridge crew already there, we didn't need a lot of time to run through the formality.

"Let's go to The Ranch," I said, taking my seat once more and kicking the festivities off after Zoya made the call.

"Hungry for a good steak, Skipper?" Zoya asked.

"I am. A good steak or maybe some lamb chops."

"I heard they've got some amazing spare ribs," Kim said.

Mr. Cartwright seems almost used to our banter, but he still didn't participate in it. I'd give him a few more jumps to get broken in.

"How soon before we can jump, Ms. Fortuner?" I asked.

"I make it just over two ticks, Skipper."

"Thank you, Ms. Fortuner. Ms. Usoko? What's the word from engineering?"

"Ms. Regyri reports the kicker is secured and the jump drives are spooled up and ready on your command."

"Thank you, Ms. Regyri. Mr. Jenson, will you be playing the game?" I asked.

He gave me a quick glance over his shoulder. "Isn't that just for the junior ratings, Skipper?"

"Open to anyone who wants to play. You'll have a bit of a leg up. But the real question isn't how much you make—it's how much you keep."

He grinned back at me. "In that case, no. I'll take my creature comforts as I find them and leave the scrabbling to others."

Zoya grinned. "I like your answer, Mr. Jenson."

"Thank you, sar."

Ms. Fortuner turned to look at me. "Time, Captain."

"Ms. Usoko, how stands the ship?"

"I've got green across the board, Captain."

"Well, then, ready about, Ms. Fortuner. Hard a-lee."

"Hard a-lee, aye, Captain." She mashed the button and the stars shifted just a little. "Jump is complete, Captain."

"Jump confirmed, Captain. We're in Tehas. Standing by for navigational confirmation," Zoya said.

Ms. Fortuner looked over her screens and nodded. "We are in Tehas, Captain. Plotting a course to The Ranch now."

"Hm. Too bad about that jump error," I said.

Everybody on the bridge turned to look at me.

"Jump error, Captain?" Ms. Fortuner looked back at her plot.

"Yes. The one that puts us at the dock just one day after the next testing period." I sighed dramatically. "You know? Sometimes the error's in your favor. Sometimes it's not."

Zoya laughed and Ms. Fortuner looked over at me with a look that was part amusement and part exasperation. "Let me just double-check that course, Captain."

"Thank you, Ms. Fortuner. I appreciate your diligence."

Zoya flipped through a couple of her own screens. "We're still going to beat the Chernyakova to dock, Skipper. By about a day depending on when Ms. Fortuner gets us in."

"Course plotted, Captain. Transmitted to helm."

"Helm reports that course has been received and locked. Sail and keel are active and the ship is responding to helm, sar," Mr. Jenson said.

"In that case, I think my work is done here. Secure from navigation stations, Ms. Usoko. Set normal watch throughout the ship."

"Secure from navigation stations, aye, Captain. But you've got the first watch."

"I'm aware. Thank you, Ms. Usoko."

She grinned at me and made the appropriate announcements and log entries while I stood and stretched a little.

Ms. Martinez brought the contest to the bridge with the usual coffee and relief break. After Mr. Keen left the bridge for a head call she shot me a shy look from the helm position. "Can I ask you a question, Captain?"

"Always, Ms. Martinez, but I reserve the right not to answer or to give you an answer you won't like." I smiled at her and she grinned back.

"Fair enough, Captain. About this contest that Mr. Carstairs is running?"

"What about it?"

"It's true, then, sar?"

"Yes. Just as he says. Whoever has the highest earned balance at the end of the voyage gets a bonus."

"Not the highest earnings, sar?"

"No. That's why you have to give him your current balance to enroll in the game. He's only interested in how much you manage to keep at the end of the voyage."

"That's like the game we play at the Academy, isn't it, sar?"

"That's the idea. It's not got as many bells and whistles, I suspect. Mr. Cartwright had a request from somebody to see if we would install the Academy game here so you could stay in practice. Mr. Carstairs thought that it would be more meaningful to just, you know, do the job and keep score by how much each of you has kept since the beginning of the game. It sounded like a good idea to me, too."

"So, it's how well we can manage our piece of the voyage, then, sar?"

"A good way to put it, Ms. Martinez."

"Won't the people with the highest share ratings have a massive advantage, sar?"

"That's the question, isn't it? They'll have maximum revenues, but what of expenses? Also consider that the shares max out at full. Once everybody has full share, the winner will be the person who finds ways to improve their own revenue while keeping their expenses down."

She looked at me, her eyes wide. "Is that possible, sar?"

"Oh, yes. Many different ways to increase your revenue in this game, Ms. Martinez." I shrugged. "Lots of different strategies."

Her eyes narrowed. "You wouldn't be willing to share a few of those, would you, Captain?"

"Take testing as an example. There are a couple of strategies. Bigger risk carries bigger rewards, but smaller risk might offer a surer one. A risky approach might be to shoot for spec/3 in your chosen specialty. If you make it, then you're sitting on full share and an improved salary. If you take it and fail, you're stuck until the next testing period. We have three more of those before we get back to Port Newmar. Those opportunities, while valuable, are limited. Picking a strategy that works for you and sticking with it might be the winning one."

She straightened around to look at the helm again. "Slow but sure, versus shoot the moon." Her words barely reached me over the sounds of the ship's blowers.

"There's a middle ground, too," I said. "Pick the best payout with the most acceptable risk."

She glanced back at me. "So if I'm confident in getting able spacer, that would give me full share, and shares are worth more than salary here. Like that, Captain?"

"Like that, Ms. Martinez. If you're not confident, then taking the ordinary spacer test and passing it will give you a leg up over everybody who shoots the moon but fails."

She settled back into the seat and gazed at the helm. I wasn't sure she saw it, but I'm pretty sure it didn't matter.

When Mr. Keen returned from his head break, they swapped places. As he settled in, Ms. Martinez asked him, "Josh, how tough is the able spacer test? Really? Like no BS." She gave me a quick glance to see if I had anything to say about it. I studied my console, flipping through some screens and wearing my bland poker face, but keeping an eye on them in my peripheral vision.

Mr. Keen shrugged. "Not that bad. The key is the practice tests. Keep taking them. Over and over. Start the day with one. Take a couple at lunch. Do them on watch. As messenger, you don't have that much to actually do beyond a few housekeeping chores."

"Are you taking one of the tests?" she asked.

He nodded. "Spec/3 ship handler." He grinned up at her. "But I'm not in the game. I like liberty too much."

She frowned. "What's that mean?"

He chuckled. "It means that I like to go ashore when I can. Eat food. Drink beer. Buy things. Unwind a little."

"Doesn't everybody?" she asked.

"Oh, yeah. But the game? It's not just about income, is it."

It wasn't a question and I saw his comment hit home more solidly than my rather veiled references.

"No," she said, biting her lip. "It's not."

She stood there for a long moment, eyes narrowed and her gaze somewhere out in space.

"Something else?" Mr. Keen asked, looking up at her.

She shook herself. "What can I do to learn the fastest?"

"Bring your tablet up here and study with us," he said, glancing at me. "That's how I did it back on the Chernyakova. If you get stuck, we can help."

She blinked several times. "What? Here? Am I allowed to do that?" She looked at me.

"I'm sorry, Ms. Martinez? Do what? Study on the bridge while on watch? Of course. You're part of this watch section all the time. You don't have to sit on the mess deck." I nodded at the other consoles around the bridge. "Any seat except the tall one in the back."

She glanced at my chair in the aft section of the bridge and grinned. "It'll be a long time before I sit in one of those, Skipper."

Mr. Keen looked up at her and whispered, "Just do it when we're docked. Nobody will notice."

She looked at him, her face blank for a moment, and then she laughed. "Is that what you do?"

He glanced at me and shrugged. "Maybe." He drew the first syllable out and grinned. "It's quiet up here unless Ms. Fortuner is working on astrogation updates or Mr. Cartwright is running the backups." He looked back at me and shrugged. "It's not the most comfortable seat on the bridge, is it, Captain?"

He made me laugh. "It grows on you after a while, Mr. Keen. Why? Think you might like one of your own?"

He looked at the chair and back at me. "I'd have to go to the Academy first, wouldn't I?"

"Probably a good start." I gave him a heartbeat to think about that. "Why? Would you like to go?"

He looked at me with his mouth half open. "Me, sar? At the Academy?"

"Why not you, Mr. Keen?" I asked.

Ms. Martinez gave him a playful cuff on the shoulder. "Yeah, why not you, Josh Keen?"

"I didn't realize you'd gang up on me."

"Answer the question, Mr. Keen. Would you like to go?"

He sighed, shrugged, then glanced back and forth between us a couple of times. "I never thought about it, sar. Aren't I too old?"

"The second highest cadet in my class is thirty-something," Ms. Martinez said. "She'd be number one, except the ranking cadet grew up on ships and learned to pilot system shuttles as a kid." She scowled. "I hate that guy." Then she laughed. "Not really. He's had all the advantages that I didn't. I can't fault him for using them."

Mr. Keen frowned up at her. "Really? I could. Is he a good guy otherwise?"

She nodded. "As good a guy as you can be and still be the top cadet, I suppose. I think you need a certain mindset to even see yourself in that position."

They both looked at me, Mr. Keen with curiosity and Ms. Martinez with a dawning horror, probably worried that she'd just insulted me.

"I think you're right, Ms. Martinez. I just wanted to graduate. I let everybody else worry about rank positions."

My answer did nothing to satisfy the curiosity I saw in Mr. Keen's face, but Ms. Martinez did everything but say "whew."

"Think about, Mr. Keen. That's an order."

"Think about it, aye, Captain." He grinned a little and went back to his helm.

"Thank you, Captain. You, too, Josh. You've both given me a lot to think about." She turned and left the bridge.

After a few moments, Mr. Keen asked, "You think she'll do it, Skipper?"

"What? Study on the bridge?"

"I was thinking 'win the game,' but sure. Study on the bridge." He shot me a grin.

"I think she's asking the right questions. It'll all depend on follow-through, won't it?"

"Got that right, Skipper."

"I was serious about the Academy, Mr. Keen. I didn't mean to put you on the spot with Ms. Martinez."

He shook his head. "That wasn't the problem, Skipper. It was the idea of me going to the Academy. It just took me by surprise."

"Why not you?"

He shrugged. "I'd have to get accepted first."

"Well, first you'd have to apply, Mr. Keen. You can't control the acceptance process, but the application is all on you."

He shrugged again. "Let me think about it a little. It's a bigger step than going for spec/3, sar."

I laughed. "Yes. Yes, it is. I was in your seat once. Take your time, but consider that you have enough officers on this ship alone to finish the application."

"I'd need three, sar?" he asked, looking over at me.

"Three is the minimum, yes."

He nodded and focused on his helm. "Good to know, sar. Thank you."

"Why aren't you in the game, Mr. Keen?"

"I told Ms. Martinez, sar. I like liberty too much."

"She might have believed that, but I don't."

He glanced at me and gave a little shrug. "I have a lot of advantages that they don't. I don't have the driving need to use them."

"You don't want to be 'that guy?'"

He laughed. "No, sar. I never wanna be that guy." He gave me another glance and a sly grin. "But I'm not against helping Ms. Martinez win."

"Just Ms. Martinez? Not very egalitarian of you."

"I suppose not, Skipper." He chuckled a little. "But she asked. If somebody else asks? I'll probably help them, too, if I can."

"Think she can make spec/3?"

He shrugged without looking at me. "I'm not sure I can, but we'll see, sar."

I turned back to my console and started the run through the ship's status reports. "I got faith in ya, Mr. Keen."

At that, he glanced over. "Thanks, Cap."

The test period ended while we lay just a day out of The Ranch. At dinner the night before we docked, I asked Mr. Cartwright about how it went.

"It went pretty well, Skipper. Some interesting strategic thinking going on."

"Like what?"

"The most challenging was Ms. Nunnelee from engineering." He shot a glance at Natalya. "What'd you do to her?"

Natalya shook her head. "I rode them all equally hard. I'm not sure how many of them are playing the game."

"Only about half," Pip said. "I don't expect anybody else to join after this port visit."

"What did Ms. Nunnelee do?" Natalya asked.

"She took three exams. Except for Mr. MacBradaigh here, that was the most anybody has taken in a single period."

Mr. MacBradaigh grinned. "Good for her. Did she try the cross-division idea?"

"No. That's what set her apart. She signed up for spec-3/power, mechanic, and engineer."

Natalya raised her eyebrows. "That's unexpected. How'd she do?"

"I let her take them in descending order. Missed the spec/3 by a fair amount but killed the mechanic test. Didn't need to take engineer after that."

"How many new full shares do we have?" Pip asked.

"Six new full, three new half. Everybody in the lower ratings who took a test passed it except for that one with Ms. Nunnelee. She was the only quarter share to even try for a specialist rating."

"Mr. Keen?"

"He passed, Skipper. As did Mr. Schulties in environmental and Mr. Franklin in the galley."

"We going to have profit enough for shares, Pip?" Natalya asked, nudging him with her elbow.

He grinned. "Plenty. Luckily we had no timed delivery bonus on this stuff." He shot me a frown. "Nice trick, by the way."

"I have my moments."

Natalya frowned, glancing back and forth between Pip and me. "What trick?"

"The captain noticed the jump error on entry," Ms. Fortuner said, giving me a smile. "It was enough to delay docking until after the test period ended."

Mr. Cartwright frowned but Natalya raised an eyebrow in my direction. "Finger on the scales much, Skipper?"

"Whole arm and part of a leg, if you ask me," Pip said.

"You have a problem with it?" I asked.

"No, actually. I approve. It seems my influence is rubbing off on you."

Ms. Fortuner lifted her coffee mug to her lips. "Maude help us."

Mr. MacBradaigh raised a hand, index finger extended. "A question, if I may?"

I nodded to him. "Go head."

"If I understand you correctly, you're maneuvering the crew to climb the ladder as quickly as possible, even though that potentially decreases the amount of share payout per person for those at the higher ranks."

"You have it right," I said. "What's the question?"

"Why?" He shook his head. "It not only reduces your own income but that of the company."

"Not exactly true," Pip said. "Owner's and captain's shares come out before the distribution. The remaining amount is divided based on the number of shares drawing them. You're correct in noting that we'll each, potentially, earn a little less." He shrugged. "Why? As I've said before, the ship is safer and runs better when everybody knows their jobs to the best of their abilities. It's not wasted money. It's invested in the crew."

"But you won't keep this crew," Mr. MacBradaigh said. "They're all going to leave the ship and you'll have to start over."

"Yes, but that investment will get distributed to the ships they eventually command. All of us will be safer, and probably more profitable, in the long run."

He pondered that for a few moments, staring at his empty plate, his brow furrowed. He looked up. "Am I also correct in understanding that the captain purposefully delayed docking by a few days so that the crew would have a chance to take the test before docking?"

"You are," I said. "Captain's privilege."

Pip nodded. "As CEO, I approve of his action, even if some of the crew might have less than favorable opinions on being kept in space for the extra days."

"By doing so, you've allowed some of them to advance to a higher share," he said.

"Yes," Pip said. "Those who were savvy about the game, or even about how to best prepare for their eventual return to Port Newmar, will have capitalized on that extra time. Literally, in this case, because they'll have considerably higher incomes than those who weren't."

Mr. MacBradaigh frowned at him. "And you see this as a good management decision?"

"I do. For the reasons already on the table. It's just good business to invest in the crew."

"What's to stop them from taking those skills elsewhere?" Mr. MacBradaigh asked. "Not the junior ratings, as you call them. Your permanent party crew? Can't they take their skills to another ship?"

"Of course. That's the point," Pip said. "You don't get good people by sitting on them. You get good people by keeping them interested, challenged, and paid well for their time. It's a strictly capitalist exchange. Their time for our credits. Since we're paying the credits, we get better value from crew with higher skills."

"Even if they're not using those skills?" he asked.

Pip frowned. "Yes. Of course."

Mr. MacBradaigh huffed and threw his hands up. "I don't understand."

"You're missing the obvious answer, Mr. MacBradaigh," Zoya said. "What happens to us if, say, Mr. Jenson gets an offer and takes a berth on a new ship? Or takes his credits and retires? He's Ms. Fortuner's right hand when it comes to astrogation and keeping our charts updated. What does the ship do if he leaves?"

"You'd have to replace him, of course, that's my point."

"Exactly. Who do we replace him with?" she asked.

"You'd have to hire somebody, wouldn't you?"

Zoya looked at Ms. Fortuner. "Kim?"

"Caitlin Heath has her spec/3. She'd move up." Ms. Fortuner shrugged. "That would leave us light on helm watch, but we could move any full share into that spot. Ship-handling training and experience would be a plus, but the helm watch only requires that the person in the seat is adequately supervised by the officer of the watch."

Zoya looked back at Mr. MacBradaigh. "By doing this, we're building a deep pool of expertise. By paying them their rating instead of their job, we gain loyalty and make it difficult for them to find a better job, at least one based on salary and share alone. There are other reasons for leaving the ship, but it behooves us to make sure the crew member feels like a valued and valuable member of the crew. When somebody does decide to leave, we have at least one person ready to step into the position, even cascading up a couple of levels. If we need to hire somebody, we only need to hire a quarter share to fill the hole."

"That gives us an incredible advantage in the market-place," Pip said.

"We've implemented the same policy on the Madoka," Natalya said, leaning forward to talk around Pip. "We didn't exactly have a turnover problem before, but there's almost zero turnover now."

"But you're going to lose these people at the end of the stanyer."

"You keep going back to that as if it's significant," Pip said. "Why is that?"

"Aren't you losing your investment?"

Pip shrugged. "Maybe. Maybe I'll be hiring those third officers to work on the ship when they graduate. In any case, we'll have new quarter shares to bring along when we get underway again. Our senior ratings will still be with us." He pursed his lips. "You've got a point, though. We're not filling in the bench by having people trained and ready to step up. That lower tier of ratings will churn." He glanced at me. "Something for future planning. We may not want to keep the Chernyakova in the program."

I nodded. "That thought had crossed my mind. Short term, we'll be fine, but I'll be recommending people to the Academy, and we'll need to fill those berths."

Zoya grinned at me. "Josh Keen?"

"Well, the whole bridge crew. Mr. Bentley in particular would make a good officer." I looked at Natalya. "You've got some, too, don't you?"

She shrugged but grinned. "Maybe. We'll see if anybody is interested after this little experiment completes the cycle."

Mr. MacBradaigh frowned up the table at her. "Are you implying that being exposed to cadets might dissuade them from attending the Academy?"

She nodded. "That's one outcome. The other is that they might give it more favorable consideration having seen the cadets first hand."

Mr. MacBradaigh opened his mouth but Pip shook his head. "Put the shovel down, Caoimhin. You can't dig yourself out of a hole."

He looked around the table, taking a moment to look at each of us, before nodding. "You've given me a lot to think about. Perhaps I should digest this a little."

"I like this plan," Pip said. "I'll buy you a beverage of choice when we get to The Ranch and you can tell me what you think of it all after you've had a chance to think about it."

Mr. MacBradaigh looked at him, a frown morphing into surprise. "I'll take you up on that. Thank you."

Pip shrugged. "Something else to think about while you're scoping out the Toe-Holds. I'd be interested to hear what you've found so far."

Natalya nodded. "I'd be interested, too."

Pip looked around. "All right. Tomorrow night. Whoever wants to come. My treat. Mulligan's at 1900 assuming the captain grants liberty." He grinned at me.

"Should be free by then," I said. "Make the reservation."

He grinned. "Already did. I try to plan ahead."

CHAPTER TWENTY-THREE
THE RANCH: SEPTEMBER 23, 2379

We cleared visa and docking just after noon. Pip's cargo crew had new cans lined up for us, and I asked Zoya to give me the first watch so Mr. Cartwright and Ms. Fortuner wouldn't be shut out of the festivities.

"I'll take the watch right after, Skipper," Zoya said. "As much as I'd like to hear what Mr. MacBradaigh might have learned, I'm sure Pip and Nat can straighten him out without me." She stood in her usual position at the doorway of the cabin, arms folded and leaning on the jamb with one shoulder.

I chuckled. "You seem to think he's developed some misconceptions?"

She smiled and shook her head. "No. I think he's probably done a good job. Alys Giggone wouldn't send us a clunker. At least not on purpose."

"What do you think her purpose was? Besides gathering data."

She glanced over her shoulder before answering. "I think it was to knock the edges off him. He's got a decent mind, but no real grounding."

"Are we helping or hurting?"

She snickered. "That's the question. I think we gave him more than a lot to think about with our take on capitalism the other night."

"Are we wrong?"

"No." She shrugged her free shoulder. "If I thought so, I'd have said something before this. Personally, I think it's brilliant."

"Did Nat really adopt the policy on the Madoka?"

"She did. Not long after we joined the crew here, in fact. It's now official RUTS policy."

"Regyri Usoko Transport Service. How much input do you have there?" I shook my head. "Don't answer if you don't want to. I've just been curious."

"She put my name in the company. She runs it. She asks me for advice, but I'm just the sounding board for her ideas. She doesn't have bad ones, but it's helpful to polish them before showing them to the public."

"What should we be doing that we're not?"

She stared down at the deck for a moment or three. "I don't know. That conversation last night freed up a problem that had been chewing its way out of the back of my mind since we started this project, though."

"Lack of depth in the crew?"

"That's the one. It's not so bad for us here on the Collins. Pip was right to be thinking about what it does to the Chernyakova."

"What's a better use of the Collins?"

She shook her head. "I don't know. This is probably the right thing. It doesn't have to produce much revenue. There are no real shareholders to keep happy. The company's only a fiction to give Pip and Alys cover from the trustees. I still don't know how long that might last." She shook her head again. "The Chernyakova? That's a different matter."

"Agreed. We're covering any monetary losses with additional revenues from the Academy, but that's not maintaining the investment in the crew. Not if we roll them every stanyer."

"We've got a good cadre over there. I'm planning to catch up with Julie Southern when they dock. See how she's doing with the captain."

"Is there a problem?"

She shrugged her free shoulder again. "Depends on how you classify problems. Beth Case is an attractive woman. Julie's on the bounce and feeling the cold, if you know what I mean."

"I do. I knew Captain Case had a breakup. Didn't know about Ms. Southern."

"She got the Dear Jill message just before Alys tapped her. I don't know if Alys knew when she made the call. It was relatively recent."

I blew out a breath. "Wouldn't be the first time for a first mate and captain."

She gave me a funny look. One I couldn't read. Part amusement, part sympathy. Maybe part sadness. "No. Nor the last. Don't have to look farther than Alys and Benjamin Maxwell."

I heard something in her voice that made me less cautious than I should have been under the circumstances. "You think Ms. Southern is making a mistake?"

"No, Captain. I think Julie is a grown woman capable of making up her own mind about what's best for her."

"Then what? There's something else there."

"Has Captain Case recovered enough to be thinking about a relationship? It's complicated."

I could feel my heart rate kicking up and had to fight to keep a professional demeanor in place. Talking about a romantic relationship between captain and first mate made me squirm in my chair. I thought about it too long.

"What do you think, Skipper? Is their relationship a problem for you?" She stared me right in the eyes, daring me.

"I think it depends on Ms. Southern and Captain Case, doesn't it?" It was the coward's way out, but I wasn't ready to be brave.

She didn't let me off the hook that easily. "What about Alys and Ben?"

"It seems to have worked for them. As for Captain Case and Ms. Southern?" I sighed. "It's really up to them, isn't it? Whether they're willing to risk the harmony of the ship to pursue a relationship beyond the professional one?"

She pursed her lips and her brow tightened in a frown. "That how you see it? A risk?"

"I do. As much as it pains me. As you said, it's complicated. Being captain? Being first mate? They're tough, demanding jobs. The power differential alone makes a relationship fraught with peril. A danger that might boil over and affect the safety of the ship."

She pressed her lips together, her frown deepened for just a moment. Her head tilted a few degrees to the left. "Do you think I should warn Julie off? Would Pip have a problem with it?"

I shook my head. "No. Well, I don't know. I don't think Pip has a problem there. From a management standpoint. You'd have to ask him. It would create a larger problem should one or the other be offered a new position, though, wouldn't it? Would Ms. Southern seek a captain's position when she becomes eligible? Would Captain Case be loath to put her up for the boards if it meant Ms. Southern would want to be a captain in her own right?"

Zoya blew out a breath, seeming to deflate just the tiniest amount. "I don't know, Captain. You're thinking about a pretty abstract position and taking a hard line on a hypothetical situation. You've seen this problem in the past, I take it? Seen those kinds of relationships sour a crew?"

I shook my head. "Firsthand? No."

"Is it because of the chain of command? You think the relationship will color professional judgment?"

"How could it not?" The conversation had my heart racing in ways I hadn't felt since—a long time.

"You really believe that."

"I did." The words slipped out before I could catch them.

Her eyebrows shot up. "Did or do?"

I sighed, feeling another layer of protective wall falling away. "I crossed that line once. It cost me. More than I ever expected."

Her face relaxed a bit. "We all know about Gr—about Greenfields."

I felt my face flush, the heat running up my neck and across my cheeks in an instant. "Who's we?"

"Everybody in the command structure. Well, except Cartwright. He's too new. I don't expect he'll ever have a need to know."

"And you do?"

She gave me that one shouldered shrug again. "Maybe. Maybe not. It made sliding in here after Al a bit easier on

Nat and me. Kim has been in the loop since coming aboard at Breakall, I imagine. Once you know the rough sketch, filling in the details becomes a matter of accessing the public records." She pursed her lips a moment. "Knowing why you sold Icarus—a wildly successful startup operation—to DST made the period that followed make more sense."

"How so?"

"Well, for one, it explained why the cabin on the Chernyakova was gray." She grinned and looked around. "You also haven't moved in here yet."

She caught me sideways with that observation and I followed her gaze around the cabin, ending looking up at the master's license above the console. "I managed to get that up."

"What about Al's painting?"

"I hung it in my sleeping quarters."

"That's it for personal effects?" she asked.

"Except for my whelkie. I think so." I realized the lie as soon as it came out of my mouth. "No, that's not right. I have some wall hangings I got when we docked at Mel's Place. They're still packed away." I shrugged.

"You have a whelkie."

"Yeah. I have a bunch, actually. Only one is mine. The rest? We'll see."

Her eyes narrowed. "You have more than one?"

"Well, no. I said only one is mine. I have a few stashed in the bottom of my grav trunk that haven't found a home yet."

"Someday you'll have to tell me how that happened."

"I've been carrying them since the Lois McKendrick docked at St. Cloud. I think that might have been the first port I went ashore to as a fresh mess deck attendant. There was a guy selling them at the flea market there."

She frowned. "That's not how it works."

"I found out later. A mystery I've never solved. They're apparently legit. Christine Maloney gave them a once-over and blessed them with her art background."

"One of these days, Skipper."

I raised my eyebrows.

"You're going to have to write a memoir." She grinned.

I laughed just as my tablet bipped. I pulled open the message. "Right now, I have to go see the brow watch."

"Problem?"

"Mr. Jacobs seems to think he should be allowed ashore."

"You really going to keep him cooped up on the ship until you release him into the wild at Port Newmar?"

The thought gave me pause. "I left the door open at his mast, didn't I?"

"You did. Yes."

I heaved myself up from the console and headed for the brow. "Lemme see what's happening."

She stepped out of the door frame and nodded. "Good luck, Skipper."

I chuckled. "Thanks."

A surly Mr. Jacobs in civilian attire and a moderately amused Mr. Jenson awaited me at the brow. "Gentlemen?"

"Mr. Jacobs here says he shouldn't be on the restricted list, Skipper. That it's a mistake and he should have been removed after our last stop."

"Really? Why is that, Mr. Jacobs?"

"I thought you only restricted me until Mel's Place, Captain." He shrugged. "Did I misunderstand?"

"Yes. Why?"

He paused there, mentally derailed. "Yes, sar? Yes, what?"

"Yes, you misunderstood, Mr. Jacobs. What I believe I said was that you'd find being restricted to ship more difficult once we got to Mel's Place or beyond. Since you're trying to leave the ship, I'm just guessing that my prediction might be coming true."

He scowled. "How long do you think you can keep me on this ship?" He added a belated "sar" at the end.

"How long can I keep you? Roughly speaking? Until I return you to Port Newmar or you tender your resignation." I shrugged. "I thought we made that clear already."

"You can't mean that, Captain. That's months away."

"No, I can mean it, Mr. Jacobs. Yes, it is months away." He stared at me in stunned silence. "Did you think this was a game? Something you can bend the rules around to your liking?"

"No, Captain. I guess I just didn't realize the extent of my punishment."

"Clearly. Tell me. Did you take the exam at the last testing period?"

His scowl deepened. "No, Captain. I did not."

I sighed. "Pity. There's no mistake, Mr. Jenson. Mr. Jacobs is still restricted to the ship."

"How long, Captain?" Mr. Jacobs asked, his scowl overwhelming any better sense he might harbor.

"You can leave right now, if you like. Pack your bag and safe voyage. Otherwise, until we get to Port Newmar, unless you straighten out your act. Maybe take a rating exam or two? Perhaps do more than the minimum required of a quarter share crewman? Is that clear enough?"

He looked like he might be willing to throw his career on the fire before he even began it, but he bit back any other response and made do with "Sar, yes, sar."

"Anything else, Mr. Jenson?"

"No, Captain. Thanks for clearing it up."

"Is Ms. Regyri aboard?"

"No, Captain. She and Mr. Carstairs went ashore shortly after liberty was announced. Would you like me to tell her you're looking for her when she gets back?"

"No need. I suspect she'll be tied up well into the evening. I'll catch her later." I turned to find Mr. Jacobs still standing there. "Shouldn't you be getting into your uniform, Mr. Jacobs? Perhaps check in with the duty engineering officer?"

He sighed and turned away, heading back into the ship without a word.

"You can't save them all, Skipper."

I looked back at Mr. Jenson.

He shrugged. "Some people just have to do everything the hard way, sar."

I chuckled. "Bitter voice of experience there, Mr. Jenson?"

He laughed. "Might have been there a time or two myself, Skipper."

"Yes, well. Carry on. I'll be in the cabin if you need me."

"Aye, aye, Cap. Carrying on."

I made a note of the exchange and sent it off to Natalya. Mr. Jacobs's willingness to be stubborn wouldn't be doing him any favors at the Academy. He hadn't learned that one of the best ways to win an argument is to not have it to begin with.

Dinner attendees in the wardroom consisted of Zoya, Mr. MacBradaigh, and me. I expected Zoya, but didn't expect Mr. MacBradaigh.

"You're not out with the party?" I asked as we sat down to an excellent casserole of penne and chicken in a creamy alfredo sauce. The aroma of cheese and garlic made my stomach rumble.

"I declined the invitation, Captain. I've lots to digest here, besides dinner, and that seemed more like an outing for the ship's command cadre." He looked back and forth between Zoya and me. "Is it a problem?"

"No, not at all. Just surprised. We haven't talked about your findings from Mel's. What did you discover?"

He took a sip of his water and pressed his lips together. "Hm. Their archives go back over two centuries. Management shifted from individual ownership to a corporate structure shortly after the move to the asteroid. Melisande maintained a tight grip on the board as chair. She made some decisions early on that I think set the stage for her later success." He paused to take a bite of the casserole, his eyes lighting up as he tasted it.

Zoya and I followed suit. The dish tasted as delicious as it smelled. The cheese sauce lent a delicate flavor to the chicken and pasta. I found some carrots and peas buried inside. After a few moments, we all looked up at the same time.

"This is really good," Zoya said. "Sorry, Mr. MacBradaigh. You were saying?"

He swiped a napkin over his lips and grinned. "It is. Early decisions. Mel hired a station manager early on and made him the company's chief executive. She hired a, well, I suppose accountant is the best description, but she was more of a financial manager than a bookkeeper. She directed the company in a series of investment transactions that allowed Colby Enterprises to flourish. That's where the credits came from for her adult sons to branch out into the neighboring systems without beggaring the parent corporation. A slow but steady growth in population and industry fostered further growth. By the time the CPJCT got around to setting up their first orbitals, they did it with Mel's Place as a jumping-off point."

"Did you run across High Tortuga yet?" Zoya asked.

He frowned. "Yes. Several references. That's the bank, right?"

"Well, banking and communications. Those two things are related. If you can't communicate among the various locations, you're limited to carrying all your credits with you from place to place." She shrugged. "A bad situation if you have trouble along the way."

He nodded. "I can see that. It explains why the bank also runs the communications. I never quite understood the connection and how one outfit managed to corner the market, as it were."

"When you've set up the first effective currency in the Annex, the rest just falls into place, doesn't it?" she asked.

"Not necessarily. I suspect that they have a strong corporate culture that, shall we say, dissuades competition? A sliver of every credit that changes hands is a lot of slivers."

"CPJCT has been trying, but the startup costs of building a duplicate are huge," she said.

"They weren't always so well thought of," Mr. MacBradaigh said. "High Tortuga. There's some kind of pirate connection with the name. A lot of people thought they were just trying to scam credits from depositors in the beginning."

"Did that show up in your research?" I asked, letting the first round of casserole settle and taking a sip of coffee.

"It did. Melisande wanted to set up the bank. As one of the earliest permanent settlers on record, she saw the benefit."

"What happened?"

"Well, I guess you could say, High Tortuga happened. Those financial transactions I mentioned? They were with an upstart company in—Ravaine? Yes. A system in the Far Shores cluster. I think I have that right. Precious metals and access to some impressive computing power gave them the leverage to finance most of what Melisande wanted to do but couldn't without help." He shrugged. "By growing her influence in trade and manufacturing, she effectively ceded the financial services to High Tortuga."

Zoya took a sip of water. "Sounds like quite a story. Any idea how you're going to spin it for the Academy?"

He took a moment to eat a few bites while he stared into the middle distance. He swiped a napkin across his lips and took a sip of coffee. "I don't have the entire story yet. I'm hoping that our visit here at Bar None Ranch will help me understand how food distribution happened."

That caught my attention. "How it happened? Wasn't it just barter in the early days?"

He shrugged. "I don't know about that. It makes a certain sense, but some early archives indicate that the interdependence of various stations led to the creation of the credit system that High Tortuga controls. If Station A needs the products from Station B? How did that transaction happen? Originally, it was probably barter, but money, currency, in this case, credits? Those are just markers for debt. We give them in exchange for labor because the worker barters their time and skills for our benefit. We recognize and satisfy that debt by paying them in tokens they can redeem for products and services they need."

"Basic theory," Zoya said. "You're suggesting that the Western Annex evolved from straight barter to a monetary system early?"

"I am. Not in the beginning, but the archives show that Mel Colby, in particular, drove the movement very early on. It irked her that she succeeded in establishing the credit but failed to control it."

"Food distribution?" I asked.

"Ah, yes. Some of the first trade goods consisted of foodstuffs. Station A has a lot of frozen corn. They trade some of it to Station B for a load of dried fruit. Staples like flour, eggs. My take is that the stations could produce enough food, but not all of them produced the right food. That drove Mel Colby to get the monetary system going in order to facilitate the growth of her own station. The system of trade fueled the resulting explosion of development and led to the expansion of the CPJCT in the Western Annex."

"So that part of the Academy's curriculum is correct," Zoya said. "They acknowledge that the Toe-Holds provided the stepping stones for the Annex's development."

"Oh, yes. The part that gets skipped over, or more accurately, suppressed, is the current state of Toe-Hold space. The Toe-Holds are, as you so correctly pointed out back in Newmar, the future of the Annex. They're the foundation on which the entire CPJCT infrastructure is built and continues to rest, if I'm reading the history correctly."

"So, what are you hoping for here at The Ranch?" I asked. "Beyond corroboration."

He finished off his meal and settled back in his chair. "Soil."

"Soil?" Zoya asked.

"Yes, soil is stupidly difficult to compound artificially. It's why all the stations rely on hydroponics to cover their basic nutritional requirements. Spacewise, it's more efficient than soil but it takes a lot of energy to keep it going. A lot of technology to even get it started and keep it running. Soil doesn't need all that, but the exact nature of soil is hard to quantify. So much of this, so much of that. Some organic. Some mineral. Some amount of absorption, but sufficient drainage. Different plants have different requirements. I'm hardly a botanist, but historically, creating soil was the biggest challenge for terraforming. With enough time and energy, you can put the right mix of gases in a dome or around a planet. Soil? That's more difficult."

"You think you'll find the answer here?" I asked.

"Maybe not the answer. Terraforming science solved the problem for planets. As I understand it, that process only works on planets in the liquid water zone of the system primary. The Traveler's Guide suggests that the founder, Arial Felder, got a load of soil from one of the Core Worlds to start his ranch. I'd like to try to corroborate that. Find out which one. Was it actually Earth? Why go back to the Core Worlds? That's a long way to ship a load of dirt."

Zoya grinned. "Take a step back, Mr. MacBradaigh. How do you think this is going so far?"

"I haven't had this much fun in ages." His grin lit up his normally serious face. "Connections and mysteries abound. I have no idea how the trading situation is going, but what I've learned in just these last few weeks has changed my perception of the Western Annex drastically. I'm still building the context and I find it disconcerting to have to be my own subject matter expert here. I'm creating the knowledge base directly from primary sources, as it should be, but there's no opportunity for peer review as yet. I'm inevitably adding my own biases to the findings, which might be problematic down the road."

"Well, replication can't happen without origination, can it?" I asked. "If you don't lay out a context, how can anybody challenge it or expand on it?"

He sighed. "This is not my field. I can tell you how to deal with sequence, with scaffolding. I can find reasonable assessment strategies within the limits of a particular system. Even suggest better systems depending on the goals. This?" He looked around the room. "This is so far outside my comfort zone, it's not funny. Alys should have sent an ethnographer. I'm just ..." His words petered out and he shrugged.

"You're just the person who happens to be in the position to do the work." I grinned at him. "Teacher, teach thyself."

He bit his lips together and gave a little chuckle. "I confess I've been trying to bone up on the kinds of things an ethnographer would be looking at. I don't even have enough to go on yet."

"What's an ethnographer do?" I asked. "I've heard the word, but what do they do?"

He sighed. "Mostly interviews. Direct observation. Particularly from the perspective of an acknowledged outsider. For example, at Mel's Place, they have a district as their main structural organization. Arts districts broken down by the forms, you know, graphic, performance, literary. General goods seem to be handled at the chandlery, but even there, they have a district for residential purchases. If you wanted a new wall screen, you might go to the chandlery but you could also go to the local electronics store. At Dark Knight, they had the one district, Main Street, and everything branched off from there. Everything from tea shops to restaurants to brothels. All cheek by jowl." He took a breath and a sip of water. "But is that organization specific to the station's founder? Something that developed over time? Mel's is older and bigger. Is that structure what we might eventually see arise at Dark Knight?" He shrugged. "All I can do is record it as objectively as possible. It'll be up to future researchers to answer some of the questions I'm finding."

"So food barter led to the credit system, which kicked off the growth of the Toe-Holds, which allowed the CPJCT to organize the High Line." Zoya nodded. "Seems logical."

"The roots of the CPJCT are more exposed here," he said. "I'd never find these connections up there. The original Board of Exploration is a footnote."

Zoya pursed her lips. "I wonder what the exchange rate is."

"Exchange rate?" he asked.

"Between Western Annex credits and whatever unit of currency they have in the Core Worlds."

He blinked several times, his head tilting slowly off axis. "I hadn't considered that."

"Is there one?" I asked.

She shrugged. "I don't know. Something to think about."

I knew who to ask, but I wasn't about to let that genie out of the bottle until I'd had a chance to speak to Maggie Stevens in private.

Zoya nodded as if reading my mind.

"It would seem logical," Mr. MacBradaigh said, seeming oblivious to the silent communication at the head of the table. "The CPJCT exists to further the interests of its members, but its original source is Sigma Draconis in the Core Worlds."

Zoya pushed her plate back a fraction and lifted her coffee cup. "You think they're making credits off the Western Annex?"

"It would be logical, but without any kind of corroborating evidence, I'm not willing to go that far." He frowned at his empty plate. "I should make some notes on this before I forget."

I shrugged. "It may be simpler than that."

Zoya lifted her chin in query.

"Humans need room to expand. The Core Worlds used the annexes to off-load those who wanted to explore. Parents launching children off into their own lives."

"Some kind of interstellar mitosis?" She grinned at me.

"Kinda."

Mr. MacBradaigh asked, "So, release valves? Are the Core Worlds so crowded?"

"Maybe they're too regulated." I shrugged. "The Toe-Holds are the antithesis of the High Line. I can see CPJCT as a kind of offshoot of a highly regulated society. They brought their regulations with them because that's what they do."

Zoya nodded. "Makes sense from a family-of-origin perspective."

Mr. MacBradaigh tilted his head. "Speaking of, how do either of you reconcile family-of-origin values with your current circumstances?"

"Never been an issue for me." I shrugged. "My mother was an ancient lit professor. We valued loyalty, consistency, and curiosity."

Zoya's eyes narrowed a little as she considered me over the rim of her coffee cup. "That was before you came into space."

"Of course. That's kind of the definition of family of origin."

She shook her head. "But your space family of origin is the Lois McKendrick. That's where your first indoctrination began under Alys Giggone and Benjamin Maxwell."

I nodded to cede the point. "My earlier values weren't in conflict with anything I learned there."

She shrugged and pursed her lips, looking down into her cup as she took a sip. A little frown appeared on her forehead.

Mr. MacBradaigh leaned forward. "What about yours, Ms. Usoko?"

"Values?" She shrugged. "Loyalty is a big one. Work ethic is another. Do it right, the first time if possible, but the second or third if need be."

"You were in command of a ship at a very young age." He raised his eyebrows.

"Yeah. I was. Only nominally, at first. I had a good guide who helped me work through the issues that a kid might not consider. Extenuating circumstances. Unintended consequences. He also taught me chess." She sighed and looked into a cup that had to be mostly empty. "I never did beat him." She tilted the cup once before putting it down on the table. "A lot of what I learned at my grandparents' knees was about how to treat people. Common decency goes a long way in the Deep Dark and it's a precious commodity. Perhaps the only really scarce item in the Western Annex."

He frowned. "An interesting observation."

She shrugged. "The Western Annex thrives on plenty. We can never mine out all the rocks. We can never use up all the gases. Taken in aggregate? Even the ravening human horde can't consume a sun." She grinned. "We've given good shots at mining out a belt, but we give up and move on rather than clear out all the rocks once we've pulled the significant metals and minerals out of them."

He frowned at that. "So the real problem is distribution?"

"Yes. I think so. Which feeds into your ideas about how the Toe-Holds came to be and supports the notion that they're the future, as well as the past."

He nodded, a few slow nods up and down. "I can see that."

Mr. Armengol stuck his head in from the pantry. "Excuse me, sars. Anyone for dessert?"

I looked back and forth between Mr. MacBradaigh and Zoya.

Mr. MacBradaigh responded first with a shake of his head. "I am replete and, with your permission, Captain, I want to get some time ashore this evening to see what I can observe."

"Of course, Mr. MacBradaigh. I look forward to your insights."

He smiled, pushed himself up from the table, and beat a retreat from the wardroom.

"Zee?"

"We have your choice of cookies, a nice mixed-berry pie, and ice cream," Mr. Armengol said, a tempting suggestion in the tone of his voice. "All, some, any, sars?"

"I'm good," Zoya said. "But I'll keep you company if you want some, Captain."

I shook my head. "Thank you, Mr. Armengol. If I could get a refill on coffee, I'll take it to the cabin and get out of your way."

He nodded and produced a carafe from the counter behind the door. "Of course, Captain." He filled my mug and held the carafe up. "Ms. Usoko?"

She nodded. "Probably good idea. I've got the overnight. I'll take a rain check on the pie, though. I bet that would make a good midnight snack."

He grinned. "I'll make sure there's a helping with your name on it here in the pantry."

"Thanks, Cisco."

"You're welcome, Ms. Usoko."

He gathered up a load of dirty dishes, mostly clearing the table in the process, and exited the way he came in.

We took our cups and climbed the ladder to officer country. Zoya split off outside the cabin. "I've got some time to practice before I relieve you. See you at 1945."

An unexpected twinge of disappointment slipped between my ribs. "Have fun. See you then."

She went into her stateroom, leaving me to ponder my life choices as I settled behind my console in the cabin. "Family of origin." The phrase wouldn't leave me alone, even after I said it aloud.

Chapter Twenty-four
The Ranch: September 23, 2379

Natalya returned from dinner with Pip just before 2200 and caught me after I got off the track but before I made it to the shower. "Good, you're still awake."

I wiped the sweat out of my eyes with a towel. "What's up?"

"Pip's taken the others out for a pub crawl. You wanted to see me?"

"Oh, right. Mr. Jacobs seemed to be under the impression that he should be allowed off the ship."

"Did he?"

"Correct me if I'm wrong, but I restricted him to the ship until further notice, didn't I?"

She grinned. "Yes. That's how I remember it."

"That's what I put in the report, too. He didn't take the test when he had the chance?"

"No. I put as much pressure on him as I could without banging him on the head with his tablet. I'm not sure that would have helped. He's got deck plating for a skull."

"How did he get into the Academy?"

She blew out a noisy breath and shook her head. "Money? Connections? He's slacking off now since he's got what he wants and doesn't see the need to exert himself any more than necessary?"

"That would explain him being in the candidate pool for this assignment." I wiped my face again, feeling the sweaty T-shirt cold on my back. "Why did you pick him?"

She shook her head. "He put up a good front. Talked a lot about making him a better officer."

I sighed. "I just wanted you to be aware that he and I crossed paths. I sent him back to engineering to see if the watch leader had any tasks for him."

She snorted. "His buddies won't give him something to do unless I'm standing there directing them. I'll find a few tasks to keep him busy."

"I'm going to take a shower and get into a clean uniform. You wanna talk after?"

"No. It's quiet hours and I'm going to get some sleep myself. I'll deal with Jacobs in the morning."

"There should be a way to light a fire under him." I shook my head. "I can't think of what it might be."

She nodded and gave me a rueful grin. "I'd try a blowtorch if I thought it would help."

I chuckled and headed for the shower.

I was still up at midnight when Pip and Mr. Cartwright came up the ladder. "Have fun?" I asked.

Pip came into the cabin and plopped down in one of the chairs. Mr. Cartwright stopped at the cabin door.

"I did," Pip said. "I don't know about anybody else." He craned his head around to look back at Mr. Cartwright.

"It was good," he said. "Thanks, Pip. Night, Captain."

"Good night, Mr. Cartwright."

He disappeared down the passageway and a moment later I heard a stateroom door close.

"Where's Kim?"

He shrugged, a light dancing in his eyes. "She's ... ah ... found a friend. She should be back in time for watch. What'd I miss?"

"Mr. Jacobs trying to leave the ship. Took umbrage when Mr. Jenson stopped him at the brow."

"Fisticuffs?"

"No. Just seemed to think that being restricted until the captain says otherwise only applied to the next port of call."

"A bit short-sighted of him, wasn't it?"

I shrugged. "I would have been willing to give him the benefit of the doubt, but he hasn't done even the simplest thing to rehabilitate his reputation."

"Like what? Take the engineman exam?"

"Yeah. Natalya says he's still being stupid. Although her exact words were 'deck plating for a skull.'"

He winced. "Yeah. That's Nat."

"Anything from the Chernyakova?" I asked.

"Nothing new. Still due day after tomorrow." He glanced at the chrono. "Well, tomorrow, at this point. Anyway, Abe's got a can waiting but we'll be ready to leave before they are."

I raised an eyebrow. "Your thinking on that?"

He laced his fingers together over his chest and stared down at his feet. "Two minds. Maybe three."

"One is usually enough, but do go on."

He snickered. "One, we drag feet leaving, giving them a chance to change cans, get some liberty behind them, and get underway. Downside, we won't need that much time to hit the Burleson limit."

"You know where we're going next?"

"No." He sighed. "Abe's can is heading for Ice Rock. We can get some cargo to go along with them, but it would barely cover the cost of taking it there. There's no guarantee we can get anything coming out. Abe will be able to snag the next can in the stack, but even for the Chernyakova, that's a crap shoot."

"Agreed."

"Two, we jump to The Junkyard. I can get a few good cans heading in that direction. Still iffy, but keeps us out of CPJCT space and puts us in a position to be able to meet the Chernyakova when they come out of Ice Rock."

"The Junkyard? That's a bit out of our way, isn't it?"

He shrugged. "Perhaps a bit, but the alternative in the Toe-Holds would be High Tortuga. I could fill the ship with cargo heading to Ravaine."

"What's the downside of that?"

He shrugged again. "Not sure there is one. I picked The Junkyard because it's a pretty laid-back station. I can't say the same for any place connected with High Tortuga."

"So you're afraid our junior ratings will get into more trouble than we can get them out of?"

"You have to admit. They've sunk below our expectations on decorum at every stop so far."

"True, but at least some of it wasn't their fault. Maybe we won't have any trouble here."

He barked out a harsh laugh. "I'll believe it when I see it."

"What's your third mind saying?"

"Gretna. The confederation seat itself."

"Back to the High Line?"

He nodded. "Alys wants us to show the flag. Gretna's got a lot of mixed industry. I'm pretty sure we can get some profit out of it. Getting profit into it shouldn't be much of an issue. One of their back doors is a finished-goods factory complex specializing in consumer electronics. They need the mining spares we can get here, so we can trade off at the back door and get a small profit on top by taking a few cans to the main port."

"Downside?"

He gave a dismissive shrug. "Only that it's the High Line. Opportunity cost for not going to High Tortuga and pushing the shares up a little. The upside is that we'd be on the same side of the Annex as the Chernyakova so we could meet up with them easier after."

"You think Beth is ready to make a run on her own?"

"Well, she has a whole crew with her." He grinned. "But yeah. We have to cut the cord sometime. This will be her third Toe-Hold. Ice Rock is about as quiet a place as she could go. Not a lot of opportunities for things to get sideways on her there. They'll have to take the next can leaving, so Abe's only job is to rubber-stamp the documents. Other than that? It's as good a 'solo' run as we're likely to find and the timing is right for us to let her take it."

"All right. What's your pleasure?"

"I'm thinking Gretna. I don't like jumping to the wrong side of the Annex with legs as short as ours." He sighed. "I can only do so much with communications. Ice Rock being Ice Rock. It's a lot more effective to negotiate in person."

"You don't think Abe can handle it?"

He shook his head. "No. I think he can. I just don't want Beth to feel like we've dragged her down the garden path and left her twisting in the tulips." He eyed me. "You have a problem with Gretna?"

"No. I'm good with any of the three. I agree with your assessment, if that's what you're looking for."

He nodded. "All right. I'll get my people working on snagging the cans to Gretna. We're still leaving in three days?"

"Yeah. Far as I know. I'll ask Kim to put the course together tomorrow."

"Good." He slapped his hands on his thighs and stood. "In that case, I bid you good night." He gave me a comically inept salute and turned for the door.

"Close it on your way out?"

He grabbed the handle and pulled it closed as he left.

I eyed the reports on my console and shook my head. They'd keep until morning. I rose, stretched, and headed for my rack. "You need a hobby," I said with a sigh.

I invited Beth to dinner when the Chernyakova made the dock and met her at 1800 at the Chernyakova's lock. She strode down the ramp, smiling. "It's my turn, isn't it?" I asked.

"It is. Thank you for remembering." She laughed. "I'd have bought if you hadn't."

"My invite, my treat. Come on. There's a chop house here that grills just about anything you'd care to eat."

"Sounds good." She fell into step with me, almost bouncing along on her toes.

"You're in a good mood."

She nodded. "I am. Quite pleased with the situation as a whole, as it happens. The shares on this leg?" She shook her head. "You tried to tell me. Nothing like seeing the deposits to make me a believer. Is it always this good?"

"Not always. I understand you're going to Ice Rock next?"

She glanced over at me. "Am I?"

"Pip seemed to think so. Abe has a can going that way."

"He said he had a can lined up. I hadn't heard where yet."
She gave me another glance. "Is that a problem?"

"Ice Rock is funny." I steered us around a slow mover
in the cargo lane and onto the sidewalk that led out of the
docking gallery.

"Funny how?"

"They don't have an open market the way others do. You
take the next can going."

"Or what?"

"Or you let another ship take the next can and you take
the next can after that. You don't get to pick which can you
take, other than 'this one' or 'wait for the next one.'"

She frowned. "That seems to fly in the face of the whole
Toe-Holds mindset, doesn't it?"

"Not really." I took the turn that led to Grayson's Grill
and she followed along. "The driving philosophy here isn't
exactly free market. It's more like 'I'm going to do things my
way.' At Ice Rock, that means you do it their way and their
way is to stack cargoes making only one available at a time."

Her frown deepened. "And that works for them?"

"Oddly, it's not that bad. There's some variation in the
kind of ore, but for a Barbell? Yeah. Almost all the cans are
raw ore, so waiting for the next one costs more than taking
the next one in line. The benefit for Barbells is that you never
have to worry about getting a can to take away."

"What about multi-freight haulers like the Collins?"

"Ah, that's the problem, isn't it." I shrugged. "Pip didn't
tell you?"

"Tell me?"

"You're going solo on this next one. We're going to Gretna
to show the flag for Alys Giggone. We'll plan to meet up at
the following port, or more likely the one after, once you know
where you're going."

She grimaced and frowned at the sidewalk. "How will you
know?"

"It's going to take us a fair amount of time to get into
Gretna's gravity well. More time coming out. If you message
Pip on the way out of port at Ice Rock, we'll know in plenty of
time for us to meet you." I shrugged. "I wouldn't be surprised

if you get a couple of stops in before we can get back out of Gretna."

"So he's cutting me loose?"

"In a sense." I stopped at the door. "This is it."

"You don't have some coded knock or something?" She grinned at me.

I pulled the door open and the aromas of grilled meat and spices wafted out. "No. Just good food here."

"Smells divine." She followed her nose in.

The host seated us at a table near the middle of the dining room without a lot of fanfare and we got drink orders placed before she revisited the subject of taking off on her own in the Toe-Holds.

"You think I'm ready to go it alone?"

"Of course. You've got Tom Reed there to keep the navigation straight. You've got some experience with the visa system now. Nobody from your crew has crossed swords with station security, have they?"

"No, but I made it policy that the new people didn't go out without an experienced guide. Your people are amazing in that regard."

"Your people now. As much as I hate that phrase." The server delivered our drinks and I toasted her with my beer. "Safe voyage."

She clinked her wine glass to mine and took a sip. "Why do you hate that phrase?"

"They're not anybody's people. They're the ship's crew. That doesn't confer ownership."

She nodded. "I take your meaning."

"The ship is well crewed, adequately provisioned. The officer cadre is coming together?" I raised an eyebrow.

"Very nicely, to be fair. Even Mr. Skaggs. I'm not sure what his problem was coming in, but whatever had him twisted up seems to have been reconciled."

"Good to know." I took another sip of beer. "How do you feel about being let off the leash?"

She snickered a little. "A good metaphor. It does feel a little like being let loose. To be honest, having that much free rein feels a bit unsettling. Not just because it's the Toe-Holds."

"You didn't have much with Saltzman?"

"None. Even the cargo chief had to take whatever Saltz-man's brokers picked for the ship, which dictated where we'd go."

"Ice Rock will feel familiar then." I grinned. "Except it'll be the station telling you what can to take."

She smiled. "That wasn't lost on me. How do you feel about having me wandering around in your ship?"

"I keep telling you, it's your ship now. I may own most of the company, but I've my own crew to deal with."

Our meals arrived and got our direct attention for a couple of ticks.

"This is wonderful," she said, leaning back in her seat to take a breath and a sip of her wine. "I have to hand it to you. You know how to show a girl a good time." She grinned.

I nodded at my plate of grilled chops. "They have a great chef here who knows how to deal with meat in general. Nothing against Chief Bashar."

She gave me a funny look and glanced over my shoulder. "Speaking of. Isn't that him?"

I glanced back and saw the chief being seated with Mr. Franklin and Laura Huber. "It is."

"How did he find the place?" she asked. "He's as new to the Toe-Holds as I am. I'd never have found it."

"Maybe Mr. Franklin brought him. We've visited enough that he'd probably know of it. It's rather the place for steaks and chops."

"Nice of him to bring his staff." She took another bite of her steak and looked over at me. "Ms. Sharps doesn't seem to take much time for herself. Has that been a problem?"

"It wasn't. Not that I was aware of. Being a day worker and department head? Her schedule is largely driven by meal times, but I know she frequently delegated portside dinner mess to Ms. Adams. Generally, cooking ahead with something that can be put on the buffet line without much trouble."

She frowned and nodded. "She mentioned something about the wardroom and being docked?"

I finished the last piece of chop and followed it with a sip of beer. "We had a policy of securing the wardroom when docked so the stewards only had to deal with the mess deck. Officers usually sat together at one of the tables. With so few of us eating aboard? It made sense."

Her brow furrowed up as she stared at me. "How did that go? Dining with the crew?"

I shrugged and chased the last bit of banapod around my plate until I could spear it with my fork. "Quite well, really. It was rare that more than two officers at a time attended any of the normal mess times except breakfast. Even then, usually only me and the OD."

She nodded, her eyebrows rising. "The crew didn't object?"

"What? To having us pollute their space?" I grinned. "No. I made it a point to invite them to sit with me when I was alone. Gave me a chance to talk to them about the ship. About any problems they might have been having without getting into the chain of command stuff. We made it clear that officers ate on the mess deck to relieve the galley crew when docked."

She sighed. "Now I feel like a jerk. It's an elegant solution to something I didn't think might be a problem. Ms. Sharps mentioned it, but I didn't pick up on the nuance."

"How many times were you the only one in the wardroom?" I shrugged. "If the new cadre stays aboard for meals, it makes sense to keep the wardroom going. Frees up the mess deck."

"Like you said. Me and the OD most of the time." She shrugged and finished her meal. "I'll have to revisit with the other officers and see what Ms. Sharps has to say about it."

I nodded. "I found it to be quite satisfying, but I started on the mess deck. I'm perfectly comfortable at one of the tables and eating off a tray."

She gave me a wry smile, picking up her wine glass and swirling the ruddy liquid around. "How egalitarian of you." She held the pose for a moment, then laughed. "Seriously, though, I need to put that policy in place. I see too many good things that could come of it to let it fall by the wayside. Thank you for mentioning it."

"Eh, you know. Skipper talk." I grinned and finished my beer, just in time for the server to stop in.

"How was everything?" he asked.

"Lovely," she said. "What's for dessert?"

He pulled a tablet out of his apron pocket and held it out to her. "I hoped you'd ask. I particularly recommend the granapple cobbler. We grow our own here on station. Well. Next station over, but locally." He shrugged.

She laughed. "Close enough." She scanned the offerings and handed the menu to me. "I'll have the cobbler. Sounds good."

"You want it with ice cream?"

"Yes, please."

I scanned down through the list. "I'll have the tiramisu and a cup of coffee?"

"Good choices."

"I'll have a coffee, too," Beth said.

"Of course. Let me just take some of these away and I'll be back in a jiffy with your desserts." He picked up most of the empty dishes, balancing an impressive load of crockery on his arm, and whisked off toward the back.

"You're not in a hurry, are you, Ishmael?" she asked. "I should have asked first."

"No. Not at all. Unless something breaks or I need to bail somebody out of the brig, my time is pretty open right now."

She tilted her head a little. "Wanna talk about it?"

"Talk about what?"

She shrugged. "Sounded a little wistful there. Like having free time wasn't actually all that great."

I snickered. "I need a hobby, I think."

She smiled and sat back in her seat. "Like being captain isn't enough?"

"What's your hobby?" I asked. "Tell me you don't have one."

She gave me a comically wry grin. "Busted. I read. I'm a sucker for a good story."

"You'd think I'd read more." I shook my head. "My mother being a literature professor and all. I never think of just sitting down to read."

"What do you think of?"

I shrugged. "I've taken up running again now that I have a ship with a track on it."

She frowned "There's a treadmill on the Chernyakova, isn't there? Didn't you run there?"

"No, that's the silly part. I used to run all the time. Bleed off stress. Get my focus. Also learned tai chi and practiced for ..." I paused, blowing out a breath. "Well, I've fallen out of practice since we got the Chernyakova going again."

"Hm. Julie crochets. Mostly just patterns, but she made me a lovely open-weave shawl."

I laughed.

"What's so funny?"

"I used to crochet a little, back on the Lois. We had a whole cottage industry going in deck berthing."

"Cottage industry?"

"Flea marketing. We organized the crew into a trading empire. Pip was the mastermind as always. We'd rent a table at whatever flea market we docked in. Divvied up the table coverage and sold off whatever we brought from the last orbital or made in transit. The transit times gave the co-ed crochet team plenty of time to turn raw yarn into salable goods."

She started out with an incredulous smile on her face and ended with quiet laughter. "That's brilliant."

The waiter brought out desserts and coffees. "That hold you folks for a while?"

"Looks great. Thank you," I said.

He nodded and flitted away.

Beth picked up a forkful of cobbler. "I never knew about the flea markets until I made second mate."

"Really? Didn't spend much time on orbitals?"

She shook her head and savored her dessert a moment before taking a swig of coffee. "No. When we got up to the orbital at Inidia, even as teens, we tended toward the entertainment venues like theaters and gaming halls. I always thought it was just an interesting phenomenon until I discovered that they're part of the orbital design."

"You never noticed that every orbital is the same?"

She laughed. "Well, yes. The docks. One rather expects that at the point where the ships have to stop. I didn't realize they all had the same number of decks."

"Same number of decks. Same layout on every deck. Every compartment has the same footprint from orbital to orbital."

She sat with her mouth open and some cobbler halfway to her mouth, eyes wide. "What?"

"Every orbital. Stamped from a mold. Every deck. Down to the compartment plan. Identical."

"How do you know this? Have you been on every orbital?" She tucked the cobbler into her mouth.

I started to answer but stopped, closing my mouth. After a thought I shook my head. "No. I haven't. I may be the victim of my own bias here. Every station I've ever visited, every space I personally saw. Those were identical. Or appeared to be."

She shrugged. "Well. The deck layouts. Sure. The two decks on either side of the docks. Industrial spaces and permanent party housing below. Retail and office space above."

"Flea markets always on the same deck," I said. "You're right. I have no idea what may be in any of those other spaces."

She chuckled and scooped another chunk of cobbler while I took a moment to savage the tiramisu in front of me.

"I should be more careful," I said, sipping my coffee and contemplating my empty dessert plate.

"What? Too many desserts?" Her eyebrows rose with her smile.

I chuckled and shook my head. "No. Generalizing on inadequate data. I assumed they were identical based on a limited sample."

She sat back and lifted her coffee cup to take a sip. "We all do it, I think."

The server came back, strolling up to the table. "Anything else I can get you?"

I shook my head and flexed my thumb. "This was wonderful, as usual."

He offered the tab and I pressed my thumb to it after keying the tip. "You've been here before?"

"Every time we dock, I try to get here at least once," I said.

"First time for me," Beth said, raising her hand as if volunteering. "I'll be back."

"What ship are you from?"

She said, "Chernyakova."

"Marva Collins for me."

"You're that Academy ship?" he asked, looking at me.

"Guilty. Why?"

"I thought she was on her maiden voyage. How have you eaten here before?"

"I used to be the skipper of the Chernyakova before she took over. That ship's been here a lot."

"How did you know?" she asked. "That the Collins is the Academy ship on her maiden voyage?"

"Kidding? It's all over the newsies. First time we ever had a ship from the Academy here. It's big news."

"It's the first time the Academy has had a ship to be here," I said. "All their other training vessels only sail on water."

"And you got her? Brand new?" He gave me an approving smile. "Good on ya."

"Right place, right time." I grinned back at him. "Or wrong place, depending on your point of view."

He chuckled and started collecting dishes. "Thanks for coming in and congrats on the new ship." He nodded to Beth. "And on your new command."

"Thank you." She rose from the table as he scurried off. "I hope you left him a good tip."

"I did. Why?"

"I'm not used to being congratulated on taking command."

"Fair enough. I can't say as it ever happened to me either."

She headed toward the exit sign. "How often have you taken over a ship?"

I had to think about it a moment.

She turned to me as we stepped out into the passageway. "So many you have to count on your fingers?"

I laughed. "Four. Agamemnon, Iris, Chernyakova, Marva Collins. Yes. Four."

She laughed back at me and we strolled back toward the docking gallery. "Chernyakova is only my second command."

"You spent a lot of time on the Saltzman ship?"

"Saltzman ships. Most of my life, seems like. Only took command the one time." Her face fell into a frown and she glanced at me. "Made it doubly hard."

I nodded. "I'm sure I can't imagine it, but what I can imagine is bad enough."

She chuckled a little and shot me another glance. "You didn't walk away from the Iris unscathed. What little I know of that situation makes me think you can imagine pretty well."

I gave her a glance back. "Yeah, well. I'm sorry either of us had to go through that, then."

She laughed. After a moment she asked, "What do you like to do besides run and manage reports?"

She made me laugh, too. "Well, the reports?" I see-sawed my hand. "Not sure about those. Can't seem to escape them. Even here."

"What makes you think you need a hobby?"

I shrugged and headed down the last passageway toward the ships. "It used to take every waking moment and some of my sleeping ones to manage the ship. Small ships in particular. Skipper is very hands-on, if you know what I mean."

"Not a lot of crew to delegate to?" She nodded.

"More than that. With fewer than a dozen people, you get thrown together a lot more closely. On the Agamemnon, there wasn't even a wardroom. On the Iris, we all ate in the galley, crew and passengers alike." I smiled, remembering. "That kind of experience is rare on a larger ship like the Chernyakova with a larger crew. It will be harder still on the Collins because there's no opportunity to develop over time."

"Sounds like you miss it," she said as we walked up to her lock.

I let the idea roll around in my head for a bit. "Someday I'll get back to it. Right now, I have a commitment to keep."

She pursed her lips. "A word of advice from a senior captain?"

I nodded.

"The commitments to yourself are more important than those you make to others."

"You believe that?" I asked.

"If you're not true to you, how can you be true to others?" She shrugged. "Just my opinion." She gave me a smile and keyed the lock open, leaving me standing there thinking about her words.

They followed me all the way back to the ship.

CHAPTER TWENTY-FIVE
BAR NONE RANCH: SEPTEMBER 27, 2379

Two days later we got underway for Gretna. First section drew the first watch underway. I stood at the aft portion of the bridge, staring at the receding station and thinking about what Beth had said about being true to yourself. We were still close enough that I couldn't see the whole thing. It felt like some kind of metaphor. How do you know if you're being true to yourself? How do you resolve conflicting truths? Was it a function of distance? The old "You don't know what you got till it's gone" idea? I'd see more and more of the station as we got deeper into space, but I sacrificed detail for scope.

"Forest for the trees," I said.

"Pardon me, sar?" Mr. Keen said.

"Sorry, Mr. Keen. Just musing aloud. Something my mother used to say about not seeing the forest for the trees." I took my seat at the console and ran a few diagnostics.

"Hard to see the whole when you're blinded by the details, sar?"

"Yes, Mr. Keen. Exactly."

He glanced at me. "Were you serious about going to the Academy, Skipper?"

"Who? When? Was I serious when I went to the Academy?" I grinned at him. "Tell you the truth, I was more scared than serious."

He laughed. "Were you serious about me going to the Academy, sar?"

"Yes, Mr. Keen. You've been sailing with us for a couple of stanyers now. You stepped into this role without hesitation. You've been helping the junior ratings, and you seem to have a good head on your shoulders."

He shook his head and adjusted his helm. "There was plenty of hesitation, Skipper."

"What convinced you to come along?"

He shrugged. "I wanted to stay with the officers I know. I'm sure Captain Case and Ms. Southern and the rest are good, but you? Ms. Usoko. Ms. Fortuner. Even Chief Regyri and Mr. Carstairs. I guess I'm just more comfortable with you."

"How do you think Mr. Cartwright is doing?"

He glanced at me. "You don't expect me to criticize an officer, do you, Skipper?"

His answer made me pause. "No. Sorry. I didn't think of the position it put you in."

He grinned. "He's all right. I don't have much to do with him, but he was really good during the testing. He's a good morale officer, I think. I know he listens to the suggestions he's getting. Ms. Fortuner did when we were on the Chernyakova, too."

"You don't have to answer if you don't feel comfortable, Mr. Keen."

He shook his head. "If I didn't feel comfortable, I'd have said so, Skipper. That's probably the main reason I decided to come over."

"Thank you, Mr. Keen."

We sailed along in silence for a few ticks. "Can I ask you a question, Skipper?"

"Of course. Although I reserve the right not to answer."

"You always say that, you know?"

"I forget who's heard it before. I find it cuts down on awkwardness later if the question is one I don't want to answer. Or can't. What's the question?"

"What should I do about going to the Academy?"

I chuckled. "That's rather up to you, isn't it? I can't very well tell you what to do with your life."

He laughed. "Not what I meant. I mean, what are the factors I should be considering? Finances, sure. I get that part. Unlike our current crop of junior ratings, I don't have to worry about funding. Thanks to Phoenix Freight. What else should I be considering?"

"Where do you want to be in a decade?" I asked.

He shook his head, glancing at me. "I don't know."

"That's a good question to think about, then." I took a breath and blew it out, racking my brain to think of a good answer. "The Academy isn't just a commitment to join the officer corps. It's a good foundational education that just happens to have a lot of use in running spaceships. You don't have to become an officer. You could become anything you want."

"What if I want to be a helm specialist?"

"A fine choice, Mr. Keen. Going to the Academy wouldn't prevent you from getting a job at helm. It might not be necessary, but you could go to the Academy and decide to let somebody else be third mate."

"What are the advantages of being an officer?" He glanced at me. "Nothing personal, Skipper, but it doesn't look like you have a lot more control of your life than I do."

"There's some truth there. I suspect you have more control than I do. Taking our personal finances out of the equation, since we could both do almost whatever we wanted at this point, you can get a job on a different ship much easier than I could. There's more demand for helm specialists than there is for captains."

"Same is true for all of the officers, isn't it?"

"For the most part, yes. Industry has a similar issue. More workers than bosses means there are more jobs for workers." I paused. "Tractors are the only ships I know of where the officers outnumber the crew. Even there, it's basically one per job."

He raised his eyebrows at that. "Really? More officers than crew?"

"Because of the regulations on how many people need to be on watch in which positions. All of the ship designers work very hard to put the fewest crew requirements on any design.

The tractor design works with an engineer, a cargo master, a captain, two mates, and three deck watchstanders."

"What does that work out to in shares, sar? Twelve?"

"Eleven, assuming the watchstanders are all full share."

"How does that work out, Skipper?"

"I liked it. There's a lot less officer–crew distinction. There's only the one berthing area with three bunks for the ratings. We all ate in the galley at the same table."

He frowned. "No steward. Who cooked?"

"Our cargo chief became our head cook, but we all pitched in on occasion."

"You sound like you miss it."

I thought about that for a moment or two. "I suppose I do. It's a different kind of operation. Chief Regyri thinks that tractors might be the next big thing here in the Toe-Holds."

He looked over, eyebrows high on his forehead. "Really?"

"There are dozens of stations we can dock in with the Barbell. More than the Collins could find cargoes for, but we'd be spending a lot of time getting to some out-of-the-way station for one can. For many of them, one of our smaller cans are all they could handle. Either as a delivery or export."

He nodded. "I guess I could see that. Not every station is as big as Mel's."

"Some aren't much more than a couple of dozen people. In order to grow, they need to be able to link in to the distribution networks for goods they need and to sell the materials they produce. Shares on one of our cans isn't going to amount to much. Margins are going to be very, very thin. The Chernyakova is on the other end of the spectrum."

"So, the can's too big for the station to even handle?"

"Coming and going," I said. "Barbell can't leave unless there's a can attached. If the station doesn't have a can of something leaving, a Barbell can't make a reasonable turnaround."

He grimaced. "And time is money."

"It isn't really." I grinned at him. "But time costs money."

"So tractors thread the needle, sar?"

"In a manner of speaking. The cans are larger than we carry but only a fraction of what a Barbell hauls. They can also maneuver without having a can, if they need to."

He nodded. "I get it. Tractors can serve more of the smaller stations that nobody else can."

"Fast packets handle most of it now, I suspect, but there's a cost benefit to getting a bulk shipment of, say, printer stock so you can print your own air and water filters."

"And to shipping raw ore?"

"Whatever they produce. Every station has to produce something. Raw ore is the base resource for the entire Annex, but there are other things. Small-scale chemical producers. Gas scoops can pick off the upper atmospheres of the giants. Those gases can be packaged for use elsewhere. If you're running on a shoestring, you need to move the small amounts of product out so you can afford to buy the things you need to keep producing and expanding."

He bit his lower lip and frowned in thought. "I hadn't thought of it that way before."

I shrugged. "It doesn't matter what you do. It has to be viable. You can't go on vacation for the rest of your life."

He glanced at me, with a grin. "Is that a challenge, sar?"

I laughed. "No. Financially, you probably could. I definitely could. Most people, probably not. The point is that if you can't afford to keep doing whatever you're doing, you need to find something else to do. Doesn't matter what it is. Doing nothing gets boring pretty quickly. Doing the same thing over and over isn't much better unless you take satisfaction just from doing it. All of that is moot if you don't have food and shelter."

He nodded. "I could see that. I don't really need to keep doing this." He looked at the helm console. "You're right, I could retire, but I'm kinda young to head for the rocking chair."

"Why do you do it?" I asked. "That's not a question you need to answer for me, but might be a good question to answer for yourself as you're thinking about the Academy and what you might do a decade or two from now."

He nodded and placed his hands on the helm controls. He nodded just slightly as if to himself. "Yeah. I can see that." He glanced over. "Thank you, Captain. I appreciate your insight."

I shrugged. "You're welcome, of course. Hope it helps."

He glanced over again. "What do you get out of it if I go to the Academy, sar?"

"The satisfaction that I helped a worthy candidate along their course." I grinned.

He chuckled and shook his head. "I don't know about worthy or course, sar, but I do appreciate the kind words."

"My first boss on the Lois was the head steward. Spec/1 chef. He told me early on, 'Pick a path before someone picks one for you.' It was good advice for me at the time."

"And now, sar?" He turned in his seat to look at me. "Still good advice?"

The conversation twisted in my head. All the advice I'd been doling out. All the talk about being worth it. All of it congealed into a fist that smacked me in the psyche. I felt physically stunned, only vaguely aware of the young man peering at me across the bridge. I cleared my throat and shook my head. "Sorry. Yes. I think it's still good advice."

He gave me a funny look and I realized I'd waited too long to answer.

"Sorry, Mr. Keen. It reminded me of something, and that train of thought left the station with me on board."

He chuckled and straightened around to face forward again. "No problem, Skipper."

I stood again and walked aft to look out. Pick a path, indeed. Was this the path I wanted, or was it simply the latest instance of somebody picking one for me? Had I ever been in a position to pick my path? I blew out a quiet breath and watched the sequence of my life play out in my head while my eyes stared at nothing.

Science Fiction

The Golden Age of the Solar Clipper

Traders Tales

Quarter Share
Half Share
Full Share
Double Share
Captains Share
Owners Share

Seekers Tales

In Ashes Born
To Fire Called
By Darkness Forged

SC Marva Collins

School Days
Working Class*
Hard Knocks*

Smugglers Tales

Milk Run
Suicide Run
Home Run

Shaman's Tales

South Coast
Cape Grace
Finwell Bay

Dark Knight Station: Origins

Fantasy

Tanyth Fairport Adventures

Ravenwood
Zypherias Call
The Hermit Of Lammas Wood

The Wizard's Butler

The Wizard's Butler
The Wizard's Cat*

* Forthcoming

Awards

2011 Parsec Award Winner for Best Speculative Fiction
(Long Form) for *Owners Share*

2010 Parsec Award Winner for Best Speculative Fiction
(Long Form) for *Captains Share*

2009 Podiobooks Founders Choice Award for Captains Share

2009 Parsec Award Finalist for Best Speculative Fiction
(Long Form) for *Double Share*

2008 Podiobooks Founders Choice Award for *Double Share*

2008 Parsec Award Finalist for Best Speculative Fiction
(Long Form) for *Full Share*

2008 Parsec Award Finalist for Best Speculative Fiction
(Long Form) for *South Coast*

About The Author

Nathan Lowell first entered the literary world by podcasting his novels. The Golden Age of the Solar Clipper grew from his life-long fascination with space opera and his own experiences shipboard in the United States Coast Guard. Unlike most works which focus on a larger-than-life hero, Nathan centers on the people behind the scenes, ordinary men and women trying to make a living in the depths of interstellar space. In his novels, there are no bug-eyed monsters, or galactic space battles, instead he paints a richly vivid and realistic world where the hero uses hard work and his own innate talents to improve his station and the lives of those of his community.

Dr. Nathan Lowell holds a Ph.D. in Educational Technology with specializations in Distance Education and Instructional Design. He also holds an M.A. in Educational Technology and a BS in Business Administration. He grew up on the south coast of Maine and is strongly rooted in the maritime heritage of the sea-farer. He served in the USCG from 1970 to 1975, seeing duty aboard a cutter on hurricane patrol in the North Atlantic and at a communications station in Kodiak, Alaska. He currently lives on the plains east of the Rocky Mountains with his wife and two children.

Contact

Website: nathanlowell.com
Mastodon: zirk.us/@nlowell
Email: nathan.lowell@gmail.com

Made in United States
North Haven, CT
08 July 2023

38711167R00222